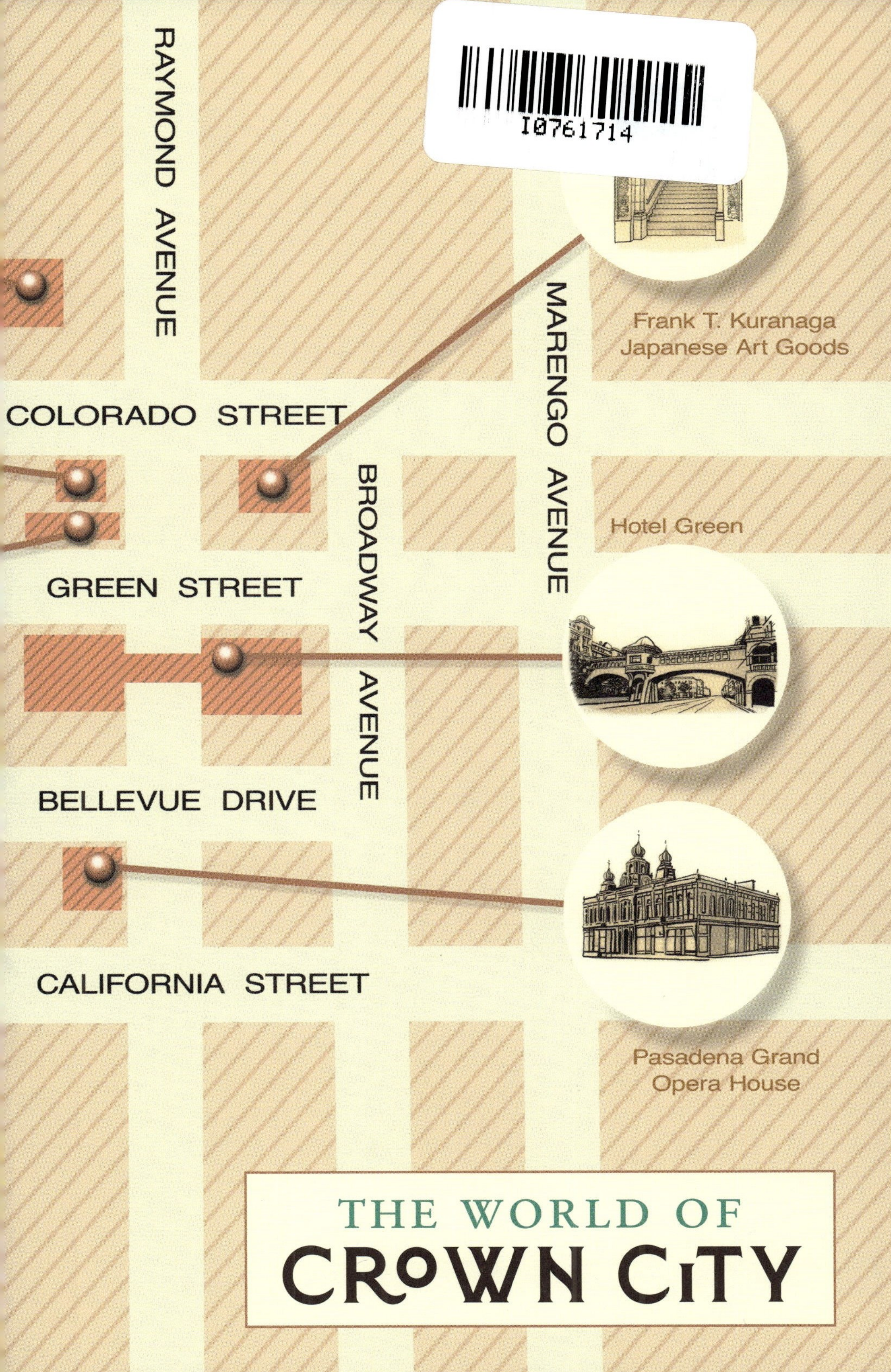
RAYMOND AVENUE
MARENGO AVENUE
BROADWAY AVENUE
COLORADO STREET
GREEN STREET
BELLEVUE DRIVE
CALIFORNIA STREET
Frank T. Kuranaga
Japanese Art Goods
Hotel Green
Pasadena Grand
Opera House
I0761714
THE WORLD OF
CROWN CITY

CROWN CITY

ALSO BY THE AUTHOR

• • •

The Japantown Mysteries

Clark and Division

Evergreen

The Mas Arai Mysteries

Summer of the Big Bachi

Gasa-Gasa Girl

Snakeskin Shamisen

Blood Hina

Strawberry Yellow

Sayonara Slam

Hiroshima Boy

CROWN CITY

NAOMI HIRAHARA

Published by
Soho Press, Inc.
227 W 17th Street
New York, NY 10011
www.sohopress.com

Photo of the Cherry Blossom dinner courtesy of the Archives at Pasadena Museum of History; GGG.4.4.14, George G. Green Collection.

Library of Congress Cataloging-in-Publication Data

Names: Hirahara, Naomi, author
Title: Crown city / Naomi Hirahara.
Description: New York, NY : Soho Crime, 2026. | Series: The Japantown mysteries ; 3
Identifiers: LCCN 2025034890

ISBN 978-1-64129-608-3
eISBN 978-1-64129-609-0

Subjects: LCGFT: Detective and mystery fiction | Novels | Fiction
Classification: LCC PS3608.I76 C76 2026
LC record available at https://lccn.loc.gov/2025034890

Interior design by Janine Agro
Map by Robert Venables

Printed in the United States of America

10 9 8 7 6 5 4 3 2 1

EU Responsible Person (for authorities only)
eucomply OÜ
Pärnu mnt 139b-14
11317 Tallinn, Estonia
hello@eucompliancepartner.com
www.eucompliancepartner.com

For the 'Dena
Past, Present, and Future

CROWN CITY

CONTENTS

Ryunosuke Wada
Gila River Relocation Center
Rivers, Arizona

Louise Wada
1122 N. Clark St.
Chicago 10, Illinois

July 8, 1943

Dear Louise,

Your mother says that I'm not thinking properly because of the valley fever. Heavy thoughts pile on top of my body, pushing down on my chest like I'm being buried alive by the desert here in Gila River. The heat that blistered your fair skin when the camp opened last summer has returned, but more families with money have installed swamp coolers for their barracks.

The Arizona horizon is dominated by the sky, as blue as one of Hokusai's prints of Mount Fuji. Except there's no majestic volcano, no pine trees. Only a craggy orangish mountaintop and strange cactus that look like lonely men standing at a distance from each other.

I am grateful, though, that you were able to give me that piece of wood you found with your brother before you left for Chicago. I know that I first scolded you two—maybe Richard more harshly. I do regret that. But you know about the shootings in Manzanar and Topaz and whatever other camps. The military police are young and inexperienced, eager to use us Japs for target practice to prepare to fight in the Pacific. Though I am sure you would do nothing more wrong than wandering around the brush, your disobedience would be an excuse to shoot at two innocent Nisei.

That dead branch is from a cottonwood tree. You and Richard would not know cottonwood from an oak. It's not your fault. I never taught you about how to dry lumber or how you must cut wood parallel to the grain for joints to achieve maximum strength to support a wall, roof, or a tabletop. You view me, your eccentric father who spent his evenings locked away in his wood shop next to the family's Model A, as a simple worker at Nippon Nursery.

One time, when you were a child, I overheard you asking your mother, "Why won't Papa let us play in the garage?"

"That's where Papa is a magician," she told you.

I know that our house was not a conventional one. When you were a teenager, you wanted kitchen tables and chairs from Sears. Not furniture made from my own hands. But somehow, you changed after you graduated from Pasadena High School. And when we were forced to leave the house, I heard you warn Mr. Carr to get renters who would take care of the furniture. "They should use coasters for their drinks," you told them. "And tell them to make sure to polish the wood on a weekly basis."

I had your mother bring that piece of cottonwood

to me when I was hospitalized. The nurses here—even your mother—don't trust me with a pocketknife, so I have to use only my hands to make this cottonwood into something of beauty. Your Houdini-san will make magic again, through the oil and the pressure of my fingers. I'm making a kobu. I think that you've seen the other Issei men furiously rubbing bits of broken branches. You didn't stay in camp long enough to see what can be created solely through the power of human touch. A rotting burl can be transformed into the bend of a woman's smooth knee. The remains of a boxwood, its trunk split open by lightning, can be shined into the curves of a cresting wave.

I learned this type of hand polishing through my father's workers in his wood shop in Yokohama. I know that I have not spoken much to you about Yokohama or him, specifically. All I've told you was that he was a carpenter, but he was actually much more than that. My mother, who was born of samurai stock, told us never to ebaru, brag about ourselves, and she was right. Especially in America, what does "master temple carpenter" mean? In Japan, our artisan family was still below samurai and farmers, but within the artisan class, we were close to the top.

Now, as I lie in this bed, my earliest memories seem to rise and dominate my reality. I don't know how much more I can write on paper. When the fever subsides, I will try again.

Sincerely,
Dad

I
YOKOHAMA
1885-1903

1.

I tell people that I'm from Yokohama, but I was actually born in the countryside of Yamaguchi, just below Hiroshima. What should my birthplace mean to me if all of my memories are from Yokohama?

I wish that I could have taken my children to Yokohama at least once. Growing up, they viewed Japan as the Old Country, because many of their friends who actually traveled with their parents to family hometowns like Wakayama, Hiroshima, and Fukuoka would return with reports of dreary places with virtually nothing to do besides fish and plant rice.

My Yokohama was nothing like this. It was full of people, sounds, and smells from all around the world—China, the United States, Holland, England, Portugal, and Australia. There were diplomats, soldiers, merchants, sailors, entertainers, and, of course, us artisans. The port was expansive, the bay filled with ships of all sizes, bringing in or taking out passengers and goods of every kind imaginable. Motomachi, a shopping area with as many signs in English as Japanese, had streets lined with fancy photo studios selling postcards depicting watercolor scenes of Yokohama. Since Yokohama was a main port of departure to South America and the United States, many

Japanese wearing their best clothing sat for a memento of life before leaving their native country.

My favorite spot to view Yokohama was at the top of the steep 102-stone steps that led to a famous teahouse. I'd come at the end of the day, when light was slipping away and docked ships were barely visible. With the sea's expanse hidden, Yokohama seemed more compact and intimate. Below, on the right, I could see the laundry hung on the second floor of the humble house where my parents, our maid, and I lived. Electric lights from Yokohama's Chinatown flashed on the left and beyond that was Kaga-cho, where my father's carpentry shop was located. Shipbuilders and traders traversed dirt roads in their wooden *geta*, either to their wood-framed homes or to alleys where women of the night plucked on stringed instruments behind paper doors. The only disadvantage of the dusk was the reappearance of the buzzing mosquitos, but I had been bitten so frequently as a child that I had become immune to their poison.

In 1885, when I was born, Japan was in the middle of a transformation, adopting more of a Western way of governing. That year, Ito Hirobumi became our first prime minister under what we call the Meiji—Enlightened—Restoration after the American naval officer Commodore Perry had forced his way into our archipelago fortress. We still had our Meiji Emperor, but no longer did the shogun or samurai hold power. In Motomachi, I frequented a store that sold woodblock prints for art dealers. As I wandered through the stacked prints awash in bright colors, I ignored the ones depicting scenes of foreigners in Yokohama, opting instead to leaf through ones capturing Nippon of old—a shogun brandishing a skull as a warning to underlings who would attempt to unseat him, or horses galloping with samurai riders who hoisted bows to launch arrows toward targets.

I would be the first to admit that I was sheltered from a lot of turmoil that this Meiji government brought to Japan. Occasionally one of my father's disgruntled workers called me a *botchan*, a Japanese name reserved for spoiled brats, specifically sons of the wealthy. My father was not rich, but our family was privileged in the sense that our positions as artisans were secured. We didn't have to worry about our next meal or a roof above our heads.

Occasionally I would encounter beggars wandering the streets. My mother merely ushered me across the street, never explaining to me how these men became so desperately impoverished. When I was with my maid, however, she would sometimes stop to give them a rice ball that she was planning to eat later in the day.

"Why did you give the man your lunch?" I asked one day after the beggar scurried away.

"He reminds me of my father," she told me. "He was a farmer in the country, but after the new leaders began to charge rent that we could not afford, my father came to the city to find work. We never heard from him again."

This was the only time our maid shared details of her past with me. Thinking back, I believe she regretted being so honest with me. The encounter with this particular beggar engendered memories of her father, which caused her to speak without thinking. She didn't make that mistake in my presence again.

Near my father's shop in Kaga-cho was an enormous factory that produced various artworks; my father did business with the owner. I sometimes walked through the factory floor with my father, marveling at the women weaving table coverings on looms and men balancing large vases on rotating pottery wheels with their clay-covered hands. I went to school with some of the barefoot boys painting flowers on plates and they were my occasional playmates.

It was in this factory that I first met Victor Marsh, an arts dealer known to my father. Victor and his older brother, George Turner or GT, were Australian—an adventurous and unconventional people. My father had had more dealings with the British and the Americans. My father always seemed to be more at ease with the British. He liked sitting down with them, eating hard biscuits with black tea in fanciful painted teacups that sat on matching saucers. They, like us Japanese, seemed more controlled by rules and restraint. The Americans, on the other hand, seemed a bit dirty and uncouth. They liked to handle our artwork without asking for permission first. I was drawn to these Americans' confidence, I have to admit. They had no tradition or national precedence to confine them. I wondered what it would be like to live life with that kind of freedom. As it turned out, I would learn for myself.

The Australians, specifically these Marsh brothers, didn't fall in either one of these broad categories. First of all, they could speak and even read Japanese fairly fluently. GT, the first white man to open a Japanese arts gallery in San Francisco, was especially skilled in language arts. His pronunciation was odd, having a rhythm like a rowboat going back and forth in choppy waters. But after you got used to his vocalization, you almost became hypnotized by his speech. It was as if he was speaking another language altogether, one that you could mysteriously understand but weren't quite sure how.

Victor, whose eyes were the color of water, rested his gaze on me for so long that I had to look away. While his Japanese-language skills were not as strong as his brother's, he seemed to be better at assessing a man's strengths and weaknesses—perhaps mostly his own.

"Your son seems like a smart one," he commented to my father.

"A little scaredy-cat," my father replied. "This one's always shaking like a leaf."

"It's all right to be afraid," Victor said. "Actually, it's a sign of great intelligence."

My mother, highly educated for a woman, tutored me in Japanese literature after my public school classes. She loved to read and took me to used bookstores in Yokohama and even nearby Tokio to buy classical books written in the Tokugawa period when she was a toddler. Although the new Japanese government told us to abandon the old and issued us new textbooks, my mother told me to never let go of the past.

2.

In 1893, when I was eight years old, my father was sent to the Chicago World's Fair to help oversee the construction of the Ho-o-Den, modeled after a pavilion of the Byodo-in Temple near Kyoto. I was only familiar with Chicago as the center of a train system that traveled all the way to the Pacific Coast. My mother had told me of a devastating fire a decade before I was born that had decimated many of the historic buildings, and said that Chicago was now creating new structures of steel frames and glass that stretched out to the heavens.

In contrast, Japan wanted to assert its world dominance by re-creating a treasured courtyard that went back to the Heian period. The Ho-o-Den was an homage to the phoenix, the mythical bird that descends from the sky to mark a new era. It would take my father months to complete the construction.

I wish that I could say that I missed him deeply, but I barely noticed his absence until he returned at the end of the year.

Once safely home, my father, as usual, did not tell me much about the exposition, but he had brought back a couple of souvenirs for me. One was a small woven American Indian blanket, the size of the open palm of his hand, from a special exhibition heralding the artwork of the native peoples of North America.

The other was a pamphlet of the Japanese village at what was officially called the World's Columbian Exposition. It was all in English and written by Okakura Kakuzo, one of the most respected arts authorities in Japan, an expert of culture and languages whom my father had highly esteemed.

My mother and I sat and perused every centimeter of that publication. Together we read Okakura's pamphlet only a paragraph a day because our grasp of English wasn't as strong as my father's. I could barely understand what Okakura was trying to illuminate about Japanese culture, but I knew what was being communicated was precious and needed to be protected.

I didn't mind spending so much time with my mother while my father embarked on his construction projects. My father was exacting and demanding, expecting high performance from anyone under his employ. I would still be drawn to his presence, albeit from a distance. Through the open sliding door in the morning, I'd watch him carefully pull on his dark blue *tabi*, making sure that the big toe snugly fit in its hold while the rest of the toes lay flat in the rest of the sock. This was the standard footwear for all carpenters as it ensured their stability when climbing up ladders and rafters. He wore an indigo-blue kimono top that was cinched at the waist by an obi sash. Even the knot around his waist was tied with a sense of deliberate efficiency that I could never hope to emulate.

Even though I was still in adolescence, I should have noticed that my mother's health was suffering. She would get out of breath often, usually instructing me to complete household errands on my own without her. Since her physical struggles worsened incrementally, I had tricked myself into thinking that nothing was wrong. One day, she could not get out of bed. I went to school as usual, but when I returned, she had been taken away to protect the household—mostly me—from her diagnosed disease, tuberculosis. She was sent to a sanatorium, its exact location unknown to me. My father still had to tend to his faraway construction projects, so at night I was usually alone with the maid. I started to turn to the huge bottle of cooking sake in the kitchen to relieve my sorrows, first in small sips and then large gulps. One evening I became so inebriated that I wandered outside only to collapse on the side of the road, almost lying in the gutter. The maid, who had been searching for me, found my drunken body and was able to help me get safely home. She insisted that I promise to swear off sake forever in consideration of my recuperating mother. I agreed, but my mother still died at the age of thirty-three. I had not gotten a chance to see her since I left for school that one day.

3.

After my mother's death, my father began to spend more time with me. He took me to local construction sites, lumberyards, and forests hours away from Tokio. He would explain the cypress, with its pinkish center, was the tree of choice to be used in temples and shrines. We stood in the middle of a cypress grove in Fukushima, tall skinny trees with dark bark.

"Breathe," my father said to me. I closed my eyes and complied. "What do you smell?"

"*Mikan*," I replied, referring to our family's favorite citrus fruit, plentiful in my birthplace of Yamaguchi Prefecture.

This is one of the rare times where he smiled broadly, revealing his crowded bottom teeth, which resembled an overgrown cedar grove.

While we youth were all required to go to school, gone were the after-school excursions to used bookstores. Instead I was to report to the carpentry shop in Kaga-cho. In the beginning, I wasn't supposed to touch the lumber or the tools, unless I was cleaning them. Nor was I to sit on the floor. I had to stand the entire time, my toes going numb in my *tabi*. My father gave me a thick hand-bound book that contained various dimensions for roof eaves, walls, and alcoves. This was the *kiwari* for Buddhist temples, my father's specialty. Anyone dealing with construction needed to memorize these measurements and I spent many sleepless nights attempting to imprint these numbers into my head.

Finally after some months, I was allowed to touch the wood. I felt the warmth of his breath as he instructed me. "This is the male joint, the tenon." He brought out a piece of timber with a projection that was about three centimeters thick and inserted it into a mortise that was cut to accommodate it. "A perfect fit. See how tight it is, yet no friction." He pulled out the tenon and had me push it into the cavity of the mortise.

I couldn't help but start to smirk. I had been exposed to the banned erotic woodblock prints that the boys at the art factory smuggled and passed around. I understood how male and female bodies were different and how they were to fit together.

My father didn't appreciate the lecherous expression on my face. "This is not a joke!" he exclaimed. "You are on the verge of being a man. Shape up and be serious!" He said it loud enough that the other workers could hear. My ears burned as the rest of the crew swallowed their amusement and attempted to hide their smiles. I would never win their respect, not to mention my father's.

In time I was allowed to smooth the rough wood surface after it was cut into planks. It was tedious work, requiring me to go over it with a hand plane. Looking down the length of the rectangular wooden box container, I made adjustments to the fit of the steel blade by hitting the end of the box with a mallet. These blades, coated with a translucent layer of iron, were special, produced by blacksmiths trained in creating the sharpest and strongest samurai swords. *Swoosh*, *swoosh*, *swoosh*. As I pulled the plane against the surface of the cut wood, the steel blade contained inside released a long ribbon, as transparent and thin as the shed skin of a snake. The middle of my back grew stiff after engaging in this work for a few hours. Luckily, because of my young age, a night of good sleep fully restored me to start over the next day.

"Oi, Ryunosuke," my father said to me the time when we were on an expedition to look for good lumber in Fukushima. He pointed at a gnarled knot emerging from the root of a decaying cypress tree. "This is the result of a sickness or stress in its life. You may see some of my workers cut it off to hand polish it for decoration. But such deformities have no place in the construction of a temple. Avoid such infected trees at all costs."

I nodded, but barely took in what he was saying to me. In spite of his exacting and mathematical nature, he sometimes had very strange ideas, causing his workers to snicker behind his back.

When I was sixteen, I was allowed to travel with him to the faraway cedar groves on the remote Yaku Island off of Kyushu. The journey to the island took many days, as we stopped by to see the original Byodo-in Temple, the inspiration behind the Japanese pavilion at the Chicago World's Fair. Most impressive was indeed its Phoenix Hall, which had winged roofs that precisely reminded me of a *ho-o* in flight. The bronze statues of the *ho-o* on the ridge of the roofs sparkled in the sun, giving the illusion that they were actually moving.

Also located on the outskirts of Kyoto was a temple that my father was helping to repair after an earthquake caused damage to the roof. He pointed to the rafters, explaining to me how the joints fit perfectly together. My workmanship had improved over the past several months and I made an offhand comment that I was ready to work on the structure for such a temple. My father became incensed, berating me for making such a presumptuous comment. "This takes a lifetime of training, you foolish boy," he said.

That incident set the tone for our travel down to Kagoshima. I kept my distance from my father, allowing his workers to dominate his time on the wood-burning train. Miserable, I felt resentment harden in my abdomen. Only when we were on a boat to Yaku Island was I able to regain a sense of wonder. I had never seen water that pristine blue, and the looming island was a most vibrant green, like algae on wet stones in tide pools. Once we debarked, we entered a moss-covered world inhabited by giant cedars whose roots emerged from the wet soil like tentacles or fingers. I felt that the trees were almost human.

My father was about three meters away, communing with

the upright cedars and considering which tree to cut down and take with us back to Yokohama. That's when I saw the burl, a knot, on the bottom of a cedar in an open area. Its face, a wrinkled knob peeking out from the green covering, seemed to call out to me: *I want to go where you are going. Take me with you.*

But did I dare? I recalled what my father had told me back in Fukushima: Burls were a sign of disease and should never be taken from their resting place. I was weary of my father's superstition; there were plenty of other carpenters who proudly extracted burls and hand polished them into works of pride. This could be my special *kobu*, my own piece of these magical cedars on Yaku Island. I took out my double-edged handsaw, which was secured at my lower waist with a cloth belt, and applied it to the tree. I expected more resistance, but the cedar knot immediately rolled free after one pull of my saw. It was the size of a *satoimo*, a taro root, like the ones our maid boiled for too many meals. This burl was covered in dark, flaky bark, and I was determined to aid in its transformation.

I was a thief that afternoon. I should have felt more guilt than I did. Not that I had stolen a burl, but that I had removed evidence that this cedar had a small blemish that might signal a larger imperfection. The loggers my father had hired were probably at fault, too, because instead of performing the grueling and dangerous work required to cut a tree down in the crowded forest, they decided to take this lone cedar in a clearing.

As I rubbed and transformed my burl, I called it Tama-chan. I always kept Tama-chan close by, smoothing out the years that had accumulated on its outer layers. I considered Tama-chan my lucky talisman for the next two years. I prayed that it could reverse the bout of bad luck that had shadowed my young life.

On my eighteenth birthday, that same cedar taken from Yaku Island, which had been air-drying in our lumber house in Yokohama, was transported to Kamakura for a temple building. My father's crew had lifted a wood slab from a train car when one of the men lost his footing. The piece came tumbling down and crushed my father, who was supervising on the ground. His neck was broken, his head almost detached from his body. He died instantly. Members of his carpentry shop said it was better than suffering a prolonged death or being indefinitely incapacitated. I didn't find any of it to be better.

For my father's funeral, I wore what my father had donned at my mother's funeral: a silk kimono and jacket as black as midnight, our family crest prominently displayed where the jacket draped over my shoulders. The funereal incense wafted over my face, hair, and clothing, and I knew that I never wanted this smell, a scent of tears, to be removed from the kimono.

As the Buddhist minister's chants filled the temple, I couldn't help but think that trees always remember. They remember the good, the heroic, the beautiful. But they also remember who had taken them.

II
ARRIVAL

Spring 1903

1.

Before I left Yokohama, I wouldn't have been able to tell you much about Pasadena, California.

I did know that the Marsh brothers had recently opened a store there. First to be recruited as a woodworker was Toichiro Kawai, with whom I had a passing acquaintance. Mr. Kawai was my father's age and had thick salt-and-pepper hair that stood up on his head like a Japanese rooster's comb. He was employed to repair and refinish artwork for a notable art-curio dealer, Deakin Brothers, which was located opposite the fanciest establishment in Yokohama, the Grand Hotel.

Mr. Kawai lived nearby in a boardinghouse owned by his wife's family. His wife had a warm, dazzling smile that could put even the sternest Japanese man, like my father, at ease. Mrs. Kawai had just given birth to their first child, a daughter, when it was announced that Mr. Kawai would be leaving soon for Pasadena, with the understanding that his wife and young child would soon follow. I heard that he would be doubling his salary in America.

I, meanwhile, was struggling with my new status as an orphan. A competing business took over my father's carpentry operation, and while his workers continued to have employment, there was no place for me. Our maid should have left me as soon as my father had died, but she stayed by my side, even paying for some of our household expenses. We rented our house and money was due at the end of the month. I needed to work.

I went to the art factory to see if I could be hired to carve decorative wood panels with motifs of Mount Fuji or pine trees. Unfortunately, the demand for such artwork was limited, explained the factory owner, who instead proposed that I take a position sweeping the concrete floors. While an experienced carpenter would earn about sixty-five sen, not even one yen a day, I would be making thirty-five sen.

Blinking away tears, I nodded my agreement. What choice did I have?

I felt someone staring at me and turned to meet Victor Marsh's impenetrable gaze.

"You are Wada-san's son." Even though I had met him years ago, he had remembered me.

"Yes. I am Wada Ryunosuke." I bowed to him, my toes curled up against the cool floor.

"You can speak English." He had switched from Japanese to English, perhaps to test my abilities.

"My parents thought it was important," I said.

"We plan to expand our operations in Pasadena. We could use more English-speaking Nipponese boys."

I started to feel lightheaded. Was what I was hearing correct? Was Victor recruiting me to work for him in the United States?

Before I could react, Victor's older brother, GT, came to his side. I wasn't used to seeing the brothers together, as they usually weren't in Yokohama at the same time. As the two brothers stood next to each other, I noted that Victor was a few inches taller. GT's face was more animated, the pointy tips of his ears reminding me of a fox's. His eyes were darker than Victor's and changed from blue to green brown, depending on how the sunlight hit his face.

"What do you think, George?" Victor asked GT. "You know this boy—he's the son of the master carpenter, Wada Ryuichiro. His name is Ryunosuke."

"Oh, my regrets, dear boy," GT said, not sounding regretful at all. He took a full visual assessment of my body. "He's not very sturdy, is he? You're of good health?"

I jerked as he clamped down on my right biceps, but nodded. I didn't mention anything about my mother's passing from tuberculosis.

"He's smart. He can speak English."

"Well, why don't we give him a try? What do you say, Ryui-kun?" GT had mistaken my father's name for mine and as a result, christened me with the nickname, Ryui, that would follow me my entire life.

Regarding the Marsh brothers' proposal, I didn't even take the time to think it over. Right now, my options were to either clean wet clay off a factory floor or embark on an adventure across the Pacific. "I say yes," I replied.

Victor had to leave for America immediately, leaving the preparation for my travel arrangements to GT. It wasn't only a matter of purchasing my third-class steerage ticket and securing my passport and visa, but also providing me with fifty dollars—which would have taken me almost a year to earn cleaning floors. This would be my "show money" to prove to American immigration authorities that I would be able to support myself in America. Of course, I would have to immediately pay most of it back to the Marsh brothers when I arrived in Pasadena.

What I didn't return would be taken from my salary, along with a monthly fee of seven dollars toward the cost of living in a boardinghouse.

As I had to check into an emigrant house in Yokohama before sailing to America, GT came to my house in a jinrikisha. I had never had the opportunity to ride in these passenger carts pulled by men instead of horses. That was the purview of bosses like my father, women, or foreigners.

The maid had left my packed wicker trunk on the first floor by the entryway where we left our *geta* and other shoes so as not to track dirt inside. On top of the suitcase was a single *mikan*, placed like an offering on Buddhist altars and New Year's decorations. Underneath it was an American dollar. In saying farewell, the maid was still looking after me.

The jinrikisha driver stuffed my suitcase into a metal harness in the back as GT directed me to sit down in the padded seat. Once I was ready to go, he presented me with a copy of Okakura Kakuzo's *The Ideals of the East with Special Reference to the Art of Japan*, published by J. Murray in London. "Hot off the presses," he said. I could tell from the lift in the pages that GT had already consumed it. "That will keep you busy on the boat."

As a jinrikisha could carry only one person, GT would see me off here at my house. I felt like an important person and wondered if the rest of my life would follow this trajectory.

Bouncing over the potholes in the dirt road, I recited farewell to all my haunts in Yokohama. *Goodbye, woodblock print shop. So long, Chinatown. Until the next time, a hundred and two steps. See you later, Water Street.*

The jinrikisha driver stopped at a nondescript building by the pier and helped me to get out of the elevated seat. Although I had passed this structure a number of times, I never knew exactly what it was and wasn't curious enough to inquire. The driver dropped my trunk on the ground and proceeded to find another rider.

This inspection stop was referred to as an emigrant inn, but there wasn't anything hospitable about it. The rooms were filled with farmers from the countryside, some who had apparently been detained for days. A doctor shined a light into my eyes for trachoma and quite embarrassingly studied my feces for hookworm. However, since I had a business visa through my connections with GT, I was released in a day. When I opened my wicker trunk to pack Okakura's book, I was surprised to see Tama-chan nestled beside my nightclothes and wool blanket. I had purposefully left my *kobu* on the windowsill of my empty bedroom. Here was my chance to start afresh in a new country as I set out on the *Amerika-Maru*. But obviously my maid had come across it and packed it in my suitcase, thinking that I had inadvertently forgotten it. I could not abandon it in this emigrant inn or throw it away in the ocean. We were destined to travel together.

I hobbled to the massive passenger ship docked at the end of a long pier. Most of the passengers had already boarded our ship and had released colorful streamers from all three decks in celebration of our voyage, which would last two to three weeks with a stop in Honolulu. My feet ached terribly from the new laced boots I had purchased a week earlier in my attempt to be a real American man. I barely made it up the plank to the deck, only to be directly sent down into steerage, with all the other passengers traveling on the cheapest tickets. I was given a few cans of food and was happy that I had packed a chisel that I could use to open them.

I found myself surrounded by beds on stilts like racks prepared for silkworms. Every single bed was taken and I had to take a spot on the hardwood floor. My blanket came in handy, as I created a nest with it. Above me were three-tiered beds claimed by six other Japanese men about five years older than me. Their dialects indicated that they were minimally educated, and from their rough conversations, I gathered that they were some kind of manual laborers, maybe farm workers. Only one of them, Keisuke, who seemed like the leader of the group, introduced himself and told me that they were planning to join a farming colony in the middle of California. After I revealed my own personal situation, Keisuke seemed sympathetic, and I even wondered if he had been a low-level samurai whose power had been erased with the political changes our country was experiencing.

The voyage was rough. I attempted to occupy my time by reading the Okakura book during the few hours of light from above, but it was difficult to focus with the way the ship was roiling. Sitting in the prow underneath curved eaves were about a dozen Chinese passengers who wore their hair plaited in long braids. One of them kept vomiting into a ceramic bowl, causing much grumbling and consternation from the Japanese passengers.

"Go outside and sacrifice yourself to the god of the sea," called out one of Keisuke's laborers.

"Ah, the stink."

"Does he have the plague?" said another.

I felt compassion for the stricken man. Many days the *Amerika-Maru* would toss and turn so violently that I shivered underneath a wool blanket, unable to focus much on what Okakura was writing about. Why had GT given me this book? To remind me that I was Japanese as I was making this trek across the Pacific?

The night before we were to arrive in Honolulu, the ship went through the worst storm yet. The world seemed to spin forcefully like it was disappearing through a drain. I held on to Tama-chan for dear life, my fingers almost frozen in my grip around it. I heard the farm workers talk about me as if I could not hear.

"How could they send the boy on his own like this?" It was the raspy voice of a laborer who had been constantly complaining the whole voyage.

"He has no one," Keisuke said. I felt a bit betrayed by his disclosure of details of our private conversation. "His father lost his head in the construction of the temple in Kamakura."

"How can he survive in America?" The rasps of Mr. Complaint returned.

The ship lurched, causing the creaking of the wood-plank floor. My grip tightened around Tama-chan. Passengers on the top bunks clung to nets hanging above their heads for dear life.

"Others his age have made the journey," Keisuke replied.

"But this one seems too soft."

I wished that I had enough energy to tear the blanket from my face and challenge the complainer. But I curled up like a worm instead, hoping I wouldn't vomit all over the steerage deck.

"Sometimes the soft ones will surprise you."

"Or sometimes you will find them on the side of the road, begging for scraps."

2.

When we docked in Honolulu, I finally was able to recover from my seasickness and get back my land legs. Keisuke insisted that I go onshore with his farm crew and I was most grateful. We went to a simple diner that offered rice balls and miso soup alongside meat sandwiches, quite a relief from the fat-laden stews we were served by the Chinese cooks on the boat. The travel money that the maid had left for me paid for my meal—how did she predict that it would be needed? The rest of the men were less enthusiastic about my inclusion, and for the most part they ignored me, which suited me just fine. They had no interest in Okakura or art. We had nothing in common.

I didn't have the energy to fully absorb my surroundings. The air of Hawaii felt surprisingly familiar and it was comforting to see some Japanese faces among the other passengers that had disembarked from other ships. Only the frilly palm trees were a sign that we were far from home. I braced myself for what we would see at our final destination several days from now.

I was sleeping when Keisuke jostled me awake. "We've arrived!" he shouted.

The rest of his farm crew had scattered up the stairs to the higher decks like cockroaches. I took my time behind the rest of the passengers, almost afraid to see the land we had reached. After we cleared the fog, the air was crisp and the sky as blue as woodblock prints; the scenery all seemed unreal. There were islands everywhere. It reminded me a little of Kyushu, when we sailed for Yaku Island, except the islands here were a sandy brown dotted with dark green foliage. We were heading toward the main landmass, along with a number of smaller ferryboats navigating in and out of the port. A couple of large vessels were docked at various piers jutting out of the bay. In the distance, I could spot buildings sprouting on the hills like barnacles.

Surrounded by foul-smelling unwashed men, I was a bit apprehensive about what I'd be entering into. But before long, I was swept up in the communal excitement. Soon, we would be standing on firm ground, exploring this world of America.

As we lined up to debark, American authorities separated the Chinese passengers, including the one who had been so ill, from the rest of the us. Keisuke, the more experienced traveler, explained that they would be taken to a special shack in a different location to be interrogated. While those with existing businesses and homes in America could enter San Francisco, newcomers from China were strictly prohibited.

Uniformed men who I gathered were immigration officials entered the *Amerika-Maru*. First- and second-class passengers, mostly Europeans and Americans, soon walked down the gangplank in droves. The rest of us pressed in, eager to follow, but our wait would be much longer.

"Do you have people that will be picking you up?" Keisuke asked.

Victor Marsh had said that he would have a man waiting for me, a Japanese man who worked with GT in San Francisco.

"They are supposed to send someone," I said weakly.

Keisuke gazed at me sympathetically, probably doubting that promise. At the beginning of our three-week voyage, his round face had resembled a baby's, but I now noticed the faint sign of whiskers underneath his nose and chin.

I thought I'd collapse from the stress of standing for what seemed like hours. Once we reached the next deck, we were called forward ten at a time.

Keisuke and his laborers proceeded before me. I couldn't see through the crowd to glimpse exactly what was transpiring, but in about a quarter of an hour, I heard the elevated bellows of Mr. Complaint and the chatter of rough-and-tumble Japanese.

I ran to the edge of the deck and watched Mr. Complaint being dragged toward the pier by a uniformed man. I was no fan of the ill-tempered laborer, but didn't relish whatever bad fortune that had befallen him.

I was one of the last to go through immigration. An American official, who looked as young and thin as me, thoroughly checked my passport and visa. He shined a flashlight into my face and made me open my mouth and stick out my tongue. After this cursory medical inspection, he asked me about my age, where I was from, my purpose for coming to America, and proof that I had fifty dollars in hand.

I had been shaking the entire time, but the official, wearing all black, didn't seem to notice. When he finally directed me to follow the others down the gangplank, I feared I might collapse, but forced my legs to keep moving forward onto the dock.

Surely, once I reach the end of the pier, there will be someone to meet me, I thought. I was dwarfed by the giant ships and thought I could be flattened by all the men rolling carts full of crates that had come from overseas. How could anyone possibly locate me, a mere teenager, in the middle of this hubbub?

I was relieved to spot Keisuke and four of his men gathered in a tight knot in the middle of the pier. They seemed deep in a serious discussion.

"What has happened?" I asked Keisuke.

"My foreman has been snatched by immigration. I told him to make sure that he brought enough show money, but he didn't think it was necessary. Now he's trapped in the immigration shed and who knows how long he will be in there."

"What will you do?" My heart resumed beating normally. I felt lucky to have been released from the ship without incident.

"We'll have to continue to our destination. We don't have enough money to stay longer in San Francisco." Keisuke registered my lone status. "Are your people here?"

"They should be," I managed to say but tears began to well up in my eyes. It was obvious that I probably was on my own.

I remembered what Mr. Complaint had been saying—that he predicted that I would become a wandering beggar.

"Keisuke-kun, don't get involved." A member of his crew tugged at his elbow.

I showed Keisuke my letter from Victor Marsh and I could tell that his comprehension of English was limited. He could make out my final destination: Pasadena.

"We can take you as far as Fresno. But you'll have to find your way down south on your own."

The rest of his men frowned and cursed. They obviously didn't share the same level of hospitality that Keisuke had.

Then I heard a voice, rough and authoritative. "Are you Wada Ryunosuke?" It was a Japanese man in a suit, tie, and fedora hat.

"*Hai!*" I answered in the affirmative, louder than I intended.

He was an older man, maybe the age my father would have been, but strong. He easily placed my bamboo suitcase on his shoulder. To the relief of not only myself but also Keisuke and his laborers, it appeared that I was being taken care of. I bowed my goodbyes and only Keisuke did the same. We knew we probably would never see each other again.

"I am Goto," my attendant said in Japanese, not bothering to introduce the woman next to him, who probably was his wife. She wore a ruffled white blouse and long dark skirt, but her swollen belly was such a contrast from her small frame that I could only assume that she was with child.

I bobbed my head to both of them as low as I could go.

My greeting obviously didn't make much of an impression, because Goto had disappeared with my carrier through a throng of people.

I bumped shoulders and elbows with Americans as I tried to keep my focus on his fedora. He was about my height, so he often disappeared behind silk flowers on a woman's soaring hat or the giant shoulders of a passerby. I didn't even think of where Mrs. Goto was, but in the end, I discovered she managed to be right behind him.

Horses pulling buggies threw dirt my way, soiling my new boots. As I had kept the boots off on the ship, my feet felt pinched in the tightness of their leather construction. I was thrown into a new world, and I had to rush to keep up or else risk being abandoned and lost. I didn't have time to process anything, much less form any opinions.

A horseless carriage weaved through the buggies and streetcars, almost toppling over a deliveryman on a bicycle. I had seen some motorized vehicles in Yokohama, but nothing like these, which didn't leave a puff of smoke behind them.

I wasn't paying any mind to where we were walking—and was not brave enough to ask my hosts. Mr. Goto finally stopped in front of an impressive concrete structure with a tall steeple that resembled the Christian church that stood on a bluff above a cemetery in Yokohama. Countless trains of different colors clanked as they emerged on a maze of tracks. The crowd of people grew even more dense and I was practically hanging on to Mr. Goto's jacket to make sure that I didn't lose sight of him.

I could finally breathe once we found seats on one of the railway cars. It was toward the back and I noticed that none of the fine-looking American or European passengers sat near us. Instead, a couple of rows down sat an unshaven man who seemed quite inebriated. His presence seemed to repel many others from sitting in our vicinity.

"What is Pa-sa-de-na like?" I asked once we had settled in, and the train had started to leave the station.

"The city of kings," Mr. Goto replied. "They call it Crown City."

Ku-ra-on City? As I thought Mr. Goto was saying "Clown City," I was confused. At the woodblock print store, I had seen a strange illustration of a traveling Italian circus with a clown dancing in a costume sporting polka dots and images of hot red peppers. His appearance was so disconcerting that I periodically had nightmares of this clown terrorizing me in dark alleys of Yokohama. I hoped that I would not encounter more of these clowns at my final destination.

Later, it was explained to me that the name "Pasadena" came from an American Indian tribal word and it meant "valley." Embraced by a purplish mountain range and later referred to as the Crown of the Valley, Pasadena was a world unto its own. Americans from the Eastern Seaboard and the middle of the country flocked to the second-oldest city in the county, incorporated in 1886, thirty-six years after the city of Los Angeles.

During our train ride, the wife barely said anything to me. But she shyly placed a paper bag on my lap as passengers continued to walk past our seats. Inside was a sandwich carefully wrapped in wax paper.

If I was a gentleman, I would have offered at least half of it to her; in her condition, she was probably in need of sustenance. But I was so famished that I stuffed practically the whole sandwich into my mouth at once.

"*Mah—*" Mr. Goto's crooked teeth were in bad shape, yellowed like mahjong tiles from probably too much tobacco. He looked both disgusted and amazed, while the wife's pale face broke out in a grin, her thin eyes almost disappearing into the outline of twin hills. That would be the only time I would see her smile.

The train ride was bumpy but still much steadier than the boat. My legs felt like limp noodles when I awoke from a deep sleep, and I was embarrassed to see that I had taken up most of the bench seat, leaving only a narrow space for the other passenger.

He was an Asian man with a long queue like those I had seen on our boat. Although I did not have any close relationships with Chinese people in Yokohama, I relished the smell of garlic and ginger being fried in woks during my frequent walks through Chinatown. I bowed to him and he bowed back. Mr. Goto seemed less than enthused about sharing our passenger space with such a man, but then he seemed the type to get easily irritated.

I could not communicate with the Chinese man through speech, but then we started writing kanji in the air with our index fingers. It became an entertaining way to pass the time as our train traveled through the length of California. Mountain. Lake. Cow. Grapes.

And finally he pointed to a cityscape in the distance and said something I couldn't quite understand. He began to write a complicated kanji with many strokes. "*Ra*," I said out loud, finally discerning the difficult kanji 羅. Related to silk? I was a bit confused because I didn't know what he was referring to.

"*Luo*," he said back to me, presumably the Cantonese pronunciation, and then I understood: He was referring to Los Angeles. Among Japanese immigrants, the city was known as Rafu, 羅府, or Silk Province.

I pointed to my nose. "I am going to Pa-sa-de-na."

The man enthusiastically nodded. "Pasadena," he repeated. I wasn't sure if he merely recognized the name or was planning to go there himself.

I didn't get a chance to say a proper goodbye to the Chinese traveler—much less find out what his name was—because as soon as the train made its stop in Los Angeles, Goto was on the move again, his wife and I hurriedly trailing after him. I couldn't help but wonder if he even cared that I was still there with him.

We transferred to a train with fewer cars than the one we had ridden on from San Francisco. As we ascended to Pasadena, the air felt dry, tightening the surface of my skin. My head pounded with stress and my mouth became parched. The sun, which was much more intense here than in San Francisco, caused me to feel nauseated. We passed endless groves of trees, which I later learned produced oranges, much rounder and bigger than the *mikan* in Yamaguchi.

In the distance were these lavender peaks that again surprised me. I had indeed entered a new world. I missed the salty, moist air of Yokohama. At least San Francisco also buttressed the water, the same Pacific Ocean that touched my home country. Could I survive away from the ocean? I had never considered how discombobulated I would feel being landlocked.

I was surprised to see many rolling hills the color of straw all around us. I didn't know what I had expected in Pasadena, but I hadn't imagined this kind of setting. It seemed rough yet welcoming, wild yet controlled at the same time. Why had Victor Marsh established his antique store in such a place? Could people in Pasadena really appreciate the art of Japan, our ancient culture that Okakura had documented?

The train slowed as we approached one of the most gorgeous Western buildings—much more impressive than Yokohama's Grand Hotel—I had ever seen. For a moment, I wondered if it was a castle, but then remembered that America did not have kings, queens, or shoguns. The towers were topped with red-roofed turrets, reminding me of photos of Turkish buildings I had seen displayed in Yokohama stores specializing in exotic art. A covered pedestrian bridge stretched over the street, connecting one structure to another. In back of one was more construction, revealing the owner's ambitious plan for expansion.

A passenger noticed my mouth wide open and commented,

"Hotel Green. The last bit of the west side should be completed by the end of the year."

"Here, get out," Goto ordered me, and I felt the pressure from my wicker carrier ramming against my shoulder. I was practically pushed out of the car, but before I could express any kind of displeasure, there in front of us, a familiar face! Victor Marsh, standing beside a grand horse and buggy that could seat six, raised his arm in welcome. Victor and GT stood out in Japan, even in an international city like Yokohama, mostly because they knew how to move through the archipelago, like albino snakes expertly gliding through low waters. He looked different in America, as I probably did myself. He seemed very relaxed, as if he could be any other gentleman in Pasadena.

I felt like collapsing onto my knees in gratitude, but remembered what the men had said in the boat. That I seemed soft and the type who could be begging for food.

So instead I made my body rail straight and bowed like a crossing gate lowered by a station agent. For an extra American touch, I extended my right hand and pressed it into Victor Marsh's open palm. I immediately regretted the handshake as it made me feel even smaller and more juvenile than I was, but based on the expression on Mr. Marsh's face, my action apparently impressed him.

"You ready to go to your living quarters?" he asked me in Japanese, as Mr. Goto tossed my carrier in a back compartment and pulled himself into the driver's seat behind the two horses. I was both surprised and worried as Mrs. Goto lifted herself next to him with some strain on her face.

I knew that he meant the boardinghouse and not his own home—which I pictured would be palatial, maybe like this Turkish-looking building called the Hotel Green. My abode, I would soon discover, would be much more humble, yet would be inhabited by some of the most important people in my young adult life.

Mr. Goto drove the carriage down what I would learn was the main thoroughfare in Pasadena, Colorado Street, which was lined with impressive storefronts no less than five stories. There were ornately designed facades with protruding window frames and thick decorated columns. Others were plainer, with only striped window awnings providing personality. Corner fruit stands overflowed with oranges. Mr. Goto's eyesight must have been a bit compromised because there were times that Victor had to call out from behind, cautioning Mr. Goto not to run over a bicyclist or a group of boys running across the unevenly paved road. Like in San Francisco, I occasionally saw a horseless vehicle making its way down the middle of the road and marveled how it could operate so smoothly.

"That one runs on electricity," Victor explained as we maintained about the same speed as the vehicle. "It's called a Columbia Runabout. More than half of the cars in Pasadena are electric." Someday, I vowed, I wanted to take a ride in an electric car.

From Colorado we turned on a different street and stopped in front of a two-story wood-framed building painted a grease-gray. It reminded me a little of the houses in Yokohama in its simplicity and spareness, only this one had a pitched roof over its front section as well as over the second floor. There were a few white and pink camellia bushes that framed the narrow porch. That bit of color cheered me immensely, as I rarely saw plants grace the doors of the urban structures in Yokohama.

Mr. Goto was still balancing my wicker carrier on his shoulder as Victor pushed through the front door unannounced. Only a cheap bell tinkled from the top of the door.

I followed my welcoming party through a small, worn parlor and past a long scuffed table that seemed to be made out of Australian cedar, plain but durable.

"Hello!" Victor called out.

We traipsed up the wooden stairs. It felt strange to step inside a house with our filthy shoes, but then the house itself looked untidy, so it seemed not to matter.

"Jack!" Victor shouted at a second-floor room located in the front of the house. "Your new roommate has arrived." The door was ajar but there was no response. Instead, a narrow door facing it flung open and an Asian man with a mop of wavy black hair appeared, the sleeves of his button-down shirt folded up to his elbows. He wore round wire spectacles and something in his nature seemed forever youthful, but when he began to speak, I could tell he was at least a decade older than me.

"I told you, Victor, that I prefer living solo. Taking on another roommate . . ." He then noticed my miserable figure. "Ah, welcome, welcome," he said, not sounding welcoming in the least. "I'm just finishing up in here."

A sulfur scent reminiscent of southern Japanese hot springs shocked my senses. Victor peered into the small room that Jack had appeared from. "The bathtub—how inconvenient," Victor said, frowning.

Jack was pinning wet photographs on a clothesline over the tub, which was about two knuckles full of a clear liquid that I surmised was some sort of development fluid. Indeed, that was confirmed by some trays, also wet and noxious, and jars of chemicals on the tiled floor.

Mr. Goto frowned, his disapproval quite obvious in the deep lines forming around his mouth. Mrs. Goto seemed more amused—no smile, of course, but her wide-set eyes seemed to twinkle.

Jack wiped his hands on a towel and then gestured toward the open door across the way. "This is a bit of a mess," he said. I wasn't sure whether he was talking about the bathroom or his bedroom, or perhaps both.

The bedroom was about six tatami mats in size. There was a mattress on a metal frame against the far wall. A clothesline, featuring more photographs, stretched above it. Sheets were balled up on the bed, indicating that my new roommate was an untidy sleeper.

On the other side of the room was a small, thin mattress with no frame. It was bare and I assumed that would be the place where I was to rest my head.

Mr. Goto attempted to find an open place for my carrier, but without many clear options, just dropped it on my mattress.

"Oh, *gomen, gomen.*" Jack apologized and turned to me. "I'm not making a great impression, am I? Torajiro Baba. But you can call me Jack." His movements were frenetic, like a plover on the seashore. "I try to use the bathtub in the middle of the day to develop my photographs. At least that's the agreement I have with the others. I hope you won't mind. And what is your name?"

"Wada. Ryunosuke." I bowed to my future roommate. "I've lived most of my life in Yokohama. But I was born in Yamaguchi."

"A Chugoku boy. Me, too. I'm from Okayama."

I felt a pang of nostalgia upon hearing the place name. Okayama, known for its black castle, was replete with white peaches in the summertime. I would have loved to bite into the firm, sweet flesh of an Okayama peach right now.

"He'll need your help, Jack," Victor interjected. "He knows nothing about Pasadena. Or even America for that matter."

Jack studied me, focusing his gaze from above his spectacles. "I'm not the fatherly type. But I'll help when I can."

I heard Mr. Goto's footsteps as he went down the stairs. Mrs. Goto at least nodded her head goodbye.

"*Domo* for the sandwich," I thanked her before she disappeared.

"Take tomorrow to rest from your journey but report to the store the following day." Victor also seemed eager to leave the cramped boardinghouse. "Jack will show you where to go. I will be away from Pasadena for a few days on business, but I'll see you when I get back."

I felt a bit panicked not to have my benefactor present to give me instructions on what my exact responsibilities were. I didn't want to disappoint, and not knowing what was expected of me could lead to my failure. Yet I said nothing. I was embarrassed to bring up such personal matters in front of my new roommate.

Once I was completely alone with Jack, he sat on the edge of his bed, sinking into his crumpled-up sheets.

"How old are you?" he said. He spoke to me in English from the beginning, which signaled to me that we were to abandon our Japanese language here in America.

I puffed my chest as large as I could. "Eighteen," I replied.

"Well, let's see who you are." Removing a pocketknife from his pants, he went to my luggage and sliced the twine wrapped around it. He then proceeded to dump all the contents on the empty mattress.

I was shocked beyond belief. This was outrageous, unacceptable behavior from a Japanese person, or any person for that matter, but then again, I would soon learn that Jack was no ordinary man.

He squatted down to get a better look at my belongings. Ignoring my clothing, he went straight to *Ideals of the East*, which he flipped through. "Okakura. Impressive. I don't think I've seen this one before."

"George Turner Marsh gave it to me before I left."

"Oh, GT. I've heard rumors that he's going to build a Japanese garden here in Pasadena."

I was confused. Wasn't Pasadena his brother's territory? But maybe that was feudal thinking.

"Do you like Okakura?" I asked Jack. I myself didn't have any strong feelings about him, and due to the rocking of the ship, I had only managed to read about five pages of the book. Maybe I could adopt the stance of someone more opinionated.

Jack shrugged. "Traditional thinker. He wants to bring Japan back to Japan. I don't have much time to preserve the old. I'm more interested in what we can do with the new." He tossed the book back in my now-empty wicker basket, then noticed Tama-chan on the mattress. "And what's this?" He grabbed hold of my *kobu*.

My first inclination was to take his pocketknife or my chisel and slash his arm to release my wooden companion. But Tama-chan's shine had been transformed to a miserable dull color, perhaps from the lack of natural oils on my palms from the ocean trip. Was my *kobu* even worth defending?

"A *kobu*! I haven't seen one of these in ages. My grandfather had a *kobu* from a cypress root that he hand rubbed into a golden sheen. He didn't let many people see it. I was one of the few. He was a Buddhist priest and I think he used it in his meditations. I don't meditate, but I like the look of this thing."

He held my *kobu* flat in his palm as if Tama-chan were a butterfly, so I was able to snatch it back into my possession. Since Jack had so boldly infringed on my space, I felt emboldened to wander to his side of the room. Propped on a chair on the side of his bed was a large box camera.

"*Sugoi!*" I declared in Japanese after inspecting the camera more closely. "That must have cost you a lot of money." I surprised myself in expressing my inner thoughts so openly.

"You bet it did. Every cent from working at Manako's, the restaurant down the street."

"You cook?"

"I clean."

"Oh."

"I think they are in need of another dishwasher, but it looks like you have your hands full with Mr. Marsh."

I couldn't imagine this eccentric photographer behind a sink filled with dirty dishes.

"Listen, I have more prints to develop before my shift at Manako's, okay? We'll chat more later."

The bathroom door slammed shut. I was relieved to end my interaction with this strange man. Had living in America made him more odd, or had he been this way in Japan already? In my father's carpentry world, men rarely spoke out of turn, deferring to their *senpai*, or masters, to direct them first. On the other hand, to speak without self-censure seemed liberating, but I was always afraid to exercise such an option. So I instead concentrated on the paint peeling from the door's surface. The moisture from the bathroom was causing damage to the door, I quickly ascertained. Someone would have to remove the paint with chemicals or else use a hand plane to sand it clean. The second option was preferable, at least in my experience.

The bell on the front door sounded again and I peered down. Entering the boardinghouse was the most beautiful girl I had ever seen. She wore a navy blue dress cinched at the waist with a flowing bustle, and she had thick hair the color of cherrywood and full voluptuous lips that made my lower body tingle.

I had seen white women in Yokohama, of course, but most of them were older with heavy upper arms and loose necks. The younger ones were the daughters of diplomats, definitely belonging to another social class and living in houses very different from mine.

She paused in the entryway to gaze up at me. "Oh, hello. You must be Jack's new roommate. I'm Rosalie Georgia Greeman. Most people call me Gigi."

I was trembling. At least the distance between us would not reveal my nervousness. "Ah, I am Wada. Ryunosuke." I added my first name because I knew Americans liked to refer to each other informally.

"Oh, my goodness, I'll just butcher that."

I looked at her blankly, not comprehending what she was saying.

"Do your friends call you by another name? Maybe something shorter? We called Jack's former roommate Eddie. I couldn't even begin to pronounce his actual name."

Somehow I felt competitive toward this Eddie, especially in the presence of this beautiful woman. "My employer calls me Ryui."

"Louie. Oh, that's quite a wonderful name. Louie," she repeated as if she didn't want to forget it. After removing her gloves, she waved them at me from the foot of the stairs. "I'll see you around, Louie." She left my sight and I heard her high-heeled boots echoing from another part of the house.

My face was a beet red as I stepped back toward the bedroom, only to discover that Jack had been observing us from the open bathroom door.

I wanted to immediately pepper Jack with questions. Who was that? Surely she didn't live here, too?

"Louie, huh?" he only said. "I guess Gigi has given you your American name." Then he laughed and returned to his photographs, again shutting the bathroom door behind him.

I was being introduced to Jack's strange habit of popping in and out of his makeshift developing room. I had been taught to respect anyone older than me, but Jack was making it difficult to do so.

I returned to our room, taking off my stiff boots at the doorway. Obviously, judging from the dirt on the hardwood floors and the worn rug in the middle of the room, Jack had not continued that Japanese practice, but I needed to be free of the tightness around my ankles.

Now alone, I took the liberty to freely examine the rest of Jack's belongings. He had taken up every centimeter of the small closet. I gave him credit for having clean and pressed clothes, at least. Being a photographer, he must value appearances. On top of a built-in bureau were a gray felt hat, a canister of brushing powder, and an empty glass holding a toothbrush. I twisted open the canister to release a scent of old earth.

In Japan, we didn't spend that much time on dental care. Until recently, upper-class married women had dyed their teeth black with strong tea, herbs, and iron tar. I cleaned my teeth with the side of my finger, which I sometimes salted for a more thorough treatment. I felt determined to learn to groom myself as Americans did to make myself attractive to women like Gigi.

A hair brush held a few of my roommate's wavy strands and I wondered if his family lineage included a European ancestor, maybe a Portuguese or Dutch trader. My own hair was pin straight, as was my parents', confirming that no intruders had entered our family lineage.

I returned to closely study the prints that he had pinned on the clothesline. Some of them were of Japanese immigrant farmers, standing next to plows, in fields of flowers, or between irrigated lines of strawberries. Even though the black-and-white images could not adequately capture the vibrancy of the brilliant red fruit or pastel-colored chrysanthemums, the hopeful and determined expressions of the farmers and their families were a sight to behold.

Other photos were of still objects: a rotting, sunken orange on a scratched surface I would later recognize as the table where we took our meals. The shadow of the metal spokes of a bicycle wheel against a dirt background. Circles on slick black liquid. They all were extraordinary. Even I, who knew little about photography, could see what he was intending visually.

My father had said that sometimes genius was very close to madness; that's why he himself didn't believe in hiring any workers with unconventional methods or vision. At the end of the 1890s, there were an increasing number of men who were trained at the Imperial University and called themselves architects rather than carpenters. They also embraced the shrine and temple style that my father practiced, but with the knowledge of Western styles such as Queen Anne and Gothic. My father feared that somehow this training of foreign design would seep into his distinctly Japanese work and he rejected them outright.

It seemed like Jack fell closer to the "breaking the rules" end of the spectrum, rather than abiding in our established traditions. However, I didn't have much choice in my living situation. Either I would share my room with a genius madman or spend the night on a muddy street dotted with horse manure.

I addressed the pile of my belongings on the pitiful bare mattress. My father had taught me the importance of making sure that our working tools—our handsaws and such—were polished, cleaned, and sharpened. Cleanliness and order were our guiding lights. I found a small built-in bookshelf and adopted it as my bureau, folding my meager shirts, pantaloons, and underpants in neat squares and stacking them up according to category. I rubbed my *kobu*'s smooth surface a couple of times before lying down with it in my hand—I was planning to only rest for a moment . . . but then I was startled by the ringing of a bell. The room was considerably darkened. The sunlight through the opaque curtains was diffused.

I wondered what time it was. There was no clock nearby, so I awkwardly pulled my boots back on to leave the room. The bathroom door was ajar and I wanted to take a bath so desperately, but judging from some strong smells downstairs from the kitchen, dinner was being served.

I went back and forth on what I should do, and since Jack was absent, I could only rely on my flesh—hunger. I slowly and quietly walked down the stairs, prepared to retreat back into my bedroom if needed.

"Well, the prince has awakened!" A woman with a flame of demon-red hair held two plates of food above the boarders seated at an oval table in the dining room. Jack was not among the diners. The apron that the woman was wearing was stained with what looked like streaks of blood and I honestly feared what was on our plates.

"I am sorry to be late for the meal," I told her.

"Thank goodness you speak English!" the cook exclaimed. "Jack's old roommate must have been a straight descendant from the samurai, judging from all the grunting he did. He wasn't too hard on the eyes, at least."

People kept mentioning the prior roommate, this Eddie. I wondered what had happened to him. I could imagine that he had tired of Jack's eccentricity and moved out.

"I am from Yokohama. Many people from the West live there."

"Yokohama, Pokohoma, it's all the same to me." She gestured for me to sit at an empty seat between two burly white men in overalls. One was a smaller version of the other and I later learned they were brothers, both machinists at the Pasadena Machine Shop on Broadway. Both of them wrinkled their noses at me in reaction to the dreadful smells emanating from my travel-worn clothes.

As I was settling in a wooden chair, Gigi appeared from a

door down the hallway from the kitchen. I hoped she would keep her distance from me; I should have sacrificed eating for bathing.

She wore a fetching green dress and in one gloved hand was a clasped embroidered bag, which looked more functional than glamorous. "Off to the opera house, don't expect me until late," she said as she walked through the dining room. She flashed me a smile. "Nice to see you again, Louie," she said, and I felt a surge of blood rush to my head.

The brothers, their mouths each filled with yet to be fully consumed dinner rolls, guffawed.

"Is she a theater performer?" I asked once the door closed behind her. Surely she was attractive enough to be on stage.

"No, she mends the costumes that the actresses wear. Either way, don't get any ideas. I don't condone any kind of fraternization between boarders. My house, my rules—that's why this is called the Riley House. I run a clean ship here." The woman who I erroneously thought was merely the cook must have picked up on the spark between me and Gigi.

"Oh, do you now," the smaller brother said and the two dissolved in laughter again. He had a strong accent that I identified as being from the British part of the world.

"I just hope that you aren't like that other Japanese gentleman who shared the room with Jack. All that man had were complaints. No meat, nothing with gravy. But he still managed to be as strong as these blokes."

"Mrs. Riley, look how wee this boy is," said the smaller man. "I'm sure that he'll eat anything that you serve." I appreciated his advocacy but was a bit irritated that he had referred to my measly frame. "And they call you Louie, do they?" he continued. I was prepared to tell him my full given name, but he then added, "That's a name of royalty, at least from our part of the world. You could do much worse."

I felt some warmth spread into my insides. If Louie was a name that commanded respect, I would enthusiastically adopt it.

"My name is Simon. And that's my younger brother, Ian."

I nodded in response, grateful for his introduction. I was finding it a challenge to piece together all these new people and cultural practices. Just to have the brothers acknowledge that I could start from the beginning with them was a relief.

As I waited for Mrs. Riley to serve me, I noticed that Ian had a very strange propensity for eating with his left hand. I only had known of one person, a talented carpenter, to use his left, but since he was able to work on certain joints better than us right-handed workers, no one tried to cure him of this curious habit. If the Boyle brothers switched seats, I would have been relieved of my unfortunate situation, two elbows being thrust my way during the meal.

My troubles didn't end there, however. I did have some occasion in Yokohama to use a fork and knife, but the silverware seemed so heavy and inelegant, nothing like the simplicity and ease of chopsticks. The meat—who knows what kind of animal it was—was tough and the potatoes were hard and not seasoned properly. The food was indeed quite terrible. I craved a simple bowl of rice with a pickled plum on top. But I wasn't going to insult the cook by complaining. Instead I forced myself to eat every speck of the horrible food, later vomiting most of it in our bathroom, which still stank of sulfur.

3.

That night sleep came to me swiftly. In the early morning I was awoken by a strange noise that sounded like wooden *geta* walking on cobblestones, only this was coming from my roommate's bed. Jack was furiously gnashing his teeth, bellowing in Japanese, "*Yamé, yamé.*" I was too afraid to intervene and covered my ears with my fists, hoping that the nightmare in Jack's head would eventually pass through.

When my eyes fluttered open again, the room was shrouded in dim light. I looked outside and spied the same scene that I had the previous night. The streetlights flickered on, guiding the motorized cars and men in wagons driving horses down the road. Had I really slept for twenty-four hours?

When I ventured down in my boots, shoelaces untied to accommodate my swollen feet, I could smell the remnants of burnt meat, which turned my stomach.

"You fortunately missed supper." Simon sat reclined in a dining room chair. "But we saved you some bread and cheese from our lunch."

Ian presented me with the food, which I gobbled without restraint.

"He resembles that rat that used to visit us in our old lodging house." Ian's ample belly jiggled with laughter. Although he was much larger than his older brother, his voice was softer and I had to concentrate to comprehend what he was saying. "Simon and I are going to play tenpin. Would you like to come with us?"

I had no idea what tenpin was, but agreed to tag along, not wanting to appear rude.

I was still incredulous that I had slept for a day and followed the two brothers in a bit of a haze. Fortunately for my feet, we only had to walk around the corner to a simple building marked with a sign reading BOWLING. Inside were four narrow lanes made of light-colored wood like pine, facing white pins set up in the shape of a triangle. We were the only players in the building and I wondered how popular this tenpin game was.

"Get your ball, Louie," Ian called out from the far wall

where at least thirty large globes sat on wooden shelves. Both he and Simon quickly selected large ones from the bottom shelf, hefting them in their hands.

I approached the shelves and noticed that there were three holes drilled in each globe—two close together like eyes and one below, an open mouth. I imitated the brothers and picked up one from the lower shelf but almost fell over from its weight. Simon chuckled and directed me to a smaller one on the top shelf, which proved to weigh much less. This ball was made of wood, and in my hands, it felt familiar, like an old friend.

"What kind of wood is this?" I pressed my hands around the globe and took a big sniff. I could not detect anything beyond oil and perspiration.

Simon crinkled his nose. "You are a strange wee lad, aren't you? It's oak, but it's not meant to be caressed, but thrown."

Ian was already standing on the edge of one of the lanes and releasing his globe down the alley with his left hand. It bounced against the hardwood and then rolled with ferocity toward the pins. The ball toppled some of them, but left four still standing.

I jumped in response to the noise of the crashing pins and then Ian's cursing. I had been exposed to drunken brawling foreigners in Yokohama late at night, so I had heard those English expressions before. It seemed the goal of the game was to knock all the pins down. Ian took another turn and was able to strike only two of the four remaining pins. More yelling. A young boy wearing a cap and suspenders appeared from the back to roll back Ian's ball and reset the pins back in their original position while Simon sat in a chair and marked Ian's score on a piece of paper with a pencil.

"Your turn." Simon instructed me to place my thumb in my ball's mouth and my middle and medicine fingers in its eyes. He first attempted to show me himself with my ball, but his meaty fingers could not even fit into the holes. I noticed that his fingernails were lined with a black residue, perhaps machine oil.

Once I was able to accurately position my hands, Simon gestured to the other side of the lane. "Just aim for the pins."

It felt strange to attempt to throw something so heavy. This was a most unusual activity. I couldn't exactly mimic what I had seen Ian do as I was using my right hand, but tried my best to be a mirror image.

"Gutter ball!" Ian predicted as my oak ball rolled past the ten standing pins into the sunken trough parallel to the wooden lane.

My feet were pulsing with pain and I pulled off my leather boots, revealing my *tabi*.

"Look at those, brother." Ian pointed at my socks and laughed, his good mood restored after his poor performance. "The feet of a duck."

Placing my fingers in another ball, I focused on the center pin, the leader. I stepped forward in my *tabi* and released. My ball curved slightly but stayed on course, knocking down all the pins in a majestic flurry.

Simon howled with glee, while Ian became glum again. "You may have some run for your money, Ian. This lad's small but he has technique," said the older brother as he scored my performance on his paper. I was given a ten. He advised, "Attempt to get a high score in your next turn to maximize your spare." He explained that in contrast, knocking all ten pins down in the beginning of a single frame was called a strike.

We continued and alas, as my arm became more weary from the weight of the ball, Ian braced up and soon his lane was raining spilled pins.

"Another strike!" called out Simon, whose score was also much higher than mine.

"He's very good," I said as we waited for the boy to reset

the pins. We were in what Simon called the last frame, and since Ian had a strike, he was afforded another try to further elevate his numbers. His ball, when delivered properly, had a magnificent spin to it; while seeming to head for the gutter, it corrected itself midway down the lane to ultimately hit the head pin and all the nine pines behind it.

"That's Ian for you. Archery, lawn bowling, wrestling, he can do it all."

And in that first game, Ian did. He scored more than 200; Simon, 167; and I, 113. Both brothers assured me that for a first effort, I had done well. Ian polished his ball with the inside of his shirt while I waited to see if we were to play another game.

"Are you from America?" I finally asked the brothers. From their rhythm of speech, I had guessed that they were from England but I didn't want to make any assumptions.

"Ireland," Simon said.

I didn't encounter too many Irish people in Yokohama. "How are you different from the British?"

"The Brits would call us hooligans. Troublemakers with no sense of decorum."

Ian nodded in agreement.

"How long have you been staying at the Riley House?" I asked.

"About a year. We were at another lodging house but it was too far from the center of town."

"Do you know Jack well? He was gone when I woke up this morning."

"Jack can be quite a vampire," Ian said. Upon my lack of response, Ian continued, "They don't have vampires in your country? They are creatures that drink human blood when you are sleeping. Jack seems the most active when the sun sets, doesn't he, Simon?"

"Oh, Jack and his secrets." Simon uncharacteristically

mumbled his response and excused himself to take his turn to throw his wooden globe.

Ian pulled his chair next to mine. "Simon doesn't like to talk much about Jack and Eddie. Their friendship didn't end well."

My stomach sank. I feared my cohabitation could result in me also fleeing the Riley House.

Simon's release was a bit too forceful and ended up only knocking down one pin on the end.

"I saw that Gigi caught your eye." Ian abruptly changed the subject.

"Pardon?" I felt my face grow hot. I was not used to someone, especially a near stranger, infringing on my privacy about such a personal matter.

"Are you interested in her?" Ian was unrelenting.

"Ah—" I stuttered.

"Simon was. Couldn't get very far with her."

Simon's second attempt at knocking down the pins was more successful, resulting in a total of eight pins down. "I think she may be a woman who would be captivated by a specimen like Louie," he said.

I wasn't sure if that was an insult but didn't probe more to find out.

"In my country, a young single woman does not live by herself in a boardinghouse," I said. I was surprised that I had spoken my concerns out loud.

"Speak of the devil, here comes her bosom friend, Josephine Carter," Simon whispered.

A lean and tall woman strolled toward us in a plain floor-length skirt and short-sleeved white shirt. Her skin was very pale and she had light eyebrows and eyelashes; like young Japanese girls, she had her hair cut abruptly above her eyes in a style that reminded me of dried rice stalks. "May I join you?" Her voice was surprisingly husky.

"Gigi's not with us. Maybe you better come another time when it's ladies' night." Simon crossed his arms as he spoke to the woman, barely acknowledging her.

The woman did not move. She stared at me for the longest time, studying my features and my *tabi*. I thought that she would ask me questions about where was I from, but she did not. She turned abruptly and headed out of the door.

"That lass is a strange one," Simon commented.

Ian nodded. "She looks a bit like an ostrich."

"Ostrich?"

"They don't have those birds in your country?" Ian extended his burly neck as far as it could go, widened his green eyes, and took a few unsteady steps as if he were lost.

I couldn't help but laugh, but Simon didn't indulge his younger brother's insulting impersonation.

"She's unfortunate looking, but there's no doubt that she'll beat you in tenpin," he said.

Ian pretended he didn't hear his older brother and I blushed, feeling ashamed that I had derived joy from such a caricature. America seemed to extract coarseness that lay in the marrow of one's bones. Time and time again, I was surprised by the wickedness that would emerge not only from other people, but also myself.

4.

The next morning when I awoke, the right side of my body felt a bit stiff. It seemed tenpin caused me to move my arm in ways that I was not used to.

I looked at Jack's bed and found it unoccupied.

I went to the window and pulled back the sheer curtains. The bright sun had returned and the street was full of bicyclists and horse-drawn carriages. I needed to get a timekeeper, but couldn't afford a watch until I could save my earnings. In fact, Victor hadn't really revealed how much I was going to get paid or how I was going to receive my wages.

The second floor seemed to be empty of the Boyle brothers, so I took the opportunity to fill the bathtub with hot water. Back in our rental house in Yokohama, we had a large Japanese tub that we heated with firewood every night. After we scrubbed the day's filth off while outside the tub, we then sank into the warm water up to our chins. I had been warned that such a luxury would be unavailable to me in America. It felt terrible to be soaking my dirty body in the same water I'd be bathing in. As my bathwater turned brown from all the layers of dirt I had accumulated over my long voyage, I could not help but think how barbaric Westerners could be.

Mrs. Riley had left me a thin towel. I dried my body and dressed myself in a simple gray shirt and pants. I had already run out of socks and would have to handwash the two pairs that I had brought.

Mrs. Riley was making a racket in the small kitchen and I hoped that her mood would not worsen when I requested her assistance. The wild strands of hair that had come loose from her headscarf resembled flames as she washed a large cast-iron skillet.

I waited until she was finished before I addressed her. "I need to report to Mr. Marsh's store. Jack is to help me—"

"And let me guess, he's not around." Mrs. Riley spoke knowingly as she finished drying the pan with a dirty rag. My belly then released a loud growl that revealed how famished I was. Apparently Mrs. Riley understood the language my body was speaking. "You remember that you need to take care of your own breakfast and lunch. I'm your landlady, not your caretaker. But I do have a pot of coffee ready every morning."

She had me sit at the dining room table while she poured thick liquid the color of tar into a mug.

I cautiously sipped the offering. The coffee was so strong that it immediately began to burn my stomach, but I was too afraid to show any dissatisfaction with it.

"If you need directions to Victor Marsh's, bring me a piece of paper and something to write with."

I didn't waste any time leaving the coffee. After a stop at my room, I presented Mrs. Riley with a carpentry pencil and a page from my travel journal. I hadn't had time to sharpen the pencil and Mrs. Riley frowned at the thick lines it produced on the piece of paper. Her fingers were misshapen and curled in different directions; later, I would notice that her gait could be unsteady. Yet she completed her physical tasks perhaps inelegantly but with finality.

"We are here." She marked a circle on the paper and then a horizontal line above it. "Colorado is the main street." I didn't quite understand why the most important fairway was named Colorado, because I had heard that was also the name of another state that was known for its impressive mountain peaks. But I suspected I shouldn't interrupt Mrs. Riley to ask. A vertical line came next, a few centimeters from the circle and crossing Colorado Street. "Fair Oaks and Colorado is the center of your compass. If you ever get lost, look for this intersection." She placed a large X on the spot.

"Thank you so much. I'm indebted to you." I carefully folded the map and placed it and the pencil in the deep pocket of my pantaloons. I then bowed to her and then gestured to the woodwork around a window above the sink in the kitchen. Because the window faced the north side, the frame was getting warped by the sun as well as the moisture from the faucet. "Once I get some more tools from Mr. Marsh, I can fix that kitchen window for you."

Mrs. Riley was speechless for a moment and her pinched face softened. I had the feeling that she didn't often get offers of assistance. "Well, go on now." She rose, swatting a small flying insect from her face. "Mr. Marsh will be waiting for you."

Mrs. Riley's map was helpful, and in fact, I kept it for months, adding new locations that I would visit around Pasadena.

I followed the map from Marengo south to Green Street—I assumed that it had been named for the man behind Hotel Green—and then east along a stretch that had been much quieter than Colorado Street. To my south, the land was underdeveloped and vast, with lines of orange groves visible in the distance. Then I neared the grand Hotel Green. What a spectacle it was, with a large, boxier building on the east side of Raymond Avenue connected by a bridge to the more Turkish-influenced addition across the way. Most of the windows were covered and dark, so I assumed the rooms were unoccupied. Would there be a time in which they would all be filled? What would bring so many people to Pasadena?

Since no pedestrians were walking on Green Street at this early hour, I couldn't ask anyone for directions, nor was I inclined to do so. I referred to Mrs. Riley's map. Marsh's emporium should have been right there on the northwestern corner of Raymond and Green facing the side of the new hotel addition. I had been concerned that I wouldn't be able to find it, but such fears were unwarranted. There, on the corner, was a pristine curved three-story building that obviously had been constructed to perfectly fit its location. The top arched windows were long, resembling a feature that I had seen in photos of Italian cathedrals. But the underside of the roof eaves had soffits with a slightly Japanese flare. The bottom floor, obviously the storefront, mimicked a Japanese building with square panes of glass like shoji wall screens.

Through the windows I recognized many of the same goods that I had seen produced in the Yokohama factories that Victor frequented.

I turned the brass doorknob—decorated with an ivy motif—and entered into my new workplace. It was even more inviting inside than outside. Water trickled in a corner from some sort of fountain.

"Welcome, Ryunosuke," said a familiar voice. The figure of Toichiro Kawai had appeared from a back room. "You must be tired after such a long journey."

Even though my father and I were only distantly acquainted with Mr. Kawai, I couldn't help but embrace this familiar person from Yokohama. When I felt the top of my head grazing his impressive mustache, I immediately dropped my arms, shocked by my own spontaneous expression of affection, but Mr. Kawai chuckled in response. I was relieved that he was not offended.

"Come, see where you will be working." Mr. Kawai gestured for me to follow him into the back room, which reminded me of the configuration of my father's smaller space for the construction of furniture. On what appeared to be a custom-made table was a row of flat double-edged handsaws, which were controlled by pulling back on the wood rather than pushing forward as was the case with the Western-style saw. On another table were hammers, mallets, and chisels. On a shelf below were various hand planes and steel blades. The far corner of the room was populated with traditional Japanese furniture in different states of disrepair.

Lining the opposite side of the room were various wood planks of different hues. As I strolled past them, I detected the faint scent of honey, flowers, and then the familiar astringency that was the hallmark of cedar. Now these were old friends.

"You have everything that we have in Yokohama," I

exclaimed, causing Mr. Kawai to beam. He obviously took great pride in emulating what we practiced across the Pacific Ocean in Japan.

In the middle of the workroom was a reddish wood post secured onto two sawhorses. I took a big sniff to see if I could identify the tree variety. It smelled of soil being turned over with a slight sweetness and zing of chili spice. I didn't think I had encountered such a tree before. "What is this wood—"

The bell on the door rang out and before I could complete my question to Mr. Kawai, a well-built young man wearing a vest and tie burst into the workroom. I suspected he was of African heritage, based on some traders I had run into in Yokohama. "Oh, you're here already. Another early bird!" His presence immediately energized the more sedate setting. "I'm Logan James, salesman." He plucked a black full-length apron from a line of other such aprons in a corner by the door, pulled his head of curly, frizzy hair through the loop, and tied the belt around his waist. He presented another one to me.

"I am Wada. Louie Wada," I said with a dash of pride. I put on the apron, which hung loosely on my body. It felt familiar, like the one I'd worn at my father's business.

"Louie, thank God. I've been practicing Ryu-no-su-ke all morning. Made a mess of it. Hey, but I think I did it." Logan's dark round eyes widened earnestly. "Ryu-no-su-ke. Ryu-no-su-ke. Sounds like a song."

I felt grateful that Logan had been attempting to embrace my Japanese identity. Hardly anyone—except perhaps my father—said my full name in Japan. "Wada is good enough."

"No, I'm calling you Ryunosuke. It's like conjuring a spell, like abracadabra." Logan grinned, and I also noticed a flash of Mr. Kawai's smile.

I was desperately trying to ascertain the hierarchy in Victor's absence. Was I supposed to get my instructions from Logan, or Mr. Kawai? "Do you know what my duties are?" I finally plucked up enough courage to inquire.

Logan explained to me that Victor handled the important customers, who usually came with an appointment, while he dealt mostly with deliveries and pickups. Mr. Kawai was in charge of all repairs and refinishings. I would assist in any way I was called for. I would work Monday through Friday and when necessary, also on Saturday.

That the enterprise could be operated by such a small staff revealed either that not many craftsmen could do what we did, or else a lack of demand for such specialized merchandise.

As I was contemplating the modest size of this enterprise, Logan made an astonishing declaration: "This Saturday you will be working the cherry blossom dinner at the Hotel Green."

"Cherry blossom," I clarified, and even repeated in Japanese, "sakura?"

Logan didn't bother to address my confusion. "The invitations just went out a couple of days ago and the whole town is abuzz."

"Pasadena has sakura?" I asked again hopefully. March was certainly the season for it in Japan.

Logan finally acknowledged my obsession with my nation's most iconic flower. "No, no, these paper ones were shipped over. And Mr. Aoki is hand making some with his girls."

I had no idea what Logan was talking about, and my confusion was quite evident.

"You've heard of Toshio Aoki?"

I shook my head.

"You're pulling my leg. I thought you were from Japan."

"I am," I said, a bit annoyed.

"Well, Toshio Aoki is world-famous. He even has his own studio in Hotel Green. Can't believe you've never heard of him."

A Japanese artisan had already made his mark in Pasadena! I was both impressed and jealous.

"He and GT are as thick as thieves. They were together in San Francisco, working on the fair over there about ten years ago. What they built is still up. I was able to go with Victor recently. The teahouse will make you feel like you're in Japan."

Why would I want to experience a reproduction of Japan when I had just come from the real place?

"Anyway, this cherry blossom dinner is the talk of the town. And as you are serving your countrymen's food, you'll get to rub elbows with Mrs. Pullman, Mrs. Pierpont, all the grand missuses . . . I heard there's a reporter, Grace Hortense Tower, who's going to be there."

Who were these people? Even though I nodded my head, as I would do in Yokohama, the expression on my face must have betrayed my innermost thoughts.

"These are money people," Logan clarified. "Or at least mostly their wives. You know, the ones who can make things happen at the drop of a hat."

I gathered that Logan was referring to the rich. Back in Yokohama, I was used to being around the powerful. Who else could afford our carpentry services, after all? Our overlords were religious leaders, who could also be quite frightening even without any weapons hidden in their robes. I couldn't imagine that anyone in this city of Pasadena could be as formidable.

"You'll be there, too?" I asked.

"No, they just need Japanese faces," he said.

Even though I had no experience serving food to anyone, I qualified.

The front door opened and Logan left the workroom to greet a society woman, who collapsed her parasol to come into the store. Using a hand plane, Kawai smoothed the post balanced on the sawhorses. *Whoosh*, *whoosh*, *whoosh*. That level of repetitive motion and rhythm was almost hypnotic, and I felt my anxiety disappear.

"Kawai-san, let me do that for you."

"*Daijoubu.*" He rebuffed my offer. "You are not familiar with this wood. Redwood from the forests north of San Francisco. The splinters are like poison; it is difficult to remove them once they enter your skin."

That sounded quite horrifying, so I relented. But I still wanted to be of help, and Mr. Kawai asked me to wait a moment until he was finished stripping the redwood of its outermost layer.

"By the way," he said to me in Japanese while he continued to work, "do not feel bad that you have not heard of Aoki-san before. He is quite well-known in this town, but doesn't have a following in Japan. I know him because we both worked for Deakin Brothers and Marsh."

Mr. Kawai kept his eyes on the piece of redwood that he was smoothing out. I couldn't determine what he himself felt about Mr. Aoki's artwork.

"Will you go to the party?" I asked.

He shook his head. "I have too much to do here." I gathered, however, there was perhaps another reason that he was not attending, but felt that it would be disrespectful to press a craftsman who was old enough to be my father about his true thoughts.

After he'd finished stripping the redwood surface, Mr. Kawai pulled out a cedar table with a missing leg from the corner of broken furniture. The table was constructed with joints and not nails, and Mr. Kawai instructed me to create a new leg from one of the cedar planks. A test! Eager to prove myself and live up to my father's legacy, I got to work.

I sharpened the tip of my pencil with one of the knives, and using a measuring rod made of bamboo I determined where to mark notches on a cedar plank about the same color as the table. After hand sawing the wood, I used a carpenter's square to draw angles of the appropriate cuts to accommodate fitted joints.

"Eh," Mr. Kawai grunted in approval, breaking the rhythm of work I had assumed. Apparently he had been watching me the whole time. "You have been trained well," he said. My heart soared. From that point on, he trusted me to complete the task without instruction. As we both worked in silence, I felt that my old self in Yokohama was returning.

A few hours passed quickly, and the sun cast a warm glow on all the decorative items on display in the storefront windows. Mixed with the intermittent ringing of the bell attached to the front door, I heard different pitches of female voices and Logan's warm timbre. I wondered when Victor would be coming and then recalled that he said he would be out of town for business. Based on how many times the Marsh brothers came in and out of Yokohama, despite the lengthy boat ride, I knew they both were constantly on the move.

"Did you bring something to eat?" Mr. Kawai asked. Clearly, he had heard the loud rumbling from my stomach. My body was certainly communicating my physical needs today.

I shook my head. Mrs. Riley had informed me that I was responsible for preparing my own lunch, but our maid had handled such duties in Yokohama and I was at a loss on food preparation, especially in a new land with different culinary practices. In America I had to face that I was indeed a *botchan*, expecting food to magically appear when needed.

"I will share my lunch today. But you must bring something every day for yourself." Mr. Kawai pulled out a parcel wrapped in dyed indigo cloth. Quickly loosening a knot tied at the top of the package with his nimble fingers, he presented me with a rectangular woven bamboo bento box. Inside were two beautiful triangular rice balls and a piece of pungent mackerel, its grilled skin shiny silver. Only a master craftsman could create such perfectly formed rice balls. I almost began to weep.

"I know of a Chinese peddler who brings his vegetables for sale on his cart once a week in Pasadena. He gave me the rice. I've become friends with a fisherman in San Pedro. He comes from Wakayama and knows how to catch fish with bamboo poles."

"Uncle," I gasped as Mr. Kawai shared one of the rice balls and half of the fish with me. I hadn't had Japanese-style rice in days since our stopover in Honolulu, and it felt like a lifetime ago. "Thank you so much."

Mr. Kawai bowed in response and said he was going outside to a nearby park to eat his lunch. He didn't extend an invitation for me to join him, so I remained in the workroom to watch over the store. It only took me a few minutes to devour my lunch, and before I knew it, Mr. Kawai had returned to the storefront.

He remained in the front room, however. The bell rang and I heard him greet a customer: "Lady Madison, so good to see you." I peeked to see a large woman standing in front of the counter. Mr. Kawai took two very deep bows, so I quickly gathered that she was a customer of import. In fact, I would eventually discover that Lady Madison was Victor Marsh's best patron, consuming teacups, dishes, and sake sets like they were sweet confections.

Once Lady Madison left, Mr. Kawai returned to the workroom, a serious expression on his face. "Ryunosuke," he said in Japanese, "I'm sorry about your father. I could not go to his funeral and I realized that I said nothing about his passing to you. Forgive me for my negligence."

I couldn't look into his eyes or else I would dissolve into tears. I took hold of the chisel and pressed it down into holes I had created for the mortise. With some gentle taps of the mallet against the back of the chisel, the hole expanded.

Even though I had not done any work that was exceedingly physically taxing, by the time I entered the Riley House at the end of the day, all I wanted to do was wilt on my mattress.

In the front parlor sat Gigi, the last bit of sunshine through a dusty window creating a halo over her head.

An otherworldly sight, until I noticed that across from her was her friend, whom the Boyle brothers and I had encountered at the tenpin alley.

Gigi was looking at me grimly; I feared that Josephine had given her a report of how we had rejected her. I was ready to escape into my room, but when I reached the base of the staircase, Gigi's voice stopped me: "Louie, may I speak with you?"

"Ah—" I turned back toward the dining room and saw Josephine slipping out the front door.

After we both took a seat at the dining room table, Gigi immediately got to business. "I just spoke to my friend, Josephine Carter. She said that she saw you with the Boyle brothers at Hare and Bray's bowling alley. You didn't let her play with you."

My face burned. I had already felt ashamed about my complicity, but to have Gigi discover it and confront me? It would be my fate to be held accountable for every wrong I committed in this new land.

Gigi noted my discomfort. "I know that it wasn't your doing. The Boyle brothers are fine, but they have quite old-fashioned notions when it comes to women." She paused, as if she were waiting for me to agree with her.

"I would have liked to see your friend perform tenpin," was all I could manage.

"I better tell you that Josephine and her mother are frequent customers to Marsh's emporium. They collect those little figurines—what do you call it, nets-something."

"Netsuke," I guessed. Netsuke was the rage among foreigners in Yokohama. Smaller than an adult's little finger, these tiny carvings were designed to hang on a cord from a kimono sash.

"Yes, those things. I thought that I would warn you to treat her properly."

"Of course," I said. "I'm happy that you took the time to tell me."

Gigi's blemish-free skin glowed with health. I couldn't help but stare at her wide mouth and bee-stung lips. "Thank you for taking the time to listen to me," she said. With that, she stood, bestowing on me another of her bright smiles. "I'm sure you need to get cleaned up for dinner. So long!"

Watching her bustled figure disappear out the front door, I breathed in the lavender scent she left behind and then wondered if my own lack of hygiene had led her to make such a comment.

I felt quite ashamed of myself as I made the trek up the stairs to my shared bedroom. I couldn't be the same passive person I was in Yokohama. But how in the world could I change?

5.

While I wanted to understand my new town—which, at the time, I was convinced would be only a temporary place of residence—I was quite fearful of exploring it beyond the boundaries of Mrs. Riley's map. In Yokohama, I encountered Europeans, Americans, and Australians on a regular basis, but we Japanese still outnumbered them. They were like white sesame seeds on a golden grilled rice ball—decoration and seasoning, but still not the main attraction. Here in Pasadena, *I* was the ornament. I didn't know if I would get smashed or spat out if I wandered into the wrong place.

Hotel Green, on the other hand, reminded me of home. I felt quite emotional about the covered walkway that attached its two impressive buildings over a busy street. It was the closest thing in Pasadena to a bridge, reminding me of the Kintaikyo Bridge in my birthplace—a spectacular creation that attracted Japanese from across the archipelago to visit and gaze at its five arches reflected in the Nishiki River.

Ever since Logan had told me that the cherry blossom dinner would be held inside of the Hotel Green, I had been overcome with excitement to actually enter the building. The party would be held in Mr. Aoki's studio, which apparently was quite expansive, large enough to accommodate seventy or so people. The studio was located on the first floor of the more flamboyant building on the west side, and I was eager to see how the interior was configured.

I was also quite worried about what I was expected to do and wear. *I cannot bring shame to Mr. Aoki or the event*, I thought to myself. I had already hurt the feelings of Josephine Carter, an offense that had even been felt by her magnificent friend. I was committed to improving my behavior.

Logan, unfortunately, had to suffer through my anxious inquiries about what was required of me at the cherry blossom dinner, but offered to take me to meet Mr. Aoki ahead of the event. He said I could pick up my uniform from him ahead of time, too.

Hearing that I would finally make the famed artist's acquaintance, I was able to work the rest of the afternoon with a sense of peace. I had completed my work on the table leg—now I was to test it, placing the tenon into the mortise to see if the joint would hold. I could hear my father's instruction. *It should be tight, but no friction.* As I pulled out the tenon, I heard the familiar slight pop, the sign of a job well-done.

Mr. Kawai was pounding a chair leg with a mallet when I heard the bell on the door. Mr. Kawai gestured for me to greet the visitor, as he often would from that point on. I eventually learned that Mr. Kawai was more comfortable dealing with wood than people. Entering the emporium was a stylish white man, with a trimmed mustache and wavy hair combed in back of his ears. Through his spectacles, light-colored eyes gazed observantly at me. "You're new," he said.

"Yes. I came from Japan this week. My name is Louie." I introduced myself with my American name and didn't provide my surname, which felt both awkward and invigorating. Was I on my way to becoming an American?

"I'm Charles Greene." The man extended his hand and I took it, surprised to feel familiar calluses on both his fingers and palms. Although this stranger looked like a gentleman, he also worked with his hands, which made me feel more connected to him. I wondered if there was any kind of link between this man and the Hotel Green. Later I learned that this man's surname ended in an *e* and was completely unrelated to the hotel.

Mr. Kawai emerged from the workroom, wiping his hands with a rag. "Mr. Greene, so nice to see you."

"Thank you for lending me those issues of *Kokka* magazine," Mr. Greene said. "I can't read the text, of course, but I'm so enamored by the images. I hope someday the Japanese publisher can offer a translated English version?"

I knew *Kokka* magazine well. Okakura, the author of the Chicago World's Fair pamphlet and the book that GT had given me, had been largely behind it, and my father had been a great supporter.

"Okakura-san—" I couldn't help but to blurt out.

Mr. Greene shifted his attention to me. A faint look of disapproval clouded Mr. Kawai's face.

I blushed. "Ah, Okakura Kakuzo. He's a famous man in Japan who helped to start *Kokka*."

"Oh," Mr. Greene responded in a confusing tone that could have signaled polite distance. Mr. Kawai then shooed me away from the man and I gathered that I might have offended him. What a fool I was! Why in the world would I expect a white man in California to know about Okakura? I must have come off as impertinent, a young know-it-all with no sense of decorum.

"Can I help you with anything?" Mr. Kawai interjected.

"Only window shopping." His hands linked behind his back, the visitor strolled around the store as if he were in a garden admiring new blossoms.

He spent a long time studying some large decorative jade green tile that Mr. Marsh had imported from China. GT went regularly to places like Shanghai and displayed that merchandise side by side with Japanese artwork, a bit jarring from my perspective.

After circling the floor, he said his goodbyes, not bothering to open his pocketbook to acquire anything. Perhaps my impertinence had led to his escape?

After Mr. Greene went out the door, Mr. Kawai let out a breath and his erect posture relaxed. I sensed this Mr. Greene was part of Pasadena's elite.

"I am sorry that I spoke out of turn," I said to Mr. Kawai, bowing my head.

"Never mind," he responded in Japanese. "Sometimes our customers don't want too much background. Better for them to ask first."

I made a note of that in my mind. If some work-related

thought floated in front of me, I had a tendency to say it out loud because I would forget if I didn't.

"He and his brother are architects in this town," Mr. Kawai explained.

"Has he spent much time in Japan?"

Mr. Kawai shook his head. "He has never gone. Neither has his brother. They both studied at MIT." He pronounced "MIT" with such emphasis that I knew it must be an institution of prestige. "Together they went to the World's Fair in Chicago and saw the Japanese Ho-o-Den."

"*Honto!*" I reverted to Japanese in a burst of enthusiasm. To contemplate that this architect had crossed paths with my father filled me with great joy.

"They are constructing a building right now farther east on Colorado Street. The Sanborn House. You should take a look."

I removed the map that Mrs. Riley had drawn for me and asked Mr. Kawai to mark the location of the building, which was several blocks east of my boardinghouse. I was eager to examine the construction of a house in America. Perhaps this Mr. Greene could teach me the ways of the West.

With Mr. Greene gone, I tried to resume the meditative nature of my work, but it was difficult to achieve such a state as I knew I would be entering the Hotel Green in a matter of hours.

Finally it was time to report to the hotel that Friday evening. Once we'd bid Mr. Kawai farewell, I followed Logan outside of Marsh's emporium and waited for him to lock the door. The sun was starting its descent and certain lights in the rooms of the Hotel Green flickered on—hardly half, by my estimation.

"It doesn't look like it's full, does it?" I said.

"It's not the season yet. That starts in November. But some people live there all year round. I'm not sure how Aoki got his studio in there. But he hobnobs with the upper crust. Let's go through the lobby so you can get a sense of the whole building."

My heart pounded as we crossed the street, my whole body tingling in anticipation of entering what seemed the closest thing to an American castle.

From the entryway, I was immediately swept up in the arches that marked both the exterior and interior. Could I learn this type of architecture, which was so foreign from the pared-down, precise craftsmanship of a Japanese temple?

We walked below the connecting bridge and turned left into the west-side structure. Suddenly, we were in the grand lobby. Oriental rugs swept the floors and elegant multi-tiered chandeliers hung from the high ceilings. Tall rounded archways, some adorned with heavy woven curtains, led to other rooms. The Grand Hotel of Yokohama was touted as the most elegant Western building of Japan, but the Hotel Green, exuding regal and rich elegance, eclipsed my memories of the seaside lodging house. Both locations, however, featured rocking chairs in their lounge areas. Why did Americans have to move even when sitting down?

The tile work on the floor mesmerized me. Small white and dark squares were arranged like the design on a textile—almost evoking an Indian aesthetic, in fact. Its pattern transported me to an exotic location far from dry Pasadena peaks. A grandfather clock stood under the curve of the wooden banister leading to other floors. The chandelier remained unlit, but the evening light pouring through the windows made the room feel inviting. Two portraits of probably very clever and esteemed men hung on the far wall, watching us.

Logan pointed to the portrait of a mustachioed man whose face resembled the current American president, Teddy Roosevelt.

"That's the owner. He calls himself Colonel Green, even though he's no military hero."

The daimyo *of this Pasadena castle.* My thoughts were interrupted by a high-pitched female voice.

"Who might you be?"

I turned to see an Asian girl standing behind me, almost challenging me. Just like with Jack, it was difficult to estimate her age—she could have been eight or in her teens. Her long straight black hair was pulled back in a ribbon, while her sky blue dress was made of a thick luxurious fabric that revealed her well-to-do upbringing.

"I work for Victor Marsh," I said, and sensed Logan's impatience as he tapped the tiled floor with the toe of his shoe. "My name is Louie Wada."

"I've never seen you before." The English language came out of her mouth quickly and precisely. I wondered if she was some sort of savant.

"Tsuru, he just arrived. Give him room to breathe." Logan pulled me away from the Japanese girl but she kept edging closer.

"My father is the one holding this party. It's in his studio," she said with such confidence that it seemed she was demanding that I kowtow to her. She ended her announcement with a pirouette, her slender arms perfectly arched and fingers intertwined above her head.

Following Logan's lead, I barely acknowledged her as we marched through the grand lobby to a hallway into the strangest world I had ever seen.

The distinctive trunk of a cherry blossom tree, striped with thick bark, was situated in a rectangular platform in the center of the room. For a moment I thought it was in full bloom, but then realized that its pink blossoms were made out of paper. On one side of the wall, painted on what looked like animal skin, was an image of a flying dragon, small demons creating mischief in its wake. A canvas banner on the other side bore a message honoring the gods, along with illustrations of Japanese peasants and samurai taking a lively stroll. Covering every other open space, even the glass windowpanes, were paintings of flowers—iris, wisteria, and, of course, cherry blossoms. On one side of the room were stacks of toy jinrikisha, rickshaws barely big enough to hold a doll, and on a table drying were flower pins made from a ceramic substance.

The room, which looked like it could comfortably seat fifty people, was full of workers. Commanding the laborers was a Japanese man with a slim build and a faint mustache. His voice reverberated as he directed them to affix the paper blossoms to the ends of the branches. It wasn't necessarily that loud, but its tone dripped with honey, making one want to listen to him even when he wasn't saying anything profound.

This must have been Pasadena's famous Toshio Aoki, the toast of the town and father of the dancing girl we had met in the lobby.

Logan boldly made his way to the speaker while I trudged behind, not desiring to be the center of attention.

"Mr. Aoki, there's someone I want to introduce you to. This is our new carpenter assistant, Ryu-no-suke, fresh from Japan."

I bowed deeply. "Wada Ryunosuke. At your service."

"Ah, Wada, so glad to make your acquaintance." Mr. Aoki bowed in response. There was a playful glint in his eyes that reminded me of childhood stories of the *kappa*, fictional creatures that lived in rivers and feasted on drowned human beings. He was wearing a thin kimono over a suit, such a curious combination. Its informal construction reminded me of a robe that a Japanese man would wear after soaking in a hot spring.

"Your arrival is quite fortuitous, as we are in need of more Nipponese to serve our guests." He brought out a folded cotton kimono, the same type he was wearing. "We are expecting a photographer tonight to take photos of our preparation, so please put this on."

I received it without enthusiasm. I would never wear something so plain at a significant event, and certainly not over Western clothing.

"Go on," Logan pushed me.

Why did I have to debase myself in this get-up? I bitterly wondered as I threaded my arms through the cotton sleeves and pulled the kimono over my shirt and pants. In fact I was very self-aware that I was one of the few Japanese laborers in attendance and, as a result, among the only ones wearing such a costume. The worst was that I was wearing this thin kimono with the work boots. I was at least grateful that no one in Yokohama could witness me like this.

"Wonderful, wonderful," Mr. Aoki murmured. "You'll be coming back and forth from the hotel's kitchen to serve food and drink to our guests—about seventy have responded that they will come. Come early to help place the party favors on the table, and you may have to stay late to clean up. And remember to wear the kimono."

He went on to supervise a group of towheaded girls who were dressed prim and proper in ruffled dresses topped by pinafores and handling scissors while seated on the floor. "Please keep the pieces of paper the same size," he insisted. The girls and their mothers were cutting long pieces of colorful paper that I recognized as *tanzaku*, a popular decoration for the festival of the star-crossed lovers. "These pieces of paper will hold special messages for our guests," Mr. Aoki explained.

Why were elements of the Tanabata Festival, typically celebrated in the summer, on display now?

To view these young white women re-creating Japanese culture in America made me feel uneasy and confused. I was certainly pleased that they were embracing the ways of my homeland, but raised without the knowledge of our centuries-old traditions, could they really understand Japanese sensibilities?

As the girls were giving me curious looks, I returned to the cherry blossom centerpiece. There, Gigi's friend Josephine and an older lady were tying more paper blossoms to the branches. They both were tall with slightly bulging eyes. The older woman had a wide forehead and a soft body. Her hair, unlike Josephine's pale rice stalks, was the brownish-red color of a Japanese maple that had received too much sun in the summer.

"Mother, not that way, this way," Josephine said to the other woman.

"Mrs. Carter, how good to see you." Logan swept in. I had almost forgotten that he was there. The ingratiating way he addressed Josephine's mother confirmed that she indeed spent as much money at Marsh's store as Gigi had shared.

"Oh, hello," Josephine said to me.

Here was my opportunity to address my rudeness from the previous night. "I am sorry that I was not properly introduced to you yesterday. I am a new worker at the Marshes'. My name is Louie Wada."

"I know who you are. Eddie's replacement," she replied. Again, the mention of Eddie! I hadn't met this man yet but I was definitely beginning to resent him.

Logan excused himself to talk to Mrs. Carter, leaving me at a loss as to what I was supposed to do. Join the women at work? But I felt so out of place just standing there in my ill-fitting kimono. Josephine focused her attention on tying more paper blossoms to a bare branch, while her mother was obviously experiencing no joy in her task. Mrs. Carter looked up frequently, monitoring who had entered the studio. Obviously my presence was not anything to take note of.

I was then engulfed in the heavenly familiar smell of lavender.

"Don't you look quite dapper in your costume."

I had to blink twice to fully absorb that Gigi was standing in front of me. "I didn't know you were a part of this," I said once I'd come back to my senses.

"I wouldn't say a part of it, but emergency seamstress. I'm glad you're here with Josephine. Hello, Jo."

"I wasn't sure how this would come out, but it's better than I expected," Josephine said in her husky voice. The two young women embraced and whispered into each other's ears, leaving me the odd man out.

I tried to pretend that their actions to exclude me went unnoticed and turned my attention to my surroundings. Standing next to the drawing on animal skin, I studied the comical expressions on the demons, which reminded me of the Kano school of art that dominated Japan before our country was forced to open up to the West. My mother relished this detailed style, reminiscent of Chinese scroll art, while my father opted for a more *shibui*, minimalist, and less humorous style. I had never seen Japanese artwork on what smelled like goatskin. That touch gave the room a more primitive feeling, which probably was what the artist had intended.

Prominently displayed next to a stack of photo albums was quite a magnificent oil painting of several ripe persimmons—the pointy hachiya kaki variety that required many days to ripen and become edible—spilling out from a woven Indian basket. I was startled by its sophistication, such a contrast to the fantastical Japanese-style images displayed around the room. Still, an earthiness did link them together, and when I looked for the artist's signature, I easily spotted "T. Aoki." *Why didn't Mr. Aoki create more works like this?* I wondered.

"Gigi, can you help me?" a young girl, her chubby face framed with blond curls, called out. She was struggling to thread the paper blossoms and held out a needle in frustration.

"Be right with you, Bernice," Gigi responded and separated from Josephine, saying, "Duty calls." As she passed me, she smiled and I felt as though I was melting again. She proceeded to elegantly move through the society girls. Even though she was dressed much more plainly in her functional navy blue dress, she, in my eyes, was a raven of exceptional beauty against a background of white.

I relished this time in which I could openly admire her. Anyone in the room would assume I was observing the work in general rather than being transfixed by one woman.

A conversation in my native tongue reached my ears, breaking my reverie. Mr. Aoki had reentered the room with another Japanese man, heftier in build and carrying a parcel wrapped in brown paper. "Is the reporter here?" the man asked, opening up his package to reveal the same type of kimono that I was wearing.

"She'll be coming any minute now. Busy at the store?"

"Slow today. I wonder how Marsh did."

They both glanced at Logan, still seated at the table, and noted my presence. I felt their eyes looking me over from the top of my head to my work boots. The two men lowered their voices.

"Who's this?" the heavy man asked Mr. Aoki.

"It's the Marsh brothers' new hire from Yokohama."

"Marsh has another employee from Japan?"

I wasn't sure how I should respond to being spoken about but not directly acknowledged.

Logan, meanwhile, having the skill of always being aware of who was in a room, excused himself from the woman he was talking to and approached the duo. Gesturing for me to join them, he said, "Mr. Kuranga, I want to introduce you to a new addition to Marsh's emporium. Ryu-no-suke."

"My name is Kura-na-ga," the man corrected Logan, his voice coated with disdain. I wondered what reason he had for his obvious dislike of Logan. Mr. Kuranaga was a man who didn't bother to disguise his negative feelings. His build, about the size of an average American, was larger than Mr. Aoki's. He had a fuller face that indicated that he was well-fed and lived a life of leisure. His embodiment of confidence suggested that he was much older than my eighteen years, but I later learned that he had not yet turned thirty. I was quite impressed by men who held themselves with such esteem as I lacked so much self-confidence myself.

I bowed. "Wada Ryunosuke. Pleased to make your acquaintance. Are you an artist as well?"

Mr. Kuranaga snorted. "I am a businessman. I have my own enterprise on Colorado Street in a most prestigious location." He said it in a way that seemed to demean Marsh's Green Street address.

"I'll take you over there sometime," Logan offered.

Mr. Kuranaga didn't even register a response and resumed speaking to Mr. Aoki in Japanese about the various news outlets that had committed to cover the dinner. I was surprised that newspapers outside of California would be interested in such a local gathering.

As they continued talking, I bowed deeply again and Logan, perhaps feeling the aloofness from Kuranaga, graciously said his goodbyes on our behalf.

Once we were outside, Logan was free to provide me with the full scuttlebutt. "Kuranaga has a teahouse on Colorado Street, but he'll be expanding it into a full art goods store. He already has related businesses in San Francisco, but I think he prefers it in Pasadena, or at least he has a reason to prefer it."

I was all ears. Logan, with all his socializing, was the repository of the most entertaining gossip, and I was soon to learn that this would be of the most delicious kind.

"He cavorts with a white woman." Logan seemed very impressed with this feat. I certainly was. "Her name is Leonna Cook. She's from a wealthy family in San Francisco. I've heard rumors that he may be getting married soon. But not in California, of course. This state doesn't allow such things, at least not officially."

I assumed that Logan himself was a product of the mixing of races. I didn't know him well enough to inquire and, in fact, would never ask such a personal question, even of a close friend.

"His teahouse is a couple of blocks away in the Richardson Building. There's not much there, and I think he's been quite envious of the Marsh brothers' success."

By this time a large streetlight with multi-pronged electric bulbs was pouring brightness onto Colorado Street. Logan needed to take an electric streetcar to the northern part of Pasadena. Before we parted ways, he told me, "Now you know some of the people behind the cherry blossom dinner. Make sure you don't act foolish tomorrow night—a lot of our customers will be in attendance."

I nodded, but inside I felt that Logan pricked my pride. I always strove to never shame my father's name in Japan; here in America, I would do the same to establish our family's reputation.

Colorado Street was quite festive, with couples in fine outfits strolling to see and be seen. Many men tipped their hats my way while their female partners greeted me with bright smiles. Pasadenans were a friendly people, I concluded.

When I entered my shared bedroom, Jack was already there, going through his prints. He stared at me over his glasses, his dark eyes narrowing. "Why are you wearing that?" His voice sounded accusatory, as if I was doing something wrong. Then he answered his own question: "Oh, Aoki's 'sa-ku-ra, sa-ku-ra' party." Jack was using the "Sakura" song, one we had all learned as children, to mock me. "I wasn't asked to be at that dinner. But if I was, I most certainly would have declined."

"We *are* getting paid." I stripped off the kimono, only now realizing that my Japanese costume was the reason why the passersby on Colorado Street had been so amused.

"There's some things I won't do, even for money."

I remained silent, feeling the sting of his criticism.

"Well, how was it? What did you think of Aoki?"

"He's so accomplished."

"Really?" Jack almost snorted. "That's your assessment?"

"I've never seen paintings like his before." The closed Edo period had resulted in ink drawings of an entranced Buddha and colorful paintings of fetching courtesans, but nothing like the wild, fevered images that Aoki had conjured up. I didn't understand Jack's disdain. "You don't like his artwork," I guessed.

"He's just pandering to these Americans. Giving them a slice of Japan that they can easily digest."

"What's wrong with that?" I thought back to Okakura's book and the difficult language he used to describe traditional arts like the tea ceremony. Maybe instead of fancy words, Americans needed to be enveloped in pageantry and action.

"You need to think for yourself, Ryui."

I resented that Jack was reprimanding me like a schoolteacher, so I was relieved that I would be free from his presence at the dinner. He reminded me of my father's veteran carpenters, who could be quite critical of structures produced by competitors.

I wasn't sure what to make of this cherry blossom dinner, including my own participation while wearing a flimsy costume. But it seemed to be my chance to establish myself in Pasadena. Without my father, there was no place for me in Japan. I wasn't old or experienced enough to continue his trade business in Yokohama. In the back of my mind, I thought I could make a name for myself in America and return to Japan as the golden boy. Could I transform myself like Toshio Aoki, unknown or even disrespected in Japan, but so celebrated in this town of invention?

That night, I missed my father more intensely than ever. I grasped hold of Tama-chan in an attempt to conjure his image. I wished I had a photograph of him. I never thought I could start to forget his features.

III
CHERRY BLOSSOM DINNER

1.

"You like Mr. Aoki?" I asked Logan as we both unloaded a shipment from Yokohama that Saturday morning. It was from the factory in Kaga-cho, which was home to my father's former carpentry shop. I almost shivered imagining my former classmates creating or at least touching the merchandise that was in these boxes.

Since I was more adept at dealing with tools, I loosened the nails on the wood crates while Logan carefully lifted out fragile items protected in straw. It became a game to discover what was hidden in the boxes—enormous vases, tea sets, rolled-up screens in silk sleeves, and carved wooden statues.

"I don't know him well, but all the ladies are charmed by him. He leaves his studio open for women and children to gawk at all day long."

"You like his art?"

"Of course! Flying goddesses, naughty demons, playful geisha. Who wouldn't want to wake up to all that? Besides, his paintings sell so well. Every household wants a Toshio Aoki."

I appreciated Logan's optimism and enthusiasm in contrast to Jack's judgment and criticism of the cherry blossom participants. To be so cynical darkened my spirits, so I decided for at least the duration of the party, from eight in the evening to midnight, I would attempt to be as sunny and upbeat as possible.

I made sure to arrive early, actually hoping that I would run into Gigi. Alas, no Gigi, but plenty of tasks. Mr. Aoki's students, who had been worker bees the night before, were not in attendance, leaving only a few of us real laborers to place one miniature jinrikisha at each place setting for the women and a ceramic figurine for the men. There were five other young Japanese men in kimono. I attempted to introduce myself to them, but they barely looked at me, so I retreated. Perhaps they felt some embarrassment over being reduced to servants masquerading in a cheap re-creation of our homeland.

One particular man seemed very disgruntled. I heard that he was a migrant farm worker who traveled all throughout the state. I wondered where he could be living—Pasadena certainly wasn't a haven for many Japanese laborers.

"This is ridiculous. An affront to our nation," he murmured bitterly in Japanese.

He had a perfectly round scar on the middle of his forehead that reminded me of the dot I once saw on an Indian mother shopping in Yokohama. Although his delivery was impassioned and loud, his vocabulary seemed sophisticated for a man of his station.

If you feel so disrespected, why don't you just leave? I thought to myself. But the same held true for myself and I wasn't going anywhere. Through Victor Marsh's assistance and connections, I had a place to lay my head and food—albeit quite horrible—to keep me alive. And whenever I worked with wood, my soul was restored. America couldn't take that feeling away from me.

"Welcome, welcome, everyone." An impeccably groomed mustachioed white man stood in front of the entrance to the studio. He carried himself with great confidence, sweeping his arms around him as if he owned the building, and later I learned that he actually did. He was the castle's *daimyo*, Colonel Green. According to Logan, he was given his honorary military title by a politician in the state of New Jersey and not by a general for any frontline exploits. Nonetheless, he was indeed a svelte version of the US president.

With Aoki's exotic murals affixed to the wall and the impressive spray of artificial pink cherry blossoms emerging from the middle of the table set for seventy-five, the guests were visibly mesmerized. The whole room was awash in pink, from pink lanterns girded around the sakura trunk to the flowers that Aoki had painted on the tablecloth. No matter what Jack thought about Aoki's motifs, he was a talented artist.

I was transfixed, too, by the older women's grand hats and the blinding white starched tuxedo shirts on the men, established scions of industry. I recognized Lady Madison, gliding through the room like an exclusive ocean liner. Whatever seemed inauthentic on the table was obscured by the pageantry of the white people. It was one thing for foreigners to make a spectacle of themselves in Yokohama. It was quite another to view this in their own country.

The other Japanese waiters were more familiar with who was who and assisted Mr. Aoki in getting them situated in the right seats, based on hand-painted place cards. Once everyone was seated, Mr. Kuranaga, dressed in *hakama* pantaloons and a *haori* jacket, strode into the room, a white woman hanging on to his elbow. She must be his future wife. She had a prominent aquiline nose and round bright eyes; most men would classify her as attractive, but I found a disconcerting quality to her countenance. Maybe it was the way she gazed at Mr. Kuranaga rather than being fully aware of her surroundings, as extraordinary as they were. She seemed completely besotted with her fiancé, and I was a bit envious that a Japanese man could command such adoration.

I noticed that the rest of the crowd had registered the arrival of the mixed-race couple. Based on the whispers and titters from various women from behind cupped hands, I guessed that their presence together was not de rigueur.

"Welcome, welcome." Again, Mr. Aoki did not speak loudly, but his voice had tendrils that moved throughout a crowd. Everyone hushed. "I am honored you have come to my cherry blossom dinner, something no American has ever seen before."

I could feel the excitement emanating from the guests. They were the chosen ones!

"There will be many courses throughout the evening. One by one, I will introduce them. For now, my friend Frank Kuranaga will tell you the meaning of the cherry blossom in Japan."

Mr. Kuranaga got up from his seat and stood by Mr. Aoki. Above them on the ceiling was the flag of the United States, with its forty-five stars, and that of Japan, the Hinomaru with the singular crimson circle representing the sun. Even though there were no diplomats in attendance, this dinner almost seemed like an official affair between two nations.

"The cherry blossom," Mr. Kuranaga was explaining, "reflects transience. As each petal falls, we are reminded of the fragility of life."

I didn't comprehend all that he was communicating, but the message was obviously touching the hearts of his audience, especially the women. I spied handkerchiefs being removed from purses to dry wet eyelashes. What a speaker this Frank Kuranaga was! I was curious about his background and wondered when he had come to this country.

Standing next to me was the unhappy Japanese laborer, releasing deep breaths to express his displeasure. "*Ou*," he kept repeating and I finally comprehended that he was murmuring the Japanese word for "king." Did he take offense to what Mr. Kuranaga was saying, or perhaps the businessman as a person?

I heard someone else snorting and stole a look over my shoulder. It was Jack, holding a small box camera made of what looked like black cardboard. Here he was at an event that he had characterized as beneath him!

He immediately read the expression on my face. "I was curious," he hissed and then pressed down on a side lever on the camera. I grimaced. The last thing I wanted was to be forever immortalized in the ridiculous costume I was wearing. I made my way to the other side of the room, seeking to keep my distance from Jack and his camera.

After Kuranaga's speech, a Japanese man blew into a bamboo flute, which he held upright from his puckered lips. The familiar music tore through me, piercing my heart. The music from the shakuhachi, often performed without any other instruments, embodied loneliness, so much that I avoided it even in Japan, preferring the lively twang of the three-string shamisen instead. It was, however, precisely my state of mind, even in the company of ten Japanese and seventy-five Americans in a room decorated with demons and goddesses and raining down with artificial cherry blossoms.

With each new course, Mr. Aoki would come forward and in his quiet but commanding voice, make an announcement. "Golden epaulets and compound salad," he said.

The diners were mystified by his strange description, as was I, and I watched as Japanese waiters brought forward trays of sliced *tamagoyaki* and raw oysters marinated in wakame. It would continue like this for the next two hours.

My job was to carry the dirty small plates away from the studio to the kitchen across the way. Part of me wanted to slurp up the remaining miso soup and gobble down the uneaten chicken teriyaki and *manju*. All I had eaten today was a piece of dry bread in the morning and more bread and hard cheese for lunch. Hardly anyone had finished the *kombumaki*, a New Year's delicacy in which thin dried strips of gourd were tied around rolls of slippery kelp. Young men in the kitchen took my trays of dirty dishes and dumped the leftovers into buckets. Just to see the amount of wasted food made me want to cry.

Tsuru was seated next to her father on the other side of the room. I was too busy to interact with her, but I did notice that she was dressed in a proper silk kimono cinched with a thick brocade obi. She was engaged in an animated conversation with a guest next to her, a woman probably five times her age with an overwhelming white hairstyle like a parrot's crown. Josephine and her mother were also seated nearby with a lanky man with the same pale features as the younger Carter. I assumed he was Josephine's father.

I searched the crowd to see if I could spot Jack, but he was nowhere to be seen. I wasn't even sure how he had been admitted because he wasn't an invited guest. A man with a camera, however, could find his way into the most restricted spaces.

I was relieved that he wasn't there to further document my shame. Is this why I had suffered the tumultuous voyage across the Pacific? To be a servant for rich white men and women? I could have done that back in Yokohama. As I picked up leftover sake in tiny cups, I couldn't help myself. In the hallway to the kitchen, I took a huge swig off two of them and felt the familiar jolt of rice wine pulse through my body, even pushing its way into my fingers and my face. My father had been a teetotaler himself because he worked so much and found drunkenness a hindrance and sometimes a danger to building a house or temple. I had promised our maid that I would give up sake after that drunken incident following my mother's death.

But this was Pasadena, not Yokohama, and I was free to make my own choices.

I continued to go back and forth from the kitchen to the studio, weaving a little in the hallway. Feeling the urge to relieve myself, I quickly visited the washroom. On my way back through the lobby, I heard an unmistakable throaty voice, reminding me of male kabuki actors playing female roles—Josephine. She and Gigi were seated in a love seat tucked behind a pillar.

"My mother is quite against their union," Josephine was saying. I took a few steps back and hid behind a giant potted palm.

"Well, I think it's quite romantic," Gigi murmured. "What do you think?"

"I believe in free will. That's why I cannot be a Calvinist."

"Oh, Josephine, you are something else." I could hear Gigi's amusement. "Do you always have to be so philosophical about everything, including love?"

"Marriage seems to benefit the man. He gets a maid, cook, and governess without having to pay any additional salaries."

I found it difficult to remain still in my hiding place and gently swatted away a palm frond.

"That is a most cynical way to look at romance! How in the world are you going to find a husband?"

"Look at yourself! You don't seem like you're in a rush to matrimony."

"If it's the right man, I will not hesitate." Gigi sounded resolute. "And like Leonna, I will not let race or nationality prevent me from love."

I could not believe what I was hearing. From a Japanese perspective, interracial couplings were not taboo, but certainly seen as unusual, sometimes scandalous, or even illicit at times. My father, of course, would have required that I wed someone who was not only Japanese, but from a reputable background. Some wealthy parents even hired private investigators to dig into their child's prospective mate's family history. Any discovery of madness, a criminal past, or financial insolvency would sever a potential marital union. But Gigi was proclaiming to her closest friend that none of that mattered to her.

This display of unadulterated emotion thrilled me, but then I realized how awful I was to eavesdrop on such an intimate and vulnerable moment. I stepped back as quietly as I could in my clunky boots, hoping not to attract their attention, to resume my work at the dinner.

While moving about the emptying room, picking up abandoned glasses, I wondered if my father's values would fade in my psyche over time. My world was turning upside down here in America, and without my father or any living relatives who cared about me on earth, I could be anyone I desired. Could I be a Frank Kuranaga?

As I considered the starry possibilities of the future, Mr. Aoki brought me back to my present lowly position. He held out a silver tray that held a bottle of whiskey and cut glass tumblers. At this late hour, he must have been tired, because he gave me a directive without any niceties. "Offer this to our male guests in the lobby," he said, practically pushing the tray into my chest.

I wasn't sure at first who Mr. Aoki was referring to, but then I saw a cloud of smoke lingering above rocking chairs arranged in front of the unlit fireplace. As I approached the men puffing on their cigars, I recognized a tall man, the one I'd assumed to be Josephine's father. His gangly legs were firmly planted on the floor, preventing his chair from rocking.

"You really should consider it. Oil, oil, oil, that's the best game in town." He pulled a brochure from his suit pocket with his free left hand and waved it in another man's face.

"I'm not sure, Sherwood." The chair rocked back and forth,

and this man, wearing a monocle in his right eye, kept his cigar in his mouth as he spoke. "Who knows when a field will gush with oil? It's all speculation."

I held out the tray to a couple of men who were not engaged in the conversation. The fresh-shaven younger one poured each of them a large glass of whiskey.

The speaker continued to be oblivious to my presence. "Why are you hesitating? Don't you want to give your children and grandchildren future security?"

"Well, of course I do."

"Doheny has already cashed in his Los Angeles petroleum holdings. Think about Olinda. That will make a fortune for a new group of men."

My ears pricked up with the mention of fortunes. In these men's lifetimes, gold had brought dreamers all around the world to California. Japan had been closed to the West at that time, but perhaps this would be our second chance. Could I someday buy a piece of land that would pour out oil and money, securing my future?

I offered the tray to the monocled man and he shook his head. The oil speculator, Sherwood, kept promoting real estate in a place called Olinda, not even acknowledging my presence. It was only when I turned back to the kitchen that he finally called out to me, "Wait a minute, boy, I'd like a libation as well!"

The tone of his voice raised my hackles. The sake, which had invigorated me an hour before, now caused my head to pound. I was not trained to wait on people, much less rude Americans, but, gritting my teeth, I returned to his side and poured him what he demanded.

I was now ready to leave the party for the Riley House. Before I could sneak away, Mr. Aoki called me over to the kitchen. "I've sent the rest of the men home, so it leaves you to take out the trash," he said.

I wanted to protest, but I had no leverage, being such a new arrival.

He pointed at the buckets overflowing with discarded Japanese delicacies. "We can't have rats roaming around Hotel Green," he said. "Place these outside for the garbage collector. He'll pick them up in the morning to feed his pigs."

At least the chef's efforts would not be totally wasted. But it was painful to think that such fine food would go to animals who would literally eat anything put in front of them.

Since there were four buckets and I was on my own, I would have to make two trips. I was weary, depleted, and feeling quite put-upon. I wasn't quite sure where to leave the buckets, but was too frustrated to get the specifics. I walked west on Green Street to Fair Oaks and left the first two buckets on the corner outside the entrance of another art goods store, this one owned by a Japanese businessman, Ishiyama. I felt ashamed to leave the slop there, but exhaustion trumped decorum.

As I dropped the buckets onto the corner, I spied the real estate man's brochure left next to the dirt road. I carefully plucked it out of the gutter. Once I'd wiped away any dirt on my kimono, I slipped it into my pantaloon pocket. A chance for riches should not only be reserved for those who were already rich.

I had never imagined engaging in such dirty work in America. I had sunk to a new low. I went back to retrieve the other refuse, cursing under my breath as I clunked those two buckets down by the ones I had left earlier on the corner.

Then came the bounce of metal and rusty gears turning, a warning that danger had arrived. A push to my back made me lose my footing and I felt my body fly through the air and then fall to the ground with a thud. Not knowing what had happened at first, I slowly got up—hearing that grinding metal again.

A bicycle circled around me. The rider was wearing a burlap bag over his head with two holes cut for his eyes, which were dark as he pedaled directly at me. I shivered in fear but held my ground, tightening my fists to prepare to defend myself against any oncoming violence. The bicyclist removed a piece of thick paper from the inside of his shirt and threw it my way. The paper landed in front of my boots before the rider cycled away at top speed.

I could clearly see its message from where I was standing: DIE JAP.

Jack wasn't in our room when I returned after the dinner. Even though he was quite abrasive, I would have appreciated his ear and advice as a more experienced man in America. No matter his personality, he was still Japanese and subject to the same prejudice that I was.

I didn't get a speck of sleep that night. I kept imagining masked men bursting into our tiny room with guns in their hands. I dreamed that I was attempting to fight back or at least hide myself, but all power had left my body and I couldn't move from my filthy mattress. In a corner sat Jack like a bat, eating rice balls and mocking me.

2.

When I awoke, I wasn't sure what was real and what wasn't. Again, Jack's bed was unslept in, some photographs stacked on his blanket. Since it was Sunday and the store was closed, I stayed on my mattress for the whole day. All the travel across the Pacific Ocean and being uprooted from my home country had continued to take their toll. I didn't even have the energy to take Tama-chan in my hands to try to make it as sleek as it was before we left Yokohama.

Early on Monday morning, I heard the Boyle brothers stomping down the stairs and I hurried out to address them.

"Hello," I called to them.

"Oh, good mornin', Louie."

"Jack didn't come home this weekend."

"That's how Jack is sometimes. Disappears from time to time," said Simon.

"Like an alley cat, he prowls all over Pasadena, especially around the Red Car stop on California Street," Ian added.

"He frequents a celestial house over there. I'm sure he'll be back. Nothing to worry about."

"After Eddie went away, we didn't see him for about a week, wasn't that so, Simon?"

"No need to bring up Eddie. Well, we're needin' to go to work now."

I nodded and watched the brothers go out the door. How I wished I had a sibling who was my travel companion. The hardships of life in America would be much easier to bear with a blood relative.

Feeling as isolated as ever, I shut the bedroom door behind me. The message was face down by my folded clothes on the shelf. I had purposely placed Tama-chan on top of the heavy paper as if the talisman could overpower the message of hatred.

I had only been in America for less than a week—who would want me dead? I had unwittingly offended Josephine but I had apologized—surely that wasn't a misdeed deserving of threats to my life? Avoiding Mrs. Riley's stomach-burning coffee, I left for work and mentally went through all the people I had met during my stay—everyone in the Riley House, the customers and staff at Victor Marsh's store, and now the organizers, workers, and guests at the cherry blossom dinner. As it turned out, I had quite a list, even more contacts than I had in Yokohama.

I needed to talk this over with someone, and with Jack's absence, I wasn't quite sure who I could turn to. The note was folded in my pocket; I couldn't leave this ugliness in the place where I slept. I didn't want to bring up this sensitive matter with Mr. Kawai. I wanted always to be in his good graces, and if I told him about the incident, I feared he'd think I had done something to deserve such animosity.

Managing a half-hearted greeting to both Mr. Kawai and Logan, who was on time for once, I slunk to the workroom.

"I was telling Mr. Kawai that all the guests are saying Saturday night was something to behold." Logan was in a particularly gregarious mood. "They feel like they just traveled to the Orient."

"It was nothing like Japan," I spouted out, harsher than I intended. Both men quieted and although I kept my eyes on the tenon that I was trying to fit into a newly created mortise of the table I had been repairing, an awkwardness filled the storefront.

Mr. Kawai, being older, seemed fine with long stretches of silence. But Logan was bothered by it and immediately confronted me when Mr. Kawai left for an errand.

"Did something happen at the party on Saturday night?"

"I served dinner and drinks like I was told."

"Balderdash! Don't lie to me, Louie. I thought we were becoming friends."

Logan was overstating the status of our relationship, especially since we hadn't even spent more than a week together. The shallowness of American intimacy both disturbed and impressed me. Being an only child, I was used to being on my own and keeping my most sensitive thoughts to myself.

But Logan was relentless and I definitely needed a confidant. Although I didn't trust him completely, I didn't have many other options.

"When I went to take out the trash at the dinner on Saturday night, I was—" I couldn't remember the exact word for it, so I said, my voice beginning to shake, "pushed down."

"You mean attacked?"

"Yes, attacked." I took the folded paper out of my pants pocket and offered it to Logan for his perusal. "He threw this at me."

The look on his face mirrored my own horrified feelings.

"He was riding a bicycle. And had a bag over his head."

"So you didn't see who it was?"

I shook my head.

"Was it a white man?"

"I don't know."

"Are you going to tell Mr. Marsh?"

"No, no." I didn't want to involve our employer. If I created too much trouble or proved to be an inconvenience, he could revoke his sponsorship of me, possibly sending me back to Yokohama.

"Who have you told?"

"No one." I had left the Hotel Green immediately without even telling Mr. Aoki what had transpired.

"It might be better that way. The Marshes wouldn't want any trouble like this. Or the whole city of Pasadena, for that matter."

"What do you mean?"

"Crown City wants to be known for being progressive and welcoming. Not for chasing Orientals out by burning down their places of business."

"What?" I had never heard of such a thing before.

"Never mind, that was ages ago, maybe even before you

were born." Logan placed the folded message in his jacket pocket. Sensing my concern, he said, "Don't think about it again, Louie."

I took a deep breath and tried to clear my mind. But one matter related to the Marsh emporium still nagged at me—money. Before Logan went to the front counter, I tugged on his elbow. "Ah, I have one question. When do we get paid?"

"Mr. Marsh didn't tell you? You'll get an envelope every two weeks."

My ignorance shamed me. There was so much that I didn't know.

3.

Keeping secrets was difficult for me. I was raised around secrets back in Yokohama. Some went back a generation; one ancestor, a samurai, had killed another's relative in a bloody battle over an ancient castle, and that was why their descendants couldn't stand to be in the same room. When my father was alive, I thought the animosity between two of his carpenters was fueled by professional competition, but after a literal clashing of chisels in a dangerous altercation, I learned that they were in love with the same woman. Being so young and naive, I was often oblivious to all the tension below the surface. It was only when the animosity erupted for all to see that our maid, a lover of gossip, revealed to me all the undercurrents.

I always felt better when the truth came to light. Deception made my stomach gurgle and my heart feel heavy. So not being open about the horrible incident made me retreat inwardly.

Finally, on Tuesday, three days after the event, Jack returned to our room smelling of smoke and some strange scent like ammonia. In anger, I barely said anything to him.

"What did you think of the 'sa-ku-ra, sa-ku-ra' party?" he finally asked in his mocking way.

"It was fine," I replied and resumed removing the mud clots from my boots with a tool I had borrowed from Mrs. Riley. I had been feeling quite abandoned by Jack. Here I had thought that he would serve at least as an elder I could turn to for advice, but he was completely unreliable. One thing that I had inherited from my father was the importance of dependability. I wanted to completely erase Jack from my daily life, but that was impossible. "What did you think of it? I thought you didn't want to have anything to do with it."

"Gigi connected me with one of those grand madams. They wanted some souvenir photos for their scrapbooks."

I smarted to hear Gigi's name. Although Jack had known Gigi a lot longer than me, I felt threatened by any direct communications that didn't involve me.

Jack must have felt my jealousy because he gazed at me with such pity. "You are so young, Ryui," he stated, infuriating me further.

I dumped a mud clot from my boot sole onto our floor. "Just don't produce your photos in the bathroom today. It's been so nice to have two days of not being subjected to those terrible smells."

Jack grunted, but I sensed that I had wounded him enough to make him take me a little more seriously. He was clever enough not to engage me in conversation again.

We did not speak to each other until the next evening, when there was a knock on our door.

Jack got up and flung open the door in his heedless manner. For a moment he was silent.

I was lying on my mattress and could not see who our visitor was. I was in no mood to be hospitable, but if a guest casts a shadow from your open doorway, what can you do? I stuffed my shirt into my pants and got up from the mattress. "Mr. Aoki!" I exclaimed and bowed. Why in the world had he come to our hovel of a residence?

"I am sorry to bother you at your home. May I come in?" He addressed me rather than Jack, when he really should have posed his request to my more senior roommate.

"You can go to Marsh's store if you want to talk to the boy." Jack continued to block the entryway.

"I wanted to talk to both of you. In confidence."

Jack was obviously intrigued and opened the door wider for our unexpected visitor.

Jack and Mr. Aoki made quite the contrast, standing next to each other. The cloud of fuzz on top of Jack's head made him look otherworldly, like one of the characters in Mr. Aoki's paintings, while the artist himself was impeccably groomed, the lines in his raked hair reminding me of formations in a Zen rock garden.

In terms of the state of our living quarters, I expected judgment from Mr. Aoki, but his attention was drawn to the photographs hanging from the clothesline. Jack had developed a few shots from the cherry blossom dinner. They featured close-ups of some female guests with their boat-like hats almost floating around the artificial cherry blossom tree and its paper flowers.

"You do have a flair for the visual," Mr. Aoki commented.

Jack's eyes softened for a moment, but he still made his voice stern as he said, "What do you want, Aoki?" I was dumbfounded by his combativeness. I knew that Jack disrespected Mr. Aoki's aesthetic but I hadn't expected him to be obviously rude.

"I'm missing a painting from the night of the cherry blossom dinner."

"I didn't take it. You know I don't care for your fake Japanese nonsense." Jack's antipathy was obviously known to Mr. Aoki, who didn't reveal any surprise.

"It's the painting of the Indian basket and the persimmons."

"Oh, that one. Your one achievement. At least your thief has taste." Jack seemed pleased with his sarcastic jab. "Perhaps this boy took it."

I couldn't believe Jack was accusing me. "I am not a *dorobo*!" I protested.

"You did leave quite abruptly. You did not even come to see me to collect your pay." Mr. Aoki pulled an envelope out of his inside jacket pocket and dangled it in front of my nose.

"I was quite tired," I said, "after all that work. I was the last one there to clean up."

"Exactly." Mr. Aoki lowered the envelope. "The perfect opportunity for you to abscond with my painting."

"I did not!" I exclaimed. To be called a thief after everything I had been through—I was wounded beyond belief.

"Was there anyone at the party who had something against you or your associates?" Jack suggested. "I've heard there is some apprehension about GT opening up a Japanese garden a few blocks south of the Hotel Green."

Mr. Aoki, seemingly repulsed by such criticism, turned his head away from Jack. "Just naysayers. The garden certainly will be good for business, however."

Mr. Aoki's business, no doubt.

"All I want is the return of my painting. And I think you can achieve that for me." Mr. Aoki turned to face Jack, who was cleaning his spectacles with a camera lens cloth.

"How could I possibly do that?"

"Nose around. Be a bit of a pest. There's no one better than you to do that, Jack."

Mr. Aoki was giving Jack a backhanded compliment, but Jack didn't seem to mind. Judging by the gleam in his eyes, he even seemed to relish what the artist was asking of him.

"Are you hiring me to be your private investigator?"

"Questioning must be done confidentially, of course." Mr. Aoki spoke in a hushed tone, as if someone could be listening to us.

I thought it ridiculous that Jack, who had no background as an inspector, was to be recruited for such a job. "What about the police? Does Pasadena not have officers?" I asked.

"I want to avoid that. They are very close to the newspapers in this town and beyond. One mention of the theft and it will probably end up on the front pages of the *Evening Star* and even the *Los Angeles Times*. We Japanese are a bit of a curiosity here. I would like all the write-ups on the cherry blossom dinner to be complimentary and not scandalous in any way."

"Yes, we wouldn't want the enterprises of T. Aoki to be tarnished in any way." Spittle sprayed out of Jack's mouth.

"Do you want the job or not?"

"Job? This is a paid position?" Jack straightened his spectacles on the bridge of his nose.

"Five dollars." I nearly doubled over. That would cover a month's rent. "As long as this incident stays out of the paper. And my painting is retrieved."

Jack took a few steps toward Mr. Aoki. "The first point, I can definitely promise you. But as for the latter, payment should not be contingent on its recovery. It may be destroyed for all we know."

When Mr. Aoki heard that ominous possibility, his face took on an even paler hue. Unlike Keisuke and his crew from the *Amerika-Maru*, or even Jack, Mr. Aoki obviously did not spend much time under direct sunlight. "Just find out who did it. I'll then mete out justice the way I see fit."

Jack seemed content with the terms of the job. "Where was this painting?"

Because I'd liked it so much, I remembered exactly where

the painting was, so I answered before Mr. Aoki could: “It was on a marble table in the corner of the room.”

“Yes,” Mr. Aoki said, “it’s usually hanging on the wall, but to accommodate the decorations for the dinner, I moved it to a new location.”

“We will need a list of all who attended your dinner.” Jack’s voice was all business. “And the boy, he’ll have to be part of this, too.”

What was Jack up to now?

“What do you mean?” Mr. Aoki asked.

“He was there all night. He witnessed everything—you heard him. And without proper payment, who knows who Louie would be talking to?”

“That’s blackmail, not business.”

“I’ll need his help. He’s part of your art world, not me.”

Mr. Aoki stroked his raked hair. “All right. I suppose that he may be useful. I’ll pay you five dollars and an additional two fifty for Wada.” He finally handed me my envelope. “Yes?”

“*Hai*,” I agreed, receiving the envelope with both of my hands and bowing. Two dollars and fifty cents would cover almost half of my monthly boardinghouse fees.

As Mr. Aoki left the Riley House, Jack was delighting in his new role.

“A private detective, imagine that! I could be the first Nipponese detective in this country.” Jack started pacing in the limited open floor space in our room, nearly brushing his dirty shoes on my sheets.

Recovering from the shock of Mr. Aoki’s visit, I had collapsed back on my mattress. “I already have work,” I said. “How can I add investigation to my other responsibilities?”

“This is America,” Jack declared. “A working man’s lot is to work all his waking hours. And not to sleep much.”

My heart sank. Is this why I made the challenging voyage across the Pacific Ocean?

Jack circled the room so rapidly that I was getting dizzy. I noticed his tendency to be overly excitable, especially about opportunities that would elevate his status. "Jack, I need to tell you something." I took a couple of breaths before continuing. If we were being tasked to solve any crimes occurring at the cherry blossom dinner, I would have to share the hateful encounter outside the Hotel Green. I couldn't easily explain in English what had happened to me so I reverted back to my native tongue to tell him about the bicyclist.

Jack was clearly annoyed. "Why didn't you tell me of this?"

You disappeared and left me on my own, I wanted to scream back at him. But instead I kept my anger at bay. "You were not around for me to tell."

Jack raised his chin and gazed down at me through the lower half of his spectacles. "I see," he said, perhaps acknowledging why I had been so upset with him. "Who else knows?"

"I only told Logan at the store. He said for me to keep quiet."

"That was probably the right decision. Everyone is worried about trouble coming to Pasadena again."

"What do you mean?" Logan had mentioned something that had happened long ago. Just the mention of the word "trouble" made the hairs on the back of my neck stand on end.

Jack went into one of the drawers in the bureau for a rolling paper and an oblong canister. He didn't look directly into my face, as if he was about to share information that could hurt me. "About twenty years ago, a mob set a Chinese laundry on fire. Only a few blocks from where Marsh's store is. They chased the Chinese out of that immediate area for a while. That's why the Pasadena Chinatown is around the California Red Car stop."

This concept of racial violence was new to me. After all, the Japanese were the majority in my home country. I wasn't raised to think about what it was like to be a minority group. "Have there been some more recent incidents like mine targeting Japanese?"

Tapping dried tobacco leaves from the canister onto the paper, Jack rolled a cigarette and lit it. He seemed to shut down his emotions, perhaps in an effort to protect either me or himself, or the both of us. "More involving Chinese. I know of a Chinese man who was being jeered at on the train. He didn't stand for it and administered some of his medicine to the bullies."

I struggled with the English idioms that he used.

"He soundly beat them. Used some sort of Chinese judo on them." Jack pulled aside the curtains, opened the window, and sat in the sill.

"How about yourself?" I asked. "Have you encountered any trouble?"

"Not much. I landed in Seattle and only encountered lumberjacks and fishermen who had no interest in bothering anyone, not even us Japanese. I've been in the countryside of Washington, too, but did not encounter many problems there. The Chinese miners, of course, faced their issues—" Jack pulled on an invisible noose and let his neck go flaccid. It was quite apparent that the Chinese pioneers had gone through much suffering in the west. "Pasadena has been fine. After all, they idolize Japanese sensibilities. We might as well take advantage of it." He tapped on his cigarette and released some ash outside. "Have you met the older Marsh brother yet?"

"GT? Oh, yes, back in Yokohama. He's the one who gave me the Okakura book."

"Oh, that's right. I keep forgetting about your long

association. Well, do you know about Japan's presence at the World's Fair in Chicago?"

I nodded. "My father oversaw the building of Phoenix Hall."

Jack stared at me with what seemed like regard. "Really? I had heard he was quite well-known, but I didn't know he was that accomplished."

I felt pride warm my stomach. To receive a modicum of respect, finally!

"Anyway," Jack continued, "GT thought up a plan to do the same in San Francisco. Not as large, of course. The Japanese government didn't support it. All their money went into the Chicago exhibition and then there was the war with China. They didn't want anything to do with the California Midwinter Exposition in 1894."

The talk of the San Francisco fair sounded familiar. Hadn't Logan mentioned that he had gone to the teahouse with Victor?

"It was all GT's doing. It was his carnival to sell his curios. And Aoki was there as his lapdog."

I wasn't sure what lapdog meant but I assumed it wasn't complimentary.

"The Japanese teahouse that GT and Aoki created was atrocious. You can go up there and see for yourself, if you don't believe me." Jack took another puff from his rolled cigarette, which was now barely visible. "And there was the jinrikisha incident."

Jinrikisha? The mini-reproductions for the female guests at the cherry blossom dinner immediately came to my mind.

"The *Kinmon* newspaper—it's out of print now—was a San Francisco newspaper operated by these renegade nationalist students. The *Kinmon* reporters went after GT, even inciting death threats."

"Over what?"

"The jinrikisha in the garden. GT was recruiting Japanese to pull the carts for visitors. Just like animals."

The way Jack emphasized "animals," I could tell that he probably was on the side of the *Kinmon* students.

"So what happened?"

"GT changed course. He hired Germans to pull the jinrikisha—I guess they didn't have the same revulsion toward being treated like horses. He made them put ash on their faces."

"To look more Japanese?"

Jack shrugged and blew out some smoke.

That didn't sound like the smart, intellectual GT I had encountered in Yokohama. But money could compromise the values of many an honest man.

Jack threw his cigarette stub out the window. "We'll need a plan for our investigation. First of all, tell me everything that you heard and saw that night."

I closed my eyes and felt my throat close up. What Jack was asking me felt too much. I was a carpenter who felt a kinship to wood and trees, not human criminals. Before I knew it, my body was shaking, including my teeth.

"*Orai-orai.* No need to get melodramatic. Take a deep breath. Take two. Maybe rest. Then you can tell me exactly what you saw that night. We then can go over there at, what—midnight, was that when the attack happened? We will re-create the crime at Hotel Green. To help you remember."

"That does not seem necessary. Who knows if it has anything to do with the missing painting?"

"We need to explore every scenario," my roommate said. His voice grew softer, as if he were speaking to a young child. "Take a nap, Ryui-kun. I'll wake you up when it's time."

I tried to protest but it was no use against Jack's urging and the way my heart pounded. I lay down on my mattress, clutching Tama-chan in my right hand. Soon I had abandoned my worries to sleep.

4.

Jack nudged me awake with the edge of his dirty boot. If he had done this when I first arrived, I would have been insulted, but I, unfortunately, was becoming accustomed to his rudeness.

Our room was enveloped in darkness. We had electricity downstairs, but the second-floor boarders still had to use gas lanterns to light our rooms.

"It's time to go," Jack whispered hoarsely, as if we were undertaking a covert mission.

Once we were outside, I looked up at the moon. It was about three-quarters full, but the evening was a bit cloudier than the night of the cherry blossom dinner.

The air was brisk and the streets were relatively empty at that late hour, which was close to midnight. Jack had been quite emphatic that we reprise the circumstances of the cherry blossom dinner as much as possible. He even made me wear the cotton kimono, which I had left on the floor after the dinner. Now hopelessly wrinkled, the kimono looked even more ridiculous on me.

We stood in the arcade archway. The garbage man had already claimed the buckets of slop and the only evidence that they had ever been on that corner was a trail of some leftovers that had most likely spilled as they were dragged to the curb.

"Remind me, how many of you Nipponese were there?"

I counted us on my two hands. Me, Mr. Aoki, Mr. Kuranaga, the five other boys, and the flute player. And Tsuru, of course. But I didn't consider her in the total, because it was ludicrous to consider her as one of us. "A total of nine, I think. Five other waiters like me. Oh, and you. So ten."

"I saw Kichihei, one of my restaurant coworkers, there. I

don't know him too well, but he seems quite disagreeable. But smart. Smarter than you."

After paying my father such a compliment back at the Riley House, why did he have to be so insulting now?

"I didn't get his name," I said, "but I think I had some interactions with Kichihei. Was he the one with a scar on his forehead?"

"Yes, that's him. I can question him later at the restaurant."

Jack examined both sides of Raymond Street, which were empty of both pedestrians and drivers. "I say the note was directed specifically to Aoki or Kuranaga. Maybe they thought you were one of them."

"But I'm so much smaller than Kuranaga."

"In this darkness, all I see is this cheap kimono. And white people can't tell us apart. I can't tell you how many times I've been mistaken for Aoki." The expression on his face told me that was a case of mistaken identity he didn't care for.

"Why would a guest want to threaten Mr. Aoki or Mr. Kuranaga?" I said. "It doesn't make sense. This whole party was about Japan and the cherry blossom." Though I wanted to help Jack, I was frozen in place as I pictured that imposing masked figure on the bicycle coming down this very street. Why did his face being hidden make him seem especially frightening? I imagined a demonic or deformed visage underneath that crumpled burlap bag.

"Look, look, what do we have here?" Jack had been inspecting the gutter while I was in my trance. Wincing in response to an especially ghastly smell, I cautiously approached him to see what he was looking at down there: a ceramic flower pin.

"All the partygoers were given those. Men put them in their buttonholes while some women placed them in their hair. Didn't you receive one?" I asked.

"I left early. I didn't have a place at the table, anyway. I just wanted to get some quick photos at the beginning." He attempted to shake the muck off the pin and placed it in a handkerchief. "This could have fallen off when he accosted you."

"I suppose." But the ceramic pin was so far from where I had been.

Jack continued his search for clues. "And what's this?"

Splinters of wood, but still recognizable as the souvenir jinrikisha. How could someone treat the elaborate gift with such disrespect?

"Those were party gifts from Mr. Aoki," I told Jack, who tore off a page of an abandoned newspaper to wrap the splinters.

While he collected evidence, I gazed up at the west side of the hotel and noted the lights turning on in a room at this midnight hour. Had we created enough noise to interrupt a wealthy vacationer's sleep?

Jack was also looking up, except he seemed transfixed by the three-quarter moon. He pressed his lips together in thought. I learned later that when Jack was quiet, it meant a dangerous darkness had visited him. "If anyone else threatens you, you come to me immediately," he said.

"Well, all right." Jack had not shown any concern for me before, so I didn't know how seriously I should take his admonition.

"No, listen to me. I need to know."

5.

When I woke the next morning, Jack was already up and pinning wet prints onto his clothesline. I could tell that he had launched into his excitable mode, like a top that had been set in motion. "I'm not sure how valuable that painting really is and who would want it. But I know someone who might be able to tell us."

I rubbed my eyes. "Who?"

"Grace Nicholson. Once you are dressed, we will go over to her store."

"What time is it?"

"Eight."

"Isn't that a bit early for us to go to someone's place of business?"

"Lucky for us, she practically lives there."

Grace Nicholson, according to Jack, was the foremost expert on tribal Indian art. She, in fact, went on solo buying expeditions to reservations in New Mexico to find the most authentic baskets, pottery, and weavings. I was curious to see what kind of woman could operate such an enterprise on her own.

Miss Nicholson's shop was located in an old paint store only a few storefronts away from Marsh's emporium. It was quite an unassuming exterior, but once we walked inside, I found myself in a most amazing tented room with a wall literally covered with woven Indian baskets. Colorful rugs and even an animal pelt were on the floor. I felt as if I had entered Indian country, even though I'd never seen an actual reservation. For a single woman to operate a thriving business, Miss Nicholson had to be no-nonsense and quite fearless. The women in America were certainly quite a different breed than those in Japan.

"Ah, Jack, this is early for you." A trim woman with dark hair and sharp eyes stopped packing a box to address us. I found it difficult to estimate an American woman's age, but based on her voice, she could have been in her twenties. The way she dressed and carried herself, however, made me think she could be older.

"Hello, Grace. I wanted to introduce you to a newcomer to Pasadena. Louie Wada."

She held out her hand and I hesitated before pressing my fingers into hers. Her hands were callused like a man's—she must have been devoted to her work.

"Are you a photographer as well?" she asked me.

I shook my head. These American women were leaving me tongue-tied.

Jack came to my rescue. "No, he's a carpenter. His father helped to build the Japanese hall at the Chicago World's Fair."

I was impressed that Jack could seamlessly share this information that he had just learned the day before. Elevating me would probably help Jack extract the information he wanted from this woman.

"How wonderful," Miss Nicholson replied. "Please forgive the mess. I'm moving to my own building soon on Los Robles."

"It will have a garden and everything," Jack said. He seemed to be quite taken with the art dealer.

Miss Nicholson smiled. "You were listening to me. I'll hire you to take some photographs once I've completed all the renovations." She pulled out a couple of wooden chairs for us. "How can I help you, Jack? For you to come so early, it must be very serious."

"This is a delicate matter. Something that should not be spoken of outside these walls."

Miss Nicholson remained expressionless. She seemed quite unflappable, which probably made her a good businesswoman. "You know I will keep the matter in confidence."

"Do you know Mr. Aoki's painting of the Indian basket and the persimmons?"

"I know of it." Miss Nicholson adjusted her cuffed sleeves.

"Would anyone outside of Pasadena be interested?"

"You mean a museum or collector?"

"Either—both. Would it have any value?"

Miss Nicholson gazed at her packed boxes in thought. "Hmmmm. Well, to be honest, Jack—I don't think there would be much interest in Mr. Aoki's artwork. I mean, isn't he a flash in the pan? He's not a true Japanese artist working in his country's tradition. He's contemporary and independent, and he lives here, not in one of the ancient cities in Japan."

"So that painting would not be worth much."

"No. I mean, some of the women of Pasadena may find it an amusing decoration. But its financial worth? Not much. Its motif is totally unrelated to Japan. Why, is he selling?"

"I was just making inquiries." Jack rose abruptly and I followed suit. He ran his hand through his unruly hair. "Thank you, Grace. I think we have taken too much of your time."

I bowed. "Yes, thank you." I spoke in Grace's presence for the first time, startling her as if she just realized that I had been there.

"Remember to come by my new place," she called out as we walked past the baskets on display.

From the dourness that had descended over Jack's demeanor, I could tell that he was bothered by Miss Nicholson's pronouncement about Mr. Aoki's low artistic value.

"I thought that you didn't think much of his artwork," I said, practically running after him.

"Look, why don't you go by Aoki's studio to pick up that list of dinner attendees. He sent word that it was ready to be picked up," he said before abruptly heading in the opposite direction of the Hotel Green. Jack was at times very difficult to comprehend. He could be so welcoming to me one day, then cold and rude the next. I wondered what I had done to make him treat me this way, and part of me wished I could speak with Eddie, his former roommate, to ask if he'd always been like this.

Resigned to follow Jack's suggestion, I made a left on Green to enter the studio from the street, only to find it locked. *I would have to come later in the day*, I thought as I turned away, only to hear someone call out to me. I looked up and saw a figure waving at me from the balcony of an upstairs room. "My father gave me something for you," Tsuru yelled. "Meet me in the lobby."

Since I greatly enjoyed being inside that grand building, I was only too happy to oblige.

On the tile floor stood Tsuru, a bit out of breath. She was holding on to a large envelope, which I assumed was the list of guests. "I was planning to go to your boardinghouse to deliver this."

I accepted the envelope, nodding my thanks. "What were you doing up there?" I asked, referring to her balcony perch.

"At times I stay with the Marshalls; they are patrons of Toshio. They live part-time in the Hotel Green. I spent the night there after the dinner."

My interest was piqued. From the balcony where Tsuru had been standing, a person would have a clear view of the corner down below. "What time did you go to bed that night?"

"I was tucked into bed about eleven. But I didn't actually go to sleep. All that excitement at the dinner! And then I heard an awful ruckus down below by Ishiyama's store."

My breath got caught in my throat. "What did you see?"

"A tramp. You know, a hobo, going through the buckets. He comes to this area quite often. The police usually pick vagrants up right away but not that night."

My emotions, which soared a moment ago, deflated.

"This one has a long beard. He looks a bit like Saint Nicholas, but skinny." Tsuru was clever enough to see that I didn't know who she was referring to. "How about . . ." She pressed a finger on her cheek in thought. "Confucius?"

"Koshi, yes." I couldn't imagine a white man resembling the Chinese philosopher, but appreciated the reference.

"How many buckets did you see?"

"I'm not sure. Maybe two?"

"Then what happened?"

Tsuru twirled a piece of her long hair around her index finger. "The tramp didn't stay too long. Not sure what he took."

"Did you see anything after that?" I asked hopefully.

"No. Did something else happen? Mrs. Marshall caught me by the window and sent me straight back to bed."

"Nothing, nothing," I said. However precocious Tsuru was, I didn't want to scare her with stories about people wishing for our death because we were Japanese, and her father obviously had not mentioned anything about the stolen painting.

Freed from her delivery task, Tsuru began doing pirouettes on a red, white, and blue Persian rug. Still a bit self-conscious about Tsuru's theatrics, I was glad that there was no one else to witness her dance.

"I'm going to be an actress," she announced.

"*Yakusha*," I said in Japanese, just to make sure I understood. How could a Japanese girl become an actress in America?

"My family came here as performers. The government said that I couldn't tour with them, so Aoki-san adopted me."

I gave her a strange look.

"You didn't think he was my real father, did you? He's so old."

It was an odd arrangement. In Japan it was a common practice for children—specifically boys—to be adopted by a branch of the family who had no male descendants. For a girl to be adopted in a foreign country by someone who was not a blood relative, on the other hand, was quite unusual. I suddenly felt more compassion for Tsuru as she, like me, was in a sense completely on one's own in America.

"Aoki-san is thinking about sending me to a boarding school in Colorado," she added.

"Won't you be lonely there?"

"No."

"I would be angry."

"Why would you be angry?"

"I think that I would feel that I was being thrown away."

Tsuru began to laugh. "You are too sensitive," she declared. Her attitudes were certainly beyond those befitting her chronological age.

"Maybe," I mumbled and made up an excuse to make my exit. As I walked to work, I felt strangely comforted that at least one acquaintance—could I even call her a friend?—had been watching that corner. I was known by someone who had seen evidence of my existence, even though it had only been buckets filled with food waste. I felt a little less alone.

6.

When I returned to our room at the end of the day, Jack was pinning new items on his clothesline above his bed. Instead of photographs, they were either pieces of paper with Japanese writing, or ephemera. He seemed quite recovered from our visit to Grace Nicholson's store. "I think we need to focus on someone who wanted to do some harm to Mr. Aoki and maybe us Japanese in general," he said. He gestured to his newly arranged clothesline. "Potential witnesses or suspects."

I handed him the list of attendees. Upon reading a name, he dug through a stack of paper and pulled out the real estate brochure that I had picked out of the gutter. I thought that I had left that in my pants pocket, and I had not mentioned anything about it to Jack. He must have rifled through my belongings again.

He clipped the Olinda oil advertisement onto the line. "Sherwood Carter. I saw he was at the dinner with his family."

I nodded. The brutish man who thought that he ruled the world. "Do you know him?"

"Never met him, but I know the name. A real estate tycoon who bought and sold land in this place called Olinda. One of the properties was a sheep farm owned by one of the Boyle brothers' relatives. I even went there to take some photographs when the ranch was in operation."

"Do you think he could have been involved in some way?"

"Who knows? Wherever he goes, he seems to get people's tongues wagging. And he certainly has a low regard for Asiatic immigrants buying up land in California."

Also on the clothesline was a photo of Gigi. The portrait looked like one Jack himself had taken because it was the same dimensions as his other work and reflected a high level of emotional authority that I didn't see in standard pictures. Here Gigi was standing next to what looked like our camellia bush in the back, her face lifted up toward the light of the sun. So much beauty and optimism. My whole body tingled. I wanted to place that portrait by the edge of my mattress so I could go to bed and wake up to her magnificent visage.

"You have a photo of Gigi," I said.

"She's modeled for me in the past. I already questioned her about what she saw."

"But I could have talked—"

"You have private motives that aren't so private about our Miss Greeman. You must leave passion at the door during investigations."

I felt ashamed that I hadn't better hidden my romantic

feelings for Gigi. On the other hand, how could Jack scold me about passion? He had no lid on his tempestuous tendencies.

"Well, what did she say?" I asked glumly.

"That there was a circle of older women led by Mrs. Gertrude Carter who were flatly against the union between Leonna and Kuranaga."

I could have told you that, I thought, recalling the conversation between Josephine and Gigi that I had overheard that night in the lobby. "If they were supporting Mr. Aoki in his cherry blossom dinner, how could they be so against a friend marrying a Japanese?"

"Their daughters are learning to be part of the ruling class by being students of Aoki. Being under the tutelage of a Nipponese art teacher is different than being related to one. Doing *sumie* painting or owning an Aoki mural makes these women feel worldly, maybe not so much under their husbands' thumb. But the line is drawn—Aoki is the exotic monkey. You can play with him, but don't make him a part of your family or social circle."

The reduction of our status to the level of monkeys distressed me. There were no young Japanese women here in California, other than the adolescent Tsuru. Was I destined to be a fatherless bachelor in this country?

I was stunned into silence for a moment. And then I recalled my encounter with Tsuru. "I do have some information of my own." I then told him about what Tsuru had witnessed from her high perch in the Hotel Green on the night of the cherry blossom dinner.

"I know that tramp," Jack said. "I've taken photos of him before."

"He posed for you?"

"He wasn't quite aware that he was my model," Jack admitted. "I have some prints in my trunk somewhere. He wanders around the Hotel Green, but I think he has someplace where he sleeps. He causes no harm. Except maybe going through garbage, but then there's less to collect, all the better." Jack tugged at the chain that was connected to his silver pocket watch and checked the time. "I'm going to be late for dish washing duty. Come with me to Manako's. With all this hard work, we both deserve a decent sandwich."

We sped down the dirt-packed street, dodging other pedestrians, bicyclists, and buggies. Ever since the attack at Hotel Green, I had become a bit skittish of crowds and especially bicyclists, but it was broad daylight and I was in Jack's company. Jack wasn't the burliest of men, but he had a discerning eye and that pocketknife, which he consistently sharpened. Although I didn't know about his full background, both in America and Japan, I had the feeling that he could ably defend himself if challenged.

Without Jack's knowledge, I had already surveyed Manako Restaurant on North Fair Oaks early one morning. I was curious about where he worked, and I found that it was a respectable enough establishment. I didn't go inside, of course, but peered through the glass window when I knew he wasn't working there. I had seen it was an expansive, clean space full of perfectly arranged wooden chairs with elegant thin vertical spindles. Even though framed posters of Japan lined the wall, everything on the customers' plates seemed strictly American.

As we neared the café, Jack told me to wait outside. Since I wasn't a paying customer, he wanted to make sure the owner wasn't around so I could come in.

"Hello, do you work for the Watanabes?" A voice greeted me from behind. It was a vegetable peddler, an Asian man, on a horse-drawn cart. There was no perceptible accent in the way he spoke English and pronounced the name of Manako's owners. He had a helper, another Asian man who was a bit younger, maybe in his late twenties. I couldn't help but notice that the younger man had some kind of injury; he limped to tie the horse to a post.

I managed to find my tongue. "I'm working for Victor Marsh, the art goods dealer on Green Street."

"Oh, is that right? They are my steady customers at their home on Euclid Avenue."

I was surprised that the vegetable man knew such personal information about Victor Marsh. I didn't even know where he lived.

"My name is Louie Wada." I extended my hand up toward the driver.

"They call me Ah Hugh." Oh, a Chinese man, I quickly surmised from his name. We grasped each other's hands, knowing full well that our true names had been left an ocean away. "That's my nephew, Ah Wang." He nodded toward the younger man who didn't acknowledge me as he unloaded bags of vegetables onto a small wheelbarrow. "Where have you come from?" Ah Hugh asked.

"Yokohama. I came last week."

"With your parents?"

My face colored. I was loath to admit that I was an orphan. "Only me."

"Well," Ah Hugh said, "that is brave. You must be stronger than you look."

Another backhanded compliment. I was getting used to receiving such comments from older men.

Ah Hugh must have noticed my reaction, as he quickly added, "I guess we all are."

At that time, Jack made an appearance from the back of the restaurant. "C'mon, now," he said, waving me in. I excused myself from Ah Hugh's presence and went inside.

I sat in the kitchen on a stool while Jack prepared a sandwich for me. He buttered two pieces of thick bread and topped them with some diced meat—he later explained it was a combination of boiled ham and tongue—before placing it in front of me. I immediately took hold of this splendid sandwich. If I waited even a second, I would be overcome with emotion over being served such a substantial meal. And weeping over a sandwich would only confirm the perception that many men had of me.

"How well do you know that Chinese peddler?" I said, my right cheek bulging with half of the sandwich.

"Oh, Ah Hugh?"

"Yes, yes. He speaks English well," I commented after swallowing.

"Not only that, he speaks Spanish and French. And I think a little Japanese, too, in addition to Cantonese, of course."

In Yokohama, I did encounter multilingual Chinese traders who specialized in selling silk and tea to Japanese trading houses. I sensed in California, Chinese were relegated to more menial labor, maybe like the Japanese migrant farm workers I had encountered on the *Amerika-Maru*. This Ah Hugh was probably exceptional.

In preparation for the dinner crowd, Jack had started to fill the sink with hot sudsy water. A busboy brought a tray of coffee cups and saucers as well as a few dirty lunch plates. I didn't want to be underfoot and chewed faster so I could get out of the way, but someone bumped right into me. Luckily my legs were entwined underneath the stool, causing me to withstand the force.

"Oh, you." It was the angry Japanese man who had been part of the serving staff on Saturday. He glared at me as if I had been an obstacle in his pathway on purpose. "Don't tell me that you'll be working here."

His dislike for me was so obvious that even Jack intervened. "Now, Kichihei, what has this boy done to you?"

"I'm not working here," I murmured, but I didn't think anyone heard me.

"I know his type. Coddled by his parents. You should have seen him kowtowing to Aoki."

I hated to be characterized as a sniveling servant, especially since I was never seen that way before coming to America.

Jack dried his hands on the apron that was tied around his waist. "When did you leave the Hotel Green that night?"

"As soon as the ice cream was served. I couldn't stand to be there one more minute."

"And why is that? Do you have something against Aoki?" Jack asked. "Have you had any prior dealings with him?"

Kichihei seemed quite put-upon by this line of questioning, but before he could respond, a Japanese man, presumably the proprietor or a manager, appeared in the kitchen and defused the tension. "Kichihei-kun. Customers."

Kichihei marched to grab one of the aprons that were hanging on the wall. He expertly tied the straps around his thin waist and ran out of the kitchen.

"He seemed happy to get away from us." I wiped crumbs from the side of my mouth with my shirtsleeve. "Is he like that with everybody?"

Jack shrugged. "Like I told you, I don't know him well. He's new. Came from the San Francisco area, I believe. Lives in a labor camp near Lamanda Park."

Noticing my blank stare, Jack elaborated, "It's an area east of here. Lemon and orange groves." He returned to the growing mountain of dishes in the sink. "He's by himself, like you. Works also in the packing shed when he's not at Manako's. He's a hard worker, and that counts for a lot."

Curious to hear more about this Japanese worker that Jack claimed to know little about, I considered assisting Jack with his dishwashing duties, but concluded that would be viewed as an affront. Sliding my dirty dish into the suds of the sink, I decided that I needed to respect his work and let him engage in it on his own.

7.

I returned to the Riley House, my stomach feeling quite satisfied for perhaps the first time since I had arrived in America. I was walking past the small darkened parlor, which I assumed was empty—but then I noticed someone sitting in a corner chair. I stifled a startled cry and stopped to see who it was. I couldn't tell the color of his skin, but both his jaw and nose were strong and broad.

"Hello, are you waiting for someone?" I asked.

"The lady of the house," he replied in a deep voice that sounded like the groans of a giant tree in a windstorm. "She's seeing if there may be room for me."

I heard the clattering of pots from the kitchen and excused myself to see what was the matter. The front of Mrs. Riley's hair had come loose into her face and she looked even more demon-like than usual.

Before I could ask what was vexing her, she spat, "Did you see him?"

I supposed she was talking about the gentleman waiting in the sitting room, and nodded.

"What do they want me to do with him? Sometimes your Victor Marsh and his kind ask too much of me."

"I do not understand."

"Didn't you see? He's an Indian! He probably slaughtered settlers for all I know. If anything, he belongs in a labor camp, but no, Mr. Marsh wants me to house an Indian at the Riley House!"

Excitement washed over me. A real American Indian! This morning I had met Miss Grace Nicholson, who had face-to-face dealings with Indians on reservations, and now I had the opportunity of getting to know an Indian of my own.

"Isn't there that extra room next to the Boyles?"

"So you're fine with it? Living on the same floor as a savage? I mean, I heard that long ago some were here doing farmwork, but I thought they died off." She thrust a soup pot in one of the cupboards, which led to the tumbling of something ceramic. If she hadn't broken anything, she was close to doing so.

I left the kitchen for a moment to sneak a peek at the man in our front room. My eyes had adjusted to the interior light, and I could see that he was wearing a plaid shirt, a plain jacket, and a felt hat. Nothing savage-like at all.

When I returned to Mrs. Riley, she seemed depleted, leaning in the corner beside the icebox. "I'm not running a welfare house here," she declared. I wasn't sure if she was talking to me, but I thought she would have spoken even if I wasn't in the room. "Mr. Marsh says it's just temporary until he finds work. Since he'll probably end up picking oranges or working on the railroad yard, why in the world should he be living in a fine boardinghouse in town?"

It was odd to hear Mrs. Riley being so prideful about her humble establishment. I didn't want to distress her further. Instead, I quietly crept out into the hallway, only to see my dear Gigi emerging from the back room. She was hatless, so I knew she probably had been home all this time. "What's the fuss?" she asked.

"We have a new boarder," I told her. "He's an Indian."

"Oh." Gigi wasn't as concerned as Mrs. Riley about the new addition to the Riley House. In fact, it seemed her mind was elsewhere. "It's good that you are here, Louie. I wanted to talk to you in confidence. Shall we go outside?"

After I managed a slight nod, she immediately turned down her hallway toward the back door. As I understood that she didn't want us to leave together, I waited a moment and then followed. What in the world did Gigi want to talk privately to me about? I was starting to feel faint.

Outside, Gigi came to a halt underneath a lemon tree. A stray piece of curly hair had come loose to hang over her eyes. Her relaxed appearance made me feel that this was indeed a moment of intimacy. She squeezed her gloveless hands together a number of times, and I could tell that she was as nervous as I was.

"Jack asked me some questions about the night of the cherry blossom dinner," she finally said. "He mentioned something about the two of you becoming private investigators."

Damn Jack. He couldn't keep quiet about much of anything.

"Not really," I responded. "We only have one client." I hoped Jack at least hadn't revealed Mr. Aoki's name or the details of our assignment.

"Is it all right for you to take on another case on your own? I mean, without Jack."

Without Jack sounded good. I nodded to signal that I was listening and waited to hear more.

Gigi inhaled before speaking again. "I'm looking for a man. A Japanese man."

I felt a pang in my heart. Could this be a lover?

"His name is Eddie Morita. He was Jack's roommate for some months."

Again, Eddie. Now I at least had a last name, but this mysterious Nipponese seemed to be a person that everyone knew but didn't want to talk about. Now I would learn more about the man who had been sleeping in my bed before I arrived.

"So you were close—"

Gigi quickly dismissed any untoward relations. "It's not

what you think. He owes me money, you see. Ten dollars. I was happy to lend it to him, believe you me. But I'm in a position now that I need that money back. I'm quite desperate."

I wished my pockets were full of cash. "I would loan you money, if I had it."

"I know you would."

I felt a warm breeze brush against my face and blow through one of Gigi's loosened curls. "Is he in some kind of trouble?" I asked.

Gigi's face flushed. "Well, that's the thing. He always seemed to be in between jobs. Working at restaurants, laundries, and even doing seasonal farmwork. But he claimed that he had found a new endeavor that he was very enthusiastic about. He said that the enterprise would lead to an immediate profit and that he would be able to pay me back with interest in two months' time. Well, four months have elapsed and now he's gone."

Gigi had obviously made an unwise financial decision, but it was in keeping with what little I knew of her. She had been the advocate for her friend who had been slighted in the bowling alley, and in the same way, she had come to the aid of this Japanese boarder with little consideration of her own circumstance.

I quickly attempted to regain my footing in our conversation. "Why do you think that I can help find him?"

Gigi pressed her fingers together at the base of her chin. "Since he's your own countryman, I thought you might be able to root out his location. You'll be able to freely move about in his circles without detection."

"I am not sure. I am a newcomer to California. I would not know where to go."

"He would spend a lot of time in a house on Pico Street, in back of a Chinese laundry." She shared these details quickly and precisely, as if she had been prepared to give these descriptions to me all along. "I don't have the address for you, but it's down on South Raymond, not far from the California Street stop. It's near the opera house where I mend costumes. It's not a neighborhood where a lady should go. Among my friends, we call it Dark California."

That certainly sounded menacing. Not a place I would want to traverse.

"I did go down there one time." Gigi's voice trembled as she recalled the experience. "I located the dirty white clapboard house. I knew it was the right location because it was as was described to me. Two stories with some kind of Oriental symbol attached to the door."

Hadn't Logan himself mentioned that the Chinese had moved near the California stop after a laundry had experienced mob violence?

"Don't worry, Gigi. I will see to it," I said as confidently as possible, although I had little idea about whether I could deliver. In terms of physical strength, Gigi might have been as capable as I was, or even more so.

Before I could leave with a semblance of bravado, her face turned ashen gray. She then revealed what everyone, especially Jack, had been concealing from me. "The only thing, Louie, you can't breathe a word of this to Jack. They were mortal enemies. Jack would not be happy if he knew you were trying to find him."

IV
SCANDAL

1.

I didn't feel quite right hiding my secret mission from Jack, but at times, I have to admit, it made me feel a bit superior, as in most instances I was the last to be informed about what was going on in our city of Pasadena. One morning when I went to the kitchen to grab a piece of hard bread and drink Mrs. Riley's most terrible coffee, I discovered the Boyle brothers and Jack had already gathered to relish a bit of scandal that I had not yet been apprised of.

"I know the Cook family. Her father sometimes comes into the shop when he's in town for spare parts for his car. She's a beauty queen, you know," Simon said.

"I heard the family is mad as hell. And to have it in the papers! One of our customers told us the mother won't leave the house," Ian added.

Jack took a big swig of coffee and grimaced. His hair was in disarray and I wondered if he had gotten any sleep last night. "Much ado about nothing. It's just two people who fell in love."

"Oh, mornin', Louie." Ian finally noticed that I had come downstairs. "Did you hear? The Cook girl has gone and married Kuranaga in Reno."

I wasn't quite sure where Reno was and my ignorance was apparent because Simon explained, "It's in Nevada, one state over."

News of the elopement sounded exciting. "Will they be living in Nevada now?" I asked.

The Boyle brothers laughed in unison. "Nothing much in Reno except for worn-out gold prospectors, miners, and railroad workers. They are already back in town," Ian said.

"Leonna is tougher than I thought," Simon said. "She's a little lass but stronger than steel inside."

"She'll have to be, to endure the hornet's nest of Millionaire's Row. They won't be happy that one of their own married a Jap," Jack concluded.

I followed Jack back to our room, feeling electrified and intoxicated by the news, and crumpled onto my mattress, forgetting to remove my shoes. Meanwhile, Jack was busy taking out papers from a low trunk underneath his bed and clipping them onto his clothesline. He had added a new photo of the Richardson Building on Colorado Street.

"What's that?" I asked, finally focusing on what was transpiring in front of me.

"That's where Kuranaga's teahouse and curio store is located," said Jack. "I've been thinking of Kuranaga. His store is nowhere as grand as Marsh's emporium. Maybe there was some jealousy involved and he stole Aoki's crown jewel of a painting."

"But they looked to be quite congenial with one another. Would Mr. Kuranaga do that to a friend?"

"You have a lot to learn, Ryui. Even in Japan, samurai at times turned on their masters."

I grew weary whenever my elders lectured me on the pre-Meiji times, as if I didn't know anything about our history, so I just huffed, getting up to take a closer look at the handsome arch of the building that I had passed at least once before.

Another new addition to the clothesline was the profile of an old white man. His long beard glistened in the sunlight and his thinning hair almost glowed like he was wearing a crown of fire.

"I think that's the hobo that Tsuru saw," Jack said. "I took a photo of him a few months ago. An arresting figure. Very photogenic, especially the beard."

As we were talking, I felt someone else's presence in our room. Jack had a habit of not closing our door properly as he went back and forth to his makeshift photo-developing room. The door, in fact, was ajar about five inches and I identified the strong jaw of our potential new boarder, the Indian. When I opened the door further to see what he wanted, he was gone.

"What?" Jack asked as I firmly pushed the door closed.

"Nothing." I returned to our investigation. Thinking of the protests about Kuranaga's marriage, I asked, "Do you think a woman could have knocked me down?"

"A child could have done it," Jack commented. I first thought he was trying to tease me but soon became dismayed when I realized that he was making an honest assessment. "Or a woman could have hired someone."

"I suppose," I said. I wasn't thoroughly convinced. Wouldn't it have made more sense for someone to lodge their disapproval to Mr. Kuranaga directly, instead of sending such a general message of hatred to a random Japanese worker at the cherry blossom dinner and stealing Aoki's painting? Of course, there had been much imbibing of sake and whiskey, so perhaps the perpetrator wasn't even thinking soberly.

"I'll meet you at Marsh's emporium after work," Jack said, dismissing our impromptu meeting. "It's time that you went to Kuranaga's."

When I reported to the shop's back room, I barely

acknowledged Mr. Kawai's presence, even though we were both engaged in repairing a large cedar chest that had gotten damaged during transport.

All I could think about was Kuranaga, whose Japanese name was Terusaburo, according to Jack. During the past few days, I had learned a lot about Kuranaga from Jack. He had been a labor recruiter in his earlier twenties. All the Japanese had to go through him if they wanted a job on the Southern Pacific, and those railroad titans had to use him if they wanted to hire Japanese.

The Chinese had been the original laborers brought in to complete the construction of the tracks, which sometimes required the detonation of explosives through mountainous terrain, Jack explained. "Many workers suffered injuries or even lost their lives."

I was unaware of the perils of laying railroad tracks in the wilderness of America.

"All these big railroad men were competing with each other to see who could come up with the best, most convenient lines. But the government began to close the doors on Chinese coming over here, so the Nipponese filled in."

And as a result, Kuranaga made his fortune, enabling him to transition into international trade.

As soon as the clock in the workroom struck five, I was out the door even before Mr. Kawai—uncharacteristic for me as I usually waited to leave until my senior co-worker was finished for the day, a common practice in Japan.

Waiting outside was Jack, dressed formally in a dark jacket, and I wondered if he himself might have been concerned about what kind of impression he would make in the presence of the moneyed entrepreneur.

As we walked up Raymond and turned east on Colorado Street, Jack continued to share the legend of Frank Kuranaga.

"He was a king of sorts. Or else he'd like to see himself as a king."

I recalled Kichihei murmuring "*ou*," or "king," at the cherry blossom dinner. That must have been what he was referring to.

Buoyed by hope, I was able to meet Jack's stride, step-by-step. Maybe if I could somehow get on Mr. Kuranaga's good side, I could be his apprentice. I knew that I had to stay for some time at Marsh's because, after all, he had sponsored me to come to America, but maybe there would come a day when I could actually work for a fellow countryman.

Kuranaga's store had a slightly disorganized quality to it, with tables full of ceramic tea sets and shelves behind the counter displaying glass bottles filled with different loose green teas. Rows of archery sets—bows and wooden quivers—hung from the ceiling while vases, netsuke, and framed illustrations, most likely done by Toshio Aoki, lined the low shelving around the store.

Kuranaga, who at first sported a jovial expression of welcome, frowned when he realized that it was us, not white customers, who had entered his place of business.

"Congratulations on your nuptials." Jack said it in the most disingenuous way possible, which Kuranaga immediately picked up on.

"What do you want, Baba?" he asked, sounding exasperated. "And you—don't you work for Marsh?" Clearly Kuranaga viewed me as a company spy.

I bowed as deeply as possible, attempting to signal my reverence. "I am at your service."

Jack seemed annoyed by my efforts to ingratiate myself to Kuranaga. "He's not here for the curio business. We are just paying a neighborly call. Nipponese to Nipponese."

"Huh." Kuranaga obviously wasn't believing that.

"Your store is very beautiful," I lied. "A fine archery collection."

At the mention of archery, Kuranaga's expression seemed to warm a few degrees. "Do you practice? I've been in competitions in San Francisco and have even started an informal club in Pasadena." I could tell from the blank look on Jack's face that he was not part of such activities, but Kuranaga was obviously proud of his *kyudo* lineage. "I've been involved in *kyudo* since my days as a boy in Saga. My father was a teacher himself."

I had watched martial artists engage in *kyudo* on horseback during New Year's celebrations. It was riveting to observe the pageantry of equestrians in full costume on galloping horses take aim at targets. Always too thin and a bit sickly, I could only hope to be an onlooker, not a participant attempting to shoot an arrow while on horseback.

"No," I murmured. "Never had an opportunity."

"Wada is from a long line of temple carpenters. I'm surprised you're not familiar with his family." Whenever Jack sang my praises, I knew it was for his own purposes, and perhaps the investigation's, but not my benefit. I was heartened nonetheless.

There was a flicker of reappraisal on Kuranaga's face. "Oh, of course," he said, but it was clear to both Jack and me that he was unfamiliar with my family's history as artisans. Still, it at least seemed to make him take me more seriously, as he left the spot behind his table. "Would you like to see?" Kuranaga removed the largest bow, a grand swoop of what looked like mulberry and bamboo, from a hook attached to the ceiling. "This one has been in my family for more than two centuries." The wood was well polished and smooth to the touch. The arc of the bow was indeed made of mulberry while the bowstring was a taut strip of bamboo. Kuranaga then lowered a box quiver of exquisite arrows, their ends lined with feathers. "Go on, take one," he said.

I had done stationary archery only twice with a friend. My second attempt had ended with an injury to my left thumb. But

I knew enough to at least hold the bow properly and position the arrow without releasing it. "Very nice," was all I could manage, awkwardly returning the bow and arrow.

Kuranaga was beaming; I could tell that his heart was more into masculine endeavors like sports and setting up enterprises than operating a tea parlor. After all, he had said that he was from Saga, on the southern island of Kyushu, the epitome of manliness and home of the most fierce samurai.

"We gather every Saturday morning in the Arroyo. Even some women have started to participate. I can even lend you a bow and arrow, if you'd like to try in the future. Only tomorrow will be the championship competition, with me as one of the competitors."

Kuranaga clearly liked the focus to be on him and his accomplishments, while someone like Logan enjoyed charming our clientele, making them feel sophisticated and learned.

"Everyone who is anyone in Pasadena will be there," he added.

Jack seemed to tire of Mr. Kuranaga's constant platitudes about his position in Crown City, and turned the conversation to his newlywed status. "You are certainly a lucky man to have wooed a beauty like your wife," he said, then launched an arrow of his own: "It's the talk of the town. I'm sure with all the congratulations on your recent nuptials, you've received some criticisms, too."

Mr. Kuranaga remained smiling but not as widely. His burly left hand tightened around his bow. "What are you talking about?"

Careful, Jack, careful, I thought.

"A painting was stolen from Aoki's studio the night of the cherry blossom dinner."

"Is that right? Toshio has said nothing to me. But I haven't seen him since I've returned."

"It's quite a confidential matter," Jack said. "I hope you understand that news of the theft cannot be repeated to anyone. That is Aoki's request."

Mr. Kuranaga seemed surprised but also flattered. Any person privy to a secret world would feel like a chosen person.

"Which painting?"

"The one with the basket and persimmons."

"Oh, that one. How could someone sneak away with it? It's quite large."

Jack rubbed the edge of his right jacket lapel. "There's no limit to what can be done with the most passionate of motivations."

Mr. Kuranaga seemed confused by Jack's cryptic observation. "I wasn't under the impression that it was especially valuable."

"Monetary gain is one motivation. Another could be harm."

Mr. Kuranaga frowned, the bow still in his hands. "Who would want to cause harm to Toshio-san?"

"Maybe someone who wanted to wound our small Japanese colony?"

Like a competitor in a furious match of table tennis, Mr. Kuranaga shot back his reply. "We are seen differently than the Chinese."

"Maybe someone who didn't approve of the union of a Nipponese man with a white woman?"

"Who has expressed opposition to my marriage to Leonna?" I practically jumped as Mr. Kuranaga's yell reverberated against my eardrum.

"Have you received any threats?"

Now Mr. Kuranaga's bottom lip was extended in anger.

"I'm serious, Kuranaga. Did you notice anything strange the night of the cherry blossom dinner?"

"I don't need to answer any of your asinine questions."

"This boy was threatened that night. Assaulted and given a message: 'Die Jap.' We were wondering if that message was aimed toward you."

Mr. Kuranaga's face softened. "That really happened to you?"

I nodded.

"Maybe in San Francisco. But not here in Pasadena." Like the gentry of Millionaire's Row, Mr. Kuranaga placed Pasadena on a pedestal above other California cities.

"I've still kept my businesses up in San Francisco, even though Sherwood is trying to get me to sell them off to make investments in his real estate scams."

"Sherwood Carter was also at the cherry blossom dinner," Jack said. "Not a typical night on the town for him."

"His wife forced him," Mr. Kuranaga explained. "But he used the evening for his own purposes."

I remember him sitting in the hotel's rocking chair, attempting to recruit investors into his real estate enterprise.

"He, in fact, is my competition tomorrow morning." Kuranaga grinned widely and a sharp dimple cut into his left cheek. This news caught both Jack's and my attention. "Sherwood spent some of his childhood in London and grew up shooting with his father." He returned his treasured bow to the ceiling display. "We'll be competing in the canyon tomorrow at sunrise." He nodded his head toward me. "You can come." And then an icy glance at Jack. "I suppose you can accompany him." Kuranaga brushed his shoulder, as if he were getting rid of a cobweb. "Now I need to close up and go home to my new wife."

2.

As soon as we stepped into our room, Jack seemed ready to leave again, putting his camera into a worn-out carpetbag. "I have to go into Rafu for a job," he told me, checking his teeth for any remnants from his last meal.

Whenever Jack went out for a photography job, I noticed that his countenance completely transformed. Rather than assuming the character of a flighty bird seeking a place to land, he was relaxed in his purpose, comporting himself with a certain level of maturity more reflective of his age.

Straightening out his spectacles after cleaning them, he was gone in a flash. Since Mrs. Riley had gone to Monrovia to visit her sister, leftovers were waiting for me in the kitchen.

The only thing worse than Mrs. Riley's hot meals was when they were eaten cold. Trying not to gag, I cut off the skin of the chicken and chewed the unseasoned meat glumly. These days I ate to survive, not for any other kind of gastronomical enjoyment.

I almost jumped in my chair when I heard the raucous voices of the Boyle brothers reverberating on the first floor.

"Hello, Louie."

"Louie, you are a brave lad to put Mrs. Riley's cold supper in your stomach."

"We're going into downtown Los Angeles. Would you like to join us for a Friday night drink?"

Actually, alcohol was a temptation, but I knew that I needed a good night's rest in order to wake up for Mr. Kuranaga's competition with Mr. Carter. "I am going to the Arroyo for the archery contest," I told them, "or else I would."

"We are planning to go as well—" said Simon.

"But that's not gonna stop us from going to the Union Bar," Ian finished. The brothers punched each other in the shoulder and laughed as they left the boardinghouse. I wasn't sure what was so amusing—again, the mysteries between brothers that I would never be privy to.

My meal was a mess and I happened to drop a piece of the

chicken skin in my lap. In my efforts to clean it up with a rag, I only made the stain smear and become even more noticeable. No sooner had I thought with relief that at least I was alone, than who came into the dining room but Gigi. She was dressed in her trademark navy blue dress but had the ceramic flower from Aoki's party fastened onto her lapel, making the outfit new again. She was wearing a hat I hadn't seen her wear before—a snug, small-lipped one that hung on the right side of her head, while her curls cascaded down from it like dancing waves. "Just the person I was looking forward to seeing," she said, making me blush. And then, in a softer voice, "Have you been able to find out anything more about Eddie?"

Oh. Finding Eddie Morita had completely slipped my mind. I was embarrassed that in spite of my infatuation, I had put her needs much below mine. "I will be doing some investigating tonight," I quickly announced.

"If you have plans—" Gigi said sweetly. I could not deny her.

"No plans. I will provide a report as soon as I can." I got to my feet and even gave her a bow as a promise.

Gigi put her hand to her mouth as to stifle a giggle. "Oh, Louie," was all she could manage before going out the front door.

I looked down at my pants. On the crotch was a blotch the size of a melon.

3.

After changing my pants, I took the Pacific Electric Red Car to the California Street stop. A number of Chinese men debarked and I followed, both fearful and curious about what I would encounter.

I spied at least three laundries around the California station, their tired facades unwelcoming. All of them were closed for the evening. I could literally hear the buildings sighing from overwork in the shadow of the setting sun. In the distance stood a rail yard surrounded by boxcars. On the left side was a long wooden structure; based on the men walking toward it, I guessed that it was probably housing.

The businesses that seemed most active were what Pasadenans called washhouses. I had been in Japan's bathhouses and enjoyed the deep communal tubs, but American washhouses were alien to me. Men coming home from agricultural work and other kinds of physical labor crowded these wooden shacks, water draining from them onto the dirt roads. I was too self-conscious to go inside and see what exactly was taking place in them—even though one of the men might have known something about Eddie Morita.

After circling the closed laundries and produce markets, I noticed a two-story structure located behind one on Pico Street. Since the sun had just gone down, I couldn't tell if it was white in color. A couple of smaller one-story buildings and a stable, judging by the neighing and smell of horses, formed a compound. I entered the courtyard to examine the taller building further. A piece of artwork was affixed to the upstairs door, and as I approached, I could see that it was the symbol for *fuku* or good luck, 福. Just like Gigi had described—this must have been the place. I prided myself for finding the location but dreaded actually approaching its inhabitants.

There was no light emanating from the building. I wondered if anyone lived there. I carefully made my way up the stairs, hearing the mildewed old pine creak underneath my feet. When I finally reached the dilapidated door with the faded good luck decoration, I barely grazed its surface with my knuckle. No one responded, of course. I exhaled and knocked louder a second time. The force of my knock caused the door to gradually swing open.

Smoke wafted from inside. I shuddered. The air seemed coated with the scent of ammonia, which brought to mind Jack's clothes. I had tried to deny it earlier, but it was the same smell that would emanate from the opium dens in the seedier areas of Yokohama. Carpenters who had fought in the China-Japan War also described the dangerous effects of this potent drug—that could forever consume your average man, enough so that Japanese commanders ordered any of their soldiers who used it to be shot.

I immediately turned away to flee, when I heard a booming voice: "Stop, boy." And then a rush of words that sounded like the Cantonese I heard on the streets of Yokohama.

Slowly, I turned to face a Chinese man with sunken cheeks, wizened like an old apple. My knees knocked, as he obviously was very displeased that I was standing in front of his apartment. "I am Japanese," I said to him and pointed to my nose.

"Ah, Japan," he declared and bellowed, "No-o-bu!"

An Asian man stumbled out of the back room. His eyes were practically closed and I didn't know how he could actually see. He wore his hair short, no queue defining his ethnicity, and he obviously had not shaved his face for a few days. "I don't know you," he said in Japanese.

"I am Wada Ryunosuke." I reverted to my polite Japanese and bowed. "I've come recently from Japan."

The man staggered forward. "I am Noboru," he managed. I was surprised that a Japanese would be sharing a domicile with a Chinese man. But they had opium in common, which superseded ethnicity. He laughed for no reason that I could fathom, then stopped in his tracks, swaying back and forth like he was a palm tree in the middle of a storm. I could tell now that the whites of his eyes were completely bloodshot. "Oh, you are living in the Riley house, aren't you?" he said in rough-and-tumble Japanese.

I was surprised that my arrival had reached his ears. Who had revealed to him that I had arrived and made my home in downtown Pasadena?

"Has that *kusotare* turned up?" he asked. I hadn't heard that word, *kusotare*, "snotface," since my childhood days; it was a bit comical to hear it coming from the mouth of an adult man with a dark shadow of a beard.

"Well, has he?"

"I'm not quite sure who you are talking about," I said in a soft voice.

"The *hinin*."

Hinin? Non-person? That term was taboo in my circles in Japan and it was almost painful to hear the slur.

"You know, from Okayama."

Jack was from Okayama. "I don't know," I said weakly. I was a terrible liar and I hoped that his inebriation had dulled his ability to reason and observe.

"I'll cut his throat if I see him."

I wanted to run, but the image of Gigi, dressed in her straw hat and clutching her satchel full of thread and needles, planted me in place.

"Are you deaf? Has Eijiro Morita shown up at the Riley House?" the man demanded.

"Ah, no," I said truthfully, but my voice held no conviction. "I'm actually looking for him myself."

"Don't play games with me!" the man shrieked. "I know he sent you. Baba doesn't have the guts to come around here anymore. Like I told him, if Morita doesn't pay up, I'll cut *both* of their throats."

I started to back away from the Japanese-speaking man. His mind was obviously quite compromised. I wouldn't be able to extract any helpful information from him.

I made my quick escape, almost tripping on the unsteady

stairs of the run-down house. The man yelled after me and then I heard a crash on the stairs. I didn't bother to check if he had injured himself and instead used the opportunity to flee. In my haste, I nearly crashed into a man leading an overweight horse into the stable.

"Ah, excuse—" I expected the man to lash out at me, but instead he examined me with surprise.

"*Ra!*" he called out. It was the Chinese man who had shared a seat with me on the train from San Francisco.

"*Luo!*" I reciprocated. I wanted to spend more time with him but, hearing another commotion at the top of the stairs of the clapboard house, I kept running to preserve my life.

V
THEFT

1.

I felt a pang of guilt when I returned to the room and Jack was there, cleaning his camera lens.

The job in Los Angeles must have gone well because he was humming some tune that, because of its upbeat rhythm, I assumed was American. The photograph storage trunk sat in the center of the room.

"I made some money tonight," he sang. He stopped his work and studied me. "Where were you?"

"Just taking a walk," I lied. I was quite confounded by the fact that there was what seemed like an opium den in Pasadena. Obviously Jack had been there in the past, but I wasn't going to inquire about his intentions. So he wouldn't catch me in my falsehood, I gestured at his picture archive to distract him. "Can I take a look?"

He proudly jutted out his chin, giving me permission.

I quickly went through the pastoral and agricultural field shots and slowed when I reached his portrait section. "You haven't taken many photos of the people of the Riley House," I commented. "I mean, Gigi, of course. But no one else?"

Jack narrowed his eyes. "Who else could there be?"

"Mrs. Riley and the Boyle brothers." *And Eddie Morita*, I thought to myself. If I had a sense of what he looked like, maybe it could help me identify him.

"I don't believe in taking photos of people who are too close to me," he scoffed. "Their truth may be obscured."

Sometimes Jack's comments mystified me; this was one of them. How could a person cover their truth in plain sight? I retreated to the bathroom and soaked my naked body in lukewarm water. Covering my eyes with a worn wash cloth, I tried as hard as I could to transport myself into a Japanese bath, but it was impossible.

2.

The sun had not fully risen the next morning, so we were surprised to encounter Mrs. Riley dusting the lamps and chairs in the parlor. Since I had first arrived, I had never seen Mrs. Riley clean anything besides pots and pans nor even be so resourceful this early in the morning.

"Hallelujah, he's gone," she said gleefully. Jack, not wishing to be inconvenienced, barely acknowledged her on his way to the door.

Out of respect for our landlord, I stayed behind. "Who's gone?"

"The Indian. He calls himself Clem."

"Oh." I didn't know quite what to make of Clem. I wanted to get to know him better—he was the first real Indian I'd ever encountered—but he kept his distance and skulked around in the shadows. I felt disappointed that I wasn't going to have more opportunities to learn more about him, but perhaps he wouldn't fulfill my image of how Indians moved through America, especially in a place like Pasadena.

"He's not on the streets, is he?" My ultimate fear for any person.

"He got a job at the rail yard. That's where he belongs."

I wasn't sure what Mrs. Riley meant by that, but at least Clem had a source of income, which was the most any of us could have asked for.

"See you later." I practiced a popular colloquialism on Mrs. Riley, but she merely narrowed her eyes with suspicion. "I'm off to the Arroyo." I liked how "Arroyo" rolled off my tongue like a Japanese word.

I was excited to see firsthand the primitiveness of the Arroyo, which I had only seen captured in postcards that we sold at Marsh's emporium. However, I hadn't considered how we were going to travel to the canyon, which was on the west side of town. I got my answer when I stepped outside and saw Jack, his camera bag around his neck, with two bicycles. He was holding on to one and the other was lying on its side on the dirt walkway.

"I'm not riding that," I told him. Until recently, only people with money could afford a bicycle in Japan. Like my weak attempts with archery, I had only dared to ride a bicycle in Yokohama once, and almost ended up crashing into a fishmonger carrying two rattan baskets balanced on his shoulders on a bamboo yoke. I refused to get on a two-wheeled cycle from that point on.

"You mean you've never cycled before?"

"I can run beside you. You know how quick I am." I stretched out my toes in my boots.

"That's ridiculous. C'mon, Ryui. Don't be a coward."

The bicycle was heavy. I was afraid that the top bar would cut me off at the crotch because of my short height, but it was angled down to the bottom gear.

"Is this a bicycle for women?"

"Perfect fit for you!" Jack laughed cruelly.

"I'm not riding that." I released it back onto the dirt ground.

"Don't be a *botchan*," Jack scolded me. "This is for the investigation."

I knew that I was indeed being a *botchan*, I hated being called a *botchan*, and Jack knew exactly what would motivate me to get on that women's bicycle and start pedaling.

Ironically, the women's configuration gave me a lot more control and freedom. At first, I swerved erratically as I bumped into the divots in the dirt road, but luckily because of the early hour there was hardly any traffic, so I didn't hit anybody or anything. Jack was taking us down a less traveled pathway, away from the busyness of Colorado Street. My fingers wrapped tightly around the handlebars and my feet pumped in a regular rhythm, somehow keeping me upright.

"You are doing well!" Jack encouraged.

The spring morning air felt good against my face. We had only traveled for about fifteen minutes east and I already noticed a difference in the air. As we neared the Arroyo, the sky was a resplendent blue cast in a golden hue. The clouds were so delicate that they seemed painted on. After we passed the mansions on Orange Grove, sounds became more hushed and I could better hear my deep breaths as I pedaled.

A line of horse-drawn carriages and one motorcar were parked along a street overlooking a ravine. I had seen the canyon below while on the train, but this was the first time for me to actually experience it in such close proximity.

I had never seen anything like it before. In Japan, our rivers and creeks cut through jagged moss-covered rocks. But here the boulders were smooth and the color of sand. The trees weren't straight cedars or pine, but tangled oaks with worn gray trunks and cupped leaves or thin, leaning trees with large leaves shaped like hands. The air was heavy with a strong, almost bitter scent; it wasn't repulsive but definitely wild.

I felt like I was floating in this environment, the chirps, chattering, and buzzing of different birds transporting me to another world like a scene in Toshio Aoki's paintings. The back of my legs felt sore from moving my body in unfamiliar ways, but that didn't slow me. As Jack and I walked our bicycles down a crooked pathway, we reached a shallow creek that tinkled like wind chimes. One man had brought his horse into the canyon and Jack stopped to get a photo of the magnificent animal taking a drink from the clear waters.

It turned out that the man was known to Jack—a fellow shutterbug and proprietor of a store that sold books and photographic supplies in Pasadena. The tall man introduced himself to me. "A. C. Vroman."

"This boy works at Victor Marsh's emporium. He is known as Louie," Jack said.

"Is that so?" Mr. Vroman immediately showed interest in me. "I haven't been to Victor's in a while. Any new netsuke?"

"You are a collector?" I immediately thought of all the netsuke collectors I encountered in Yokohama. This mania for netsuke had apparently reached the shores of California.

"Yes, I have that illness. I'll be going to Japan and China this year and hope to pick up more. The craftsmanship is unparalleled. I'm especially keen on Tokoku."

"So you know Tokoku." I was honestly impressed by this gentleman's knowledge about a specific netsuke artist. Suzuki Tokoku was a master of detailed work, able to represent full figures in a few centimeters of ivory, boxwood, and bone.

"Indeed, I know of Tokoku's mastery. If you come across any of his pieces, please let me know. My store is on Colorado."

I nodded. Jack and I bid our goodbyes and continued down the trail while Mr. Vroman stayed in the creek with his horse.

"How do you spell his name?" I asked when we had walked quite a distance away.

"It's odd. Begins with a *V* like Victoria. *V-R-O-M-A-N*."

I had studied Mr. Aoki's invitation list for the cherry blossom dinner several times, and that name hadn't been on it. "He wasn't invited to the dinner."

"Well, he's not the type to socialize with Aoki, despite his interest in netsuke."

"He's not here for the competition?"

"No, he's a naturalist. He'd rather commune with the trees and take photos of the Hopis and Navajos than spend his Saturdays with blowhards like Kuranaga and Carter."

I understood the attraction. Since the Japanese liked to embrace the notion that our archipelago was formed by the sun goddess, I had grown up thinking that we were in the center of the universe, that life started with us. But for these boulders to be so smooth and polished, they must have been washed by storms and rain over centuries. And these oak trees—one even seemed almost five stories in height—had to have existed for generations. For the first time, I considered that perhaps America, as a land, was older than we all imagined. Perhaps the universe didn't start with Nippon—could that be possible? To be fully cocooned in the beauty of the Arroyo made me feel that perhaps another supernatural force—beyond rulers and nations—was behind our creation.

By the time we had reached a clearing where the competition was to be taking place, a small crowd had already gathered. I looked for the Boyle brothers but they were nowhere to be found. It was just as well, as they would have felt out of place; most of the white men were old enough to be their father, and were wearing tailored clothing that appeared to be made from fine fabric. No overalls or plaid shirts here.

Jack and I weren't dressed that way, either, but we represented the Japanese contingent and therefore had different rules to follow. I saw Mr. Aoki and bowed to him, while Jack hung back.

"I trust everything is proceeding smoothly," the artist said to me.

"*Hai*, we are working hard." I knew that this was not the time or place to openly discuss our arrangement. And to be honest, I didn't have much to report as we didn't have any definite leads on who had stolen his painting.

As Mr. Kuranaga had told us in his store, this seemed to be an exclusive affair, with only about a dozen men in attendance. I felt quite honored to be included. After leaning my bicycle against one of the oak trees, I looked for an open place to watch the contest. Jack had already wandered to the eastern edge of the clearing to engage in a conversation with a very eccentric-looking white man with a huge gray mustache that lay on his face like a dead rat. Soon both of them were smoking together.

I caressed the trunk of one of the oak trees in the back of the clearing. Climbing was one skill that I excelled in from all the time I had spent in cypress forests as well as working with my father on the roofs of temple buildings, and this tree, with its low, strong branches, seemed perfect for the task. Before I knew it, I had climbed from one branch to another until I was about two stories high. I pulled at some leaves in front of me and soon I had the best seat to view what would transpire in a few minutes.

Two targets featuring red concentric circles had been placed on the other side of the clearing. My heart started to race. I hadn't watched a sporting competition since I had attended an outdoor sumo match with my father at a temple in Tokio three years ago. I had been drawn to the exhibition of masculine athletic prowess, and although I myself had none of that, for a few moments I could pretend that I inhabited the wrestlers' enormous bodies. And now watching the two archers, I could sense their focus and determination even from my perch in the oak tree.

"Positions, gentlemen," I heard a voice call out, and the crowd quieted, only releasing smoke from their mouths and their pipes.

Mr. Kuranaga and Mr. Carter both broke away from their conversations. Even though I was quite a distance away, I still recognized Kuranaga's family bow, tremendous in size. Mr. Kuranaga took his position on the right-hand side, while Mr. Carter came into view wearing the most ridiculous top hat. Since he was tall already, he towered over Kuranaga. I could imagine that the hat would get in his way while pulling back the bow, but it remained on his head.

Plop, plop, plop, plop, plop. Sherwood quickly released his five arrows, one at a time, toward his target. The bright yellow ends of his white arrows were crowded around the second circle, with only one having reached the center.

Kuranaga, on the other hand, was more deliberate. Like the samurai warriors of the past, he held the bow higher, pulling the arrow back above his head before launching. The arrows whizzed with great speed and almost all hit the bull's-eye.

The crowd cried out and applause erupted through the canyon.

Sherwood was standing still—I wasn't sure if it was from shock or shame—when I heard a whoosh coming from a neighboring oak tree a few meters away from me. Turning to follow the sound, I spotted a pale, burly right arm holding a bow after apparently launching an arrow. The man scampered down the tree, scattering leaves and tiny branches behind him. Another smaller man followed him. I didn't see their faces, but my heart sank as I recognized the sandy hair and the uneven gait of the two young men in overalls.

Meanwhile, on the ground, spectators yelled and scattered to hide themselves. Had what I had seen really happened? I stayed frozen in place, not making a sound. I didn't want to draw any attention to myself for fear of being pierced by an errant arrow. Jack, I assumed, was in the middle of the chaos with his mustachioed companion.

"There! There!" A younger man had reached the oaks where I was hiding and ran up the path after the overalled men escaping up the canyon. He seemed to be the only man fit to give chase.

Finally, after some minutes, all I could hear was the chatter of the birds again. Nature ruled over man.

"It's safe now." Jack stood below the tree with our two bicycles and waited for me to climb down.

I quickly scurried from one branch to another and jumped down into a spot beside a low rock. "What happened?"

Jack gestured with his chin toward the two targets. On Mr. Carter's were his white arrows. And then pinned in the center was his top hat pierced by an arrow with red feathers.

I clamped my hand over my mouth. Had the archer next to me in the oaks shot his arrow deliberately through Sherwood's hat? My hands shook as I claimed my bicycle. Had I been a witness to an attempted murder?

We trudged up the trail with our bicycles. The air, which had felt so liberating during our ride to the canyon, made my eyes sting. When we reached the top, a handful of men, including Sherwood Carter, were gathered in a tight circle. We learned from Jack's unconventional companion that they were waiting for the police to arrive.

"I still think it was some youngsters," one was saying to the group.

"But a youngster who had such a command over a bow and arrow."

"I think you were targeted, Sherwood."

Mr. Carter, who was looking quite emasculated without his top hat, bobbed his head. He had quite a receding hairline and his forehead was getting pink in the sun. He finally noticed us and aggressively approached me first.

"I've seen you before. You were the boy pouring the whiskey at the cherry blossom dinner. What are you doing here?" Was he accusing me of taking aim at him?

"I don't know much about archery," I meekly said.

Mr. Carter's attention then focused on Jack. "And do I know you?"

"I'm a dishwasher at Manako's restaurant."

"Oh, Jack, don't be so humble." The man with the dead-rat mustache spoke up. "This man's a true talent. A photographer. See this camera he's carrying? He's even taken photos around your property in Olinda."

"Olinda? Why were you there?"

Before Jack could answer, two police officers in dark uniforms approached on horses.

"Did you take any photos of the match?" Jack's friend asked him.

"Not anything that would be helpful," he replied. "C'mon, Ryui, let's get back to the Riley House." He quickly got on his bicycle and pedaled south, the opposite direction of where we needed to go but away from the police officers on horseback.

When we were a good two blocks away, Jack abruptly stopped. I wasn't doing so well controlling the bicycle and had fallen at least a couple of times in the dirt.

Jack's eyes looked somber through his spectacles. "What did you see up there, Louie?"

I took in a deep breath and exhaled slowly. "I didn't see a face, but I saw the arms. It was a white man who uses his left hand."

"Unusual," commented Jack.

I didn't have to say it out loud, but I did. "It was Ian Boyle."

When we arrived back at the Riley House, the Boyle brothers had not yet returned. We sat and waited on the edge of the porch; Jack was smoking and I was sucking on an orange that Jack had given to me.

Finally, after about half an hour, the two brothers limped up our walkway. Neither one was carrying a bow and I wondered if they had taken the time to abandon the weapon before they returned.

Simon forced a smile when he saw us. "Mornin'."

Ian was less skilled at hiding his nervousness. Smeared in sweat and dirt, one side of his suspenders broken, he resembled a giant infant who had been playing in the mud.

"You two look like you've been busy this morning. Were you at the Arroyo for the archery competition?" I could see Jack expertly laying down traps for the brothers.

Ian's mouth fell open and he deferred to his brother for guidance.

"We were planning to—but we had to go into work for an emergency. Thorny problem with a customer's engine." Simon's answer didn't explain why they were covered in dirt and not oil.

"Funny, because there were two men who looked exactly like you running from the Arroyo. After there was an attempt on Sherwood Carter's life."

Ian began shaking his head back and forth like a wet sheepdog. "Oh, no, no. It wasn't like that at all."

"Quiet, Ian." Simon's teeth were clenched and I could envision smoke coming out of his ears.

"I was just there to scare him."

"Ian!"

"But why?" Jack asked. I wanted to know as well.

"Because he's a scoundrel, a thief, a lying con artist." Ian spat the words, mucus appearing on the sides of his mouth.

"All right—" Simon gave up trying to keep his brother from talking. "We'll tell you the truth, but can we take this conversation somewhere more private?"

That place ended up being the Boyle brothers' room. I had never been invited to enter their room before, and I was surprised how neat and tidy it was, especially in comparison to ours. Two identical beds stood on metal frames beside each other. I imagined that their arms and their ankles would hang over their tiny mattresses when they slept. There was nothing on their walls except for a crucifix above the dresser.

"Carter stole from our family. Made a windfall on some land behind our bedridden uncle's back," Simon revealed.

"You mean the lot in Santa Ana?" Jack asked.

"Aye, the one you took pictures of before the sale." Simon went into the bottom drawer of the dresser to pull out Jack's print, which he placed on the wool blanket on top of the bed on the right. "Well, they found oil on the land a week after buying it for a mere pittance."

I glanced at the photo of sheep grazing together with oil derricks in the distance. Such a pastoral shot. What a contrast of peasant life and man's innovation and discovery.

I stared at the fluffy white sheep, particularly a large one in the back with prominent horns. Its coat had both white and black markings.

"The whole thing is fishy. We tried to talk to Sherwood about it, but he's been refusing to talk to us," Ian explained.

"Son of a bitch." Jack had used a phrase that I had never heard before, but I was able to ascertain that it was the ultimate insult.

"Aye."

"When we heard about the archery competition, we thought we could finally confront Sherwood. But when we saw the fine carriages parked by the canyon, we knew that we probably couldn't get close to him. I brought my bow and arrow, just in case, if the competition opened up. Then we got the idea to give Sherwood a little scare." A smile slipped onto Ian's face, which he immediately tried to suppress, considering the accusations that Jack had posed.

"The police came to the Arroyo. No doubt they are investigating as we speak," Jack said.

"Are you going to report me?" Ian asked.

"You are fortunate that no one died. Or got hurt," I said.

"Ian here was a champion archer back in Ireland. He's in perfect control of his bow and arrow. If he wanted to put an arrow in Sherwood's head, he would have," Simon maintained.

Ian sat on the bed on the south side of the room, the mattress crushed by his weight. The adrenaline of the morning escapade had clearly worn off, and now he wore traces of regret. "No, you're right, Louie. I did wrong. I promise I won't do anything like that again. On our dead mother's grave."

The mention of dead mothers was effective. We were both young men without the comfort or wisdom of a maternal force. How many mistakes would we make in this country without that guidance or forgiveness? I didn't have wisdom, but I could extend mercy.

Once Jack and I were back in our disaster of a room, we didn't talk for a while. It was as if we didn't want to come to any quick conclusions or perhaps were constrained by knowing the Boyle brothers were only separated from us by one thin wall.

Finally, after the Boyle brothers had left the boardinghouse, I turned to Jack, who was sitting on his bed and sharpening his pocketknife. "What do you think?"

"I don't think it was a murder attempt. But I also plan to sleep with one eye open."

2.

I slept fitfully that night and the next and so did Jack. At times he ground his teeth, which reminded me of the sound of roasted soybeans being thrown outside our doors to keep demons at bay during our annual Setsubun festival in February.

I woke early on Monday with the weight of guilt on my chest. I had made a promise to Gigi that I had not delivered on.

I knocked on her door at eight o'clock and waited patiently as I heard noises in her room. She finally opened the door in a pink robe and I lowered my eyes in embarrassment.

"I have no news yet about the man I'm investigating for you."

"Oh, don't worry about that anymore. I forgot to tell you. He wrote me that he would be soon sending me my ten dollars."

"Really? Did he say where he was?"

Gigi shook her head. I couldn't help but notice that her unrestrained breasts hung loose underneath her robe. "It was postmarked in Pasadena, however, so he still must be in the area. I have no idea why he mailed it instead of dropping it off in person."

"Maybe he wanted to avoid Jack." I forced myself to lift my head and look into her eyes.

"Well, that certainly could be."

"Do you know what the source of their disagreement was?"

"I never was privy to it. But I thought it was probably none of my business."

How virtuous my Gigi was! I vowed that I could be half as principled and attempted to banish Eddie from my mind.

"Anyway, I'm glad you came by," Gigi said. "Do you like Shakespeare?"

"I'm not sure. He writes plays, yes?"

Gigi wrinkled her nose. "You need to get educated," she said, laughing.

I burned with both embarrassment and offense. I had gone to my share of Bunraku puppet shows and even one Kabuki performance with my mother and considered myself very cultured for my age.

"Don't be angry." Gigi softened her voice, abandoning her usual playful tone. "I have an extra ticket to *The Tempest* at the opera house tomorrow night. And I'd like to invite you."

Of course, I said yes. Or at least nodded my head vigorously because I was so shocked by her invitation that no sound came out of my mouth. That was followed by an extreme dizziness that brought to mind my seasickness on the *Amerika-Maru*.

As I walked to work, I was hit with the most horrible realization. I had absolutely no idea how I should conduct myself on an evening outing with a beautiful young white woman. Would she take my arm as I saw ladies doing with their male companions as they strolled along Colorado Street? I thought I would literally collapse if she did such an intimate thing.

My experience with eros was nonexistent. In Japan, I was under the constant supervision of my parents when I wasn't in the classroom—whether it be in one-on-one tutoring sessions with my mother, who had been quite educated by her scholarly parents, or with my father in his carpentry workshop. Since the Meiji government prohibited pornography, my only exposure to female private parts was the banned erotic woodblock prints that the boys at the art factory smuggled and passed around. I had never laid eyes on a real naked woman's body.

There was also the perplexing matter of my clothing. That morning I took special note of Logan's clothing—the starched white shirt, the black silk tie loosely knotted at the base of the neck, the dark jacket with the small rounded lapels, the shiny pointed leather shoes. He always presented himself in the most fashionable clothes, not too flashy yet very distinguished for a young man who was a low-level salesman.

I considered asking him for advice on what to wear to the theater, but didn't want to face his probing questions or serve as his amusement. I sensed that he was a bit of a ladies' man as I would sometimes see women waiting for him outside at the end of the day. They were all of African descent like him, and some looked about ten years older than he was, which didn't seem to be an issue for either person.

Dejected, I thought about declining Gigi's invitation. Although I wanted nothing more than to be in her presence, I was in no position to step into the shoes of an American suitor. I had to admit that Mr. Kuranaga had a certain level of confidence I could never hope to attain. While the morning had started with such a jolt, I was depleted by the end of the day. My head down, I pushed open the door of our room. Jack was there, hanging more prints on his clothesline.

"You look like a stray dog who's ready to drop dead. What's wrong now?"

I was completely resigned. Who cared what Jack might think of me? "Gigi has invited me to Shakespeare at the opera house. And all I have to wear is this." I gestured to the gray pantaloons and plain cotton shirt I was wearing.

I thought Jack would tease me for my shabby wardrobe, but he instead became energized. He wrangled a large box from the depths of his closet and dumped out clothing, props like fans, and multiple hats. In a flurry, he tossed men's shirts, pants, ties, and jackets at me. Most were much too large, but I finally settled on a white shirt that had a hole—maybe from a cigarette burn—on its elbow. "This will cover that." Jack handed me a pinstripe jacket. "Got that from a customer. His teenage son outgrew it." Another hand-me-down from the same person was a pair of gray trousers. Jack pushed a black bowler hat onto my head. "That becomes you," he exclaimed with delight. After fastening a polka-dotted tie around my neck, he held a hand mirror in front of my face for me to get the full effect. "You've become a gentleman."

I was pleased, truth be told, but I was also shocked by my appearance. Of all the people to save me, it was Jack Torajiro Baba. No longer did I resemble a bedraggled Japanese carpenter but instead looked like an impressive American man. All the next day, I was buoyed by my style transformation. When I walked down the stairs of the Riley House that Tuesday night, I could tell from the flush in Gigi's cheeks that she was also dazzled by my appearance.

"Hello, Mr. Wa-da." It was quite electrifying to hear both "mister" and my surname from her lips. I was happy that the Boyle brothers were gone for the weekend to visit with their uncle so that I wouldn't have to endure any teasing from them.

We had met early because she wanted to stroll down the Pasadena Cycleway from the Hotel Green. It was a strange elevated pathway, ending in a bare area; I thought it was only for cyclists, but Gigi corrected me. "It's also for lovers to take strolls." I nearly collapsed in response.

It was fifteen cents a round trip, which I insisted on paying. The young ticket seller with a rash of freckles on his face and lower arms glared at me with impatience. Even when I handed him the coins, his lips were pressed into a frown. I wasn't quite sure if there was something else that made him so irritated.

As we strolled down the cycleway, Gigi and I passed other couples, their arms intertwined. They were too consumed with one another to give us more than a passing glance of curiosity.

I slowly lost my self-consciousness.

"You are looking quite dapper, Louie," Gigi commented. Instead of shrinking into false modesty, I jutted out my chin in agreement.

Halfway to the opera house, incandescent electric lights flipped on and I felt my heart soar. Gigi was right—the Pasadena Cycleway was for lovers, too.

Once we arrived at the opera house within the next half an hour, I felt my newly adopted confidence dissipating. I was bathed in scents—fancy women and men doused in high-quality and expensive perfume and cologne. I, on the other hand, smelled musty and a bit sour from my secondhand wardrobe.

Gigi, familiar with the venue, quickly located our seats and I found myself enveloped in grandeur. Magnificent chandeliers hung from painted frescoes on the ceiling. Gigi warned me that Shakespeare used a type of English that I wouldn't understand well—she herself had comprehension challenges, but always read summaries before she attended such plays. She was about to share the premise behind *The Tempest* when the auditorium darkened. A noisemaker offstage boomed like a storm as the play began.

I practically leapt and grasped onto the arm rest for support, only to find my hand over Gigi's delicate gloved fingers. I expected that she would pull her hand away but she didn't. Instead, she turned her hand over and her palm pressed into my flesh. My breath caught and my head pulsated so hard I thought it would explode. After a squeeze, she released her grip. But before long, her hand returned to cover mine. With these intimate touches, I couldn't concentrate on the play at all; my focus was only on Gigi, her intoxicating smell, and her gloved hand warming my sweaty grip.

I was sorry when the play ended, mostly because Gigi finally withdrew her hand to give a rousing round of applause to the actors. I did the same, clapping more for the romantic interlude in the darkness of the opera house.

Gigi excused herself for the powder room before we left. I was grateful to be alone because who should approach me but Tsuru with an older white woman.

"I didn't know you followed the theater!" Tsuru's cheeks were pink and her face was as animated as ever. "I acted with my uncle's troupe in San Francisco. I played a boy!"

Was Tsuru making up a story? Male actors played women all the time but for a girl to assume the role of a boy was highly unusual. It would be quite bold for her to make such a fabrication in the presence of her companion, who turned out to be Mrs. Marshall, Mr. Aoki's loyal patron.

Mrs. Marshall offered me a ride home in her carriage, but I demurely declined, making up a story that I had to stop by a nearby friend's house. The fact that the ladies' powder room had been so crowded benefited me as Gigi finally appeared much later, after Tsuru and Mrs. Marshall had gone to find their carriage. I didn't want to face any prying questions from Tsuru and I knew she would show no discretion in sharing that she had seen me with Gigi.

Outside, the lights on the cycleway were dark, so we opted to take the Pacific Electric home. The car was crowded with drunken revelers of all ages and colors, but even that was most stimulating, as Gigi had to stand so close to me, her dress brushing against me. Our hands grazed each other as we reached for the straps above us to steady against the jerks of the streetcar. Is this what it meant to be a romantic couple in Pasadena? If so, I could do this forever.

After piling out of the Pacific Electric on Colorado Street with most of the other passengers, we strode down the fairway side by side. We dared not hold hands or display any kind of affection to each other so publicly, but whenever Gigi jostled me to move away from an oncoming party, a shot of electricity traveled through me.

When we finally arrived at the Riley House, I exhaled, releasing all the tension and excitement of the evening into the dark night. Stars were barely visible through smears of clouds, but the ones I saw seemed to celebrate our intimacy.

Before I could properly thank Gigi for her invitation to the play, she tugged on my jacket, leading me to the other side of the camellia bush. Before I knew what was happening, she pulled me to her face—easy since we were about the same height—and pressed her full lips onto mine.

I had never seen my father kiss my mother and could not even imagine it. That's how sacred kissing was in Japan, even within a family house. Who knew what happened behind a closed sliding door? As a sheltered young man of eighteen, I was certainly not aware.

The kiss was brief and before I could ask for more, Gigi had left me alone in the darkness. It was past the season of camellias in Pasadena and the decapitated heads of a few wilted white blooms lay on the ground.

My whole body pulsed. I was in love. My mind whirled forward, imagining the consummation of our union. I was convinced that someday I would travel to Reno, Nevada, and marry Gigi.

I practically floated up the stairs. I was still so drunk on my feelings that I didn't notice how quiet the second floor was. Our door was unlocked and ajar; did Jack again forget to properly secure our room when he escaped to who knows where?

I couldn't see the condition of our room in the darkness. But as I took a couple of steps toward our gas lamp on a table near the window, my boots caught on something on the floor.

After I stumbled to reach for the lamp and light it, I couldn't believe what was before me. A pile of clothes—seemingly Jack's—were on the floor. The closet doors were wide open, revealing an empty cavern containing an overturned box of costumes. The clothesline that held Jack's photo was ripped from the walls. Clothespins were still on the line but the photos were missing.

I glanced at the built-in shelves. My meager clothes were still there. But Tama-chan was gone. My only physical proof that I had been to Yaku Island with my father. It couldn't be. Who would want to abscond with my burl?

I fled to the Boyle brothers' room and pounded on the locked door. No light emanated from under the bottom of their door. They still hadn't gotten back from Santa Ana.

I didn't want to awaken Gigi, especially after our sweet kiss this evening. I wanted her to see me as a strong, stoic man, much like my father, instead of the weak, frightened boy that I really was. I was too repelled to reenter our room, which had been tainted by an intruder who was perhaps out to take my life. Instead, I firmly closed our door from the outside and circled into a ball like a cat on the hallway floor, hoping for sleep to finally descend and remove me from this nightmare of reality.

3.

"*Oi*, Ryui, what are you doing out here?"

My body jerked awake. I was at first startled and then

relieved to see the familiar figure of my roommate standing over me. His wavy hair was in complete disarray, as if he had walked through a typhoon, and the smell of ammonia was overwhelming. He was carrying the bag that held his camera.

"I—" I struggled to find my words as I pulled myself up to my feet without Jack's help, accidentally crushing the bowler hat that had fallen off my head. He already sensed that I was afraid of something inside our room and brushed me aside to go in.

"*Chikusho!*" he yelled, reverting back to Japanese for a moment as he observed our belongings in such disarray. He pulled at the clothesline like a fisherman desperate for the catch that got away. His narrow trunk, normally full of his most treasured prints and stored underneath his bed, had been pulled out and was now empty. His actions confirmed that he had not taken his photos—they had been stolen.

"Who did this?" His dark eyes bored into me. His glasses sat a bit askew on the bridge of his nose, making his right eye look bigger than his left.

"I do not know." I barely managed to get out the words. In the light of day, the damage to our room looked even worse than last night. "No one was here on this floor."

"How about Mrs. Riley? Or Gigi?"

"Well, I was out at the opera house with Gigi."

Jack had already forgotten about this monumental engagement and that he had helped me prepare for it.

"Riley!" he bellowed, tripping down the stairs almost two at a time.

Mrs. Riley emerged from the back hallway in a long cotton nightgown, parts of her hair rolled up in rags. "We better be on fire. Do you realize the time?"

"A thief broke into our room last night."

"You don't have anything of value to steal." Mrs. Riley's tongue could be extremely cutting.

"My photographs."

Mrs. Riley was silenced by this piece of information. Even she knew how precious Jack's photographs were to him.

"And my *kobu*," I added. Mrs. Riley only responded by giving me a blank stare.

"Did anything suspicious happen last night?" Jack demanded. "Did you see anyone stalking around the house?"

"Him." Mrs. Riley's eyes widened, accentuating the dark circles on her face.

"Who?"

"The Indian."

"Mr. Clem?" I couldn't remember his surname.

"Yes. Clem Moro. He came to the house about six-thirty. Said that he wanted to talk to you two."

Jack and I locked eyes.

"I told him that you were both out and shooed him away." Mrs. Riley raised her shoulders to her ears and shuddered. "What an odious creature."

Could Mr. Moro have done such a thing? But why? We hadn't had any real interactions with him.

"Where does he live now?" Jack asked Mrs. Riley.

"As far as I know, he's staying at a labor camp at the Pacific Electric rail yard. South of the California stop."

The sun was barely rising above the hills in the east but that wasn't going to stop Jack from confronting Clem.

I would have preferred taking the streetcar to the rail yard, but Jack was in no mood for waiting for transportation. He traveled by foot, each step powered by retribution. The outline of his knife bulged out from his pocket. His photographs were his everything; concordantly, he would do everything to get them back. I practically had to run to keep up with him. A part of me hoped that we would not find Clem, because if we did, the Indian's life might be at risk.

We strode underneath the cycleway, which wasn't open yet. Eventually the familiar opera house was to our right. It looked less majestic with a prominent sign advertising the Mount Lowe Railway company more noticeable in the sunlight.

A flicker of excitement reignited in me as my lips burned with the memory of Gigi's kiss. I shook my head, pushing away my lust from last night, hoping that it wasn't a brief fantasy. I certainly had to attend to important matters before I could relive my time with my beloved.

We passed the California station, lean-to storefronts, and the clapboard house that I had visited that Friday evening. Some Chinese and dark-skinned laborers, early risers, had already left their homes in work clothes. Many of them seemed to be heading south for the rail yards like us.

Jack headed into the large shack built out of weathered wood that I had previously noticed. Once inside, he stood in front of the half-occupied bunk beds and bellowed in a language that I did not recognize.

Some dark-skinned men responded in what I presumed to be the same language. A few Asian men lying on the north side of the shack tossed and turned in irritation. Obviously, it was too early to create such a commotion. One of the dark-skinned men gestured toward a bunk bed next to him.

Jack marched to the lower bunk and pulled a moth-eaten blanket off the man sleeping there. Clem, rumpled and disoriented, leapt up.

"Where are they?" Jack demanded, digging his hands underneath the mattress.

Clem was much larger than Jack and quicker in his own

way. He didn't waste any motion or words and clamped down on Jack's wrists in one swoop, holding him up like a yellowtail tuna. "What do you want with me?" he asked.

Jack struggled, attempting to get loose from Clem's grip.

"Mr. Moro, please, he doesn't mean any harm," I interceded. "It's just that something precious was stolen from him. And we heard from Mrs. Riley that you had been at the Riley House last night."

My pleading must have been effective because he practically dropped Jack onto the dirty wooden floor of the bunkhouse. "You are accusing me of being a thief. Me. A thief." His immense chest shook—at first I feared it was rage—but I soon saw that he was overwhelmed with laughter. He bent down, steadying himself by holding on to the frame of the top bunk.

"It's not a laughing matter." Jack, rubbing his wrists, was obviously annoyed, insulted by Clem's merriment over a most serious crime.

Clem finally caught his breath. "What's missing?"

"My photographs. The photos that I have taken over these past three years of my life in America."

Clem instantly became more sober. "Your photos are beautiful," he declared.

"You've seen them?" Jack said. In spite of the circumstances, he could still be charmed by compliments.

"You kept your door wide open while you were out. I couldn't help but see them when I passed by your room."

That was certainly true. For a man who prized his photographs, Jack was very cavalier when it came to security.

"I would never take another man's creation," Clem said with such authority that I didn't doubt him.

"Then why did you come to see us last night?" I asked.

"I knew you were looking for that tramp. The one with the

white beard who goes through the slop buckets near the Hotel Green."

I then recalled seeing Clem's face through our open door when I was telling Jack about what Tsuru had seen the night of the cherry blossom dinner.

"What about him?"

"He lives here. In the rail yard."

We followed Clem through a trash-ridden field to a rusty black boxcar on the edge of the yard. It looked like it hadn't been used for years, but it was probably too expensive to move it—and then again, where would it be moved to? Vines and weeds had grown over the side facing the afternoon sun. From the inside, someone had pushed a plank of wood covered in moss over its opening—a very ineffective barrier, as Clem easily pushed it forward.

It was dark in the car, so we couldn't see if anything alive was inside. The smell was terrible, a mixture of mold and an intense sourness; I was loath to imagine its source. My shoes bumped into some half-filled slop buckets, which didn't fall over because they were surrounded by piles of clothing.

"He's there." Clem pointed to a far corner. Jack, seemingly not bothered by the filth in the car, started rummaging through the clutter in search of anything of value, whether his photographs or Aoki's painting. I didn't join him. If Tama-chan was the hobo's latest acquisition, there was no way to locate it in such chaos.

Underneath an army-issued blanket, a figure moved. I could see a long white beard peeking out. I braced myself for a violent response to our trespassing, but the hobo merely turned over, his back now to us.

Usually I would wait for Jack to take action, but the matter of my assault was my business. I slipped and slid across the sticky metal floor until I finally arrived at the side of his makeshift bed. I cringed at his rancid smell. He probably had not bathed for months. I didn't know what to call him and I couldn't wake him up with the heel of my now very soiled shoe.

"Grandfather," I called out. That's what we called all male elders in Japan, whether they were blood relatives or not. He didn't respond, so I repeated louder, "Grandfather!"

The man then adjusted his body toward me. The morning light was now starting to reach the far corners of the railcar and I could see his eyes, as dark as coal. His hair was coated with so much dirt that the strands were turning a dark gray color.

"What do you want with me?" he finally asked, blinking hard to focus on my face.

"You were on the corner of Fair Oaks and Green Street two Saturdays ago. It was about midnight. A series of crimes happened at that time. What did you see?"

He didn't move for a moment. I wasn't sure if it was because he was concocting a story or trying to recollect. I feared that this interrogation was a complete waste of time.

"Ryui," Jack called out. Standing beside a mound of junk, probably "treasures" that the hobo had collected throughout Pasadena, Jack held up a burlap bag marked with two round holes, positioned for a person to see out of.

"You?" I wanted to grab him by the neck and shake him, but I was afraid that any sudden moves would unleash sleeping rats. "Why did you do such a thing?"

"It wasn't me. My bicycle days are long over," he said without emotion.

"So you saw—you know who attacked me?"

"Not his face. He pulled that off after he rode by. I took his mask because you never know when you'll need one."

I studied the hobo's broken body. He was right. He wasn't capable of riding a bicycle and threatening me at the same time.

"Did you see anyone leave Hotel Green with a large item the size of a painting?" Since I had given up on my interrogation, Jack took over.

"I mind my own business," said the hobo.

Jack sneered in disgust and gestured for us to go. Even he was uncomfortable being in a contained space that was in so much disarray. Clem had already stepped out, probably thinking that his duty in directing us to the witness was over.

I exhaled, trying to breathe out of my mouth. There was no point in thanking him or apologizing for our trespassing. I turned toward the light of the outdoors.

"You didn't ask me about the bicycle," the hobo said. He sounded as if he had entered the netherworld that Japanese folktale heroes often had to visit before finding freedom. "I've seen those bicycles before. Boys ride them to make deliveries."

I closed my eyes. I recalled the bounce of metal—yes, a rusty frame connected to the front of the bicycle where a basket could be placed to transport items. How could I forget that detail? I had been more fixated on the menacing mask and the message on the piece of heavy paper.

"Thank you." I bowed to the hobo and he bowed back—either making fun of my Nipponese heritage or attempting to respond in a way that would be relevant to me.

As I tripped out into the sun again, Jack was waiting for me with Clem, who apparently had not left. Jack held out the offensive burlap sack. Even with the holes, I could read LAMANDA ORANGE AND LEMON GROWERS ASSOCIATION.

"The Lamanda Park packing shed uses delivery boys on bicycles," Jack said. "I've seen them on Colorado Street when I'm going to work."

Could the offender be a worker from the orange groves?

I wasn't sure where Lamanda Park was located, but instead of focusing on that, I turned my attention to Clem, who had endured Jack's unwarranted rough treatment and accusations. I bowed deeply to him. "Thank you, Mr. Moro, for your help."

Jack, surprisingly, did the same. "Forgive me for rudely getting you out of bed."

"I understand," Clem said. "You want your stolen property to be returned."

Jack's shoulders rose as he took a deep breath. All inquiries over, we made our way back to the train station. After his bow, Clem made his way back to the bunkhouse, where he slept underneath the weight of another working man.

I glanced at Jack's pocket watch, which hung from a chain attached to his pants, once we boarded the Red Car. "I'll have to report to Marsh's now."

Jack slumped in one of the empty seats and covered his eyes with the crook of his arm. It was as if he finally realized that his stolen photographs might never be recovered.

"Go ahead," he said. "We will go to the orange groves in due time."

I wished I could tell him his photographs would eventually end up in his grasp again. But I wasn't the type to speak falsehoods, so I pressed my lips together and we rode back to downtown Pasadena in silence. Disembarking on Colorado Street, we separated. I was still half dressed in my borrowed clothes—the hole in my white dress shirt was now exposed because I had left my jacket at the opera house. I rolled up my sleeves to hide the damage and ran my fingers through my tangled hair. I had taken a bath before my outing with Gigi, so at least I was free of the dirt and oiliness that seemed to accumulate on my scalp thanks to my lifestyle in Pasadena.

The bell at the top of the door rang as I entered Marsh's emporium, only to have Logan sound a low whistle. "A fine time for you to look presentable for once," he said. He walked to me from behind the counter and adjusted my tie. "Lady Madison's netsuke have arrived. She's in a hurry to see them and has asked that we hand deliver them. I would do it, but I have an appointment with a new customer in an hour."

"Oh," I merely replied.

I wasn't sure why Lady Madison was called "Lady," a title I had heard British people use when referring to royalty. But then apparently Colonel Green, the owner of the hotel, wasn't really a military officer but an inventor of medicinal elixirs sold to cure a multitude of illnesses. In America, or perhaps especially in California, people could be transformed into anyone they dreamed of being.

"Here's her address. She lives in one of those mansions along Orange Grove." Logan handed me a wooden box that probably contained around half a dozen netsuke.

Tasked with this delivery, I was indeed grateful that I was dressed better than usual. I knew about the thoroughfare called Orange Grove, also referred to as Millionaire's Row, but never felt compelled to stroll there, fearing that a policeman might stop and interrogate me. It was obvious that I didn't belong there unless I was trimming trees or planting flowers. I arched my back as straight as possible as I walked past giant Victorian homes, the box of netsuke resting in my hands as if I was to present a gift to a queen, until I reached the house number Logan had told me. I paused in front of the mansion before proceeding along the neat walkway that led to a massive porch.

A dark-skinned man opened the door. I introduced myself and informed him why I was there.

"Who is it, Frederick?"

"A delivery from Victor Marsh, ma'am."

"Is it Logan?"

Lady Madison approached the open front door. "Oh, Louie."

I was surprised that Lady Madison even knew my name.

"Good afternoon, Lady," I said, holding out the box to her.

"Please come in. I'm hosting a morning tea and my guests would love to see what netsuke you've brought me."

I didn't want to interact with Lady Madison's guests. I tended to get tongue-tied in certain social situations and feared not being able to answer any questions that might come up about Japanese aesthetics. Still, I felt that I could not refuse Lady Madison, one of Marsh's most frequent customers.

We walked past a mural in the hallway, most likely painted by Mr. Aoki. I recognized his detailed, playful style—this one was a goddess riding on a giant moth. A vase featuring the design of two persimmons hanging on an indigo-blue branch was displayed on a high wooden table that could have been Mr. Kawai's handiwork.

Scattered through the main room were European-style couches and chairs, on which Lady Madison's friends were assembled. At first I thought they were all older women, but then recognized Josephine sitting next to her mother on a love seat embroidered with peacocks. She looked quite distraught, and when I heard the ongoing conversation, I understood why.

"Just can't believe that he convinced her to run off with him like that," Mrs. Carter was saying to the other women.

"She was entranced. Who knows what those people put in their tea?" said a woman wearing a lavender fascinator that drooped down like stalks of wisteria.

"I've become quite wary of these Nipponese," Mrs. Carter continued boldly, even though I was in the room. "In fact, I've decided to pull Josephine from Aoki's class." Mrs. Carter mangled the artist's name, pronouncing it "Eye-Oh-Key," at first making me think that she was talking about someone else.

"Oh, that's a shame. Don't let Mr. Kuranaga's misdeeds unduly influence you," Lady Madison interrupted. I felt more foolish than ever standing before the white women with the box of netsuke. They looked at me not with suspicion, but with indifference. I could have been a new Japanese vase rather than a living, breathing person.

"It was quite unfortunate what happened to Sherwood at the archery competition with Mr. Kuranaga," one of the women, wearing what resembled a nest on her head, commented.

Mrs. Carter whipped her head toward the speaker. "What in the world are you talking about?"

The woman shrank in her seat, looking like she regretted her offhand comment.

Lady Madison cleared her throat politely. "Oh, men will be men."

The butler carried in a velvet footstool and placed it in front of me, effectively ending the gossip about the archery competition.

"You can display my netsuke here," Lady Madison ordered me.

Luckily, unpacking and packing valuable merchandise was my forte and I quickly removed each netsuke—two carved from boxwood, one from ivory, and two from bone.

"Oh, this one is so delightful." Lady Madison, with her sophisticated eye, immediately gravitated toward the boxwood netsuke featuring a blind, destitute masseur, a popular figure in eighteenth-century Japan.

I couldn't help but think of the boxcar hobo when I saw the netsuke. The figure, half naked and dressed in only a cloth undergarment, was crouched over a large stone. To represent his poor and emaciated condition, the outlines of ribs were carved in the beggar's back.

What was unusual about this netsuke was that a hole was

placed in the beggar's eye through the bottom of the stone, where a cord would be threaded through to hold a purse called a *sagamono* in place.

"In Japan, the blind often serve as masseurs." Lady Madison spoke with much authority, even pronouncing "masseurs" with a French accent. "It's really quite a dear practice to give the less fortunate some work."

The women cooed over the intricate craftsmanship embodied in a fox netsuke made from the bone of a bovine.

"If one strikes your fancy, I may be willing to part with it, but tell me now."

Even Mrs. Carter seemed beguiled by a netsuke of two kittens engaged in play. I gathered she was a cat lover.

"You can't buy anything, Mother," I heard Josephine whisper into her mother's right ear, its fleshy lobe weighed down by costume jewelry. "You remember what Daddy said."

Josephine's odd admonishment failed to discourage Mrs. Carter from asking about its price. Just moments ago, she and some of the other women had derided my nation, but that was now forgotten. The appreciation of art could transcend ethnic prejudices. Even though Japan could wage war against China over Korea, there was no doubt that a Chinese scroll or Korean-made vase held great value among my countrymen. It was almost as if the object lost any connection to who had created it.

My delivery of the netsuke had apparently been the highlight of the morning. I was starting to say that I needed to return to Marsh's emporium when Lady Madison told me to wait. From a sake cup on her table, she retrieved a nickel and pressed it into my palm.

"Thank you, Lady Madison," I told her. I didn't do a deep bow but managed a bend in my neck, worth five cents.

"You're quite welcome. And I'll be seeing you tomorrow at the emporium," she said, waving me off.

I was not quite sure what Lady Madison's husband did for a living or whether he made his home in Pasadena. As I looked down at the stately mansions of Orange Grove, it dawned on me that although the gardens were wonderfully manicured, they seemed a bit too exacting and imprisoning. The netsuke that Lady Madison had acquired transported her and her friends to an exotic location full of half-naked Japanese beggars without setting foot out of Pasadena.

As I carried the box, which should have been empty, I heard something sliding back and forth inside. I stopped at the intersection and opened the lid. I discovered that I had neglected one netsuke, which had been hidden underneath some balled-up newsprint. This one was an utter masterpiece, even more magnificent than the carving of the beggar. A young flute player carved in white ivory leaned into the protective flank of a giant ox created out of dark wood. Since I was well-versed in connecting joints without nails or any kinds of adhesives, I knew the artisan had done the same with the boy and the ox. I flipped the netsuke over to study its bottom. Even the flute player's minuscule ivory toes were perfectly rendered. And then I spied a red square seal—TOKOKU, it read.

An undeniable Tokoku! Wasn't it the bookseller with his horse who said that he had a passion for Tokoku? I contemplated returning to Lady Madison's mansion but didn't want to subject myself again to their cold treatment. Lady Madison hadn't mentioned anything about a missing netsuke. Perhaps our mutual lapse would be Mr. A. C. Vroman's gain, I thought.

Once I returned to Marsh's emporium, I put it on a shelf for special orders and wrote VOOKMAN, as I had forgotten how Jack had instructed me to spell the bookseller's name.

4.

I awoke the next morning to the strong scent of tobacco. Jack, seated on the sill of the open window, was smoking a cigarette, which he held tightly in his long, immaculate fingers. Maybe because he was constantly dipping his hands in development solution, his fingernails were always clean and pristine, unlike other smokers I saw in Pasadena.

Jack seemed to have returned to his normal, cynical disposition. "It's Kichihei's day off. The perfect time for us to extract information about whether he was the one to don the Lamanda Park mask," he said after releasing some smoke.

"But my work—"

"I've informed Victor that you are under the weather today."

"What?" I didn't like lying to my employer.

"Victor won't follow up. He's preparing to travel to Mexico, anyway. Hurry, let's get going."

We took the eastbound Pacific Electric streetcar. I was entranced by the rows and rows of stout trees, full of green leaves and adorned with brilliant oranges. They looked playful to me, almost as if saying "*ohayogozaimasu*" to me. "Good morning," I murmured back, only to have Jack shoot me a quizzical look.

At the Lamanda Park stop, we passed an open packing shed, which was manned by a mix of white and what I assumed were Japanese workers, based on their shorn hair. I wished we could have spent more time watching as they sorted fruit from a conveyor belt into wooden crates labeled LAMANDA PARK, but Jack wanted to attend to our business.

"You seem to know this place well," I said, running to keep up with his fast pace.

"Any Nipponese in Pasadena worth his salt has picked

an orange," he replied, pointing out that I myself had never worked as a manual laborer.

He brought me to a bunkhouse, which was smaller than the one that Clem Moro was staying in. This one, which had six bunk beds, seemed to exclusively lodge Japanese bachelors. Instead of making a spectacle of himself, he quietly approached one of the workers, and I even heard him murmur inquiries in Japanese. I hadn't heard Jack speak Japanese that often. His speech was surprisingly refined, reflecting an educated and maybe even high-class upbringing. The worker, on the other hand, had a strong Hiroshima accent, which was only a little more understandable than the dialects spoken in the far southern parts of Japan. After receiving a coin from Jack, the worker pointed to a bottom bunk away from the window. The bed was neatly made, covered with a sheet and worn blanket. I watched as Jack quickly ran his hands underneath the mattress and even checked underneath the wooden frame. No painting or photographs.

Next, Jack, gesturing for me to follow, walked through the front door toward the back, where a bathtub sat outside without any connection to plumbing. A naked man squatted in the empty tub while he poured a bucket of water over his head, plastering his fine black hair to his scalp. I saw that it was Kichihei who blinked away the water. He began scrubbing his armpits with a dried *hechima*, a type of natural sponge that I often used in Japan to smooth out the calluses on my feet. He obviously wasn't going to let our unexpected visit ruin his bathing ritual.

"We need to talk to you about some incidents at the cherry blossom dinner," Jack said.

"What kind of incidents?" His heels were being treated to a good *hechima* rub.

"Ryui was knocked over and his life threatened because he is Japanese."

"Welcome to California," Kichihei said a bit sarcastically. "What do you want me to do about it?"

"The culprit wore a Lamanda Park orange grower's sack on his head."

Kichihei picked at his left toe, its thick nail black from perhaps an accident. "You are searching for the culprit here? Those burlap bags can be found at any restaurant or delivery service. Although there are some Jap-haters over there." He inclined his head toward another bunkhouse about a few meters away. "Anyway, I hadn't heard anything about the incident. Why have you remained quiet about it?" His eyes burned into mine.

I was too shocked to answer.

"It's silent Japanese like you who stop progress from happening. So happy to twist our culture to make it more palatable to white Americans. Say nothing about injustice."

Kichihei's words burned, even causing my eyes to water. Was I that complicit? Was I indeed mealymouthed, too afraid to speak my truth?

Jack, thankfully, spoke up, diverting the conversation back to our investigation. "You haven't hidden your loathing for the cherry blossom party. And especially Aoki and Kuranaga."

"We know you thought Mr. Kuranaga lorded over other Japanese. You don't like him," I added.

My statement surprised Kichihei so much that he stopped grooming himself. "Why should I like him? He made his fortune on the backs of poor Japanese men. He was the sole labor contractor of Japanese for the Southern Pacific Railroad. I wrote about men like him when I worked for the *Kinmon*. Back then, he thought he was the king of San Francisco, and now he wants to rule Pasadena."

Kichihei's mention of *Kinmon* jogged my memory and Jack picked up on it. "The infamous *Kinmon* and its takedown of Marsh and the San Francisco fair. You probably also detest

Aoki. It would have served your purposes to cast a pall over his cherry blossom festivities with an anti-Japanese threat." *Or with the theft of the painting*, I thought.

Kichihei cackled, vertical lines creasing his thin cheeks. "I don't have time to waste on such juvenile pranks. And I certainly wouldn't cover my face in a sack. I have more self-respect than that."

I felt some truth in his statement. Kichihei seemed impetuous and not the type to conceal his identity, not even when committing crimes.

"What's the other incident?" Kichihei asked.

"What?" Jack frowned.

"You spoke as if there was something else."

"A painting was stolen." I was surprised to hear Jack reveal our secret mission.

Kichihei spat, brown liquid coming out of his mouth and water dripping from his soaked head. "For what purpose? Even if I stole it, I wouldn't be able to sell it—his paintings are hideous." He made that statement with absolute conviction. "Look, I left the party early. I couldn't stand it anymore." Kichihei squeezed excess water out of the *hechima*. Although he was thin, ribs visible on his chest like that netsuke beggar, he had a very strong grip. "I took the train to Rafu. I met my friends at a Japanese restaurant. You can talk to them if you don't believe me."

"We might just do that," Jack said. His cigarette had now burned completely down to his fingers and he flicked the tiny stub onto the dirt, then gestured to me that we were leaving.

We were a few meters away when Kichihei called out to me. "Eh, boy!" Standing in the tub, he had wrapped his torso with a worn towel that was almost see-through. "The more time you spend with our oppressors, the more you will start to look like them."

Again, an accusation that I had no backbone. Was there any shred of evidence to these recriminations?

As I followed Jack on his way back to the street, I noticed a rusty bicycle leaning against the bunkhouse. It had a wire basket in the front to hold packages. The same kind of bicycle that my attacker had ridden. A few meters away, a young white man in overalls sat on a weathered stool, attempting to carve a piece of wood with a pocketknife. His technique was terrible and it was only a matter of time before he would cut into his own skin.

"Kichihei was a *Kinmon* writer," murmured Jack as we neared the trolley stop.

I jogged beside him. Whenever Jack's head was on fire with a consuming thought, his stride was especially fast. "What does that mean?"

"It confirms that he is as smart as I first suspected. And that he's not afraid to cause trouble."

"Do you think he stole Mr. Aoki's painting to cause him pain?"

Jack shook his head. "No, that seems too subtle. I think our man likes to make a clear statement."

A low, guttural voice then sounded behind us. "Baba!"

Jack's demeanor changed instantly from analytical detective to targeted prey. "Go, go!" He pushed me forward, causing me to almost trip over a large rivet in the muddy street.

It was the same man who had scared me off from the white clapboard house. He now was grabbing hold of Jack's shirt. "*Ku-so-ta-re*," he panted. "Tell me where Morita is."

Jack whipped his arms back and forth to finally force the man to release him. They engaged in a standoff like two rebellious stray dogs. "I don't know," Jack said.

"You lived with him, didn't you? You made the introduction."

"That's all in the past. I know nothing about Eddie anymore."

"He's gotten the wrong people angry. People in Rafu. Chinatown. They won't be as patient as me."

"I'm not his keeper!" Jack bellowed, so loud that the man shuddered and fell backward. "He tried to kill me, goddammit, so I hope to never see him again."

As I assisted the man back to his feet, Jack jumped on the streetcar without me.

I ran after the trolley, hoping that one of the passengers would reach out and pull me into the car. Jack, however, had disappeared to the front of the trolley.

I looked back at the man who had attacked Jack. He seemed to have lost all desire to apprehend him. "Are you friends with Jack?" he asked me.

I shook my head. Jack wouldn't claim me as a friend, so why should I?

"Be careful. The road to hell is paved with lies," he warned. "And Jack is full of lies."

I walked the distance back to the Riley House, the blisters on my toes feeling tender in my leather shoes. I knew I had to broach the topic of what had just transpired with Jack, but I was loath to do so. This was, however, serious business. Jack had said that Eddie had tried to kill him. Was he being his dramatic self again, or did Eddie really want Jack dead? My clothes drenched with sweat, I confronted him in our shared room. "Did Eddie really try to threaten your life?" I asked.

Jack, who was seated on his bed, waved his hand in front of his face. "That was just a story I told Noboru. That man's mind has been poisoned with opium. I wanted to get him off my back."

"I've encountered that Noboru in the past," I said. "He said Eddie was a *hinin.*" I was almost afraid to say the word and my fear was apparently justified. The blood drained from Jack's face.

"When did you speak to him?" Jack asked.

"A few weeks ago. On the Red Car," I lied. "Somehow he knew that I was your roommate."

Jack extended his palms to silence me. "We won't speak of Eddie Morita anymore, Ryui. I never want to hear his name again."

The next day I was relieved to be alone with Mr. Kawai in the emporium, away from Logan's prying questions and constant banter. We could only hear water trinkling from a fountain in a corner model of a purifying pool, a re-creation of a feature in tea gardens.

All my fondest memories of Mr. Kawai come from these moments. This was before his wife and his oldest daughter, Kimi, came via the *Gaelic* a year later. From there, his brood multiplied to seven children. Kawai continued to make his artistic mark on Pasadena, from producing traditional Japanese structures like giant torii gates, bell towers, and moon bridges to creating Rose Parade floats on behalf of the Japanese community. I remember when Kimi was transformed into a Roman goddess standing next to the form of an erect grizzly bear made of pine needles.

On this Friday I gathered my strength to ask Mr. Kawai what I had been ruminating on since yesterday. "Kawai-san, do you know about the outcasts? I think they are known as *hinin.*"

Mr. Kawai frowned, a fierce line marking the bridge of his prominent nose. "Why do you bring up such things?"

I couldn't tell him that Eddie was supposedly such an outcast, at least according to that crazy man's accusation. Mr. Kawai wasn't part of the Riley House and would look unkindly on any gossip surrounding a fellow Nipponese.

Mr. Kawai showed no emotion other than pressing his lips together before speaking. "During my father's era, they were the ones to bury the dead. Samurai didn't want to touch cadavers," he told me.

"How would someone know if another was an outcast?"

Mr. Kawai steadied his gaze on my face. A searing feeling pierced my body as I was reminded of rare heartfelt conversations with my father. "We know," he said, and I immediately concurred. In Japan, so much did not have to be said. Expectations were ingrained in our everyday life. How we walked down the street, addressed one another, cleaned up after ourselves. We didn't have to speak to discover how someone felt or what class they fell into. We knew it from the air that we had breathed since infancy.

"Better not to concern ourselves with such unpleasant matters," Mr. Kawai said, and I felt relieved to brush aside this uncomfortable discussion about outcasts. "We want to devote our lives to making beautiful things, yes, Ryunosuke?"

I bowed to him. "*Hai*."

VI
THE BODY

1.

I returned home quite depleted and confused. The investigation I was involved in seemed to be at a standstill, and though Gigi had told me to drop my case on Eddie, I could not fully feel at ease without knowing more.

Over the next week, I decided instead to distract myself with my favorite diversion—being alone with Gigi and stealing kisses behind the camellia bush, past its blooming season. I was living in a floating world, suspended above my mundane activities at Marsh's emporium or inside the Riley House.

Jack was keenly aware of my obsession. "Concentrate, boy, women can weaken you," he warned. I noticed that he had at least temporarily curtailed his late-night outings and was returning to the room to sleep after work. He even woke up when I did and even occasionally cooked meals in Mrs. Riley's kitchen.

Saturday morning, before the Christian holiday of Easter, Mrs. Riley had gone into town for an errand, so Jack endeavored to make a full breakfast of eggs and sausages, a leftover treat from Manako's, for me and the Boyle brothers. No work for me because of the holiday weekend.

We had tentatively patched up our relationship with the

Boyles since the archery competition at the Arroyo. Now that the sale of the sheep farm in Santa Ana to Sherwood was out in the open, they freely shared news with us, the latest being quite curious. "Before the sale, my uncle's prize ram had disappeared." Bits of Simon's breakfast were close to falling out of his wet lips as he spoke. "And yesterday, its carcass was discovered in the foothills, half eaten by mountain lions."

Lions—my mouth dropped open. I had seen lions in paintings from Africa but didn't know they could be found in California.

"Poor creature. Maybe he sensed that he was to be sold and wandered on his own to his unfortunate demise." With a butter knife, Jack arranged the cooked eggs onto the back of his fork. For all his uncouth habits, his table manners were uncharacteristically highbrow.

Ian kept eating with relish while his older brother continued with the story. "The thing is, when they examined his skull, it looked like someone had shot the ram between his eyes."

Ian's plate was now empty. "Some kind of mischief," he said.

Jack didn't seem convinced. "It seems like a lot of work for mischief."

My mind still remained on the lion and I wondered if I would ever get an opportunity to see one with my own eyes.

The bell tinkled from the front door and we heard Mrs. Riley's frenetic steps toward the kitchen.

"Well, nobody informed me of an early Easter banquet this morning," she said, her arms full of white lilies wrapped in newspaper. She peered into the frying pan and seemed delighted to see that one sausage was left over. After dropping her bag onto the wooden floor, she addressed Jack. "I'm glad to see you alive and well. A dead man can't pay his rent."

Jack frowned, his brows disappearing behind the frames

of his glasses. We didn't understand why Mrs. Riley had made such a comment before our breakfast could be properly digested.

It all became clear when she revealed: "Officer Wilbur McEnroe had come to see me to tell me that one of my boarders had been found dead in the Arroyo. A Japanese man. He thought it was you."

All four of us around the table stopped what we were doing and stared at Mrs. Riley.

"But I told him I had just seen you this morning. Then he described the body. Around his thirties with a good build. I told him that sounded exactly like another boarder, one who had stayed with me for several months. Your roommate Eddie Morita."

I never thought Jack's face could get paler than it already was, but it had turned a ghostly green. Usually when he encountered a conundrum, he became more excitable, like a wind-up toy whose key had been turned one too many times. But after hearing Eddie Morita's name, he became almost comatose, unable to even move from his seat.

"Eddie's dead?" Ian asked.

"Officer McEnroe wanted me to accompany him to the Arroyo to identify the body. I wasn't about to go on his horse in broad daylight like a criminal, and anyway, I'm not from Eddie's country. This is a task for the family. I told him that I would send you, Jack. Because you are probably the closest thing to family."

Jack still didn't respond. The fact that he was so silent concerned me. I supposed we could have traveled on the bicycles that Mrs. Riley kept in her shed, but I feared that Jack wouldn't be able to get out of his chair.

Simon, a man of action, got to his feet. "I'll see if I can get a buggy to take Jack," he said, and headed for the front door.

"Go to Louie's employer, the Marsh curio store on Green Street," Mrs. Riley instructed him. "The owner has one."

I remained by Jack's side. Judging by those who knew him, Eddie Morita had been quite controversial. I wasn't sure what he was to Jack, but I sensed that he needed my assistance to get through what was to come. I managed to get him up and lead him to the porch.

Marsh's buggy arrived in record time with, surprisingly, Mr. Goto in the driver's seat.

"You are back in town," I said to him as I got in the back seat with Jack.

He barely grunted.

Our ride was uncomfortably quiet, as if we were traveling to a funeral. Actually, considering the circumstances, we practically were.

The policeman was standing on the edge of the cliff. A badge looking like a shining sun was sewn onto the right-hand side of his chest. Gold buttons lined the front of his jacket. On his head was a puffed-up felt hat shaped like mochi expanded under a flame. This was the first time I had ever seen a law enforcement officer in America.

"You Jack?" he asked me as I jumped out of the carriage first.

I shook my head, afraid to directly address an American law enforcement officer.

"I'm Jack Baba." Jack had found his voice, and, in the presence of the policeman, had regained his usual rebellious affect.

After the uniformed officer identified himself, he led us down a steep dirt pathway in between the rocks. Once we balanced on the side of a boulder over a wash of water, the entire body came into view. The lower half of him was underwater, his legs and arms swollen and lifeless. His face was terribly blistered and the flesh of his right cheek and lips had been ripped off, probably by a hungry predator bird or land creature.

I wanted to hide my eyes, but I couldn't look away. Although my parents were both dead, I never laid eyes on their corpses. Jack got on his knees, the water soaking his pants and boots, to get a closer look at the body.

"Is that him?" the officer asked.

"Yes." Jack's voice was surprisingly steady. "It's him."

So this was the notorious Eddie Morita. Even with his destroyed face, I could see that he had been a handsome man. I couldn't help but wonder if there had been something romantic between him and Gigi despite her vociferous denials.

"Does he have family here?"

"No." Standing up from his position, Jack addressed the policeman. "How did you know to contact Mrs. Riley?"

"He had this in his shirt pocket." Officer McEnroe displayed a damp yellowed calling card, the edges rounded. I gingerly took it so I could pass it along to Jack. TORAJIRO "JACK" BABA. PHOTOGRAPHER EXTRAORDINAIRE, it read. Underneath was the address of the Riley House.

"That's why I thought he was you. But Mrs. Riley explained that you were fine, but there was another Japanese man about the same age who used to live at the boardinghouse."

Jack stared at his calling card in his palm and for a moment, I thought that he was going to cry.

"Do you know how to contact his relatives? Does he have any in America?" The policeman tipped his pencil against a small notebook that he had removed from his top pocket.

Jack shook his head vigorously. "There's no one. No one here. No one in Japan."

"Where is he from in Japan?"

"Okayama," Jack replied.

I felt my throat close. It was as the ranting man in the opium den had said. Jack was finally confirming it. Okayama, home of the famous Blackbird Castle, was a very specific prefecture, not known for sending many emigrants out of Japan. Was it a mere coincidence that two Okayama men would be living in Pasadena in the same boardinghouse room?

Another policeman arrived on the scene. "I questioned the garbage man and sent him on his way," he told his colleague. "He's pretty shaken."

"I'm sure he didn't expect to find a dead man while gathering debris."

As the two law enforcement officers continued to update each other on the discovery and identification of Eddie's body, I spied Jack wading through the water, picking up something, and then approaching the officers.

The other officer didn't bother with a notebook or pencil, and instead examined Jack with his steel-blue eyes. "When's the last time you saw Eddie?" he asked.

"About two months ago," Jack said. "I haven't heard from or seen him since."

"What did he do for money?"

"Odd jobs. He picked oranges and lemons in Lamanda. He was what we Japanese called a blanket man, always moving with only a blanket to sleep on."

"Would there be reason for anyone to harm him?"

"No, no one would want to hurt Eddie," Jack said. It wasn't until that moment that I realized my roommate was indeed a convincing liar.

I could tell Jack wanted to leave the premises as soon as possible, but I wanted to linger in curiosity. I hadn't been in Kamakura when my father had been killed and often wondered what it was like for his employees to gather around his mortal remains. I wondered how the police officers came on the scene, and how they determined that he was really dead. I know those thoughts were gruesome and morbid, nothing that a son should imagine about his own father, but without that information, it was almost like I didn't believe what was told to me.

More officials—some in plain clothes—arrived on the scene with a gurney, followed by a man carrying what looked like a medical bag. Now, having some distance from the initial shock of seeing Eddie's body, I noticed what he was wearing—a mustard-yellow shirt and tweed jacket with a brown tie. Quite dapper for a blanket man. He must have fallen into some money, or perhaps inherited or stolen his wardrobe. Did he come to his demise as a victim of a random robbery? Was it because he was Japanese? Or was this more personal?

I wanted to discuss possible scenarios with Jack, but it was obvious that he was not in the proper state of mind to think analytically. As we finally made our way back to Marsh's carriage, I couldn't help myself and said to him, "Shouldn't we have told them about the Nipponese man who was obsessed with Eddie's whereabouts?"

Jack shook his head. "We aren't real detectives, Ryui. Let's leave it to the proper authorities to investigate."

For our ride to town, I sat in the front next to Mr. Goto. "How is Mrs. Goto?" I asked him in Japanese.

"I am a father," he said and smiled broadly. This time his tobacco-stained teeth didn't look as horrifying, but even charming. "A son. Born in America."

After congratulating him, I considered what the birth of his child would mean for future generations of the Goto lineage. Odds were that it would not recede back to the other side of the Pacific Ocean. Was that the Gotos' plan all along? Or did it just happen unexpectedly with a result that would completely alter the path of their family tree?

Eddie Morita, in contrast, had no blood relatives in America. I wondered whether his remains would be buried here. If not, someone needed to deliver them to Japan and I doubted that Jack would volunteer to do so.

At the Riley House, Jack locked himself in the bathroom even though I was sure that he did not have any new photographs to develop. I wandered to Gigi's door to see if she was home, but apparently Mrs. Riley could sense what I was up to. "She's not here," she called out from the parlor, making me feel both self-conscious and embarrassed. Did everyone in the house know I was utterly besotted with the seamstress on the first floor?

I felt a loss and a sense of disconnection when I went into our room. I yearned for the comfort of Tama-chan in my hands. Why had the thief taken my dear *kobu*? I thought only I was intimately aware of its magnificence, but this villain had somehow spotted its subdued beauty.

I went into the kitchen to search for anything edible and found only a heel of hard brown bread, which I attempted to soften with some water and then warm in a frying pan. A most dreadful and unsatisfying lunch. Mr. Kawai had given me green tea from Japan and I decided to treat myself on this most tumultuous day.

I was sipping the tea in a chipped coffee cup in the dining room when Gigi returned to the Riley House with her straw hat in her hands, her hair uncharacteristically disheveled.

"What's happened? Our neighbors are talking about Mrs. Riley being questioned by police," she said.

I quickly swallowed the bread, feeling the mass get stuck

in my throat along with the words I had to tell her. "Eddie Morita's body was found in the Arroyo. He's dead."

Gigi pressed her gloved hand over her crimson mouth. "Was it some kind of accident?" Tears pooled in her eyes and slipped down the sides of her face. She seemed overly emotional about a fellow boarder.

"I don't know." I placed my hands in my pockets as I didn't know how to comfort her. I was actually quite surprised by her response.

"When did you last hear from him?"

"I received a remittance for the money owed to me a couple of days ago. But that's after he sent me the note apologizing for his tardiness."

The timing of the return of her money and his fate seemed strangely coincidental, but I prevented my mind from entertaining the possibility that she could be involved in his death in any way. "You never mentioned his appearance to me."

Gigi stopped crying. "What do you mean?"

"Anyone would say that he was a well-proportioned man. Better than most."

"Well, yes." A frown line appeared on her usually flawless, smooth forehead. "And—"

"You told me that you were not that well acquainted with him. Is that true?" My insecurities bled from my mouth before I could clamp down on my lips.

"Louie, you can't be jealous of a dead man, can you?"

I realized how ridiculous I sounded. But my attachment to Gigi continued to grow deeper and I couldn't stand the idea that any other man had exchanged intimacies with her the way I had.

"Sometimes—" Gigi tore her gloves off her hands. "Sometimes, Louie, you are quite exasperating!" She stomped past me to her room.

2.

Since I was not part of any Easter celebration, my Sunday was quiet. I had tried to read *Ideals of the East* at least a dozen times during my stay in Pasadena, and I attempted to do so again, but eventually threw the book to the other side of the room. Okakura had experiences in America, but I doubted that he had associated with the likes of people that I had. As I remained on my mattress, the room darkened considerably. Mrs. Riley insisted that she be the one to turn on the electricity to reduce costs, and she was gone for the entire day. A shiver went up my spine. I had been threatened because I was Japanese and now Eddie Morita was dead. This surely could not be some sort of serial crime, could it?

I felt alone and vulnerable. Jack seemed very out of sorts and I had only one person who could give me support and protection: my benefactor and employer.

Victor lived on a street called Euclid. A few weeks ago I had shown Jack Mrs. Riley's map, which was getting very worn from constant usage, and he placed a dot on the approximate location of Victor's house, several blocks from our boardinghouse.

The neighborhood was not as manicured and fussy as Millionaire's Row. There were no rounded rooms or high pitched roofs. The buildings were indeed large, occupying a lot of space, but not as densely built, allowing for the growth of fig and ficus trees in between houses.

Victor Marsh's house was constructed of plain brown wood like the farmhouses in rural Japan, giving it a comfortable, homelike feel. I went up the stairs to the porch and tentatively knocked on the door.

The door opened to reveal Victor Marsh, not wearing a tie, but a relaxed cotton shirt and loose pants. "Ryui."

"I'm so sorry to bother you at your home," I said in Japanese after bowing.

I smelled a delicious fragrance emanating from inside and concluded that the family was getting ready to eat a home-cooked dinner, presumably to celebrate Easter.

"Come in, come in."

The interior of the house was appointed with mostly Japanese furniture and artwork. I let out a deep breath. Being in a somewhat familiar milieu, even though it was my employer's domicile, gave me strength.

Victor gestured me toward a low chair upholstered in leather, while he settled on a longer wood-framed couch across from me. "Now, what brings you here today?"

"I'm not sure if you heard about what happened at the Arroyo—"

"Ryui!" Entering the dark living room was a magnetic presence—GT, Victor's older brother, who had gifted me Okakura's *Ideals of the East*.

"Mr. Marsh!" I rose and bowed to him.

"Oh, enough of that, we are in America now." He extended his right hand, tufts of dark hair visible on his forearm, and I took it in mine. It felt strangely intimate to grasp his warm palm.

"I didn't know you were in Pasadena," I said.

"I just arrived on the *China-Maru*. It was a dreadful voyage. We hit a terrible storm and I thought my life was going to come to an end."

His brother scoffed. "You always say that, George, yet how many dozens of times have you made that trip perfectly unscathed?"

"Well, one of these days, I'm not going to make it out alive." GT shrugged playfully and gave me a wink.

When I remained unamused, Victor spoke up. "Be quiet, George, I think Ryui has come here about a serious matter."

I was thankful for the younger Marsh brother's intervention. "Yes." My voice began to tremble. "A boarder at the Riley House—someone from Okayama named Eddie Morita, who had stayed in the same room I'm living in—ah, he was found dead in the Arroyo."

GT's face fell. "Not Eddie." I was surprised that GT was acquainted with him.

"What happened?" Victor leaned forward on the couch.

"A drunken incident, perhaps?" GT obviously wanted it to be explained away nicely with the least frightening cause.

"The police are investigating."

Both brothers grew silent.

"There's more." I directed my apology to Victor. "I'm sorry, Mr. Marsh. I should have told you sooner. But something happened to me after the cherry blossom dinner at Mr. Aoki's studio."

GT's eyes looked more brown than blue as I unraveled my story of the bicycle rider's message of hate and the burglary of our room.

The room was hushed. I could hear pans and plates clattering from the kitchen.

Victor stroked his chin in thought. "Maybe I need to move you out of the Riley House. I'm sure I can find some other housing for you."

I thought about not seeing Gigi's rosy face on a daily basis. I was willing to sacrifice my safety to be close to my beloved. "No, I'll be fine. Really."

Victor still seemed uncertain while his older brother nodded his head encouragingly to me to assume a posture of strength. I had abandoned hope that the Marshes could help me. I wanted Victor to tell me that everything would be all right. GT downplayed the danger, but that didn't seem to lessen my worries, either.

After I bowed again, GT placed his hand on my shoulder. "We will have to talk more later, Ryui. I'll tell you all about the Japanese garden that I'm building a few streets below Hotel Green."

"Yes, yes," I replied, but inside I wondered if GT, just like in his enthusiasm to create a prominent Japanese presence at the San Francisco Midwinter Exposition, was making an error that would lead to more trouble. I walked back to the Riley House not realizing that my problems would be getting worse much faster than I feared.

VII
THE ARREST

1.

When I neared the Riley House, it was obvious that something was amiss. Three horses were tied up in front and five police officers were milling around. Jack was outside, too, taking multiple puffs from his cigarette in rapid succession.

What now? I didn't think I could withstand many more unexpected events.

Before I could ask Jack what happened, Ian emerged from the front door, his burly arms shackled in front of him. He was dressed nicer than usual. Two law enforcement officers, holding on to clubs, led him down the walkway.

Simon followed behind. When he saw us, he charged forward, brushing against a policeman. "You know what kind of man Ian is," he said to Jack. "He wouldn't hurt a fly."

Jack's jaw was locked, his mouth stretched in a straight line. *What was he thinking?* I wondered.

Inside the boardinghouse, I noticed some of the furniture had been pushed aside, perhaps to accommodate the arrest. Mrs. Riley was attempting to sweep up the mess that the police had left behind, but in her nervousness, her broom didn't even touch the floor. "First an Indian and then a possible assassin. I don't know if my heart can take this," she murmured in distress.

Simon remained at Jack's side. "You have to help him, Jack. This is all Carter's doing. He's claiming that Ian was out to kill him. You rub elbows with important people. Can you find an attorney for my brother?"

"You know you two were being complete fools that day. What exactly did you think you would accomplish?"

"We just lost our minds for a minute, that's all. We were having some fun."

"Don't tell the judge that," Jack advised. "I'll see what I can do."

Since it was Easter, Jack couldn't arrange an audience with a judge. Jack, Simon, and I found our way to the jail, which turned out to be no more than a shack with bars on Colorado Street. A pigeon pecked at a crumb on the dirt next to a young uniformed officer seated on a stool underneath a tree. He looked incredibly young with no sign of facial hair like me. It made sense that working at a makeshift jail like this was a job for the most junior member of the Pasadena police force.

Jack had been there before and even knew enough about the procedure to pick up food that was on its last legs from Manako's for Ian. "It's a bit small-town, but that's the way it's done here in Pasadena," he said, handing a parcel wrapped in a gingham towel to the officer. "The local restaurants pitch in with meals for the prisoners." For a moment, I felt the prisoners were quite fortunate to be fed better than working-class men like me. But upon seeing Ian hunched miserably on the bed in his cell, I was happy that the food could at least temporarily relieve his discomfort.

Before the meal was presented to Ian by the police officer, Jack neared him, squatting so that he could look into the prisoner's eyes. "Tell me again what your intention was when you launched that arrow through Mr. Carter's hat." Jack's voice rose to a timbre of religious authority.

"I swear to sweet Jesus and Mother Mary that I wanted to scare him, not hurt him. Get me out of here, Jack. I don't know how long I can survive behind bars."

His older brother released a moan, and I was starting to feel faint as the stench of urine from a pail beside the bed reached my nostrils. I was even more ashamed for coveting his confinement.

While Ian began to eat, the strange man with the hideous gray mustache from the archery competition arrived. Jack introduced him to us—he was a criminal lawyer and amateur photographer. Thanks to Jack's pulling some strings, he was now representing Ian. His name was Savage, which seemed quite appropriate as his appearance seemed more animal-like than human.

The four of us moved to an olive tree a few meters away to have a more private conference.

"What's the case against my brother?" Simon asked Mr. Savage.

The sun was starting its descent, creating shadows on the lawyer's grizzled face. His atrocious mustache looked more disgusting than ever. "They have a witness."

"Who?"

"A hobo. Named Artemis Brown. He was walking down Raymond with a bow. He claimed he found it on the morning of the archery competition."

"Are they sure that it's Ian's?" Jack asked.

"His name is carved in the wood."

Simon looked sheepish.

Mr. Savage continued. "When the police brought him in, he reported that he saw a large man running from the Arroyo with a bow after the archery competition. He followed him and found the bow underneath some benches around the grand oak."

The hobo's testimony certainly implicated Ian, at least circumstantially.

"The police are questioning everyone who attended the competition. It may be only a matter of time before they ask the two of you to come in." Mr. Savage gestured toward me and Jack.

"I didn't see anything!" I yelled too loudly, causing the officer to glare at me from his stool.

"What are you talking about?" Ian called out through the bars.

"Visiting hours are over," the guard called out.

"Visiting hours, that's news to me," Mr. Savage murmured querulously to us, but changed his tone with the policeman. "We will be on our way."

Ian clutched at the prison bars with his sausage fingers while Simon vowed, "Hold steady. We'll get you out of there before you know it."

I, on the other hand, was fixated on whether I would be called in for questioning.

The four of us reconvened at the Riley House later that evening, crowded in the brothers' room, which was lit by two gas lamps. Simon retrieved a bottle of whiskey from the closet, twisted the lid, and offered the drink to us. Both Jack and Mr. Savage declined, much to my dismay. I couldn't take a swig when my elders had demurred. Simon took a long glug, the sound of the amber alcohol swishing against the glass.

"I won't mince words—it doesn't look good for your brother." Mr. Savage took off his jacket and folded it neatly over the back of a metal bed frame. "The police have the weapon and it's clearly Ian's. The witness, of course, is questionable, but there's no motive for him to lie."

Simon took another drink and, after wiping his mouth, demanded, "Why is Sherwood Carter making such a production? All that was damaged was his hat. And we are prepared to pay for it."

"I have a feeling that the wife is the one pushing for Ian's prosecution."

Shame was a powerful motivator. Mrs. Carter was obviously a woman who was concerned about what other people thought of her. I gathered there was some kind of stress between husband and wife, but I wasn't sure what it was. As the three other men continued to discuss Ian's legal defense, my attention turned to Jack's photo of the Santa Ana sheep farm, which was now framed and placed on the brothers' wall by the closet. I wandered over to take a closer look.

There was definitely something odd about the grand ram's appearance in the background. "Jack, does the animal look right to you?"

Jack got up and came over to take a closer look at his photo, pulling down his spectacles to study it with his bare eyes. He got so close that his nose almost brushed against the image.

"What is it?" Simon asked.

Jack slipped out the door and returned with a magnifying glass from our room. After studying it some more, he finally declared, "I don't think those are his real markings."

Simon joined us by the photo, forcing me to stand back. "Oh, that's not his natural color. He was white as snow. He probably got into some mud."

I didn't say it out loud, but I could see on Jack's face that we had come to the same conclusion. "Simon, do you think that could be oil?" Jack asked.

Simon peered through the magnifying glass. "Are you telling me the land was already bleeding oil and the ram got into it?" The implications of this documentation finally hit the elder Boyle brother. "Sherwood Carter knew about the oil and stole the land underneath my uncle's nose?" There was a moment of silence as the four of us absorbed this accusation.

Did Mr. Carter suspect that Jack had perhaps taken a photo revealing oil on the premises before the sale? Was he the one who had trespassed into our room and absconded with Jack's photos? The mere thought of that froze my heart. That offense would cause Jack to lose his mind.

"Wait until I get my hands on him," Simon threatened.

Such an encounter would be sure to be a disaster and seal the fate of both brothers instead of only one.

"I wouldn't directly approach Mr. Carter," advised Mr. Savage.

"I can't stand back and do nothing while this hoity-toity thief robs my people. And who knows what more he is capable of?"

Jack placed his hands on Simon's shoulders, which was uncharacteristic, as he seemed to avoid physical touch with most people. "You stay out of it, Simon. Your brother is in enough trouble as it is. Let me and Ryui take care of it."

I stood more erect upon hearing my name. I had an important role in all of this. I was not Jack's younger twit of a sidekick but his equal partner.

2.

Early next morning, Jack used the boardinghouse phone to make sure Sherwood was in his office in downtown Los

Angeles. It was amazing how Jack could disguise his voice to sound like a white man.

We took the train and got off at the La Grande Santa Fe station, a building that was even more Turkish in style than the Hotel Green. People in Southern California seemed obsessed with the architecture of the Orient. As we walked down Second Street, I kept gazing back at the station to fully absorb the strange collection of standard brick structures around fanciful towers and an impressive dome. It was as if this hodgepodge creation was the result of an architect's fever dream.

My reverie of red domes and spires was eventually broken upon the sight of a tall reddish tower with a peaked roof in the distance. I would have asked Jack about what we were approaching, but he was about two meters ahead of me and I struggled to keep his gray hat within my line of vision. Finally, at a wide boulevard called Broadway, Jack abruptly turned left and I ran after him, grazing the shoulders of men in suits and women in high heels. Even for recreation and shopping, Americans in Los Angeles dressed immaculately, as if they expected to run into people they knew.

The red tower was part of a more expansive brick and red sandstone structure that reminded me of a European cathedral I had seen in a book. The skinny chimneys reached up to the heavens, and I wondered if Los Angeles had earthquakes like the ones that plagued Japan. I had been around ten when a temblor jolted Tokio, collapsing some homes and even injuring residents in Yokohama. The temples that my father built, in contrast, suffered little structural damage, which he attributed to the strength and flexibility of the wood frame and also the *shinbashira*, the central core of pagodas, sometimes made from a single trunk of an ancient tree. This brick tower, subjected to the same force, would have most likely crumbled.

The storefronts on Broadway reminded me of the ones on

Colorado Street in Pasadena, only these were much grander and more expansive. Jack halted in the middle of the sidewalk, almost causing a newspaper boy to trip behind him. "Hey, mister, watch out," the boy called out, and then attempted to sell a morning broadsheet to him. Ignoring the boy, Jack fixated on the street numbers on the buildings through his spectacles, murmuring odd things in Japanese under his breath.

"Ah, here." He backtracked to a two-story building a couple of doors down. We rushed into the building, which had a simple lobby too narrow for a receptionist desk. A sign indicated that our destination was on the third floor.

Bypassing the elevator, we took the stairs to the third floor, where we found SHERWOOD CARTER REAL ESTATE stenciled on the window inset in the door. Jack barged into the office and I followed.

Sitting tall behind a heavy oak desk was Sherwood Carter. The sun streamed through the windows behind him, making it difficult for me to initially discern the details of his face.

"Hello." Even Jack's one-word greeting sounded like a threat.

"Who are you looking for? The immigration lawyer is on the first floor."

"I was the one who called you this past hour." Jack had again adjusted his voice to sound like a white man.

At first Sherwood didn't recognize us. But after a few seconds he said, "You two." He grabbed at an item in his top drawer and I almost feared it would be a revolver. But it was only a letter opener. "What kind of ruse is this?"

"No ruse. Just here to ask some questions." Jack flicked a card at him.

Sherwood placed a pair of glasses over the bridge of his nose. "JACK BABA. NIPPONESE DETECTIVE EXTRAORDINAIRE. Is this some sort of leg-pull?"

Although I was offended that Jack didn't include me on his new calling card, this was not the time to argue about it. "No, this is no hoax," Jack said. "We are looking into a number of strange occurrences. The first being your acquisition of a piece of land in Santa Ana previously owned by an Irish sheep rancher."

"You mean Aeneas Connolly?"

"Precisely."

"He sold his land. Fair and square."

"You knew there was oil on his property. His ram's coat was covered in it. But you made arrangements for the ram to be kidnapped and then destroyed."

Sherwood began to laugh, releasing hee-haws that evolved into a coughing fit. I quickly grew tired of his dramatics and my mind wandered as I looked around his office. A wooden stand holding a trench coat and a top hat—perhaps a replacement for the one that had been destroyed in the archery competition. A line of trophies displayed on a bookshelf. And there—on his windowsill, next to an Indian doll, was Tama-chan, my companion of two years.

Surprising both Jack and Sherwood, I wasted no time in snatching the *kobu* from the sill, protecting it in my closed fist. "This is mine," I declared.

"That's just a random Japanese trinket. You can't prove that it's yours." For a moment Sherwood looked afraid and gripped the letter opener with such force that his hand began to shake.

"Jack, he must have stolen your photographs."

"You son of a bitch"—that phrase again—"give them back!"

Sherwood became stone-faced. "I don't know what you are talking about."

"You hate us Japanese. You want to bar us from buying land."

"That's the work of politicians—"

"Who are your friends."

"I don't care about politics. I will buy and sell from anyone. I'm all about free enterprise."

"Free enterprise to line your pockets. We know what you did to the Boyles' uncle. And now you are out to destroy Ian Boyle." I had never heard Jack speak this loudly. I was simultaneously impressed by it and frightened of what would transpire in the heat of this argument.

"That ragamuffin tried to kill me. There are witnesses, you know."

Including us, but Mr. Carter didn't need to know that.

Jack blew out some air. "If he wanted to kill you, he would have. He's a champion archer in his country. You would have known that if you had let him join some competitions."

"You and your miscreants at the Riley House." In his anger, Sherwood had revealed too much.

"So you are well acquainted with where we all live."

Sherwood turned away from Jack to stare at a document on his desk.

"I know you are the one who stole my photographs," Jack declared. "The photo of that oil-soaked ram, proof that you did not pay the Boyle brothers' uncle the full value of the land. But beware—other people have copies of that one." For a moment Sherwood looked afraid, and Jack wasted no time to push further. "Where were you this past weekend?" Jack's interrogation of a white man was making even me jumpy.

"What business is that of yours?"

"The body of a Nipponese man, someone I boarded with at the Riley House, was discovered yesterday at the Arroyo."

Based on the incredulous look on Sherwood's face, he had not heard of Eddie's demise. "What would that have to do with me?"

"All I'm saying is that there have been some curious incidents targeting the Nipponese. Getting soundly beaten by Frank Kuranaga in archery probably did not serve your ego, angering you to go after another Nipponese."

"You are ridiculous. If you must know, I was in Riverside at the Mission Inn with my daughter. A hundred people were in attendance at a special dinner on Saturday. And we stayed the night." Sherwood grinned after sharing this ironclad alibi. A hundred witnesses could vouch that he was nowhere near Pasadena.

My heart sank. I had harbored hopes that we could prove that Sherwood was behind this treachery against Eddie and end his immoral business activities.

Sherwood sensed that his revelation had derailed Jack's harsh line of questioning. "Get out of here. I don't want to see either of you in my offices again."

Jack would not leave without a parting shot. "You may not know, but we are a literate people. The Japanese have many newspapers in the state. In fact, one is starting here, not too far from your offices. We will be revealing the truth of people like you."

"Too bad your truth is now ash in my furnace."

"*Chikusho*, you bastard—" Jack combined insults in both Japanese and English. I positioned my body in front of him to keep him from striking Sherwood.

"You don't want to end up in jail, too," I told him. He finally relented and went out the door.

On the train ride back, Jack's bloodshot eyes focused on the back of the seat in front of him.

"*Shikata ga nai, desho*," I murmured, clutching my *kobu*. But something had happened when Tama-chan had been on that windowsill, baking in the sun. My burl's bark was flaky and rough, as if the moisture had been baked out of it. It no longer felt like it was from home.

• • •

When I returned to the the Riley House after work, Gigi was sitting on a rocking chair on the porch, a parasol shading her face. I felt a pang of shame at the way I had ended my last conversation with Gigi. Sometimes I could not bear to be in the presence of myself. In the openness of California, I could not hide my weaknesses, both physical and emotional. I hung my head, my hairless chin brushing against the white shirt with the burned sleeve that I adopted from Jack's costume box. "I am sorry for doubting your devotion," I said softly.

I thought Gigi would welcome me back into her bosom. But instead she squinted at me with a curious look on her face. "Come to my room. I'll fix that shirt for you."

I was glad that Mrs. Riley was not puttering around the first floor of the boardinghouse because she clearly would have been able to see how excited I was to be allowed entry into Gigi's private room. Mrs. Riley made it clear that she disapproved of members of the opposite sex entering a boarder's domicile. And, of course, I never wanted to malign my beloved's reputation, although in the darkness of my own room, there was plenty of decadence that I created in my mind. I felt myself torn between reverence for Gigi, and unchaste desires.

My hands twitching, I followed Gigi into her room, which was narrower than Jack's and my abode and much more beautifully appointed. Her wallpaper was obviously newer, with a pattern of blue cornflowers, and her single bed was on a wooden bed frame with long reeded posts with sharp ends. And there was that familiar scent of lavender, although more potent and intoxicating.

"Take off your shirt," she instructed.

I was frozen in place.

"How else am I going to mend that hole?" she asked, her eyes twinkling.

My heart pounding, I slowly unbuttoned my shirt from the bottom, but was unable to loosen the top button. Gigi came to my rescue and with her delicate, adept fingers slipped the button from its hole. She stood so close to me that I wanted to steal a kiss but I was terrified what it would lead to. Staring into my eyes, she pulled off one sleeve and then the damaged one. I was still wearing a short-sleeve undershirt but I felt as if I stood naked in her presence.

Sitting on her bed with my shirt, Gigi retrieved her sewing bag from a small chair with an embroidered seat. I took this opportunity to let out a deep breath and gather myself. It was certainly not manly to be quivering like a leaf over this. In my dreams, I had swept Gigi off her feet, unleashing passions that she herself was unaware of.

I turned my head from her to moderate my breathing. On a small round table next to her bed stood a framed photo—at first I thought it was a painting by a European master. But upon closer inspection, I saw that it was a photograph of Gigi.

She was completely naked and held a large fan of feathers over most of her torso. The edge of her left breast, however, was visible, and if you stared long enough—which I did—you could identify a pert nipple in between two feathers. She stood barefoot on a Persian rug, like the one Jack had rolled up underneath his bed. No, it couldn't be. I then recognized the edge of our window frame, the opaque curtains in the background. There was no doubt—this photograph had been taken in our shared room.

I was so shocked that my mouth fell open and I could not speak for a moment. "Jack," I finally managed, pointing at the photo, intense with the dramatic lighting that was Jack's photographic hallmark.

"Hmm?" Gigi looked up from her mending. "Oh, yes. Jack took it. That was last year. He's remarkable."

I could not believe that Gigi was speaking of the obscene image as if every woman would be willing to take her clothes off for an eccentric Japanese photographer. And to proudly display it so openly in her room. How many people, specifically men, had seen this pornography?

"I cannot believe that you did this."

In her right hand was her needle. "He paid me good money. I had no idea it would come out this beautifully."

I felt tricked, deceived. "What else have you done together?"

Gigi laughed, her voice now sounding like a saw breaking through old wood. "I wasn't his lover, Louie. Just a model."

Why was this hidden from me? Why didn't Jack tell me after all this time? He knew that I adored Gigi. But he had stolen her innocence before I could even imagine this level of intimacy.

"How could you do this to me?"

"I didn't even know you. Why are you getting so upset? This is art. Aren't you an artist?"

"I am a carpenter." The work of a premier carpenter was sacred, reserved for the purest buildings of worship. I had learned that it wasn't for prurient passion. The work was measured and exacting, a tongue perfectly fitting into a groove, not for pleasure but for utility. What I saw in Jack's photography was unbridled, teasing a man's lust. For the first time since I had met her, I felt great disdain for Gigi. She was only an American from Ohio.

The softness around Gigi's eyes had all but disappeared, leaving defined lines of anger. "I didn't know you were like this, Louie. Just like my parents. Small-minded. Since you are from the Pacific, I thought that your thinking would be expansive."

"I am not Louie! Ryunosuke. That is my given name. But you cannot say it. Because you are just a barbarian."

Before I knew what was happening, I felt a hot slap on my left cheek. Gigi's dainty fingers proved to be a powerful weapon when stiffened together like an oar.

Part of me wanted to retaliate with a punch of my own. But this was my dear Gigi, and that realization stopped me from acting out of pure anger.

Gigi could still sense what I was repressing. And although I didn't physically harm her, the mere thought of it proved enough to snuff out our relationship right then and there. Her dark eyes filled with tears, grieving, at least I thought, what could have been.

She did not have to tell me to get out of her humble room. I fled like a ghost that had been banished.

I ran upstairs in my undershirt, completely forgetting about the shirt that Gigi was mending. The bathroom door was closed, so I had our room to myself. I scooped Tama-chan into my hand, pressing so hard that my fingertips pulsed rosy pink and then red.

How could Jack betray me like this? Is that why he warned me to stay clear of women, but maybe specifically Gigi?

I despised being here in the Riley House, living with the fringes of American society who had no sense of decorum or respectability. Thinking of being so far from my native Japan, where, even in the transition of the Meiji era, we had some sense of where we belonged and what was expected of us, I wept. Yes, many strata of society had changed places, like mahjong tiles being moved from one place to another, but there was still a structure that I could depend on.

Where could I escape to? Returning to Japan was an impossibility, not to mention I had no money for my return voyage. San Francisco, which seemed like a beacon of possibilities from the vantage of Yokohama, had lost its romanticism in my mind. Los Angeles overwhelmed me. It seemed like the American regions that had the biggest concentration of Orientals were the targets of the most heinous violence.

At least there were trees here. The oaks and the sycamores. They were my surrogate fathers who could hold me in their branches and shade me from extreme heat.

I felt like punching the walls of our miserable room, knocking over Jack's box of ridiculous costumes and his canister of tooth powder. With Jack, everything was about image, the exterior, the perception. Carpentry was the exact opposite. A building didn't support itself through imagination, but carefully chosen wooden limbs that were exactingly measured, cut, and polished. The present was informed by the past. It was only through the past that we knew how to proceed forward.

I had been a fool to put all my trust in Jack. To view him as my *senpai*, my elder, my teacher. We obviously didn't hold the same values. I wasn't sure who he was when he arrived in America, or even the reasons why he came. America must have coarsened him, made him reject the principles of Japanese tradition. But as much as he viewed himself as a citizen of the world, America only saw him as an outsider and, as he himself sometimes casually said—a Jap.

I felt like a trapped animal in our tiny room. My pacing whipped faster and faster. As I held Tama-chan, it seemed like the blood stopped circulating in my hand. I was in such a fevered state that I didn't hear the bathroom door open. But I did see Jack's figure in our doorway, his mouth looking lopsided on his face as if he was going to make some sort of insulting comment about me. I was tired of it all. Before he could say one word, I aimed my *kobu* right between his eyes and released.

• • •

There was blood everywhere, down his nostrils, the lines outside his mouth. The force of the impact had ejected his spectacles from his face onto the floor by the window. The left lens was cracked and the wire frame had snapped in half.

After my *kobu* hit his forehead with a resounding crack, Jack crumpled like one of the cypress trees that my father cut down on Yaku Island. But he didn't lose consciousness. His dark eyes stayed on me, not in a scowl but almost with respect, as if thinking, *You finally grew some balls.*

For a moment, I didn't move. I was shocked that I had caused such harm. Now I wonder if Tama-chan had possessed my mind, because I would never have done such a thing when my father was alive. I finally found the presence of mind to run downstairs for help. "Mrs. Riley, Mrs. Riley!"

Instead of Mrs. Riley, Gigi ran into the hallway.

"Jack needs help!" I yelled.

Gigi rushed past me, the hard heels of her boots hitting each stair like beats of a thunderstorm.

She then began screaming. "What have you done? What have you done, Louie?" I have never forgotten her shrieks, which would haunt me for months.

From there, everything spun into a dizzying haze. The doctor, the same one called to the Arroyo to examine Eddie's dead body, arrived, remaining upstairs with Gigi and Jack while I stayed downstairs.

"Why is Dr. Battles's horse tied up out front?" Mrs. Riley entered the parlor, dragging her arthritic hip more awkwardly than usual.

I couldn't speak at first, just gestured up the stairs. "Jack," I said.

She dropped her bag on the floor and plodded up to the second floor.

I couldn't stay there a minute longer. I ran all the way to the relaxed wooden house on Euclid Avenue.

GT, a smaller figure than his brother, opened the door.

"I need to move out of the Riley House," I told him without explanation.

He studied me quickly, observing the sweat dripping down my face and into my eyelashes, causing me to blink incessantly. "I'm sure Toshio Aoki can accommodate you."

VIII
THE STUDIO

1.

As it turned out, Jack did not die. He was not even hospitalized. He told Ian, in fact, that he had such a hard head that nothing could break it, not even a wood projectile that was as dense as stone. His nose, however, was quite broken and, according to Ian, he strolled around town with two black eyes.

Mr. Aoki, who was also from Yokohama, but had left for America before our family arrived in the port city, agreed to let me stay in his studio for a month or two. Ever since the cherry blossom dinner, orders for murals, classes, and custom paintings had multiplied. He could use a part-timer to help clean the studios and manage evening appointments. Of course, I was still employed at Marsh's emporium, so these tasks were on top of those.

"I can no longer work with Jack on finding your painting," I told Mr. Aoki, who didn't seem bothered by this new development. "However, I would like to try solving the theft on my own."

"Why not?" said Mr. Aoki. "Then let's change the terms of our financial agreement. I will no longer be paying both of you, but only the one who locates my stolen artwork."

Gone was my initial infatuation with Hotel Green. Living in the studio was an odd arrangement; there was no kitchen, and just a washroom with a toilet and sink. Even though the bathroom at the Riley House left a lot to be desired as it also served as Jack's photo development room, at least it had a bathtub. At Mr. Aoki's studio, I was given a basin for my ablutions. And also told by Mr. Aoki to keep the bathroom spotless. No one was to actually live in his studio, so he was technically breaking rules. I felt both exceptional and criminal under these living conditions.

Mr. Aoki's studio was quite different in the darkness of night than it seemed when he was fulfilling a private sketch appointment in the golden late afternoon. Sleep was difficult on the uncomfortable love seat, and many times I was awakened by the wild laughing of carousing men walking past the windows or the haunting calls of lonely birds resting on the balcony. It was then that the wild-eyed tattooed demons and goddesses clutching rabbits on the wings of giant moths came alive in the room. They flew above me, sometimes grazing my hair or mischievously twanging their stringed instruments in my ear. Suffice it to say, my sleep was never deep, bobbing on the surface of wakefulness.

This is my penance, I thought, *for harming my most intimate friend in Pasadena*. I deserved this. After attempting to wash Jack's blood from my *kobu*, I confined it to my bamboo suitcase, afraid that it might incite me to act on my base instincts again. And although I wished to reside in almost any other place, even that abandoned railcar with that recalcitrant hobo, I committed myself to my new daily rituals.

As the Riley House and Manako's were only a few blocks away, I went out of my way to walk around the back side of the hotel to avoid running into Jack. I was walking on the south side of Colorado Street when I noticed a bookstore with VROMAN'S in cursive script on the front of the building. The storefront was neat, simple, and sophisticated, advertising BOOKS, STATIONERY AND LEATHER GOODS. And the word KODAK was featured prominently; I learned later that it was a popular American brand for both box cameras and supplies. It was no wonder that Jack and Mr. Vroman were well acquainted. I had paused in front of the store window, gazing at the books on display, when the bearded proprietor appeared from his double doors.

"Louie, right? Do you have any good news for me?"

I knew instantly that he was referring to his beloved netsuke artist. "Ah, yes. We received a Tokoku netsuke in a recent shipment."

"Come in, come in. I want to hear more."

I was hesitant at first because I wasn't in a position to buy anything in his fine store, but I was curious to take a look and entered his retail enterprise. This was an intellectual man's space. Books, like soldiers in formation, lined the shelves. On one side of the shop were rows of various box cameras and shallow metal drawers which I assumed held photographic paper.

Mr. Vroman continued to look down at me with such expectation that I could not keep him waiting any longer. Lady Madison didn't know of the Tokoku, and all that mattered to Victor was a legitimate sale and money in hand. Mr. Vroman's dark eyes shined as I explained that this particular piece integrated both ivory and wood.

The bell on the door rang and who should come through the double doors but my former roommate. I could see that he was still wearing his spectacles, but they were fastened together with a cloth bandage in the middle. He looked even more peculiar than ever, but in an odd way, his aura was even more magnetic. Instead of being fearful of him, passersby would be drawn to him, wanting to know his story.

Desperation overcame me. "I must go."

"Wait, should I come by the store—"

I rudely ignored Mr. Vroman's question and went around a shelf to extricate myself from his space.

"Ryui!" I heard Jack call out.

I knew I needed to go by the boardinghouse to apologize. Say "*moushiwakegozaimasen-moushiwakegozaimasen*" over and over. If we had still been in the samurai days, I would have been expected to offer to commit seppuku.

That would have been the right thing to do. But I needed someone to despise.

No matter how offended I had been by Gigi's photo at first, I couldn't bear any ill will toward her. In my heart of hearts, I didn't believe she'd had an affair with Jack. And I knew that my infatuation had completely destroyed my ability to exercise rational thought. If I didn't direct my hatred toward Jack, who else would there be? Not the mystery man who had accosted me the night of the cherry blossom dinner, as we still had no real idea of his identity. There would be only one person. Me. If I allowed self-hatred to overcome me, I would be one step closer to flinging myself over the cliff into the Arroyo. Or breaking into the Boyle brothers' room to drink all of Simon's whiskey. I'm not sure why, but like a hard grain inside a dry yellow rice stalk, I was determined to survive. If that meant separating myself from Jack, so be it. I felt embarrassed making such an awkward exit from Vroman's bookstore, but by this time, Jack surely had revealed to the bearded proprietor the bad turn in our relationship.

2.

I did continue to see Ian at the jailhouse. I went when I knew Jack was at work at Manako's. I also timed my visits so I arrived in the early evening, after a meal from a local restaurant had been delivered to him. Ian noticed how I had become thinner (who knew Mrs. Riley's food was in some way sustaining?), my chin now ending in a sharp point, and always shared some of his meal with me.

"Jack won't tell me what happened, but I know you really walloped him," Ian said as he munched on a piece of fried chicken. "I didn't think you had it in you."

I licked my fingers clean of all the oil from a chicken drumstick. "I did not do it with my hands. I threw my *kobu* at him."

"Whattsa *kobu*?"

"It's a piece of wood from the root of a tree. I brought mine from an island called Yaku in south Japan."

"All the way from Japan? Must be very special to you."

It was easy for me to talk to Ian. With his innocent naivete, he was not judgmental in the least. He did not think it was strange that an eighteen-year-old man had clutched onto a piece of wood like a pet.

After a few minutes of eating the chicken, Ian wiped his greasy lips with the edge of his hand. "I was able to learn something interesting about Eddie," he told me. "I overheard two police officers talking about the investigation. They tested a bottle of Green's elixir, which was found on the riverbed. It was laced with cyanide."

I knew cyanide was some sort of poison, but my knowledge of it was limited. "Is that what killed him?"

"Maybe the inquest will reveal the cause of death."

"Inquest? What is that?"

"In America, there's a doctor called a coroner. He cuts into the body to see what really killed someone."

I immediately felt compassion for the dead Eddie Morita. Not only was his body found decomposing in the most disgraceful way, but now his remains would be cut like a piece of meat.

3.

Since I spent many hours of unsupervised time in Mr. Aoki's studio, I had the freedom to examine his art materials and even snoop around his personal life. In that way, Jack, or even America, had rubbed off on me; I was acting like those American merchants who barged into Yokohama showrooms and factories, handling everything with their bare hands as if the qualities of the object could not be believed without touch. Anyway, it was a good opportunity to see if any of his customers might perhaps be the culprit who took his painting.

Mr. Aoki had created some sort of altar in the corner of the studio. On a round marble tabletop was a framed portrait of a handsome mustached actor in an ornate kimono costume reminiscent of ancient Japan. It wasn't Mr. Aoki; this man had a perfectly oval face, large eyes, fiercely thick eyebrows, and an aquiline nose. From his elevated perch, a few centimeters off the ground, he gazed down emotionally at a child dressed as a prince. The child looked familiar, and I took hold of the photograph to confirm that it was definitely Tsuru. When I saw her at the opera house, she had told me that she had been onstage in San Francisco as a boy. At the time, I had doubted the veracity of her account. But based on this publicity photo, it looked like she had been telling the truth.

A fat royal blue album was also on display on the table. It was filled with pasted newspaper clippings that had faded over the years. The news accounts, all either on Mr. Aoki or featuring his drawings, were quite incredible. I carefully unfolded an issue of the *Los Angeles Herald* to full-page spreads of Mr. Aoki's caricatures of elite men and women of the city.

While the countenances were of older white people with wrinkles and sunken cheeks, their bodies were in full Japanese historical regalia. A gentleman named Mark Sibley Severance was transformed into a *daimyo*, a samurai general, protected by long plates of armor connected with cords. A woman identified as Mrs. Sumner P. Hunt was described as a geisha in the middle of a Noh dance. I couldn't reconcile the fan and kimono stance with an aged Western face. Why would these members of American high society want to be cast as Japanese warriors or female entertainers? Jack had shared how the Chinese had been chased out of Pasadena after a fire engulfed a laundry. And now I was subjected to messages telling me to die. If we Asiatics were so despised, why would the gentry want to don our costumes? It was one of the many American contradictions that I could not fully comprehend.

A newspaper clipping from 1895 bore a self-portrait of Mr. Aoki seated at a table under the heads of Chinese men dangling from a rope. I was quite shocked to see that Mr. Aoki had publicized his great disdain for the Chinese, reflective of the nationalistic sensibility of some extremists that I saw in Japan. But he was here in the US where most Americans didn't seem like they would be able to tell the difference between a Japanese and a Chinese.

Maybe he changed his mind, I thought. The year the clipping was published, 1895, was immediately after the war between Japan and China. I had been only ten at the time and couldn't relate to such thinking. But maybe the carpenters who worked for my father were right—I was a *botchan.* Like the child Buddha, I was raised in a protected fortress, unaware of the injustices and suffering beyond the walls. But like Buddha as an adult, I had finally ventured out and seen the truth.

I heard delicate footfalls on the step outside the door and then the turning of the knob. I quickly folded the articles back into the blue album. While visitors were probably welcome to freely leaf through his accomplishments, Mr. Aoki would likely view such actions by someone like me, the help, as invasive.

"We are here!" said a high-pitched female voice.

I was surprised to see Mrs. Carter appear in the doorway with another white woman about her age. While Mrs. Carter's hair was the color of red maple leaves, this woman's hair was black as a raven's. She was wearing a ridiculously high hat, heavy with giant red silk blossoms, that rested above her forehead. They closed their parasols and left them in the corner by the door.

"Where's Mr. Eye-Oh-Key?" Mrs. Carter seemed flustered, her wide-set eyes more unfocused than usual. She obviously didn't recognize me from the cherry blossom dinner or the netsuke delivery at Lady Madison's house.

"He will return shortly." Mr. Aoki was helping GT with some plans for a Japanese garden party in his home in Mill Valley, a wealthy community north of San Francisco. Apparently GT had an impressive garden called Miyajima surrounding his house.

"I made a two o'clock appointment with him, Emma," Mrs. Carter asserted to her companion.

I quickly checked his Sunday calendar. I had written nothing down for this time period, but Mr. Aoki himself had written three question marks in the space.

"It's fine, Gertrude. You were kind enough to indulge my requests. Coming here to Pasadena is a wonderful respite from the hubbub of Los Angeles." The woman cooled her exposed neck with a fan that she pulled from her purse.

"No, no. You wanted a caricature and you should have one." Mrs. Carter was quite adamant. "We will wait." She made herself at home on the love seat that I slept on every night and invited her guest to take a seat beside her.

I was quite disoriented by Mrs. Carter's presence. Hadn't she announced at Lady Madison's that she had pulled her daughter from Mr. Aoki's classes and, in fact, was ending any involvement with my countrymen in protest of Mr. Kuranaga's marriage to

Leonna Cook? She had obviously changed her mind. Perhaps in service to her friend, who, judging by her overwhelming hat, must have been quite wealthy?

The two women exchanged some pleasantries about the weather of Pasadena, before Mrs. Carter addressed me: "Don't you have anything to offer? Like tea, perhaps?"

I knew Mr. Aoki had a tin of biscuits that he kept on his art table when he was working on long-term projects. Flustered, I opened the tin awkwardly, almost causing the whole lot of them to fall on the ground. I was able to find two plates that had been decorated by Aoki and presented the women a biscuit on each one.

Mrs. Carter took a bite first. "These are hard as rocks!" She spit what was in her mouth into her handkerchief. "Emma, don't partake. You might break a tooth."

Her companion seemed unbothered by my substandard offerings. Instead, she was mesmerized by her plate. I hadn't paid any attention when selecting them, but now I saw hers featured dancing vegetables with faces and legs. I blushed. No other Japanese artist would ever produce anything so gauche and silly. She began to chuckle softly, getting louder until she was releasing guffaws that would rival any man's reaction. "The designs on these plates are absolutely diverting. Tell me I am able to purchase some here."

Before I could answer, Mr. Aoki rushed into the studio. "Oh, Mrs. Carter, forgive me. I got delayed at my last appointment."

Placing her plate with her half-eaten biscuit on a side table, Mrs. Carter rose as if she was the queen of England. "This is Emma Summers from Los Angeles."

Mr. Aoki bowed to the woman and briefly squeezed her hand. "Yes, yes, the Oil Queen of California. I am honored to have you in my humble studio."

"The honor is all mine, sir. My friends have shared your

clever drawings with me, and when I mentioned a Japanese artist in Pasadena to Gertrude, she said that she could introduce you to me. And here we are."

I carefully retrieved both plates to make their conversation more at ease.

"Sit here, please." Mr. Aoki gestured toward a parlor chair facing his artist table. I positioned his easel in between them. An attached piece of cardboard was ready for his drawing.

"Should I remove my hat?"

"Oh, no. Please keep it on."

His brush moved effortlessly and quickly as the two women talked.

"So how is Sherwood doing?" As Mrs. Summers spoke, she was careful to keep her face still.

"Oh, wonderful," Mrs. Carter said brightly. I caught almost too much optimism in the way she spoke. "But he has been quite busy traveling. He's hardly been home."

I nearly knocked over the plates. Jack and I had seen Mr. Carter ensconced for a few weeks in his downtown Los Angeles office.

"I heard more oil was discovered in Olinda. He must be ecstatic."

"Well, ah, he sold some of those properties."

I stopped cleaning the hand-painted dishes in a basin of soapy water. What? The Boyle brothers' relative's land had been sold already?

"Oh, what a pity. He probably lost some money on that transaction. Have Sherwood consult with me on future sales. I've told you that I'm available to help him."

I snuck a look at the female companions. Red patches appeared on Mrs. Carter's pasty face. She definitely seemed unwell.

The room became quiet, filled only with the soothing sound

of Mr. Aoki's brush touching his cardboard canvas. The smell of the paint overwhelmed the strong perfume the two women were wearing. Mrs. Carter excused herself to go to the ladies' room, and when she returned to the studio, she seemed much more settled, which was a relief.

Finally, after a few minutes, Mr. Aoki stopped painting and placed his paintbrush on the table.

"You're already finished." Mrs. Summers seemed delighted that she didn't have to keep still that long. She struck me as the kind of person who felt compelled to initiate action rather than allow events to happen to her. The oil baroness got to her feet to see Mr. Aoki's final creation. "Oh, this is most delightful," she cooed at the artwork on the easel. Mrs. Carter rose, too, but slower, with less enthusiasm. "Is it dry enough for transport?"

"Not quite yet," Mr. Aoki replied.

"Gertrude and I have an appointment at a nearby millinery. My driver can pick it up later and keep it safely in my vehicle." Mrs. Summers clapped, expressing her contentment. "This is such a wonderful treat. Thank you, Gertrude. I never do anything amusing and this is a wonderful diversion from my work."

"You are certainly welcome, Emma. And I'll purchase two of the plates for you, too."

"You shouldn't, but it does give me pleasure."

Mrs. Carter's smile weakened as she saw me open up Mr. Aoki's book of receipts and tally the purchases on an abacus like the one I used at my father's carpentry shop. I wrote up the cost of the items as Mrs. Carter made her way to me.

"Can you put that on our tab?" Mrs. Carter was speaking so softly that I could barely comprehend what she was saying.

"Excuse me?"

"You know, our account."

Mr. Aoki only had accounts with his most regular customers.

For the two weeks that I had been staying at the studio, this was the first time I had seen Mrs. Carter here.

I flipped through Mr. Aoki's account book until I did locate a section for Mrs. Carter. The sheet included a list of art classes—all unpaid for. With Mrs. Carter already in arrears, was I to add this portrait session and the two plates?

Although Mr. Aoki was engaging in a lively conversation with Mrs. Summers, he noticed that I was a bit flummoxed. He came to my side and I explained the situation to him in Japanese.

"*Daijoubu*," he whispered in my ear. As he never spoke Japanese to me, I felt off-kilter for a moment. But he had given me permission to add these latest charges to her account, so I did so.

Mrs. Carter, meanwhile, was holding her head high, raising her slightly bulbous nose toward the wall molding. However, I noticed her hands were shaking.

Mr. Aoki bowed first to Mrs. Summers and then to Mrs. Carter. "Thank you so much for coming."

"You very much live up to your reputation," the Queen of Oil complimented Mr. Aoki. The two women gathered their folded parasols and made their way out.

Once they were gone, I commented to Mr. Aoki, "Mrs. Carter owes you quite a bit of money."

Mr. Aoki nodded. "I was surprised that she even contacted me. I didn't think she would show up. I heard her husband had encountered some financial difficulties."

I couldn't help but observe: "With everything that happened at the archery competition with Kuranaga, I don't think she's a fan of us Nipponese."

Mr. Aoki seemed completely unconcerned about the rumors concerning Mrs. Carter's antipathy toward us. "She's the type to change when the wind changes direction. I even heard she hired a Japanese worker to remove one of my murals from her wall."

"And yet you did her this favor of drawing her friend!" I was amazed.

"I did it for me more than her. The Queen of Oil is quite influential. If she places the drawing in her Wilshire home, who knows who will be contacting me next?" Mr. Aoki, always the businessman, gave me a wink.

I went to his art table to retrieve his dirty brushes, an excuse to examine his drawing.

There was Emma Summers, her jet-black hair swept into a typical Japanese geisha arrangement and decorated with a sumptuous red flower, seated on the floor in a full kimono, her hands resting on a shamisen. The transformation was unbelievable. Half of me wanted to gasp in amazement, while the other half wanted to collapse in embarrassment. Even though I did not say a word, observant Mr. Aoki read my mind.

"I know that your man Baba doesn't think much of me. He doesn't like art that a common person could like or understand." Were these wealthy women common? Well, their tastes certainly were.

"I just try to draw from my heart," he continued. "I'm not trying to copy what I learned as a boy. Or get my head too involved." He made a fist with his right hand and pounded the left-hand side of his chest. "The heart. Don't forget the heart, Wada. It's inside of you. Don't forget." He smiled and went to retrieve his jacket before he left for the day.

I was stupefied by Mr. Aoki's comment. For a Japanese man to speak of heart! For us, our essence lay in our bellies. That's where the blade pierced the samurai when committing seppuku. Where our rage and shame were hidden. Had this immigrant artist become so Western that he had forgotten the source of our being?

4.

Tsuru made my time at Hotel Green more bearable, as she brought spontaneity and surprise to my late-afternoon routines. This day she came in holding an ivory envelope by the tips of her fingers, her name written on it by a clearly talented calligrapher. I admired the delicate swoops of the English lettering as she announced, "I've been invited to a birthday party on Thursday at five."

"What kind of party?"

"You know, *tanjoubi*. Birthday."

"But it is April."

"Yes, my schoolmate was born in April."

I was confused. In Japan, all birthdays were celebrated on January first, as the new year marked when we all got older.

Tsuru seemed a bit exasperated. "In America, we celebrate birthdays on the day the person was born."

How cumbersome, I thought. Depending on how many people you knew, that would be a lot of celebrations.

"I'd like to bring one of Uncle's paintings as a gift." She headed for the storage area and began examining various canvases. She finally stopped at one of Mr. Aoki's more conventional illustrations—a kimonoed Japanese girl holding a parasol.

When Mr. Aoki entered the studio a few minutes later, Tsuru explained her gift proposal, which her surrogate father enthusiastically endorsed.

"Wrap up the painting," he instructed me. "In fact, on Thursday, transport the painting to the party, Wada."

When Tsuru met me at the studio on Thursday, she was quite critical of my appearance. As I was washing my clothes in the washroom and hanging them in the storage area to dry, all my garments had taken on a dingy quality.

"I'm just a servant," I told her, but she was still determined that I make a good impression, no matter my role.

She went into the studio closet and pulled out some of Mr. Aoki's clothing: a tweed vest, a long-sleeved checkered shirt, and pleated brown trousers. This was a much more conservative outfit than the one I had worn to the opera house with Gigi. I felt I had aged twenty years wearing it.

Upon our arrival at the house, located a few blocks north, the birthday girl's mother insisted that I stay at the party.

"Oh, he's just a servant." Tsuru repeated the word I had used earlier to identify myself.

"Please, there will be cake."

With that, I joined the party.

It was odd to be with youth much younger than me. In Japan, children were always at the service of their parents or other adults, but this event was to honor a girl turning thirteen.

There was a total of seven of us, including me. I felt self-conscious because I was obviously an unexpected guest, but the birthday girl, Carolyn, graciously welcomed me and even sat me beside her in the parlor. Three siblings came from one family and the oldest brother was fourteen and taller than me. Still, I was relieved that I wasn't the only male guest.

We were each given a cupful of red liquid called punch. It was unbearably sweet, but before I knew it, I had drained my glass. Carolyn quickly refilled my cup with more—I could have spent the rest of the afternoon drinking that addictive beverage. Alas, that wasn't to be, as we had to move our chairs into a circle for a series of games. Tsuru explained that one was "tongue twisters," in which the players took turns contorting their mouths to recite a series of words that sounded similar but had very distinct meanings. Tsuru barged in when it was my turn, making some excuse that I had just recovered from a cold and shouldn't put my voice under any duress for fear of losing it. I was touched and relieved by her effort to shield me from any embarrassment. Again, Tsuru exhibited a maternal sensibility beyond her years.

After we finished the games, Carolyn's mother emerged with a round dessert with lit candles and everyone in the room clapped before the thirteen-year-old blew out the candles. I left the table feeling strangely emotional, as if I was mourning the loss of an experience that I could never have. The cake was indeed remarkable and worth the disorientation of the birthday party.

Next, Carolyn ripped open her handful of gifts. A locket, elegant stationery, and some kind of fragrance. Tsuru's was the last to be unwrapped and Carolyn responded with all the enthusiasm that we had hoped for. "My own Nipponese girl! I will treasure it forever," she called out, telling her mother that she wanted it displayed above her bed as soon as possible.

We were among the first to leave; it was obvious that the other children had a closer relationship with the birthday girl. I wondered if Tsuru felt a bit like an outsider among her white friends.

We walked below pepper trees as the sun went down, casting an orange glow over the wood-framed homes on the street.

"Do you ever want to return to Japan?" I asked Tsuru.

"I guess I could someday. Maybe I could go back with a husband."

I was surprised that Tsuru was even thinking of marriage. She was still only eleven! "An American man?"

"Oh, no," she said. "They are fine for conversation, but otherwise?" She openly shuddered. "They say too much of what's on their minds. They would be awful to live with. All that talking."

I laughed, thinking that Tsuru herself was quite garrulous. But then I considered that perhaps her speechmaking was a type of public performance.

I wondered what had happened to her parents. Obviously for her to be adopted by Mr. Aoki meant something tragic had most likely occurred. Since Tsuru was so open to volunteering personal information, I took a risk and asked, "What was your life like in Japan?"

"I don't really remember. My uncle and aunt brought me here with their acting troupe about four years ago. I wasn't even seven yet. My parents are dead," she said, "just like yours." Sometimes her straightforward talk was disarming. I felt a pang in my heart. "Have you heard of my aunt, Sadayakko? She's quite famous. She was adopted by a geisha when she was young and became a top geisha herself. That's how she got into acting. When she married my uncle, who was also an actor, they made plans to bring Kabuki to Europe."

What a peripatetic life. No wonder Tsuru seemed made from a different kind of cloth.

"In San Francisco, I made my stage debut in America playing Masatsura Kusunoki, the son of a rebel soldier. I even had dialogue—Masatsura tried to convince his father to let him fight on the front lines. Of course, everyone commits suicide in the end." Tsuru shrugged before skipping ahead. When I caught up with her, she continued her story. "I didn't care for San Francisco at all. Boys spat at us and even threw stones. White women didn't want to sit next to us on cable cars. People were very mean. My cousin was called a 'Jap' and the older men were accused of being *s'kebei*."

I frowned. "You mean *sukebe*?"

"Yes, 'nasty men.' I don't know how the Americans knew that word. But they did, and they used it all the time."

I hadn't encountered any racial slurs or incidents during my brief sojourn through San Francisco. Of course, I had been with the Gotos, who had perhaps guided us through more desirable areas of the city.

"Luckily only Japanese people saw me perform in San Francisco. In other theaters, the police were rounding up all the child actors, saying that adult managers were taking advantage of them. My aunt and uncle knew they had to do something. They went to longtime friends, Christian missionaries, who were on the *Gaelic* ship with us coming to San Francisco. Those people knew Uncle Toshio and trusted him. That's how Uncle Toshio became my guardian."

These details were informative since I had never heard of a Japanese girl being placed in such a position with a virtual stranger back in Japan. Tsuru continued to defend her family's actions. "Times were very desperate, you know. One theater owner—and he was Japanese, too—ran off with the money we were due. Most of our troupe was kicked out of their lodgings and had to sleep outside in a park underneath palm trees. My uncle was able to get them into a cheap Japanese inn near the docks. Luckily, the three of us were able to stay in a hotel for a short time."

My respect for Tsuru, who by chronological age was a mere child, soared. She had experienced more than people three times her age. "Mr. Aoki has no children of his own, does he?"

"No. But Uncle Toshio can be like a child himself. He would have loved Carolyn's birthday party. His heart is young. Maybe that's why he gets along with children so well. I think my aunt and uncle saw that. And Pasadena, that was a big reason."

"What do you mean?"

"Everyone knows about Pasadena. All the rich people from the East Coast are coming to spend their winters in Pasadena. They think there's something magical about this place. The mountains, oranges. And the trees around the Arroyo."

I could not argue with that.

"They think Uncle Toshio is magic, too," Tsuru said with

such emphasis that I knew that she was also a believer. For a moment, she seemed to revert to her biological age.

Mr. Aoki didn't seem like a father or even a grandfather figure. He seemed like a creature who had imagined himself into being.

Seeing a stray cat resting under an oak tree by the side of the road, Tsuru ran ahead of me. I remembered what she had once said to me: that she desired to become an actress in America. At that time, I dismissed that as the whim of a silly girl. But now, getting to know her better, I thought it was altogether possible.

IX
ELIXIR

1.

One of my tasks was to collect the studio trash and place it in burlap sacks for Mr. Goto to transport to a new incinerator located in the north part of the Arroyo. With Mr. Aoki so busy, the rubbish over the past couple of months was piling up. I began to consolidate items. As I went through the trash, a square with familiar writing—DIE JAP—fell onto the studio floor. My heart jumped. Feverishly, I went through the other sacks. In the end, I found ten pieces of heavy paper with the same hateful message.

I didn't know what to think. Mr. Aoki himself couldn't have produced these squares, could he? The writing style wasn't his and the paper was of a much lower quality than we stocked in the studio.

The next evening, when he came in to do a late-night sketch, I confronted him with my discovery. "Aoki-san . . ."

Mr. Aoki's eyes locked on the stack of messages I had collected.

"You see I have a devoted fan who leaves me love notes on a regular basis," he said sarcastically.

"Aoki-san, if you want me to be your personal detective,

you need to tell me everything." I surprised myself by speaking forcefully to my benefactor.

"What would this have to do with my painting being stolen?"

I took a deep breath. "I was accosted the night of the cherry blossom dinner by a masked person carrying the same message." I went on to share the specifics of what had happened to me.

"That is why you left without saying goodbye."

I nodded. "I guess both of us have not been completely candid." One of the demons in Aoki's painting seemed like it was taunting me. "Do you have any idea who could be sending you these threats? Even if it's merely a feeling."

"Maybe an unhappy customer who felt they were overcharged for my services? Or a spouse who secretly resented me? But I haven't lost any customers and any business misunderstandings have been resolved. I've been receiving these notes for the past year."

"The police don't know about them? Not GT?"

"Oh, no. GT and I have gone through this countless of times, targeted by both Americans and Japanese. My skin is quite calloused by now."

"Doesn't it bother you that you are so unwelcome?"

"I long ago determined to fix my mind on the positive, not the negative, in this country. If I think of everything our Nippon is going through right now in this age of so-called enlightenment, I don't want to be there. I'd rather dream of what it was than what it is going to be. It's easier to preserve the past in Pasadena." He brought out a charcoal brazier that he kept in the corner. "Colonel Green doesn't like me to use this inside, but I think that this can be an exception."

I watched, dumbfounded, as Mr. Aoki stuffed the brazier with the paper squares. Surely he wasn't going to destroy evidence?

"Perhaps I should be resolved that the painting is lost." Mr. Aoki lit a match that he had retrieved from a small metal case in his pocket. Soon the little furnace was ablaze and together we watched as it turned bright orange and then finally dark again.

2.

A few days later, I was dusting the canvases of Mr. Aoki's paintings in the corner of the studio when Colonel Green entered in obvious distress. He waved a folded newspaper above his head. "It's a travesty," he declared. "A total travesty! How can this rag connect my elixir to a dead man?"

Mr. Aoki, who had been painting at his art table near the window, took the Pasadena newspaper from his landlord to read the offending article. "Colonel Green, I would not worry. I have heard of this Eddie Morita. He was not a reputable man. His illness was probably a result of the company that he kept."

My curiosity was obviously piqued. I couldn't imagine what the article stated.

"He lived in the Riley House, yes?" said Colonel Green. "With that snake, Jack Baba."

I nearly knocked over a painting in my shock at the colonel's disparaging remark about my former roommate. What had Jack done to him? I hid behind a canvas so Mr. Aoki could not see that I was eavesdropping on their conversation.

"Oh, how that man made my life a living nightmare! Even protested my elixir outside of the entrance to the hotel." Colonel Green was practically howling. "And he had the audacity to attend the cherry blossom dinner. He fled before I could give him a piece of my mind." He started pacing on the Oriental rug on the floor. "It's quite obvious this Eddie Morita's days were numbered. Jack was probably the close associate quoted in the article. I know the newspaper publisher and I'm going to insist that whoever wrote this article be terminated immediately."

Mr. Aoki remained seated, clutching at his paintbrush in thought.

"What? Do you think that it's not the correct course of action?" Colonel Green pulled at the ends of his mustache.

"I've worked closely with a number of newspapermen." Mr. Aoki spoke in his deliberate way that made Americans hang on his every word. "I think bringing attention to a certain point in a story may lead to a result that you do not desire."

"You are saying that I should do nothing?"

Mr. Aoki quickly ran his brush over the newsprint. "Today's newspaper will be a hobo's toilet paper," he said and gestured to the colonel to view what he was drawing.

Colonel Green approached the table and narrowed his eyes. After a minute, he grinned, revealing perfect teeth with a whiteness that seemed artificial. He doubled over in laughter and then, catching his breath, pointed a finger at the Japanese artist. "Eye-okey," he said, "you are absolutely right. No one reads this paper anyway, and even if they do happen upon this article, the details will be forgotten tomorrow. Let us go into the lobby and share a bit of whiskey together."

Mr. Aoki wasn't a drinking man, but he clearly liked to be in Colonel Green's company enough to agree. He retrieved his jacket from a wooden coatrack near the door. Since he didn't have any appointments that evening, I assumed he wouldn't be returning to the studio that night. Whether or not he knew that I was still in the room, he chose not to acknowledge my presence before he left.

As soon as Mr. Aoki closed the studio door, I rushed over to the table to retrieve the newspaper, still soggy from the black ink. Along the right column was Mr. Aoki's drawing of a bearded tramp revealing a naked bum. It flanked a brief story:

CORONER DETERMINES THAT DEAD JAP KILLED BY CYANIDE WAS RIDDEN WITH INTERNAL CANCER

PASADENA. A 35-year-old Jap man whose dead body was found in shallow water in Arroyo Canyon was determined to be poisoned by cyanide but also ridden with internal cancer. Coroner Hughes came to Pasadena and declared that the man, a wandering laborer, would have died in a matter of days from his malady without the help of the deadly venom.

According to the dead man's close associate, the victim was a regular partaker of Colonel Green's August Flower Syrup to address his fatal illness. The police discovered that a bottle of Colonel Green's August Flower Syrup found near the body contained remains of cyanide and have determined the Jap hastened his death at his own hands.

It was that final paragraph that had antagonized the colonel. From my reading, it wasn't his elixir that had killed Eddie, but the cyanide, but I supposed if I was the owner of the elixir company, I would be irritated. It certainly wasn't good publicity for the syrup to be portrayed as an ineffective way to treat internal cancer, despite its claims to be a miraculous cure.

I had seen that syrup in the studio washroom; there were three tiny bottles by the sink, presumably samples. Next to the samples there were cards that declared the medicine effective to treat dyspepsia, liver ailments, and heartburn. I had no idea what dyspepsia was, but it sounded painful.

What was most disturbing to me was that Eddie was merely identified as a "Jap" and a "victim," as if he had no name.

Perhaps that was the practice of American journalism: Non-whites didn't deserve anything more.

Since it was the dinner hour, I locked up the studio and rushed over to the jail. Perhaps Ian knew what Jack had done to upset Colonel Green.

The end of a bacon sandwich was waiting for me when I arrived at the shack. I had gotten used to the smell of urine, so I ate happily while taking breaks to ask Ian about Jack and the colonel.

"Jack was on a crusade against that elixir. Eddie spent a fortune on those bottles, and Jack said that it did him no good. Only took money out of his pocket." Ian began to crack his knuckles, a habit that both brothers engaged in.

I nodded thoughtfully, chewing. "I'm not sure of the details, but I think Jack even confronted the colonel. In broad daylight in front of the Hotel Green. Maybe that's when Colonel Green took a strong dislike to Jack."

"Jack brought that newspaper article to me this afternoon." Ian pulled a chunk of chewed food out of a space between his teeth. "He was almost proud of it. Said that he was the one who found the August Flower bottle near the body and brought it to the police. He told the story to a reporter, too."

Ah! So that was what Jack had fished out of the water. "It's not like Jack to go on a campaign for the benefit of another man," I commented.

"Not sure about that. Look what he's doing for me. I wouldn't have the benefit of an attorney without him, that's for sure."

Maybe it was more that Jack would not advocate for me.

"Anyway, Jack knew Eddie from before."

"Before the Riley House?"

"Before America. They knew each other from Japan. Or else their families did."

My heart began to race. I knew it could not have been a coincidence that the two Okayama natives had come to live together in Pasadena. *What was the nature of their relationship?* I wondered.

"The morning before Eddie disappeared, they had a terrible row."

"Row?"

"Aye, argument. They didn't come to physical blows, not like you—"

"Yes, yes." I didn't need Ian to repeat my transgression. "What did they fight about?"

"I'm not sure. But I believe it had something to do with their homeland. Eddie didn't speak English very well. And Jack was speaking Japanese." Ian chuckled. "It was strange to hear that from his mouth. I sometimes forget that he's from Japan."

To be honest, I did, too, as his actions were so atypical for men from our native country. But to hear that some kind of ancestral legacy haunted him was revelatory. What in the world had happened between the Baba and Morita families back in Okayama? It had to be severe enough for ghosts to occupy Pasadena.

My head filled with everything Ian had shared, I excused myself, saying that I had something to attend to at the studio. Once there, I went to the washroom and discovered that the three samples of August Flower were still there by the sink. I hesitated for a moment before I twisted the cap from one and poured the contents into my mouth. It was a strong concoction, thick and sweet. I returned to the studio and lay down on the love seat. The hard edges of my life circumstances instantly softened, and for an hour or two, I felt like I was floating on water. I had a difficult time waking up the next morning and felt muddled the whole day at Marsh's emporium. It didn't stop me, though, from returning to the washroom to claim the two other sample bottles and hide them in my wicker suitcase.

3.

It was dusk when I heard a pounding on the door that opened to the street. Mr. Aoki usually kept that locked except for special occasions, preferring for people to walk through the grandeur of the hotel lobby to access his studio.

"Who is it?" I called out.

"It's me," a scratchy high-pitched voice replied. "Your former landlord."

Seeing Mrs. Riley standing in the shadow of the Hotel Green was bewildering. In fact, I had never seen her outside of the boardinghouse. Here, she looked much smaller and even impoverished. I might even have mistaken her for a beggar woman on the street if I didn't know her.

She had covered her head with a large cotton scarf and was holding a basket. "Well, aren't you going to invite me in?"

"Of course, of course." As soon as I pulled open the heavy door, she rushed in, the scarf falling from her head and revealing her unkempt hair, the color of old pennies in the fading light.

"I heard that you were practically starving, so I brought you some food."

The smell, a mixture of soot and rotten eggs, was undeniably unique to Mrs. Riley's culinary offerings. When she pulled up the cloth that covered her food, I couldn't quite identify the contents of the basket.

"You did not have to do this," I said.

"No thanks necessary. You are all skin and bones." She dropped the basket on the Oriental rug and proceeded to inspect my living space. After going into the back area where

Mr. Aoki's canvases were stored, she returned to the front. "Where do you sleep?"

"Here." I indicated the curved love seat.

"You're a little bitty thing, but you aren't a cricket. How can you sleep on that?" She plopped down on the seat and frowned. "Hard as a rock."

Mrs. Riley had a point. "It is good to see you," I told her. I didn't want to discuss my new living situation further, but I was happy to be in her presence. In this world I had joined, it seemed that all the adults hid their true intentions, but Mrs. Riley always said what was on her mind.

"Jack misses you," she announced.

"How do you know that?"

"He always asks Simon to tell him everything about you."

"I have not talked to Simon since I left the Riley House."

"You've been seeing Ian every day."

Of course. I should have assumed that everything I said to Ian would be shared immediately with Simon and the rest of the Riley House.

Mrs. Riley traced her faint eyebrows with her hands, a sign that she was tired after a busy day. I had never noticed how her fingers were marked with arthritic knots, freckles, and wrinkles, and her nails were rimmed with dirt. "Jack has completely healed. That lawyer fellow even bought him new spectacles."

I was surprised that Jack had accepted charity from Savage. Had he fallen that low?

"And there's some news about Eddie," she said.

What now? I had never met the man, but his secrets were still plaguing me.

"He was known in Japan by a very different name," she revealed. "But I don't think that was a surprise to Jack."

"Ian told me that he thought Jack and Eddie knew each other in Japan."

Mrs. Riley had folded her hair scarf into a square on her lap. "Mr. Marsh would know."

"Victor?"

"No, the older one. I think his name is George. I saw the two of them talking to each other at times. Conspiring like thieves."

My stomach churned. Was there a connection between Eddie, Eijiro, or whatever his real name was—and GT Marsh? I couldn't believe GT would be involved in murder, but based on what I had done to Jack, I now understood that passion and rage could cause a man to do things he never imagined.

X
JAPANESE GARDEN

1.

The next day when I arrived at Marsh's emporium, I found the back workplace empty. "Mr. Kawai is helping GT with his special garden project," Logan told me. "They've ordered a Japanese show house and GT will be meeting with a few American builders to see where it would be best to construct it. Go now to survey the area. You may spend a lot of time there."

I had already endured enough change as it was and didn't relish my duties being altered.

I walked through the park that was being constructed south of Hotel Green. It was an open field below the cycleway and close to the California Street stop. I couldn't imagine that the Pasadena highbrow would want to venture there to pretend that they had set foot in Japan. And could Pasadena really support two Marsh enterprises in the neighborhood? Up above I heard bicycles rolling up and down the cycleway and thought grimly about my romantic stroll with Gigi many weeks ago. How moments of bliss could evaporate so quickly.

"*Oi*, Ryunosuke," Mr. Kawai called out from the northwest corner of the block. It seemed the prospect of assembling a traditional Japanese house had prompted Mr. Kawai to address me as if he were in Japan.

Mr. Goto, a cigarette dangling from his mouth, was also on the premises and barely acknowledged me.

"*Hai, hai.*" On the hunt for GT, I said the bare minimum so as not to be rude.

Fortunately, he was easy to spot in an off-white linen suit as he stood in the middle of a plot of dirt. He had a roll of papers underneath his arm while he framed his hands to study different spots of his new property.

"Mr. Marsh, I need to talk with you."

He pointed to a spot that was completely flat. "Ryui, imagine this. A Japanese teahouse over here on a hill. A pavilion there. And a goldfish pond there. What do you think?"

I thought Mr. Marsh had lost his mind. "I think it will be a success," I told him.

GT clapped. "And you, my boy, will be a vital part of the project. Maybe I'll even have you work here full-time, serving tea and fixing up the place. Would that be wonderful?"

I couldn't imagine anything more horrifying, but I had more pressing matters at hand. "Mr. Marsh, I have something serious to discuss with you."

"What is it, Ryui?"

"You didn't tell me how intimate you were with the man who called himself Eddie Morita."

GT's usually animated face became still, with only his irises, now registering a brilliant blue, flashing in the sun. "I didn't really know him well. Had a few conversations."

"He was from Okayama, as you know."

"Yes, the home of the Blackbird Castle." GT reached for a handkerchief that had been folded in his inside pocket and dabbed at his forehead. "Have you spoken to Jack about this? He's an Okayama man as well."

"Ah, we had an incident . . ."

"Of course, of course." He gestured toward a fig tree that was across the street. "Let's go in the shade over there."

I felt much more secure conducting our conversation at a distance from both Mr. Kawai and Mr. Goto. GT must have felt the same.

Instead of looking at me directly, he gazed at his property across Fair Oaks. "I was fifteen when I first set foot in Japan. It was in 1873. Many years before you were born. Did your parents ever speak of the time during the great transition?"

I knew about the new Meiji government taking over and the samurai being stripped of their power.

"Some things," I responded, but couldn't recall any personal stories.

"Japan was adapting to Western ways," GT elaborated. "Public education for all. Mandatory conscription of all men. And rights for the outcasts for the first time."

A small dark fruit plopped down from the fig tree, closely missing my head. *Not enough water*, I thought.

"You know about the outcasts, right? *Burakumin*, *hinin*, *kawata*. Those who handled dead bodies and animals."

I flinched to hear the words come out of a white man's mouth.

"Eddie didn't tell me explicitly, but I think his family were outcasts," he continued.

If GT knew, that meant Eddie's low status was not such a secret.

"I told him that this was America. He could be anyone he wanted to be. Look at me. In Yokohama, the Brit traders call me an antipode, but here in California, I'm a success. This is a state for reinvention, renewal. Especially here in Pasadena."

I found GT's talk of reinvention both odd and inspiring. He had found his success in planting Japan in America. Did he make that happen or was he fortunate to be here when it was happening?

A vehicle parked on the other side of Fair Oaks. Emerging were two men who GT obviously recognized. "Ryui-kun, I need to talk to those men." He excused himself and called out to one of them. Again, I was abandoned for people who were rated higher in importance. A reminder that here in America, in spite of my father's heralded position as a master carpenter, I was a mere working-class man.

I prepared to leave when I spotted Mrs. Goto walking with her son in a baby buggy on my side of the street.

"Goto-san, hello," I said to her. Even though she wasn't that much older than me, in that moment, she reminded me of my mother. I felt a deep ache in the bowels of my heart and wanted to extend our interactions.

We exchanged bows and I gestured toward the buggy. "Many felicities. I heard from your husband." I wasn't that interested in babies, but I could at least fake a cursory interest in the doughy infant who resembled every Nipponese newborn in Japan. To my relief, he was sleeping.

"You've been well?" Mrs. Goto asked. It was the first time I had heard her voice, and I was surprised that it was so low in tenor.

I was going to respond with the perfunctory "*hai*," but I stopped myself. I was in the most downhearted state possible, perhaps only surpassed by the deaths of my mother and father. "No," I replied in English. "No, I'm not well."

Mrs. Goto didn't express any words of comfort, but a line of concern appeared in between her eyebrows.

"I lost the company of the woman who I thought would be my wife." I couldn't believe that I was confessing my most intimate pain to a person who was practically a complete stranger. "And then I lost the only friend that I might have had in America."

"*Ah, sou*," she said. The baby, waking up, was starting to fuss, and she pushed the buggy back and forth to comfort him.

I felt so foolish. I knew Jack would have sneered at me at that moment. *Buck up*, he would tell me. *Act like a man, not a lady.*

Our conversation would not progress further unless I carried it. I had nothing left to say and regretted saying what I had. I bowed awkwardly goodbye and walked away as the Goto baby screeched louder and louder.

2.

As the excitement for GT's upcoming garden was rising, Victor was in the store more often, delighting our regular customers who felt they were receiving first-class treatment from the actual owner. Logan, on the other hand, had to spend more time in the workroom with me and Mr. Kawai, but he didn't seem to mind, as orders were coming in, fast and furious.

Life seemed to regain a new balance for me. Mr. Aoki was busy with a potential project in New York City and he didn't bring up his missing painting, so I, too, felt my interest in the investigation wane. *Let Jack find it*, I thought, knowing he probably had abandoned the effort as well. I had finally come to the conclusion that Mr. Aoki was correct—that the painting theft and the proliferation of the DIE JAP messages were two different crimes.

I also didn't go to visit Ian in the jailhouse as often. Without regular exercise, he kept gaining weight; the middle of his soiled overalls was starting to bulge. Also, the lack of sunshine gave his skin a greenish tinge. I felt guilty every time I saw him, because I knew that I wasn't doing enough to help him get released.

With this return to some normalcy, I felt the need to have Tama-chan back in my presence. I took it and the two samples of Colonel Green's August Flower out of my wicker suitcase.

At night, I would take a few sips of the elixir and hold the *kobu*, imagining flying goddesses carrying me back to Yokohama, to the vibrant streets full of international traders and the smells of sauteed garlic from Chinese eating establishments, and the Pacific Ocean, with boats of all sizes over its waters.

With the arrival of May in Pasadena, strange-looking native poppies with egg-yolk centers and the lavender flowers of jacaranda trees were in full bloom. After finishing my work at the emporium on Friday evening, I didn't want to return immediately to Aoki's studio. Instead, I wanted to spend as much time outdoors as I could. Since Mr. Aoki and Tsuru had accompanied GT to his Mill Valley house to prepare for his Japanese garden party, my time was much more free.

I took a stroll east on Colorado Street. Even though some of our customers had returned to their main homes on the East Coast and in the Midwest after the winter season, the streets were as crowded as ever. Pasadena seemed to be attracting its share of new residents. I passed the Fujiyama Restaurant, where I occasionally treated myself when I couldn't stand eating what Mrs. Riley dropped off on a regular basis and had a couple of extra coins to spare.

The farther I walked, the less developed the streets were. I could see the orange groves in the distance and more horses and buggies instead of vehicles. After I had walked for about half an hour, I found myself standing in front of a construction site.

As it was the end of the day, there were no signs of builders or carpenters at work. The frame of the two-story house, massive by Japanese standards, had been largely constructed. I stepped into the framing, relishing the smell of lumber. I wasn't sure what kind of wood they had used so far, but it was lighter in color than the red pine that my father gravitated toward.

"You are the one who works at Marsh's emporium."

I jumped in response to a voice that I had heard before. The architect, Mr. Greene, wearing a straw hat and work gloves, smiled at me.

"I did not mean to trespass," I said to him, my cheeks flushing. "Mr. Kawai thought that I could learn about Western architecture by studying your building."

"Please, come and see." Mr. Greene beckoned me farther into the construction site. "This is the first house my brother and I have designed with a new sensibility in Pasadena. We are thinking of ways for people to commune with the outdoors while still in the home."

I wouldn't say it was an unconventional house, except for the long open eaves that would provide shade for those sitting by the second-floor windows. It was, however, definitely a complete change from the Turkish designs of the Hotel Green and the train station in Los Angeles, as well as the turrets found on Millionaire's Row.

"What do you think?" he asked.

The inquiry caught me off-balance. It sounded like one professional asking another for an honest assessment.

I didn't want to merely issue platitudes in deference to Mr. Greene's position in Pasadena. The design of the structure was fine but, in my opinion, uninspired. I tried to think of a diplomatic way of answering. "My father built temples in Japan," I told him. "Not homes."

The mention of Japan sparked Mr. Greene's interest. "Ever since my brother and I went and saw the Japanese village at the Chicago World's Fair, I've been quite taken with your nation's architecture."

"My father was there." My voice started to tremble. "He

helped build the pavilion." Memories of perusing Okakura's brochure on the pavilion with my mother rushed over me. I could even feel her presence now.

"What an incredible coincidence," Mr. Greene said. "I had never seen anything like that in my whole life." It seemed, too, that Mr. Greene was traveling back in time in his mind.

"Everything is done with joints." I pointed to some nails that had fallen on the dirt. "Not nails."

Mr. Greene nodded. "The craftsmanship was exquisite. I hope to emulate those techniques someday."

Now my whole body felt warm. It was a healing balm to hear that our aesthetic was so revered by this white American.

"You didn't answer me. What do you think of this building?"

"It seems like one step toward tomorrow," I finally said.

Mr. Greene laughed, and I expelled a breath of relief. I had not insulted him, yet I also did not compromise my own artistic standards.

3.

My sunset interaction with Mr. Greene made a profound impact on me. The encounter with a real American architect and carpenter, a man who understood the bend of wood, confirmed my own calling to one day build houses. I coveted the respect that Charles Greene and his brother, Henry, had in Pasadena, yet as a measly repairman and clerk I was so far from my goal.

I had not traveled all the way from Yokohama to play a weak imitation of who I was in Japan. I didn't see how I could progress in a climate that despised my kind. I could not always be looking over my shoulder, afraid of who might destroy me. I wished I could be more like Mr. Aoki, brushing aside the bad and wrapping it tight to store in the deep recesses of my mind. But for better or worse, I was not built in that way. Strong winds blew through my rafters and I wasn't sure if my *shin-bashira*, my center core, could withstand great stress.

That night, I tossed and turned on that uncomfortable love seat, clutching Tama-chan so hard my hand grew numb.

Two days later, by the time a streak of morning light fell between the meeting of the heavy curtains, I had made my decision. I could not wait any longer. I, with Tama-chan in my pocket, would discover the offender who had frightened me that evening of the cherry blossom dinner.

Since I had a few extra coins, I treated myself to an early streetcar heading toward Lamanda Park, the site of the orange grove ranch. We passed the construction site of the Greene brothers' project—I saw two men in suits, in addition to some workmen, already on the premises. I envied them for having such a concrete and communal purpose. Sometimes working with disparate men on temple projects was a headache. Strong egos and domestic issues could get in the way, but in the end, we were committed to a single purpose: to complete the building. Despite whatever problems either personal or technical may have occurred, the finished structure, at least at first glance, didn't expose these obstacles.

I got off at the Lamanda Park stop. Men were already sorting oranges in the packing shed and I noted that they were all white this time. *Perhaps the Japanese ones worked different shifts?* A couple of them seemed to glare at me, but I deduced that the cause was the morning sun, which seemed much more intense than usual. A couple of boys wheeled away from the packing shed on their delivery bicycles. I was convinced, more than ever, that the terrorist must have come from here.

Would I burst into the bunkhouse, like Jack had done in Clem Moro's labor camp? If I did that, I was sure to be strung up like the Chinese in downtown Los Angeles years ago. All of this was an ill-conceived idea fueled by hubris. I turned on my heels to return to the trolley stop when a middle-aged white man with long sleeves rolled up to his elbows stopped me. "Hello, are you looking for work?"

"Ah—I already—"

"I'm the manager here." He introduced himself as Volney Craig.

"Louie Wada."

We shook hands and I felt more American than ever.

"I thought you might be Japanese. Just wanted to tell you that you and your countrymen have nothing to worry about. I'm looking into the incident and I'll make sure it doesn't happen again."

I was confused. "The incident?"

"Oh, I thought you all had read about it in the newspapers. Gunshots were heard in the middle of the night. Too much imbibing, I'm sure. I wish your people hadn't run off because of it. I could use more workers."

"I have employment at Marsh's emporium."

The manager had no reaction. The Marsh brothers and Japanese curios were obviously unknown to him. In Pasadena, celebrity status depended on which world you belonged to.

"I also work in a studio in the Hotel Green," I told him.

The mention of Hotel Green got his attention. "I should have known you were an artist," he said. "With your skinny frame, you aren't one for manual labor."

At this point, I was starting not to overreact to insults levied by either Americans or Japanese about my body. Let them think what they wanted to think. Perhaps being underestimated could be advantageous.

"If you need some more work, let me know. You Orientals are hard workers. I don't care what anyone else says."

I gave the manager a quick bow, relieved to be released from his presence. At both Marsh's and the studio, I was rarely privy to negative comments like he was referencing. In my Pasadena world, being Japanese was like being a figure in Mr. Aoki's paintings. Mystical and fantastic—a creature who delighted and entertained.

I continued down the path toward the streetcar rails when I spotted the same white worker Jack and I had seen recklessly carving a piece of wood last time. His left hand was wrapped in a dirty cloth, possibly confirming his lack of skills with a knife.

"You aren't wanted here," he mumbled under his breath.

I heard him perfectly, but I kept walking forward.

"Jap, did you hear me?"

I stopped in my tracks. I reached for Tama-chan in my pocket. I probably shouldn't have brought the *kobu* with me, but my lucky charm served to fortify and feed my anger. "Yes, I heard you," I spat back at him.

Abrupt footsteps on the dirt. Normally I would have run, but I was ready for what was to come.

"Don't think of working here." He approached me from behind and then leered into my face. He had fleshy cheeks like a cow's and blue-green eyes that didn't seem human. "We have too many of you as it is in Pasadena."

I didn't want to give him the satisfaction of telling him that I wasn't going to work for the packing shed.

"We were able to run the Chinamen and Hindus out. And now the Japs."

Two boys pedaled delivery bicycles down the path, interrupting the man's tirade.

"You attacked me," I accused. "On a bicycle."

He smirked, not only admitting that I had been a victim of his attack but obviously relishing it. "Yeah, and I'll come after you again."

As the bicycles rushed past, the bully tore one from a delivery boy, causing the rider and a crate of oranges to tumble to the ground. The delivery boy didn't make a fuss, which confirmed to me that this had happened before; he just blinked away tears as he gathered the orbs of fruit. I assisted him the best I could, but since the open crate was still on the bicycle, there was no place to deposit the oranges.

Meanwhile, the man's steering of the bicycle was completely erratic. He had no control of it and eventually circled into himself and almost toppled over. I studied his build from a distance. He was pudgy with a thick waist, nothing like the nimble figure who had seemed to appear out of nowhere late that night of the cherry blossom dinner. Even though he claimed to be my attacker, based on his inability to ride a bicycle and his size, this man was not him.

I was surprised to see Logan already at work when I reported for duty on Monday morning with Tama-chan in my shirt pocket as my talisman. Logan's hair was curled into a frizzy halo and he seemed worn out from the weekend, whatever activities he had partaken in.

"Mrs. Carter wants all her Japanese merchandise to be returned and resold." His hooded eyes were mere slits as he spoke. "She's going to take a loss, but she doesn't seem to mind. I was just about to go to her house to recover the items."

"I can go," I volunteered. My weekend activities had invigorated me and I didn't relish being relegated indoors again.

"Are you sure? I think her household's Japanese period is quite over. She's a bit hostile, in fact."

The whole notion of Japan being a temporary passion and interest was fascinating to me. I, for instance, could not abandon my Japanese essence even if I wanted to. "Yes, I will be fine," I told him. If I could deal with a threatening brute at the Lamanda Park packing shed, I could certainly handle an unhappy old matriarch on Millionaire's Row.

Mr. Goto, who had returned from Mill Valley, brought Victor's buggy to Green Street and I hopped in next to him up front. He seemed in an especially foul mood, so I didn't even attempt to engage him in a conversation, not even to inquire about his young son.

I had never gone to the Carter mansion before. Of course, especially after Jack's and my impromptu visit to Sherwood's office in downtown Los Angeles, I didn't expect any invitations.

The house was on the southern end of Millionaire's Row. The Carter residence was not spacious like Lady Madison's mansion, but it had a similar-shaped turret room with a pointed roof. I hoped Mr. Goto would accompany me to fetch the items from inside the house, but he seemed quite happy to remain in the driver's seat.

Mrs. Carter startled me by opening the door herself—I was used to domestics handling such mundane duties at these wealthy homes. There was a weariness on Mrs. Carter's face. She was wearing a worn housecoat and her visage lacked any color.

She did not disguise her disappointment upon seeing me. "I thought Logan would be coming."

"He was otherwise engaged." I used the phrase that Mr. Aoki had taught me to ward off unwanted customers.

"Well, come in, I suppose."

As I followed her through the mansion, I immediately noticed the interior's spareness—not like the intentional Japanese quality of *shibui*, but more of a lonely absence. Visible were the outlines of paintings that had once graced the walls. Aside from a glass table that displayed a number of photographs, the rooms were empty of furniture. The Carter household definitely had hit hard times.

One wall along the hallway looked freshly painted, while all the other walls were covered with wallpaper. Only the bottom trim in the hallway revealed a mysterious dark gray color. Mr. Aoki had told me Mrs. Carter had paid someone to cover up a Japanese mural in her home—I supposed that must have been what I was seeing.

Five crates, one especially large, lay in the center of the main room.

"I need those taken away," she said, as if she couldn't stand for them to be in her house for even another minute.

One by one, I carried the crates out to the buggy. Mr. Goto stayed put in the driver's seat, smoking a cigarette and reading a folded newspaper. He did not assist me even once with lifting the crates into the buggy. By the fourth one, sweat was dripping down the sides of my face. I must have looked a bit bedraggled as a man polishing a car in the open garage called out to me, "You need some help, lad?"

He looked familiar to me, but I didn't know where in the world I would have encountered the Carters' driver.

Under other circumstances, I would have declined, but I wasn't sure where Mrs. Carter had gone and the crates were heavier than I expected. The last remaining one was bulky and would require another pair of hands to carry out. "Yes. Thank you so much."

I reentered the house with the driver, who introduced himself as Adam Wilmington and cheerily told me that his position with the Carters was ending soon, while we considered the best way to grab hold of the final crate.

At last, we hoisted it into the air. As Adam was about a head taller than me, the weight of the crate shifted to my side. I shuffled as fast as I could to keep up with his stride until we deposited the crate onto the floor of the buggy.

I walked back to the house with Adam. Now that all of Mrs.

Carter's Japanese treasures were packed in the buggy, I had no further purpose in her abode. "Can you tell your mistress that I completed my task?" I bowed to him. "Thank you for your help."

I was out the door on the porch when Adam spoke after me. "By the way, were you friendly with Eddie Morita?"

I turned around. "I beg your pardon?"

"I don't mean to make any assumptions, but you are the only other Nipponese I have encountered in Pasadena . . . besides at the archery competition, of course."

"You were there?"

"It was quite a spectacle, wasn't it? I was close to catching the archer in the trees."

"I saw you there." I recalled the fit young man running after Ian. I wasn't sure if he was engaging in conversation with me only out of curiosity, but now my interest was certainly piqued. "You mentioned Eddie. You knew him?"

"Yes, yes, I couldn't quite communicate with him, but he was a good worker. I'm sorry that I couldn't speak directly with him."

"Eddie was in the Carters' employ?" I tried to slow my mind down to fully comprehend what the driver was sharing with me.

"Yes, a couple of weeks before his body was discovered in the Arroyo. Quite shocking. Eddie was hired to get rid of a mural painted in the hallway. A Nipponese scene, in fact. The missus said it was giving her nightmares. I told her that she could cover it up with wallpaper, but she said that would not be enough."

I could not believe that Eddie had been right here on Millionaire's Row this whole time. "How did Eddie get the job?"

"Eddie was going door-to-door, telling mistresses that he was well-versed in materials that Japanese artists used. When

Missus Carter said that she needed her mural removed as if it was never there in the first place, Eddie was only happy to do what she wanted."

Did Eddie despise his countrymen so much that he was more than willing to extract our presence from Crown City?

"Louie, I need you to retrieve one more box." A coolness ran down my spine. Mrs. Carter's voice sounded especially brittle and I wondered if she had overheard my conversation with Adam.

"I will come back," I called out to her from the doorway. The buggy was full, after all.

"No, now," Mrs. Carter insisted.

Adam rolled his eyes. I understood his expression to mean that this demanding tone was not unusual.

I walked back into the house, but there was no sign of Mrs. Carter or the box. I didn't feel comfortable wandering around uninvited, so I stayed in the main room and glanced at the framed photographs arranged on the table. There were at least two of Josephine, but there were no images of the family together, which I found curious. I thought I spotted Mr. Carter in some athletic function, but upon closer inspection, it was Mrs. Carter standing with a line of other women before a row of round archery targets. In their hands were bows and arrows.

I had assumed that the husband was the only Carter who was skilled in archery. But based on the photographs, it was the matriarch, too.

The empty room seemed too quiet. I looked down the hallway to see Mrs. Carter positioned by the blank wall. Her right arm was stretched back, holding an arrow in place on a bow. The tip of the arrow was aimed at me.

Initially I didn't feel frightened, but confused. "I came for the box," I said weakly.

"You must be enjoying all of this," she said.

I was convinced that Mrs. Carter had mistaken me for someone else. "I am Louie Wada. Victor Marsh's worker."

"I know who you are," she said. "You were there at the archery meet. I saw you laughing. And you were amused again at the studio when you saw how much money I owed Toshio. I heard that Japanese chatter between you two."

I shook my head. "I do not take any pleasure in people's financial difficulties."

Her arms were starting to shake from holding the bow and arrow for such a long time. I imagined the deadly release of the arrow. At this point, whether or not she intended to harm me, there was a distinct possibility that I would not fare well.

"Mr. Carter has left us. All Josephine and I have are his debts."

"I am sorry."

"Don't make me out to be a fool! You were in cahoots with Eddie Morita, weren't you? Wanting to squeeze every penny from me. Well, I took care of him, and you are next." Mrs. Carter narrowed her eyes at me, her target.

"No, no." I raised my hands in surrender. "I didn't even know him."

"Your kind always sticks together. I know how you are. Aoki, Kuranaga, Morita. I've watched how you operate."

"Please allow me to leave." I tried to keep my voice steady, even though my hands were trembling. My legs were starting to feel so weak that I could have collapsed right then and there.

Mrs. Carter's body also seemed to sway under pressure.

"Mother!"

A crackling sound, and a force pushed me back and toppled me over onto the Oriental rug. The hot breath of someone—Josephine—on my face. Above me I could see the red feathers of an arrow.

I felt a dull ache on the left side of my chest and was afraid to look down. The middle of my pocket was torn open. I expected a river of blood pooling down my body, but there was none. Mrs. Carter's arrow had speared my dear Tama-chan. In its sacrifice to save me, my *kobu* had been split in two.

The shock of it all overwhelmed me. Instead of losing consciousness, I vomited twice on the Carter family's Oriental rug. I felt the floor move and heard some kind of commotion, but I was unaware what was happening. Every time I was able to blink open my eyes, I saw Josephine staring at me with concern from under her overgrown bangs.

"Let me go! I demand you let me go!" The shrieks rang out through the empty house.

Eventually, I found enough strength to get on my elbows and see that Mrs. Carter had been restrained with rope around her waist, wrists, and legs. The driver stood over her with a very pleased look on his face.

Mrs. Carter didn't relent. She screamed for what seemed like an hour. I wasn't sure who she thought would rescue her.

Finally, the police captain and three officers arrived through the doors.

"Thank goodness," gasped Mrs. Carter, her voice raspy and rough. "My driver has bound me into submission. And this Jap boy has been terrorizing me."

"Mrs. Carter shot an arrow at the boy. I saw it all," Adam declared, unfazed by his employer's accusation.

The police captain addressed Josephine, who rose from my side. "Is it true? Did your mother try to kill this man?"

Josephine nodded, her face looking waxy and lifeless. "She hasn't been well lately."

"She, she—" I attempted to share what she had revealed—that she had also killed the man who called himself Eddie Morita.

"Boy, save your energy." The captain, who seemed familiar with the Carters, spoke crisply in a no-nonsense matter. "I will send an officer to come by your place of residence later to document your side after you have recovered. Now where are you residing?"

"Hotel Green," I told him. "Toshio Aoki's studio."

One of the officers came with a box camera—I was reminded of Jack. I remained prostrate as he took photos of the arrow held in place by Tama-chan's two halves.

There was mention of calling the doctor, but I shook my head. I was able to get on my feet and showed the police officers that I could take steps on my own. I wasn't sure if any of my ribs had been broken, but based on similar injuries that had taken place on construction sites in Japan, I knew nothing could be done about that.

"*Oi*, I'll take you back to the hotel." Mr. Goto had finally pried himself from his seat on the buggy. I had forgotten that Mr. Goto had been outside the whole time. Had he witnessed Mrs. Carter's treachery? I later discovered that he had been the one who notified the police.

I couldn't return to Mr. Aoki's studio. Mrs. Carter and her ilk were his regular customers and I didn't know if I would be blamed for what had transpired. Besides, I was tired of all the shenanigans of the rich. "Take me to the Riley House," I told Mr. Goto.

The first to greet me was Mrs. Riley, who was covered in a white substance, which I guessed was flour. "Louie!"

I leaned on Mr. Goto as we entered the boardinghouse.

"What has happened?"

"Some trouble," was all Mr. Goto could manage to communicate.

Mrs. Riley helped me up the stairs to my old bed, the mattress on the floor.

I didn't have a chance to say much or even check whether Jack was in the boardinghouse. My right ear sank into the mildewed mattress and before I knew it, I was asleep.

The next morning my chest was still throbbing and I noticed red marks like crushed strawberries over the left side of my torso. I could still, however, take deep breaths. The room was exactly how I had left it, with even my unlaced boots cast off on the hardwood floor. The bed on the other side was empty. No sign of Jack. Relieved that my lungs seemed to be able to hold air, I ventured outside of my room to find Simon.

"Good morning." Simon looked like he was freshly shaven and was about to enfold me in an embrace when I stopped him.

Since I didn't know the word for rib in English, I pointed to my chest, leaning a bit forward. "Hurt," I said.

"I heard that you got into a bit of a scrap yesterday. Because of what happened, Mr. Carter has dropped all charges against Ian. Doesn't have the time or money to press his false charges."

My head was starting to spin. Mrs. Carter's arrest led to Ian's exoneration?

"I'm going to meet with Savage now." Simon's face was flushed, the color of a ripe peach.

"Will Jack be at your meeting?"

"No." Simon fumbled with the suspender on his overalls. "Truth is, he hasn't been at the Riley House for a couple of days. I told him to stay away. A couple of brutes from Los Angeles came by the Riley House to demand money that Eddie owed, so Jack's been hiding out in that opium den on Pico Street."

The weathered clapboard house with 福 on the door.

"Did Jack have anything to do with Eddie's debt?"

Simon shook his head. "I don't think so. But he felt obliged to Eddie. Almost as if they were brothers."

The police arrived soon after Simon had left. It was the same officer, Wilbur McEnroe, who had led us to Eddie's wasted body in the Arroyo.

"It took us a while to track you down. You told the captain that you were residing at the Hotel Green," he said.

"That was a temporary arrangement." As soon as I said it, I felt that a weight had been lifted. I would not spend a lifetime under Toshio Aoki's employ.

"Mrs. Carter's driver and daughter have both provided us with a full report about what transpired yesterday. But we still need more information about why."

There was something in Officer McEnroe's voice that signaled doubt. My pulse quickened.

"Did you have many dealings with Mrs. Carter before?" he asked.

I shook my head. "Just at the studio. A few times at best."

"Why would she want to harm you? It must have been for a reason. Did you provoke her in some way?"

Anger rose to my ears and I began to shake. Surely, Mrs. Carter hadn't fabricated some lie that I had threatened her. "She killed Eddie Morita, too," I blurted out. "She confessed to it—ask her daughter. She doesn't like my kind."

Officer McEnroe seemed dismayed at my accusations but still scribbled something in his police notebook. "Fine. Just don't make any plans to leave Pasadena."

I weakly agreed. Where else was I going to go?

Before he left, I gathered enough courage to make a pressing request. "I'd like to get my *kobu* back." McEnroe furrowed his brow, causing his felt helmet to pitch forward slightly. I clarified, "The wood in my pocket that saved me from Mrs. Carter's arrow."

"It's considered evidence. You'll have to wait until the trial is over."

Now alone, I was burdened by my thoughts. I was completely mystified by the man who called himself Eddie Morita. What was he to Jack? Jack had said that Eddie had tried to kill him. Even with Eddie dead, I felt that Jack was still not safe.

With my either bruised or broken ribs, I knew I should stay at the Riley House to fully recuperate. Mrs. Riley kept coming upstairs to tend to me and I was touched by her maternal care. I couldn't help but think of Gigi, though. She must have known I was back in the boardinghouse but seemed to be avoiding me.

I didn't blame her, yet I had hoped that perhaps she'd had a change of heart, at least enough to forgive me in my darkest hour. It looked as if that hope would not be realized.

I rested for the entire day, thinking about Eddie's death. He had been in ill-health, cancer choking his body. He was desperate for money—maybe to pay his medical bills? But based on the evaluation of the coroner, it didn't seem like he was receiving any treatment.

I finally heard Simon's steps on our stairs toward dinnertime and called out to him to find out the status of Ian's legal case.

"Ian will be let go tomorrow." The lines on his face had softened and he looked more like his twenty-three years than a man a decade older. "Mrs. Carter was the one who had insisted that Ian be prosecuted for attempted murder. She couldn't bear to see her husband shamed in public like that. For the life of me, I don't understand the people on Millionaire's Row."

"Has Mrs. Carter been charged with anything—"

"Attempted murder, of course, for shooting that arrow at you."

"Is that all?"

"What, has she done anything else?"

I didn't have the energy to bring up Eddie's demise. "Later," I merely replied, and Simon seemed relieved. As the weight of his brother's arrest had lifted, he was feeling quite spent and excused himself to rest.

The sun had gone down, blanketing my shared room in darkness. Still no sign of Jack. I had a bad feeling that he was in desperate trouble. In spite of my own health limitations, I felt compelled to locate him. I put on a jacket, slipped on my boots without properly lacing them, and went out the door.

XI
JACK'S STORY

1.

I didn't have the energy to walk to the California stop, so I took the Pacific Electric car. When I jumped out at my stop, the neighborhood was eerily quiet, as if it were warning me to retreat. A line of crows sat on the telephone wire, and I got the feeling that they were wondering whether my measly body would be delicious. They concurred that I probably wouldn't provide much enjoyment and flew off toward the Arroyo, perhaps for better options.

I walked down Pico Street, the smell of hay and dung stinging my nostrils. A horse somewhere in a stable softly neighed. It was obvious that something bad had occurred in the opium den. I could tell the house had been cleared out even before I reached the last step on the wobbly, stained staircase. The door was wide open, hanging off its hinges. A shoe was left on the upstairs porch. I recognized the black oxford, its toe stained by photography chemicals. It was Jack's.

I was afraid to look inside, but I continued. As there was no electricity in the house, I had to reach out to make sure that I wasn't walking into anything. Despite my best attempts, my legs hit something and I cringed as the force reverberated up to my bruised ribs. I felt a chair. The seat was covered with something slimy. With effort, I bent down to pat the ground and then recoiled with horror. There was no doubt that my hands were on a human body.

"Jack!" It took me at least a minute to compose myself, but I knew there was no time to waste. I ripped down the soiled curtains to let some diffused light into the room.

Dark blood had congealed from a deep gash in the back of the body. The hair was long and matted—not like Jack's fuzz of waves. As I rolled the body over, I saw that it was an Asian man I had never seen before. I held my hand over the man's face, which almost looked angelic. No breath touched my bloody hands.

Had Jack killed this man in self-defense?

I got back to my feet. I was able to see now that the staircase was not only stained with dirt but also a trail of drying blood. I tiptoed to the edge of the porch to see if I could spot where Jack had gone, making sure that I didn't put my full weight on the termite-infested railing. A mosquito buzzed in my ear. Below were the two smaller houses, completely dark, and the stable—no sound of a horse now.

"Jack!" I called out. "Torajiro."

I thought I had heard a rustle. But perhaps it was one of those American squirrels, which were much larger than the ones in Japan.

"*Luo*—" I heard a distant voice from the horse stable. And then louder and more definitively, "*Luo*."

"*Ra!*" I yelled back into the darkness. "*Ra*."

The response, which sounded ominously like a mourning dove: "*Luo*, *luo*."

Wincing, I ran down the stairs and inched my way to the stable. "*Ra*," I murmured.

Past the backs of several horses, I spotted movement in the last stall. It was Luo, who lit a small gas lantern, casting an orange glow over the matted brown hay.

I blinked a couple of times before I was able to focus on what was before me. "Ah—"

Lying like a rag doll on the dried hay, Luo crouched over him, was Jack. His face was in extreme shambles this time. It looked like his nose was broken a second time, and in more places. He was without his spectacles and he was wearing only one shoe.

I ran to his side. "Jack. *Daijoubu?*"

No response.

This time, I shook his shattered body good and hard.

"Ryui." Jack's mouth was swollen and I noticed that one of his bottom front teeth was missing. He would be upset to see how his gorgeous teeth, his pride and joy, were ruined.

I gently clasped his scuffed hand. The skin on his wrist was torn, probably due to being bound.

With his free hand, he gestured toward his middle. I thought it was because he was experiencing pain there, but I saw that he was attempting to withdraw something from a cloth belt that had been tied around his belly.

"It's all right. Please rest," I told him.

But he kept clawing at the belt until I pulled out the package, which contained folded papers. The outer piece of paper was addressed to me.

He squeezed my hand weakly for a moment and then fell into unconsciousness.

Luo stepped away to the neighboring stall and came back leading a heavy old horse by a rope around his neck. There was no saddle on him, only a woven Indian blanket. Positioning two orange crates on either side of the animal, Luo gestured for us to get Jack onto the horse's back. Taking deep breaths, I forced my way through the pain to do what he was requesting. It was good that the horse was so old because he did not move even though it took us several tries. Jack's arms hung over one side while his legs dangled from the other. Luo, hanging on to the mane, easily swung onto the horse right in front of Jack's collapsed body, and gestured for me to climb onto the back.

I had never ridden a horse before and was intimidated by the animal's sheer size. But again, he remained still as I slid myself up on his smooth rump, my left side throbbing. I hung on to the Indian blanket for dear life as we slowly made our way out of the stable.

It didn't occur to me until we were in front of the Riley House that Luo had guided his horse here without instruction. He tied up the horse on the post in front of the boardinghouse and pulled Jack's body onto his shoulders. He was much stronger than he looked. As he carried Jack, his tunic came loose around his middle and I was shocked to spy a knife dangling from a chain around his neck. The blade was crusted in blood.

Mrs. Riley, hearing the echo of boots on her parlor floor, emerged in her nightgown and hair rags, carrying a lit gas lamp. "What's happened now?" I expected her to react to seeing a strange Chinese man in her house, but she was obviously familiar with him. "Lord, Jack," she murmured like she was reciting a prayer. "Here, place him on the rug." She stomped her foot in the middle of the parlor. Luo gently lowered Jack. I cradled his mangled head while Mrs. Riley held on to his legs as we deposited him onto the floor.

"Good gracious." Mrs. Riley ended her prayer.

I was just happy that he was alive. At least for now.

I turned to thank Luo, but he had disappeared. When I stepped out of the Riley House, the old horse was gone from the hitching post.

When I returned to the parlor, Mrs. Riley had placed a pillow underneath Jack's head and a blanket over his body. We both watched his chest expand and contract to make sure that he was still breathing.

"Do you know that Chinese man?" I asked Mrs. Riley.

"Yes, that's Ah Lu. He does odd jobs for a number of us widows at the church."

I looked up, curious. What was more surprising—that Luo or Mrs. Riley attended church?

"You'll be staying, won't you?" Mrs. Riley said. "Jack will need a nurse."

"Ah—" Before I could fully respond, Mrs. Riley had made her way down the hallway to her room.

I wasn't sure what I could do, but I was at least prepared to spend the night. I sat in one of the parlor chairs and with the help of the gas lamp, I located Jack's letter addressed to me and began to read.

The Confession
By Torajiro Baba

I've wasted many good sheets of paper to write you, Ryui, my lad.

I've never felt the need to sire an heir, because what would that heir receive? Now that I've lost most of my photographs, my treasures are slim. I do owe you, however, the truth. With the pen shaking in my hand, I proceed.

My father was a low-level samurai in Okayama. He never did anything heroic during the time of Tokugawa, at least not that I'm aware. I'm the second son and second child. There were five of us, all living with our parents within the confines of the castle grounds.

If anything was my god, it was the castle. The black exterior gave it a threatening demeanor that I could relate to. My oldest brother bullied me mercilessly and as the second son, I had nothing. As a result, I escaped through my mind. When I think about it, I was always taking pictures, even before I had a camera, attempting to capture a flash of emotion, whether it be joy, sadness, or rage.

Our world began to turn upside down after the last Tokugawa shogun was overthrown in 1868. I was only five at the time, but even at that young age, I could see the change in my father. He was not a kind man to begin with, but when his status as a samurai was stripped away, he lost all sense of his identity. The government filled up the moats. The castle itself was not maintained. My father became a bitter, bitter man.

The transformation was momentous for us, the children, as well. All of us had to go to public school with the other children. Peasants felt the brunt of their oldest sons, their most productive workers, being forced into the military.

What angered my father the most was the liberation of the outcasts. He liked the order of the Tokugawa times. Samurai at the top, followed by farmers, artisans, and then merchants. Below the merchants were the outcasts, those who slaughtered animals for food or the production of leather or were gravediggers. These jobs were unclean and involved death—not keeping with Buddhist principles for honoring life. Surely those people had committed wrongdoings in their past lives or their present ones to have such a polluted existence. Their punishment? To live in ghettos or on fallow land. In Okayama, they had to identify themselves by wearing plain clothing without any adornment of family crests. They were barred from wearing geta and had to be barefoot when meeting other classes of people. That way we knew exactly who they were.

We, on the other hand, had benefited from being in the samurai class. Now we were nothing. And then when I was eight, the Meiji government decreed that the outcasts would be liberated. There would be no difference between them and us.

After the liberation, I had friends who were outcasts. I went to school with them. I was especially close to the Yanai family. The second son was named Ryoji and we were in the same class.

In 1873, when I was ten, all hell broke loose. All the momentous changes during the new Meiji rule were finally leading to people protesting, including my father. He joined other samurai marauders who were angered that the military would be open to all people. And again, at the new status of the outcasts.

They went out with swords and even guns. My father didn't own a gun, so he brought with him a torch. My mother tried to stop him, but it was impossible. My oldest brother went with him. I followed. I didn't know what I thought I could do, but even at that age, I wasn't the type to stay home when riots were going on outside.

There were hundreds, maybe even thousands, of angry men in the streets of the city. They broke into schools and ruined them. They set out for the homes of government officials. And then they went for the homes of the outcasts.

I was confused and got turned around, carried by the current of the mob. I could hardly keep up with my father and older brother. And then I finally discerned where I was. In front of my classmate Ryoji Yanai's home.

My father's torch had already been lit for a while. It was becoming dim, but it still contained fire. He ran to that wood house and touched the flame to the roof made of dried grass. The house was immediately ablaze.

And then I realized that the Yanai family was still in the house. I ran toward it, but my older brother tackled me to the ground. The cracking of the burning house and human shrieks melded together until I didn't know what I was hearing.

By the time my brother released me, the house had burned to the ground, smoke choking my eyes and lungs. My father had left. My older brother was gone.

I turned to leave, too, but where was I to go? Then I saw Ryoji's younger brother, only five, covered in soot, emerging from the smoldering ashes of the thatched roof.

Did he understand what had happened?

I am sorry, I told him.

I don't know why I said that to him. I was admitting guilt. But he was a child. He would not remember anything, I thought.

After that, I knew that I wanted to leave Japan as soon as I could. I couldn't save my mother from my father's abuse, so I saved myself. Ever since I was your age, Ryui, I have been selfish. But maybe that's what kept me alive.

I was a stowaway on the Miike-Maru to Seattle. There was another Nipponese stowaway, and we helped each other steal morsels of food. We were caught at the end of the journey and interrogated fiercely. But in the end, the government officials didn't want to waste the time or money to send us back, so we were released.

I became a blanket man, doing odd jobs in the state

of Washington. Cutting down lumber and helping fishermen. I hated doing hard labor. Someone I worked with told me about a strange Nipponese man living in the Washington state countryside making a living taking photographs. I had never heard of such a thing. I set out to find him and I did.

He was a man who liked to work and live alone, yet he had become a beloved figure in both the white and Indian communities. The Indians came to him to get their photographs in traditional dress as well as Western clothes with their families. He taught me how to develop photographs in a bathtub. But more importantly, he taught me what to look for. To use sunlight to make people look their best. To stand still and wait for the action to come into the frame.

After a while, he told me to set off on my own. I think, actually, he had grown tired of me. He was only a few years older than me and I needed to be more independent. I didn't blame him.

He recommended that I go to Los Angeles and specifically Pasadena, where rich Americans lived. He told me photographers were drawn to that part of America, and the only way I could continue to improve was to be in the company of other photographers.

Through a famous photographer in the Arroyo, I was introduced to the Riley House. I couldn't quite afford a room to myself. No American wanted to live in the same room as a Nipponese. It was worth not eating a few nights a week to have the room to myself. But one day when I came home from Manako's, I discovered that I had a new roommate.

He introduced himself as Eijiro Morita. He had just arrived from Japan. He said that he was from

Hiroshima, but I knew immediately that was a falsehood. He didn't speak with a Hiroshima accent, and there were other signs that he wasn't from Hiroshima. He had a passion for sardines like many of us Okayama people do; I saw him save money to buy a tin of them for special occasions. He pronounced words like I had heard back in my village in Okayama.

Finally, I confronted him. You are not from Hiroshima, I said.

And he admitted it. He was from Okayama like me. But he had moved with his family to Hiroshima, so it was easier for him to tell Nipponese in America that he was from Hiroshima since there were so many of them here. Mostly, I think, he was trying to build a new identity, like a spy on a private mission.

I was the one who gave him the nickname Eddie. Everyone needs one, I told him. He resisted at first, but finally gave in after so many Americans could not pronounce his name. When I told him that "eddy" also meant whirlpool, he was amused. He liked the idea of moving in a circle in water. He said it reminded him of home.

Then Eddie's health began to suffer. He was a strapping man, handsome, but his skin started to look yellowish. Sometimes he was doubled over in pain. He vomited constantly. He couldn't get out of bed some days.

I told him to go to Dr. Battles, but he said he didn't believe in Western medicine. One day he partook of Colonel Green's elixir, the August Flower, despite his better judgment. It was a miracle, he told me. The pain in his stomach disappeared. He felt strong enough to move mountains—that was what he actually told me.

I knew that he was being delusional, that his euphoria could not last. But he didn't heed my advice. He kept buying bottle after bottle, spending two weeks' salary for one. He couldn't do hard labor, so he began consorting with criminals. That's when he agreed to be part of a scheme to issue lottery tickets in Pasadena, a practice that was outlawed in Rafu. Of course, he didn't have the discipline to spend less money than he had. Everything was spiraling out of control.

One late morning I felt pressure over my whole body. Eddie was on top of me, my pocketknife in his hands, dangerously close to my throat.

I thought it was the August Flower taking over his mind and body. But then he revealed his true identity. His name was not Eijiro Morita. He had fabricated that. His real name was Rentaro Yanai. Ryoji's little brother. The one who had witnessed the atrocity that my father committed.

I had placed my memories of the Yanai family in a locked box, hoping never to revisit that time and place. But Rentaro had followed me across the Pacific to avenge his family's death. He had intended to kill my oldest brother first, but he had died in the war with China. My father had died from tuberculosis long ago.

He was able to find out my address from one of my younger sisters. I had to give him credit for not hurting a woman. I, on the other hand, had been there at the scene of the crime and had done nothing to stop it. If he killed me, perhaps the burning in his body would be extinguished.

I was prepared for him to do it. Even relieved. This was my fate. I waited. But he couldn't go through with it.

He dropped the knife and ran. I couldn't let him take the coward's way. I chased him down the stairs and out the front door.

Do it! I implored him. The sins of the father follow the son. Do it! Don't be a yellow-bellied coward. I tried to give him the knife to finish me off.

But he instead screamed for me to release him. I had never heard such noises emanating from a human being. All the agony of seeing his family being burned to death. I soon began yelling, too. How could we extinguish that moment from our bodies?

He then left the Riley House. Every night I searched for him in his regular haunts at opium dens. He had left his scant possessions behind, including his passport, bearing his true name: Rentaro Yanai. Place of birth: Okayama, Japan.

I ask you, my dear Ryui, what is our past, the legacy of our fathers?

What happens when our feet touch this new ground of America? Do we become new people? Can we forget our past?

If I had the strength, I would have killed myself long ago. But I told you that I'm selfish. Part of me will protect myself at all costs.

I don't blame you for throwing that kobu at me. I don't agree with your silly sense of morality, however. That photo of Gigi was a masterpiece. Perhaps you sensed that something deeper was wrong with my character. Evil that was passed down from father to son. You did what Eddie could not do: fought back with fury. For that, I thank you.

Do not carry shame with you about any of this. It will not help you in your future. For better or worse,

America is our home now. All things are possible in Pasadena. A quack doctor can call himself "colonel" and build a castle. A woman can become royalty merely based on her family's or husband's wealth.

I know that I am quick to judge. It's one of my many faults. If you must follow the path of Toshio Aoki, so be it. I will not criticize you. But there are not only two artistic paths—his and mine. There is one for you, Ryunosuke Wada. Only you yourself can find it.

Baba Torajiro
Your Jack

As I had gotten accustomed to the darkness in Mr. Aoki's studio, the morning light shocked me awake.

The pages of Jack's letter were covering me like fallen sycamore leaves and I gathered them back together, even taking the time to properly order them. More than ever, I wished Tama-chan was with me.

"Where's Ah Lu?" Jack whispered as he still lay prostrate on the floor.

I dropped the pages onto the rug. "Jack, you're awake." I knelt by his side.

"Ah Lu?" he repeated.

"What?"

"The Chinese man who saved my life."

Oh, Luo, I thought.

"He's gone," I told Jack.

"Good. He'll need to hide out somewhere for a while." There was no white in Jack's eyes—only blood red.

"How about you? Who was that dead man?"

"One of those *yogores* in Rafu that Eddie had gotten mixed up with."

"Won't they be looking for you?"

"I don't know. I think they didn't expect that anyone would fight for me."

I felt ashamed that I hadn't. "The police may find out that you were at that house." And me, for that matter.

"The police won't put energy into it. It's not Millionaire's Row. Just another dead yellow man in an opium den. Everyone has cleared out. It will be quiet there for a while." Jack nodded his damaged head toward the freshly stacked pages of his letter. "I see you've read what I wrote to you."

I swallowed some emotion to keep my voice steady. "It wasn't your fault," I told him in Japanese. "The burning of his house. You were only ten years old."

"I could have at least apologized." Jack had let go of all his bravado and cynicism. All I saw now was a broken man with regret. "I should have fallen at his feet and begged for forgiveness. And when he appeared at the Riley House, I could have helped him more. Looked out for him."

"He chose his path," I said. "We all have. We do the best we can."

"I came to America to run away from what my father did. I came to become a new person. Why did you come here?"

I took a deep breath. I myself hadn't known the reason until quite recently. "I came because I thought the trees had cursed us. I thought the farther I traveled from Yokohama, the farther I would be from the pain. But the curse followed me."

"I think curses stay only when we allow them to," Jack said, his eyes barely open. In a matter of minutes he fell asleep again, snores released from the depths of his chest.

My lips and throat felt dry and I got up slowly and softly so as not to disturb Jack. I walked through the dining room into the kitchen, where Gigi was preparing some tea.

She looked like she had lost weight. Her face was pale and a bit gaunt, and there were lines on her neck.

"Hello," I said to her.

"Hello."

I got on my knees and bowed, pushing my arms onto the unpolished hardwood floor. I felt splinters enter the pads of my fingers but I did not flinch. "I am so sorry. I am a wretched man."

"Get up, get up." Gigi attempted to pull me up but she was too weak to do so.

"Forgive me." Again, I kowtowed on the floor.

"I forgive you—" She stood above me and my lungs again were filled with the scent of lavender.

I remained on my knees, hopeful.

"Louie, I forgive you, but I can't forget. I came to California to feel free. Not to be branded and placed in a cage."

I pulled myself to my feet, rotten wood from the floor clinging to my pant leg, my palms, my shirt. "I've changed. Or I am changing."

"Maybe so. If we met a year, two years from now, it would be different."

I felt that my heart was literally breaking.

"I'm moving," she then announced.

"You don't have to—"

"I've been offered a job in San Francisco. At a theater there. It could be my big break."

Falling, falling. Gigi's announcement sent me down a dark, bottomless hole. For Gigi's sake, I needed to mask my agony. "That's wonderful, Gigi," I said. "I wish you the very best. Truly."

XII
HOME

1.

In a matter of days, Ian was released to the Riley House. He rejoined his brother a great deal bigger, excess flesh hanging from his jawline and even from his upper arms, but the biggest development was that he was now an engaged man.

Jack was the most skeptical about the proposed union. We had moved him upstairs to his bed to mend, but he couldn't stay hidden and attempted to get up on his own a number of times. I finally brought one of the parlor chairs to our room and set it by the window so he could at least gaze at the sky and birds, and the horses and buggies going down Marengo.

"Who's heard of a man accused of attempted murder coming home from jail with a future wife!" he muttered. "And what kind of woman would be attracted to such a man?" He was back to smoking again; he could quite conveniently place the cigarette in the gap where his bottom front tooth once was.

I didn't understand his objections, because everyone in the Riley House knew that Ian had had no intention of killing Mr. Carter. I concluded that Jack didn't believe in marriage or any kind of romantic pairing between a man and woman. He was much more comfortable in the company of bachelors.

Ian's bride-to-be was Emily, who worked at a restaurant

across the street from Manako's; she had dutifully delivered dinner to the jail most nights. In that smelly, mildewed jail cell, love blossomed between the two. The restaurant's owners were of the Quaker religion, which Mr. Vroman apparently belonged to as well. I wasn't sure how exactly these Quakers practiced their faith, but I knew good works were at the forefront of their values. Emily's deliveries sustained not only Ian but myself as well, and I was most grateful.

I had the opportunity to meet Miss Emily for the first time that evening. Simon was hosting a special party to welcome his brother back to the fold. He had asked Emily to cater the event instead of subjecting the celebrators to Mrs. Riley's food. Of course, he didn't tell Mrs. Riley his true reasons. "Yer needin' a break, Mrs. Riley," he told her, patting her gnarled hands.

Mrs. Riley did provide drinks and libations, including ginger ale, lemonade, and beer brewed in Los Angeles. Simon brought newly purchased whiskey. There were platefuls of fried chicken, mashed potatoes, and sweet peas. I filled up my plate and shoveled the food in without taking a breath, while the others were listening intently to Ian's tales of cohabitating with rats, possums, and raccoons in his jail cell. Nobody mentioned the Boyle brothers' uncle, because even though it was clear he had been victimized by Sherwood Carter, there would be no financial restitution.

Emily, who wore her flaxen hair in curls around her angelic face, then tried to lead us in songs, but everyone's pitch was a bit off-key, causing us to dissolve in laughter.

As Gigi was working at the opera house, she had an excuse not to attend. It was also too much for Jack to be part of a raucous gathering. He, too, was probably relieved that he didn't have to be part of anything related to Ian and a woman as a couple.

Miss Emily brought her older sister, Virginia, with her, and based on the way that Simon was looking at her, I began to think that there might be two weddings at the Riley House. It made sense that the Boyle brothers would be attracted to sisters. They seemed to have to do everything together.

"Who would have thought being imprisoned would turn out to be a blessing?" Ian asked before placing a heaping spoonful of mashed potatoes in his mouth.

Coming late to the party was Savage, whose arrival was celebrated with multiple cheers and a repouring of whiskey. I was imbibing like the rest of the party, but tried not to overindulge. I could see how Rentaro's dependency on Colonel Green's elixir had only increased his desperation, and I didn't want the same to happen to me.

"After the daughter began to talk to the police, then the mother started to as well," Savage explained. "It was like water shooting out of a firehose. Josephine had suspected that her mother had something to do with the death of Morita, or whatever his name really was. I guess Mrs. Carter does have a conscience, so she came clean."

"Why did she kill Eddie?" I spoke up because I felt this might be my only opportunity to find out the truth.

"He was blackmailing her," said Savage. "When he was working on removing Aoki's mural from the wall, he became aware that her domestic world was falling apart. Only when he'd finished did she admit that she didn't have the money to pay him. He told her to ask her neighbors on Millionaire's Row for the money she owed him. If she didn't, he would spread the news to all the workers on Orange Grove."

How in the world was Rentaro able to communicate his threats? I wondered. Desperate people had their desperate ways.

"He was quite dependent on Colonel Green's elixir to treat his internal pain. That's why he needed the money. She lured him into the Arroyo with the promise of the August Moon. She was able to get her hands on some sample bottles that she laced with rat poison, and he began drinking it right then and there in the canyon."

I flushed when I heard about the sample bottles. Did she get them from the ladies' room at the Hotel Green?

"She's quite a devious woman. She was probably the brains behind her husband's real estate business."

During this whole account, Emily's huge blue eyes had filled with tears. "And my Ian was caught in the middle of such treachery." She clutched at his fleshy forearm as he rested his head on her shoulder. The unbridled affection that Americans and white immigrants displayed in the open was indeed quite overwhelming.

"Oh." Mr. Savage directed his attention solely to me. "That Officer McEnroe told me now that Mrs. Carter has confessed, you can pick up your belonging at the police station. I think it's some kind of wood art piece. Is it valuable?"

I nodded. "Very much so."

The party continued at full tilt. I wanted to leave but I was too tired to move my body from my seat.

"Oh, a package was delivered to you earlier today, Louie. In preparation for this party, I plain forgot." Mrs. Riley went to her room and reemerged with a large rectangular parcel wrapped in newspaper.

"Who dropped this off?" I asked.

"Josephine Carter herself, in fact."

I promptly took the package up the stairs to my bedroom and tore the paper off in front of Jack. A note fluttered to the ground. Before Jack could respond, I announced, "Josephine Carter. She was the one who took the painting."

To clutch the actual painting in my hands was a dreamlike experience. I could see the subtlety of colors, the muted oranges and browns that reminded me of the last days of autumn. A couple of the persimmons looked overripe, their dried stems having fallen off. Was Mr. Aoki, in a rare moment of self-reflection, contemplating his own limited days on earth?

In her note to me, Josephine wrote:

> *If you could not reveal my identity to Mr. Aoki, I'd appreciate it. My family is in enough trouble as it is. I thought the painting could fetch some money to rescue my family from financial ruin. As it turns out, only the people of Pasadena know of Toshio Aoki. It belongs back in his studio. I am so sorry.*

After reading the note out loud to Jack, I said, "What will we tell Mr. Aoki?"

"Tell him that his painting found its way back to him, like a child to his father. Due to the complications of the case, we cannot reveal details. And remember to collect the money owed to us."

2.

I did muster enough strength to pick up Tama-chan from the police station and return it to my shelf, a talisman for recovery. My broken rib was healing quite nicely—Mrs. Riley said that I had youth on my side. I still wasn't quite ready to return to work at Marsh's for physical and emotional reasons. I was a boy that a society woman had attempted to kill. Did other customers of Marsh's harbor any such animosity toward me?

I still needed to clean up loose ends at Aoki's and return his

Indian basket painting. I was approaching the studio entrance when I spotted a delivery bicycle leaning by our exterior door. *Strange*, I thought, because most deliverymen knew to leave items in the lobby. A broad-shouldered Asian man was leaning over our sunken entryway. He rose and studied both sides of the street before getting on the bicycle and pedaling his way toward Fair Oaks.

I crossed the street to the studio and saw that a piece of paper was lodged in the bottom crack of the door. I couldn't pull it out, so I used my key to unlock the door. There, quite visible on our doormat, was the familiar message: DIE JAP.

I knew I had seen that figure before. After stuffing the message in my pocket, placing the painting on the love seat, and locking the door, I ran to Fair Oaks Avenue.

The vegetable delivery cart was still parked in front of Manako's. I took an enormous gulp of air and steadied my heartbeat. Instead of running, I now walked briskly with purpose.

Ah Hugh, the vegetable peddler, had emerged from the restaurant, brushing his hands on his apron and starting to untie his horse from the hitching post. His nephew, the Asian man I had seen at the hotel, was with him.

"It was you." I blocked the pathway of the nephew, whose name I had forgotten. The basket of his bicycle was taken up by a bulky burlap sack marked LAMANDA PARK ORANGE AND LEMON GROWERS ASSOCIATION.

We were about the same height but different builds. Nevertheless, I'm sure, we would be mistaken for each other even though our countries were at times enemies, fighting over influence in Korea. Ten years ago, when I was eight, I had heard news that my small archipelago had claimed a surprising victory over the much larger China. In the same way, I prepared myself to take on the nephew, who, despite his limp, was probably at least twenty pounds heavier.

He attempted to get back on his bicycle and make his getaway, but I held fast to the handlebars. We wrestled for control of his transportation, the delivery basket banging into my ribs, which were just starting to heal.

He finally abandoned the cycle and ran north. I chased after him, feeling sharp stabs from my injured chest. His dragging right foot slowed his speed such that after a block I was right behind him. I lunged at his legs, causing him to fall flat on his face and squeal in pain. Sitting on his back, I brought out the paper square. "You did this," I said. I pushed his face to the side against the dirt so he could see what I had.

Ah Hugh had caught up to us in his cart. He came to a stop and jumped off. "What are you doing?" he said, pulling me off his nephew. "Ah Wang can't understand what you are saying."

"He's been leaving anti-Japanese notes at Mr. Aoki's studio. Many, many times. And in March after the cherry blossom dinner, he gave me one of these, too, and even threw me to the ground from his bicycle."

With Ah Hugh's help, Ah Wang got to his feet. He attempted to charge at me, but his uncle reprimanded him. A furious exchange ensued between the two men. As it was in their home language, I could not understand. After a good couple of minutes, the men had completed at least their first round of arguments.

Ah Wang crossed his arms as Ah Hugh communicated what his nephew had shared.

"You see his damaged foot." Ah Hugh pointed at his nephew's right limb. "He was hurt in the war with Japan."

I felt badly that he had suffered an injury that might affect him his whole life. "But why choose Mr. Aoki as a target?"

"It's the talk among the Chinese that Mr. Aoki has not spoken so kindly of us in the past."

I remembered that illustration of the hanging Chinese heads in the *Los Angeles Herald* newspaper. I couldn't defend Mr. Aoki, nor did I feel that I had to. "I have nothing to do with all that," I said. I put my palms out in front of the two Chinese men so both understood that my hands were not sullied by Mr. Aoki's politics.

"He heard about the cherry blossom dinner and thought he had to do something more. He confused you with Toshio Aoki when you came out of the Hotel Green."

Jack had been right, then. The attack was a case of mistaken identity.

The nephew glared at me, a pink mark spreading on his right cheek from being squashed onto the ground. His eyes, although piercing, were rimmed with some regret. Was he sorry that he had mistaken me for Mr. Aoki, or did he wish that he had disabled me for good?

The two continued to speak in their language. Their tones became softer and more conciliatory. A small crowd had gathered around us, and I was embarrassed to be seen in the middle of this hubbub.

Finally, Ah Hugh looked away from his nephew and turned to me. "I'm telling him that you are not Japanese. At least not the kind he fought against in the war."

I did not know if this distinction was in my favor. What kind of Japanese was I? "Get him to stop," I said.

"He will. You won't tell Marsh about this, will you?"

I recalled that he'd said Victor was a regular customer. If he knew Ah Hugh's nephew had been behind this hate campaign against Mr. Aoki, would he continue to order lemons and vegetables from the peddler?

"I'll have to talk with someone else first. But I will consider your request." I went back to retrieve Ah Wang's bicycle. I wheeled it back to him, but he didn't want to take it from me at first. In the end, he grudgingly relented.

• • •

Later that night, I told the whole story to Jack, who was feeling well enough to start developing photographs again. He wasn't agile enough, however, to regularly manage a change of clothes or get into the tub himself for a complete wash. Despite his lack of hygiene, he didn't smell that bad. In fact, he had the scent of an old relic, stored in a box for long period of time.

"The nephew had lost full use of his foot from fighting in the China-Japan War," I explained.

"So he wanted to exact revenge and Aoki was a good enough target."

"Jack!"

"I'm joking." Jack lit a rolled cigarette and took a big puff. "I don't believe in any kind of violence to solve problems. It's usually the weakest who pays the biggest price."

I had given this recent course of events a lot of thought. I felt so much pride about being Japanese before I arrived in California, but Jack and Ah Wang had shown me that our ways of doing things had also created great harm. "I don't know about Japan going into other countries like China and Korea," I commented.

Jack shrugged as if to say, *And you're coming to this conclusion now?*

"Ah Hugh has asked me not to reveal that his nephew had been behind the messages."

"And why should we say anything?"

"The Marsh brothers will want to know the truth. And how about Mr. Aoki?"

"The truth is up to interpretation, don't you think? Aoki got his painting back. And from Ah Wang's perspective, Aoki is the enemy."

"We can't say that to them!"

"Then let's keep our mouths shut. You, my good boy, have handled it all very professionally. Maybe there is hope for you in America."

The whole series of incidents was like a dream. I would never forget the defiant look on Ah Wang's face, just as I would never forget seeing the corpse of Eddie Morita—no, Rentaro Yanai—floating in that stream in the Arroyo. The story of his life was so tragic. All of us newcomers carried the weight of our pasts in our home countries or states. After all, only those who had experienced a catastrophic event, or were propelled by wanderlust or ambition, would find it worthwhile to travel thousands of kilometers by boat or train to America. Yet, after everything Rentaro had been through, he still managed to return the money he owed Gigi. That shred of morality he honored before he died.

3.

A few days later, Gigi left the Riley House. I had no idea she was gone until Mrs. Riley announced that Ian's fiancée would be moving into her old room. "I was hoping that Emily would be getting rid of all that flowery stuff, but she wants to make it her fairy-princess castle." Ian rolled his eyes as everyone around the table chuckled. I forced a laugh, too, but I felt quite empty inside. I had lost my first love.

I was, however, able to sleep much better in the boarding-house. My body held on to weight more and my face looked fuller in a matter of days. Business at Marsh's emporium was brisk, and I was happy not to have my evening job at Aoki's studio anymore.

When I reported to Marsh's on Friday morning, Logan was reading a newspaper at the counter.

"Good morning," I greeted him.

"It is a particularly good one—we are all getting a paid day off."

I was puzzled into silence.

"So you haven't heard? The president is coming to Pasadena today! He's going to lunch at the Raymond Hotel, and then he'll speak at Wilson High School."

"What president?" I asked.

"Our president. The US president. Teddy Roosevelt."

"Eh!" I was shocked. The president of the United States would be gracing our city of Pasadena.

Logan tapped the newspaper. "He's also going to stop by President Garfield's widow's house on Millionaire's Row. Garfield was assassinated, right inside a train station, a couple of decades ago in Washington. His widow moved here a few years ago."

I had not heard of any of this. A political leader being killed in public sounded like our days of the samurai.

Logan began to ruminate about our current president. "Teddy Roosevelt is quite unusual. He's enthusiastic about all things Japanese."

"You mean the president might visit Marsh's?"

"Don't be preposterous, Ryunosuke. But Victor is giving us the day off to go see him at the high school. Go change so you look more presentable."

I rushed back to the boardinghouse to get dressed in my one formal outfit.

"Did you hear about the president?" I asked Jack, who was cleaning the lens of a small new box camera that he had purchased at Vroman's.

"That's all everyone seems to be talking about."

I quickly buttoned the white shirt Gigi had mended before she left. "You are not going?"

Jack adjusted his new spectacles and continued to focus on his equipment.

"Imagine the photos you could take," I said, attempting to reform my crushed bowler hat.

That did it. Within a few minutes we were out the door.

Marengo was electrified, with pedestrians crowding the walkway underneath full pepper trees. A massive archway made up of greenery and calla lilies was suspended over the intersection with Union Street. We had to press through on our way to the high school, frustrating others who were standing shoulder to shoulder. Jack was determined to get to the front of the platform so he could get a photo of the president.

I had never seen the high school so beautifully adorned. There must have been an inch of red rose petals layered on the road to welcome the president's carriage. Heavy garlands of what looked like ferns and more brightly colored roses hung from the school building like a wealthy woman's jewels. Most curious was a giant stuffed bear standing upright on the stage.

There was no moving closer to the platform where city leaders were seated. I spotted a few customers, including Lady Madison, but did not see Victor Marsh or Mr. Aoki. Mr. Kuranaga and his wife were not far from where we were and I attempted to get their attention, but they either didn't hear me or chose not to react. I hadn't had much contact with the couple after the archery debacle.

Jack was lifting up his box camera, but as he was constantly jostled from behind, it was close to impossible to get a good shot of the festivities. Finally, the whole crowd cheered in unison as the American president, barrel-chested with a full mustache, took the stage next to the stuffed bear.

As he spoke in short sentences with simple words, I was able to understand most of what he said in his speech. He spoke about the beauty of the region, the irrigated fields, and the majestic mountains. He mentioned war and soldiers as well as how Americans needed to conduct themselves. "We need to stretch out a helping hand to others." I absorbed his message. All that I had seen in Pasadena taught me that all of us, even independent Jack, needed help.

After finishing his speech, the president got into a four-wheel carriage that was decorated with flowers. As I watched the carriage travel down the rose carpet, my heart soared with pride. I had nothing to do with the celebration, but I felt part of it nonetheless.

As the crowd slowly disbanded, I saw a man in a straw hat bump into a gentleman in front of him and expertly lift a wallet from his victim's back pocket.

Jack had seen it, too, and wasted little time taking hold of the pickpocket's arm. "This man has gotten hold of your purse," he declared to the victim, an elderly man whose beard was all gray.

"You think these Chinee know anything?" The thief attempted to get loose from Jack's grip, while the old man patted the back of his pants only to discover that his wallet was indeed missing.

Jack plucked the thief's hat from his head and there lay the stolen wallet, which dropped to the ground. The now hatless man ran through the thinning crowd, making his escape. Both Jack and I were tired of chases, so we stayed back, returning the man's wallet to him.

"Why, thank you. May I give you a little reward for your efforts?" The old man began going through his wallet for a bill.

I wouldn't have minded some remuneration, but Jack adamantly refused. "No payment necessary," he said. "Just spread the news of the greatest Nipponese detectives in Pasadena."

The bearded man nodded, even though he probably had

little idea of what Jack was referring to. Jack, now wearing the culprit's straw hat, began to whistle through the gap in his teeth and wandered to an oak tree to take some photographs.

As I walked south into the business section of Marengo, I passed an alley where a couple of slop buckets were placed outside the back door of a building. Kneeling beside them was the hobo whose railcar we had barged into in what Gigi called Dark California. Our eyes met. At one time, I had feared that my fate in America would follow his, but now I saw him for who he was, unrelated to me. "Hello," I greeted him. He grunted in response. We didn't know each other's names, but we recognized that we were both part of the landscape of Pasadena.

I continued on my path back to the boardinghouse, following a group of girls all dressed in white cotton dresses. When I finally caught up to them before Colorado Street, I discovered one of them to be Tsuru.

I hadn't seen her for several days and her appearance lifted my spirits. "Uncle Toshio hasn't stopped smiling since you delivered that painting to him," she said. "You still don't know who stole it?"

"We were able to retrieve it after a series of complicated negotiations," I told her. I don't think she believed a word of my mumbo jumbo.

"We will be leaving soon for New York City. Uncle Toshio is designing a backdrop for a play. I'll probably take ballet lessons there." She did a pirouette in front of me on the rose carpet. I gathered that her classmates were used to her dancing antics because they didn't react at all.

"How long will you be in New York?" I asked.

Tsuru shrugged. "Not sure."

I was going to miss her. There was something about her boldness that made me less afraid.

"Don't have such a sad face. It's not like you adore me."

"Of course not. You could be my little sister."

"More like your *nesan*." Tsuru used the Japanese word for big sister to emphasize her elevated status, at least in her mind. She burst out in her bright laughter, the song of sparrows, and I could not help but dissolve into joy as well.

I didn't see Tsuru often after that. She eventually went to Pasadena High School and kept busy with her teenage activities as well as gallivanting across the nation with Mr. Aoki to art exhibitions.

It wasn't until my wife and I went to see a moving picture at Clune's Broadway Theatre that I was able to gaze upon Tsuru's face again.

By that time, she was also married—to the silent film star Sessue Hayakawa, a sensation who even ran his own movie studio. Together they starred in the movie *The Dragon Painter*. Sessue was playing an artist who could not paint after entering into wedded bliss with Tsuru's character, Ume-ko. I found it quite amusing watching Tsuru defer to her husband's talents—even faking her own death so he could paint—when I knew that in real life, she would be the one at the forefront creating art. When I told my wife that I once knew Tsuru, she didn't believe me, saying why would such an esteemed and famous silent film star know a humble nursery worker? I ended any discussion of Tsuru. That was another lifetime, at the turn of the twentieth century.

Years later, I read in the *Pasadena Star News* that Tsuru and Sessue had adopted a mixed-race boy, Yukio. He was actually Sessue's biological son with a white actress, born out of wedlock in New York City. It didn't surprise me that Tsuru had willingly adopted him along with two girls and raised them as her own. After all, Mr. Aoki had been her surrogate father under most unusual circumstances. Her time under his care must have prepared her for her chosen lifetime role as an adoptive mother.

My time with Jack was limited as well. One day before the height of summer, Jack disappeared from our room, along with his cameras and all his other worldly possessions. I think he had only remained in Pasadena to learn the fate of his childhood acquaintance, Rentaro Yanai. And now that he knew, he felt the freedom to move on. While there was a vibrant photographic community in Los Angeles, he left it—for Chicago, New York, or perhaps Seattle, where he had first arrived in America. I went to every single photographic exhibition in Tropico and Little Tokyo, hoping to spy a print from my idiosyncratic and visionary roommate. But his name was never listed under the contributing photographers.

2.

I remember one of my final conversations with Jack. The Boyle brothers had constructed a couple of chairs for early evenings near the camellia bushes with their romantic partners, but Jack and I often enjoyed the outdoor seats ourselves. That night, Jack and I took up residence in the chairs after dinner. Jack, wearing his new spectacles, was looking over some prints from his small box camera while I was perusing the inaugural issue of a local magazine, *Pasadena Town Talk.*

On the cover was a black-and-white watercolor painting of a Japanese goddess suspended in air. Her flowing dress whirled around her as butterflies positioned themselves on the top of her head and below her feet. In her hands was a potted plant.

Inside was an essay that Mr. Aoki had written:

> *Once upon a time, many years ago, a famous artist, named Ho-Sai, from Kyoto, was sitting in his flower garden, of which he was very fond.*
>
> *He began to sketch, but soon, because of the warm and beautiful day, he fell asleep, and in his dream he saw a beautiful woman riding a butterfly.*
>
> *And from this was first painted the now-famous "Flower Goddess." Flowers in Japan are said to be like women, beautiful and tender and graceful.*

I noticed that Jack had craned his neck toward the magazine, reading over my shoulder. His breath was cool and smelled like soil and peppermint.

"Such rubbish, don't you think?"

I took my time reading the English essay over and over and studying the magazine portrait of Mr. Aoki dressed in a jacket and ascot, posed with a long, skinny brush in his right hand, his pinky held out.

"I've never seen anything like a flower goddess in Japan," I finally concluded.

"Precisely!"

"But he does say that the artist was dreaming. He means he is the artist, right?"

"Yes, a famous artist," Jack said, scoffing.

I remained quiet for a moment, almost afraid to express my true feelings. Now that Jack and I had healed our divide, I didn't want a petty disagreement to separate us again. But I also realized we wouldn't have much of a partnership if I kept my mouth closed.

"During my lunch breaks, I go to the park across the way, and if no one is around I even lie on the grass," I said.

Jack didn't make fun of my lunchtime activity. He probably would have enjoyed doing the same.

"The sun here feels different. I know it's the same sun over Yokohama. But here, it's brighter, always lifting me up. One day when I woke up, I saw a beautiful red-and-black butterfly resting on a bush. I had never seen a butterfly like that before."

"And your point is—"

"Maybe it's all right to dream. And paint what you dream. Even if it's not what we learned back home. That's what you do with your photography, isn't it?"

"Hmm." Jack closed his lips and continued to go through his prints. He wasn't going to waste his breath on giving any credit to Mr. Aoki, deserved or not.

On my way home from the president's visit to Wilson High School, I had, in fact, seen Mr. Aoki walking down Green Street, his sketchbook in his hand. I first wondered if he had been there to listen to the speech, but I realized that Mr. Aoki had probably not been present for that. He didn't like to see reality, the world of complicated politics and shifting attitudes. He, like the goddesses he painted, was riding on the wings of the moth or kingfisher in heavenly realms that only he had created.

Mr. Aoki eventually left his beloved Pasadena for San Diego, where he died about a decade after I first met him.

The next morning after my conversation with Jack, I removed the two halves of Tama-chan from my shelf. I held my *kobu* tightly in my fist, but as the burl could not be aligned perfectly into its original whole, the halves cut into my palm.

Jack was still asleep. Under the blue light of sunrise, I went outdoors, hearing the mourning doves cry to each other.

I set out west for a long walk. Soon I had entered the shade of the oak and sycamore trees in the Arroyo, hearing small birds chirping and the steady trickle of water below.

A couple of white men were letting their horses take a drink at the creek. I was surprised to see one of the men was Mr. Vroman. He was carrying a small box camera like the one Jack had recently purchased. When he saw me, he pressed the shutter on his camera. I hoped that my pitiful figure wasn't captured on film.

"Sir, I forgot about your Tokoku netsuke," I apologized to him.

Mr. Vroman smiled broadly as his horse continued to dip its head toward the water. "I got it from Logan. He was able to locate it on the special orders shelf. You had written 'Vookman.' Quite ingenious." He shared that he had some Tokoku pieces already. "Along with, in total, hundreds of netsuke."

"You do?"

"I have a special chest for them at home and I admire them on a regular basis. You are welcome to come see them anytime."

I had my fill of Japanese antiques at Marsh's emporium. "Why do you collect?" I asked the bookseller. My family didn't have that much space in our house, and we never entertained even friends at home. I wondered why Americans like Lady Madison were so obsessed with things Japanese.

"Well, it's not for resale, as I'm not intending to exploit the netsuke for financial gain. It's simply a personal pleasure."

"Pleasure," I repeated.

"Yes."

"What is the purpose of pleasure?" I was honestly curious what brought Americans to our emporium doors every day, and it was easy for me to speak with Mr. Vroman, especially under the liberating shade of the oak trees.

"To hold a masterpiece in the palm of your hand. There's nothing like it."

I started thinking of Tama-chan and how I felt a sense of wonder when we had been together back in Japan.

"Again, you can come to my home and see my netsuke," he offered.

"Yes," I responded out of politeness, though I had no intention of accepting his invitation.

I followed the creek, passing limp orange poppies, the only survivors of the late spring season. Sitting in the middle of long grasses was a familiar former boarder at the Riley House, his jaw even more defined perhaps due to hard labor.

"Oh, Mr. Clem!" I called to him without thinking whether this might be his moment of solitude, and swiftly apologized for interrupting him.

But he returned the greeting. "Good morning. Don't worry, I come here almost every day before work."

"Is that right?"

"It settles me."

I wished I lived closer to the Arroyo. I would visit more often if my schedule allowed me to.

I nodded my farewell to him and he did the same.

I found a spot where the current was steady. I took the two halves of Tama-chan from my pocket, remembering the tasks we had done together on construction sites in Japan, our wild voyage across the Pacific, landing in the Riley House, and, of course, my *kobu* ultimately saving my life at the Carter estate.

Eddie, or Rentaro, and even the Carters had attempted to make a new life in California. All of their efforts failed. Mine could possibly end tragically, too, but I couldn't carry Tama-chan with me anymore. I had to let it go to seize new cultures and traditions. In a sense, over all these weeks, my grip on my *kobu* had loosened, anyway. Tama-chan and I deserved a new destiny.

I nestled the two halves of the polished burl among river stones of a similar size. The cool, clear water covered Tama-chan and soon it was difficult to differentiate the polished wood from the neighboring rocks.

As I watched the running water, I was reminded of Japanese gardens built around teahouses. At a shrine near our house in Yokohama, the water flowed from a piece of bamboo into a stone basin. Using a wooden ladle, we washed our hands to purify ourselves before entering into a building.

Every time I walked through the Arroyo after that, I stopped by that bend of the creek, although over the years it has changed. I wasn't sure where Tama-chan was now—whether the two pieces had fossilized like rock or rolled downstream.

I stayed in Pasadena, as did the Greene brothers until 1922. While I wasn't enthused by their Sanborn residence, in five years' time, they would produce a masterpiece for the Procter & Gamble scion, David Gamble, a stone's throw away from Millionaire's Row. Like the other grand houses that they would be known for, the Gamble house would embody Japanese sensibilities like sloping roofs and carved wood images of mountains, flowers, and birds. And all of this would be created without the brothers' making a single trip to Japan. Their Japan had been contained in world's fairs and our community in Crown City.

The Marsh brothers didn't remain in Pasadena that long. The emporium only lasted about seven years after the time that I had arrived. By 1910, more Japanese had settled in Pasadena, opening laundries and nurseries. After leaving the Japanese art goods business, I was one of the first hires of Nippon Nursery, not far from where Mr. Kawai would build his home.

GT Marsh did make his commercial Japanese garden a few blocks south of Hotel Green, only to encounter financial struggles around 1911. Serendipity arose in the form of railroad magnate Henry Huntington, who was looking to create his own Japanese garden on his ranch in nearby San Marino. From GT, Huntington's ranch superintendent acquired some of the greenery and stone statues and, most importantly, the Japanese house, which Mr. Kawai and others dismantled to eventually reassemble in its new location. By this time, I was working at Nippon Nursery and only watched on the sidelines from Raymond Avenue as the workmen carefully pulled out one wood joint at a time.

I couldn't destroy my *kobu* because it was part of my story within this larger story of Crown City. But I couldn't keep it, either. Maybe the water trickling down from the San Gabriel Mountains had purified Tama-chan, completely altering its elements—or perhaps the *kobu* had changed the composition of the water forever.

Richard Wada
21-5-A
Gila WRA
Rivers, Arizona

Louise Suzuki
1025 W. Wolfram St.
Chicago 14, ILL

September 8, 1945

Dear Louise,

Mama and I have packed up our things and sent most of them to the house in care of Mr. Carr. He's even sending a sedan for us. I don't know what we would do without him.

I can't wait to be back in Pasadena and see my old buddies. Sometimes I wonder if they'll pretend that they don't know me, but with all the American Friends Service has done as well as Mr. Carr and Hugh Anderson, we are more confident that our move back home might go smoother than it would have in other places like the Central Valley.

I know you're still feeling sore that you couldn't make it to Dad's funeral. First we get locked up in this furnace in Arizona against our will. Then the WRA tells you to move out to Chicago, and then when you want to attend your father's funeral, they deny your request to enter because there isn't enough time for clearance. It makes my blood boil, too, but for Mama's sake, I've been trying to put a lid on my anger.

Anyway, right before Dad died, he kept telling me to send this wood thing to you. I think he hand polished it from that branch that we collected for him behind the barbed wire. Remember how mad he was? More at me than you for breaking camp rules. But you were his favorite, anyway. I didn't bother to tell him that it was your idea.

During his last days, Dad was pretty looney. I told him you wouldn't want the polished wood, but he insisted. I promised to do it, but then he died and there was the funeral in camp and everything, so it slipped my mind. Then, when I was cleaning up our barracks, I found it underneath Dad and Mama's mattress. I was going to throw it out, but I remembered the promise that I made to him. Maybe it's your influence, but I couldn't break my word to him, even though he's gone. He told me that you would know what it is and what it's about.

Maybe when you and Joe come for a visit to Pasadena, you can tell me sometime.

Your brother,
Richard

OUR CAST OF FEATURED CHARACTERS IN PASADENA

**based on real characters*

Toshio Aoki*, a wildly popular Japanese artist in California

Tsuru Aoki*, Toshio's young adopted daughter who later becomes a silent-film actor and marries another Japanese film star, Sessue Hayakawa

Torajiro "Jack" Baba, a photographer from Okayama

Simon and Ian Boyle, brothers who work at Pasadena Machine Shop and live in the Riley House

Artemis Brown, hobo

Gertrude Carter, Sherwood Carter's wife

Josephine Carter, Sherwood and Gertrude's daughter

Sherwood Carter, a real estate magnate specializing in oil properties

Mr. and Mrs. Goto*, employees of GT Marsh

Rosalie "Gigi" Georgia Greeman, seamstress who lives in the Riley House

Colonel Green*, manufacturer of an elixir and owner of Hotel Green

Charles Greene*, architect

Ah Hugh*, a Chinese vegetable farmer in Garvanza, an area near Pasadena

Logan James*, a mixed-race Black employee at Victor Marsh's store

Toichiro Kawai*, pioneering woodworker at Victor Marsh's store who came to Pasadena via Yokohama

Kichihei, a Japanese itinerant worker

Frank Terusaburo Kuranaga*, former railroad labor contractor from Kyushu Prefecture who owned Japanese art goods businesses in San Francisco and Pasadena and marries a white woman, Leonna Cook

Ah Lu, a Chinese man whom Ryui encounters when he travels from San Francisco to Los Angeles

Lady Madison, a grand dame of Millionaire's Row

George Turner "GT" Marsh*, an Australian import dealer who opened the first Asian art goods store in San Francisco

Victor Marsh*, GT's younger brother who operated his own Asian art goods store in Pasadena, California

Clem Moro, a member of the Cupeño tribe who had lived on a reservation in San Diego

Eddie Morita, Jack's former roommate

Grace Nicholson*, renowned arts dealer who sold artifacts

Mrs. Riley, operator of the Riley House boardinghouse

Mr. Savage, attorney

Adam Clark "A. C." Vroman*, bookseller and photographer

Ryunosuke "Ryui" Wada, an eighteen-year-old carpenter who spent most of his life in Yokohama

Ah Wang, Ah Hugh's nephew

Adam Wilmington, Carter family's driver

Cherry Blossom dinner, Hotel Green, Pasadena, circa 1903. (Courtesy of the Archives at Pasadena Museum of History; GGG.4.4.14, George G. Green Collection.)

AUTHOR'S NOTE AND ACKNOWLEDGMENTS

Crown City is full of real people as well as some key fictional ones. It was a delicate balancing act to accurately depict historical figures yet also provide a dramatic throughline that would make for entertaining reading.

There was an actual Toshio Aoki. He was indeed as celebrated in Pasadena as I depicted in *Crown City*. His biographical background is a bit scant; there are reports that he was married to a white woman at one time. Professor Chelsea Foxwell wrote a groundbreaking article on Aoki, "Crossings and Dislocations: Toshio Aoki (1854–1912), A Japanese Artist in California," which has been referenced by many others.

With more interest in this Japanese immigrant artist, institutions have either begun to exhibit his work or collect it. I was lucky enough to peruse some of his more notable paintings at the Cantor Arts Center at Stanford University. My thanks to both Professor Marci Kwon for providing the opportunity and Kathryn Cua for showing them to me.

Tsuru Aoki, who in my mind is a heroic figure, came to America with her biological uncle, Otojiro Kawakami, and aunt, Sadayakko Kawakami, on a theater tour. In a very unusual arrangement, she was adopted by Aoki.

She went on to become the first silent film lead actress of Asian descent. She married another Japanese immigrant, Sessue Hayakawa, who would become one of the most successful silent film stars of his era. She left America and her movie career to return to Japan and raise three adopted children, including Sessue's biracial son, Yukio, whom I had the pleasure to work with at *The Rafu Shimpo*. Although I never discussed his parents with him, I did meet with another former

Rafu employee, Cynthia Endo, who had worked closely with Yukio, to gain more insight on what kind of person his mother, Tsuru, was.

Lesser-known Japanese figures are Terusaburo "Frank" Kuranaga, whose activities—both professional and personal—made the front pages of newspapers throughout the nation.

The aesthetic and commercial influence of the two Australian brothers, George Turner (GT) Marsh and Victor Marsh, on the state of California has been largely forgotten, but they enabled the elevation of such artisans as Toichiro Kawai and, of course, Toshio Aoki. As GT had a home in Mill Valley, California, materials on him can be found at the Mill Valley Public Library.

Glenn and Judith Mason, who operate the ephemera online seller Cultural Images, kindly gave me an overview of the significance of the Arts and Crafts movement in the West Coast from the 1920s, in particular the Pacific Northwest. Glenn has cowritten with Lawrence Kreisman on precisely this topic. A brief conversation with Mayumi Tsutakawa, the daughter of renowned Seattle artist George Tsutakawa, was also appreciated. Meher McArthur provided her Japanese cultural expertise.

I took advantage of the multiple tour offerings at the Gamble House, the Greene and Greene brothers' signature building, and I would recommend that anyone visiting Pasadena takes a tour. You won't be disappointed. Other institutions to visit are the Japan House in Hollywood, which hosted an illuminating exhibition, *Masters of Carpentry: Melding Forest, Skill and Spirit* in winter 2025, and the Olinda Oil Museum in Brea.

The Pasadena Museum of History, a gem in my hometown, was invaluable in providing me with concrete details such as 1900–era addresses and photographs. The archives, led by collection manager Anuja Navare, has a fantastic crew, which includes archivists Patricia Zeider, Susan Beeler Anderson, Iris Shih, Donald Bergmann, and Judi Shur. Patricia and Susan, who perused the manuscript, aided me in locating information on Toshio Aoki and Colonel Green.

Pasadena's Central Library was closed for seismic work while I was writing *Crown City*, but its online newspaper database directed me to articles related to Japanese pioneers in the city. Thank you to Sian Winship for digging out old articles regarding Lamanda Park.

Huntington Library, also a stone's throw away from my domicile, is a treasure trove of information—for my purposes, mostly photographs and correspondence. Here you can find the archives of the Greene and Greene brothers, GT Marsh, and Grace Nicholson, a fascinating woman whose commissioned building is now the home of the Pacific Asia Museum. Academics connected with Huntington Library—art curator Yinshi Lerman-Tan and especially curator of Pacific Rim Collections, Li Wei Yang—helped to breathe life into historic figures and provide period details. Li Wei was the one who dug out evidence to unlock the mysterious origin of the old Japanese word for Los Angeles, *Rafu*. (As implied in the book, its roots lie with the early Chinese immigrants who adopted 羅省 *Luosheng*, a shortened version of the transliteration of Los Angeles, 羅省枝利 *Luosheng zhili.*) The library and its peaceful environs gave me a place to focus on writing and rewriting this manuscript. My thanks to the library, its curators, and staff.

Friends of Castle Green, which supports the preservation of what was known as Hotel Green, enabled me to actually experience the building through its various seasonal tours, such as its 125th anniversary celebration on January 16, 2024. Susan Futterman, active with the organization, has been a wonderful resource.

Kendall Brown, an expert on Japanese-style gardens in North America, had invited me to write an essay about the people behind the Japanese tea house at the Huntington Library for the book, *One Hundred Years in the Huntington's Japanese Garden*. I will always be grateful that I was able to do a deep dive on Toichiro Kawai, GT Marsh, and Chiyozo Goto, the groundskeeper, for that volume.

Completely fictional are the characters of Ryunosuke "Ryui/Louie" Wada and "Jack" Baba, as well as all the other individuals who lived in the Riley House. At Bouchercon 2023, Ron Scherman of Minnesota purchased the naming of a character after his late partner, Rosalie Georgia Greeman. As a result, Rosalie "Gigi" Georgia Greeman came to be.

While I did discover a mention of an Ah Hugh in the Pasadena newspaper, the nephew, Ah Wang, is made up. There was a mixed-race African American employee of Victor Marsh's store named James Logan, who, unfortunately, was found murdered on the Hotel Raymond golf course in 1906. A tailor, who was described in period newspapers as Logan's "deadly enemy," was later acquitted in the murder trial because of insufficient evidence.

And while there was a report of the chasing out of Japanese workers from the Lamanda Orange Growers' Association, other criminal incidents were fabricated. Toshio Aoki's organized cherry blossom dinner was indeed held at his art studio in the Hotel Green in spring 1903. It was this event and a corresponding photo that initially pushed me to understand why Japanese culture and aesthetics were so embraced in Pasadena at a time when the anti-Asian movement was gaining steam in California.

Pasadena Roving Archers, a field archery aficionado club, has regular competitions and practices in the Arroyo. Target archery didn't have a presence in Pasadena until the 1920s, so I took liberties with the timing and moved it backward to 1903.

Conversations with David Welter, a Fort Bragg woodworker, and my brother, Jimmy Hirahara, an artist and craftsman who produced custom doors for a South Pasadena woodworking company when he was about Ryui's age, provided visceral and sensory details on handling different kinds of wood.

Simon Rowe, a fellow mystery writer who lives in Japan but grew up in both Australia and New Zealand, shared his experiences and observations of being from Down Under like the Marsh brothers.

Academician Susie Ling, our local expert on Chinese American history in Southern California, can always be counted on to provide cultural context, as she did again for this project. Eddie Wong, who has done work on the Angel Island Immigration Station in San Francisco, gave me guidance on early entry of Chinese newcomers into California.

I did make a trek to the original spot of the Japanese Pavilion at the 1893 Chicago's World's Fair, which is now known as the Garden of the Phoenix in Jackson Park on the Wooded Island. Chicagoans Bob Kumaki and Mary Collins bore the heat and tall grasses to locate our destination. My always dependable Chicagoland expert, Erik Matsunaga, helped to add more authenticity to addresses in both Chicago and Gila River concentration camp.

Regarding the actual writing of the book, I must acknowledge my sprint partner, Sarah Chen, as well as the Sisters in Crime sprint program. While I was miles away from my fellow sprinters, we set specific times to sit in front of our computers and produced words. This has proven to be very helpful in bringing more structure to this solo creative life. An in-person option, Daycare for Writers, was useful on literally the last week of writing.

Thank you to all who helped to make *Crown City* a better book. That includes my agent, Susie Cohen, as well as editors Juliet Grames and Taz Urnov, managing editor Rachel Kowal, art director Janine Agro, copy editor Julie McCarroll, and proofreader Thomas Dennis. I appreciate all at the Soho Crime imprint who touched the book in terms of artwork, marketing, and sales. At home, it's the usual suspects: my husband, Wes, and Mookie, who both put a smile on my face even after a rough day of writing and rewriting.

Love to all my fellow 'Denans. We've been through hell in 2025, and I hope when this book is published in 2026 our community will be experiencing rejuvenation, rethinking, and restoration.

MORE READING AND RESOURCES

Crown City required much research, and reading ranging from the Arts and Crafts movement to early Japanese immigration at the turn of the twentieth century.

Here are some recommended essays and books if you are interested in digging deeper into the world of *Crown City*.

First of all, the cherry blossom dinner at the Hotel Green—again, that really happened in March 1903—and besides various articles reporting the details of the event, *The Good Housekeeping Hostess*, published by Phelps Publishing in 1904, provides an exhaustive description, including the menu. You can easily access these pages, written by Grace Hortense Tower, online.

There hadn't been much information on Toshio Aoki until the publication of University of Chicago Professor Chelsea Foxwell's ground-breaking article, "Crossing and Dislocations: Toshio Aoki (1854–1912), A Japanese Artist in California," published in *Nineteenth-Century Art Worldwide* 11, no. 3 (Autumn 2012). Jonathan van Harmelen's article on the website Discover Nikkei, "Toshio Aoki: The Wandering Meiji Artist and Father of Tsuru Aoki," also includes photographs of the artist and his works. I was able to track down a reprint of a book, *Log of a Japanese Journey: From the Province of Tosa to the Capital*, written by Tsurayuki with artwork by Toshio Aoki.

Some of Tsuru's background—her childhood years as well as her later years in Japan—has not been written about widely in the English language. Regarding her impact on cinema, I can recommend Sara Ross's "The Americanization of Tsuru Aoki: Orientalism, Melodrama, Star Image, and the New Woman," in *Camera Obscura* 60, Volume 20, Number 3, published by Duke University Press.

Probably the most detailed information of Tsuru's biological relatives and her arrival to the US can be found in Joseph Anderson's *Enter a Samurai: Kawakami Otojirō and Japanese Theatre in the West, Volume One* (Wheatmart, 2011).

Daisuke Miyao is the premier US-based expert on Sessue Hayakawa. For this project, I perused his books *Sessue Hayakawa: Silent Cinema and Transnational Stardom* and *Japonisme and the Birth of Cinema*. Professor Denise Khor has written about Japanese silent films in Southern California in *Transpacific Convergences: Race, Migration, and Japanese American Film Culture before World War II* (University of North Carolina Press, 2022). She was also instrumental in rediscovering the 1914 silent film *The Oath of the Sword*, which made its world premiere through a screening organized by the Japanese American National Museum at the Academy Museum in 2023.

Dragon Painter, the 1919 silent film starring both Sessue and Tsuru, can be easily viewed online from sources like Kanopy.

In spite of GT Marsh's impact on California's Asian aesthetic, I could not find one biography on him. Steven Pitsenbarger discusses GT's Japanese-style refuge north of San Francisco in "Connections: A Family Tree of Japanese Design" in the Spring 2022 edition of *Mill Valley Historical Society Review*. GT also penned books, both nonfiction and even fiction: *Citizenship for Nations*, co-written with Harry W. Wyckoff (1931) and *The Lords of Dawn: A Novel*, co-written with Ronald Temple and illustrated by renowned Issei artist Chiura Obata.

My favorite book on Yokohama is Leslie Helm's family memoir, *Yokohama Yankee: My Family's Five Generations as Outsiders in Japan* (Chin Music Press, 2013). Ann Yonemura's *Yokohama: Prints from Nineteenth-Century Japan* includes some splendid woodblock prints. And Eric C. Han penned the first English-language monograph on Chinese in Yokohama called *Rise of a Japanese Chinatown, Yokohama 1894–1972*.

Dennis Reed has written most extensively about Issei photographers, whose artistic heyday was in the 1920s and '30s. His descriptions of these artists can be found in Japanese American Cultural and Community Center's *Japanese Photography in America 1920–1940*; Japanese American National Museum's exhibition catalogue, *Making Waves: Japanese American Photography, 1920–1940*; and Oxford University Press's *Pictorialism in California: Photographs 1900–1940*, which he cowrote with Michael G. Wilson.

A fascinating profile of a frontier Japanese photographer can be found in JoAnn Roe's article in *American West* (March/April 1982), "Frank Matsura: Photographer on the Northwest Frontier," which is an abridged version of her book published by Madrona Publishers in 1981.

There are countless books related to the Gamble House, Greene and Greene brothers, and Japanese woodworking. The ones that I found the most helpful were the following: Esther McCoy's *Five California Architects*; editor Frances Miriam Reed's *Japan 1908: The Adventure of Fourteen-Year-Old Clarence James Gamble*; Randell L. Makinson's *A Guide to the Work of Greene and Greene* and his *Greene & Greene: Creating a Style*, cowritten by Thomas A. Heinz; Kiyoshi Seike's *The Art of Japanese Joinery*; William H. Coaldrake's *The Way of the Carpenter*; and Peggy Landers Rao and Len Brackett's *Building the Japanese House Today.*

To capture the interiority of a Japanese American master builder, I read George Nakashima's *The Soul of a Tree: A Woodworker's Reflections* and *Nature Form & Spirit: The Life and Legacy of George Nakashima*, written by his daughter, Mira.

Terusaburo "Frank" Kuranaga is a fascinating character whose successful labor contracting enterprise is noted in Yuji Ichioka's seminal work, *Issei* (not be confused with Kaoru Ito's equally important scholarship under the same title, which is key in understanding the seafaring journey from Japan). His more splashy activities can be found in newspapers, for example, his archery competition in the *San Francisco Examiner* on November 17, 1894, and his divorce from Leonna Cook in the *Los Angeles Times* on February 5, 1915.

Before and related to the "Orientalism craze" were the collecting and selling of Native American art. One illuminating analysis is Erika Marie Bsumek's "Exchanging Places: Virtual Tourism, Vicarious Travel, and the Consumption of Southwestern Indian Artifacts" in *The Culture of Tourism, the Tourism of Culture: Selling the Past to the Present in the American Southwest*, edited by Hal K. Rothman. *Dwellers at the Source: Southwestern Indian Photographs of A.C. Vroman, 1895–1904* by William Webb and Robert A. Weinstein showcases the spectacular prints taken by my hometown bookseller.

For more Pasadena-based details, I referred to Robert Winter's "Pasadena, 1900–1910: The Birth of Its Culture" in *Southern California Quarterly*'s Fall 2009 issue and Victor Cass's *Pasadena Police Department: A Photohistory 1877–2000*. Regarding the future home of GT Marsh's Japanese garden and a history of the Japanese American community in Pasadena, take a look at my article "From Japan to America: The Garden and the Japanese American Community" in *One Hundred Years in the Huntington's Japanese Garden: Harmony with Nature*, edited by T. June Li for the Huntington Library.

For information on early Chinese immigrants in Pasadena, see Susie Ling's "The Early History of Chinese Americans in the San Gabriel Valley," in *Gum Saan Journal* in 2005.

Regarding Japanese outcasts, a subject that has not been adequately explored in the English language, there are George De Vos and Hiroshi Wagatsuma's *Japan's Invisible Race: Caste in Culture and Personality* (University of California Press: Berkeley and Los Angeles 1966) and Gerald Groemer's

"The Creation of the Edo Outcaste Order" in the *Journal of Japanese Studies* 27, no. 2 (2001). Also in the 1979 issue of the same journal is Keiji Nagahara's "The Medieval Origins of the Eta-Hinin." Ian Neary writes of "Burakumin at the End of History," in the 2003 issue of *Social Research* 70, no. 1. A more layperson's explanation of the status of outcasts is in Tom Ashbrook's October 16, 1986 *Boston Globe* article, "In Japan, an Ancient Bias Endures."

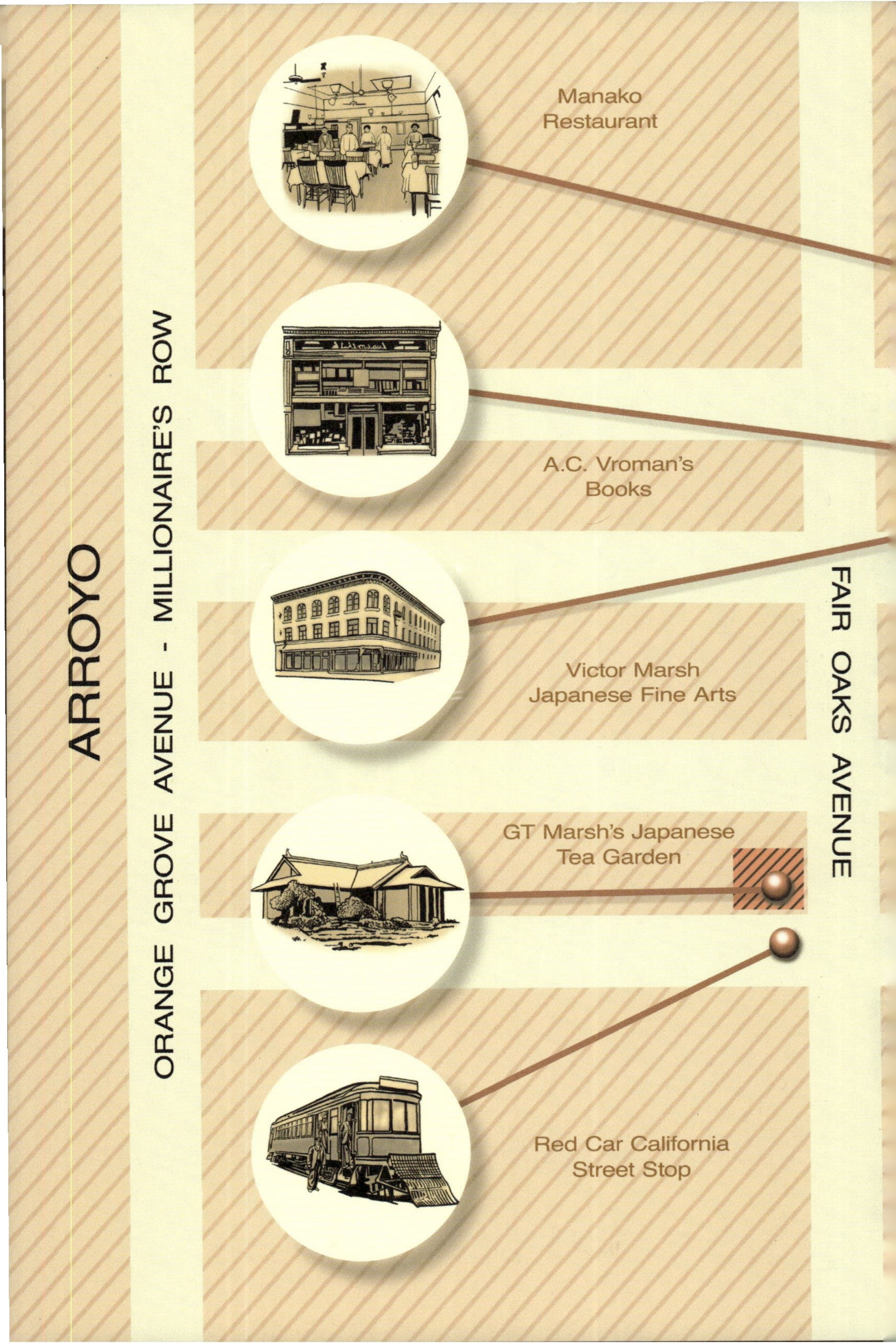

ARROYO

ORANGE GROVE AVENUE - MILLIONAIRE'S ROW

Manako
Restaurant

A.C. Vroman's
Books

Victor Marsh
Japanese Fine Arts

GT Marsh's Japanese
Tea Garden

Red Car California
Street Stop

FAIR OAKS AVENUE